BY C. C. BENISON

Twelve Drummers Drumming
Eleven Pipers Piping
Ten Lords A–Leaping

Ten
Lords A-Leaping

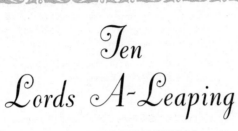

Ten
Lords A-Leaping

A FATHER CHRISTMAS MYSTERY

C. C. Benison

DOUBLEDAY CANADA

Doubleday Canada and colophon are registered trademarks of Random House of Canada Limited.

Library and Archives Canada Cataloguing in Publication

Benison, C. C., author
Ten lords a-leaping / C.C. Benison.

Issued in print and electronic formats.

ISBN 978-0-385-67017-3 (bound) ISBN 978-0-385-67018-0 (epub)

I. Title.

PS8553.E5135T45 2013   C813'.54   C2013-903084-0
                                                 C2013-903085-9

Book design by Karin Batten
Jacket design: Marietta Anastassatos
Jacket art: © Ben Perini
Printed and bound in the USA

Published in Canada by Doubleday Canada,
a division of Random House of Canada Limited,
a Penguin Random House Company.

www.randomhouse.ca

10 9 8 7 6 5 4 3 2 1

For the Earl and Countess of Orkney,
for many years of friendship and hot dinners

Cast of Characters

Inhabitants of Eggescombe Park

Hector Strickland, tenth Earl of Fairhaven	
Georgina, Countess of Fairhaven	His wife
Maximilian	Their son
Marguerite, Dowager Countess of Fairhaven	
Roberto Sica	Her lodger
Michael "Mick" Gaunt	Butler-valet
Ellen Gaunt	Cook-housekeeper

Visitors to Eggescombe Park

The Reverend Tom Christmas	Vicar of St. Nicholas Church, Thornford Regis

Miranda Christmas	His daughter
Madrun Prowse	His housekeeper
James Allan, Viscount Kirkbride	
Jane, Viscountess Kirkbride	His wife
Oliver fforde-Beckett, seventh Marquess of Morborne	
Lady Lucinda fforde-Beckett	His half sister
Dominic fforde-Beckett	Their cousin
Derek Bliss	Detective Inspector, Totnes CID
Colin Blessing	Detective Sergeant, Totnes CID

Allan—ffordi-Beckett Family Tree

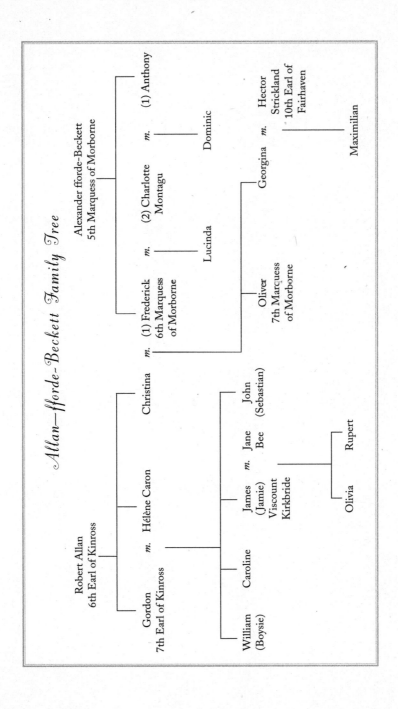

Ten
Lords A-Leaping

The Vicarage

Thornford Regis TC9 6QX

6 AUGUST

Dear Mum,

Short note this morning as it's the big day! Mr. Christmas has to be up and out to Plymouth airfield early so he and the others from the village can learn how to properly jump from an airplane without doing themselves an injury. He has looked a bit green about the gills the last few days, I must say. I was fetching a loaf at Pattimore's yesterday morning before I dropped your letter at the post office and I thought Roger looked a bit off, too, and I said so. He came over all huffy claiming it's the weight he's lost so he can fit into one of those ~~leotards~~ jumpsuits they have to wear. Ha! I thought, but didn't say anything. I don't think his mother is best pleased her son is going to throw his 16 stone into thin air with only a scrap of silk to ~~boy bouy~~ buoy him up. Enid was very quiet, and I could sense she was working herself up to one of her little "turns." I said to Karla when I got to the wicket at the post office, £10 and a quarter of choc limes if Roger doesn't pull out at the last minute. But Karla wouldn't take the bet. As you know, she's set herself against the Leaping Lords fund-raiser for the new church roof, thinks it's not proper, although I'm not sure now whether she means it's not proper for St. Nicholas's or the church council or Mr. C. or the peerage—or her! Perhaps she means everyone. Anyway, I've come around to Mr. C.'s point of view, as it should raise a very good sum quickly and let work start sooner than later on the roof, before water starts to drip on someone's poor head at Sunday service. I haven't told Karla I've shifted my views, though, as she is apt to get her back up. I don't blame her at any rate for not wanting to jump from an airplane. Neither do I, as I've said, and told Mr. C. before he even asked! He has been very good at chivvying folk in the village to join in, though, getting everyone on the PCC (except Karla!) to sign up and get pledges and getting dozens more in the village, too, although some of the attraction I think is the treat of a day at Eggescombe Park where there's to be a summer fair, too, and the chance to meet the peerage— once they've landed safely on the ground, of course. Ten lords have signed up at last count, Mum, a good job on the part of Lord Kirkbride. I am looking forwards to the day! I've never been to Eggescombe Hall, though it is not far.

Have you? I can't remember if you've ever said. Of course, I've seen pictures, and they did film one of Agatha Christie's books there not long ago, The Seven Dials Mystery, I think. Eggescombe Hall stood in for "Chimneys." Anyway, I'm driving Miranda to Eggescombe in Mr. Christmas's car later this morning after he and the others take the coach they've hired to the airfield. And then he and Miranda will take the car later this afternoon or evening and start their journey to Kent for their holiday. They're stopping overnight in Exeter with Miranda's Aunt Julia—did I mention before? I wonder if we shall ever see her at the vicarage again? But I expect not—after everything that happened last year when poor Sybella Parry was found dead in that big Japanese drum. Anyway, I mustn't dwell on past afflictions. The Met Office says the "barbecue summer" is to continue through the weekend (with chance of late-evening showers in the southwest). The Met is often wrong, of course, but I have my fingers crossed, as I expect all who shall be parachuting do, as leaping into dark clouds might be rather alarming. The sun's shining right now on the lovely blooms I have in your old ~~golddish~~ goldfish bowl on the window ledge. Of course, it will be grand to have some time away from Thornford R myself and it was so thoughtful of Ellen to invite me to stay a few days with her and her husband at Eggescombe. I'm staying with them at the Gatehouse rather than at the Hall, it turns out. Which is just as well, as I would feel odd bumping into Lord or Lady Fairhaven coming out the loo or the like. It was good of Lord Fairhaven to let their housekeeper have an old friend (me!) to stay, though it may be a bit of a busman's, Mum, as Ellen told me on the phone yesterday their best daily can't help at the weekend as she has had a family tragedy. I won't mind, I don't think. It will be like being "in service" as great-Grannie was up at the Big House in Thornford before the Great War—only with a dishwasher and a microwave and the other mod cons, of course. It will be good to see Ellen again, too. Hard to imagine it's thirty years—more!—since we were at cookery school together in London. I was never quite sure why we stopped writing, so I'm looking forward to a catch-up! Well, must go, Mum. I'll have to see that Miranda is properly packed for the trip and try to get a decent breakfast into Mr. C. He might be a bit squiffy this morning. I popped into the pub last night where all our "skydivers" were gathered having a bit of a knees up and there was much fortifying with Dutch courage, I must say! There's going to be a few thick heads on the coach this morning. I shouldn't care to jump from an airplane with a dicky tummy, but there's always a price to be paid, isn't there! Cats are well as is Bumble, who will be minded while I'm away by one of the Swan children from the pub, though they haven't sorted themselves out as to whom ~~who~~. Love to Aunt Gwen. Glorious day!

Much love,
Madrun

P.S. I can't believe that mobility scooter I ordered for you last month hasn't arrived yet! Aunt Gwen was telling me on the phone yesterday. I'll have to leave it be for the days I'm at Eggescombe, but when I return I shall let ScootersPlus have a piece of my mind!

CHAPTER ONE

"The things I do for the Church of England," Tom murmured, thinking he might as well have shouted it aloud. One could barely hear a thing anyway what with the fearsome roar. He could hear his heart crashing in his chest, though. It sounded like a big bass drum, accompanied by a simmering tintinnabulation along the fibres of his nerves, and he rather wished he could exercise some control over it—but he couldn't. The messy, squashy, beaty thing was coursing inexorably to a horrible bursting point. He would surely die before it was his turn. He would leave his daughter fatherless. It was too cruel. Miranda was already motherless.

His eyes raced around the fuselage with its great girdling ribs. The belly of Jonah's whale would have seemed like this, if the beast were aluminium and tore through the air at alarming speed. As a calming strategy, as the queue shuffled towards the beast's open jaws—to doom, surely—he focused his attention on the back of Mark's head, which was squashed into a leather helmet reminiscent of a Roaring Twenties aviator farce. Mark Tucker, faithful husband, young father, brilliant accountant, budding novelist, the best church council treasurer a priest could have. *What if something unthinkable happens? How will I ever bear Violet's reproach? Those fearsome pinprick eyes of hers.*

But Violet was young. She could marry again. Mark would have set her up nicely with insurance. Her rich in-laws doted on her. She was not without education. She could find work, keep herself occupied. Oh, it would be dreadful at first. Too, too dreadful. The grief, the pain. He knew these things. But time heals. It does. She would carry on. You do, don't you. Well, don't you?

What have I done?

This is all my doing, Tom thought. *I'm the one who pressed for this.* But it seemed the right thing at the time. Anything to avoid years' worth of bring-and-buys and carboot sales and karaoke nights to raise funds for church repairs. Something that would bring the cash in a flash. It's always such a bore lying awake at night worrying more about stones than souls. And it would be enormously satisfying to rid St. Nicholas's churchyard of that ghastly plywood thermometer. It insulted him every time he walked up the pea shingle path to the church, with its sad little red plastic capillary and its unaccountably inelegant hand lettering. He had fought members of his church council against having such a thing set up by the north porch, and had lost. If funds raised from today's event proved insufficient, well . . . The village had among its citizens a lovable kleptomaniac. Perhaps it had a likable arsonist.

The queue shuffled forwards. Tom stared past Mark's shoulder towards the gaping portal. Strong light, undifferentiated and cold, seemed to pour towards him and sear his startled eyes. *Might this be what our moment of death is like?* One of his parishioners in Bristol had described it thus, urgently, wonderingly, in a state of euphoria as she faded in and out of consciousness on her deathbed. The light, Father, the light! she'd rasped, her fingernails digging into his palm. I can see Our Lord, oh! And, look, is that Ivor Novello?

Mark bent forwards slightly, and what greeted Tom's eyes, try as he did to look away, was neither beckoning Jesus nor disoriented matinee idol, but tidy tiny patches of warm greens and golds knitted together like a fancy patchwork coat. How delightful! Heaven might look exactly like Devon. And look, off in the distance, the patterns of colour merged into a crease of soft grey brushed by a transcendent haze. Wasn't that . . . ? My God, it was! The Channel! How high in the air were they?

And then there was a terrible shout and Mark vanished. Tom shuffled forwards, to the head of the queue, into the full ring of light, and said a silent prayer. Now it was his turn. Blood roared in his ears; his heart swelled in his chest.

Some little time passed—really, *very* little time (plunging through the ether did rather tend to play havoc with time)—when it dawned on Tom that all might not be kosher. Not frighteningly, horrifyingly not kosher. More worryingly, troublingly not kosher.

He had done everything as he ought to have done, as instructed by their skydiving teacher at the airfield. When the jumpmaster next to the door of the airplane roared at him the "go" command, the fear that had punctuated his waking thoughts for the last week, the fear that had grown through their four hours of on-ground instruction, the fear that had gripped him in the fuselage of this airplane, had hurtled to a crescendo. His heart leapt into his throat like a flapping fish and in a blinding moment of panic he'd seized the frame of the door like grim death. But the jumpmaster gently tapped his shoulder. It felt like an angel's grace, and his fright ebbed. He vaulted into the sky, somersaulted, gaped with wonder at the dome of hard blue and wispy white, and—he astonished himself entirely—felt a mighty whoop exit his throat as the adrenaline terror coursing along his veins turned to joy and he embraced the wildness of the moment. Air rushed past his popping ears—a new roar—as he executed his opening stance—legs up high behind, back arched, back up—while he tumbled. He was upside down in the sky! And then, in a second, he was facing the horizon, gasping as the line between earth and sky seemed to rise higher and higher and higher. Yet oddly, he felt suspended, held in place only by the whipping wind that pressed against his body.

The free fall was over in a seeming instant. Novices, he and the other villagers weren't as high in the sky as the Leaping Lords would soon be. Tom pushed down on his rip cord, felt a sudden tug along his body, and heard the distinctive *whump!* of rushing air suddenly trapped. It was exultation. His whole body lifted into the sky as air filled the cells of his canopy. The feverish rush of noise and wind stopped. The thrumming in his veins settled into a giddy groove as a kind of peace flowed through, above, and around him. All was silent but for the hum of the vanishing airplane, above, and the popcorn pops of other opening chutes. Thin clouds hovered over the Channel, he noted as he pulled at his steering toggles, but over this patch of Devon the sky was clear, allowing an unimpeded view of the collage of fields, ripe with golden grain this early August, of the dark green coombes riven by streams glittering in the sunlight like tinsel thread, and of the snug groupings of houses, their slate roofs turned to flashing planes of silver. Below him, too, like flowers flung from a balcony, fluttered the bright canopies of the other skydivers from the village who had risen—bless them all—to this sponsored fund-raising challenge: eager Mark, for instance, who had needed no persuading; tentative Roger Pattimore, who had strained to lose a stone to come below the maximum allowable weight; undaunted Jeanne Neels, who wouldn't let being born with one hand stop her; octogenarian Michael Woolnough, untroubled by his advanced age—all of them members of his parochial church council, the entirety of which, but for one, signed on for the adventure, along with forty more from Thornford Regis.

Tom tugged his right strap, sending him in a gentle twirl. Puzzled, though not concerned, he wondered a little that no one—in the air or on the ground—had tried to communicate with him on his squawk box, the radio nestled above his chest strap. *Jumper Number Nine, you should be preparing to land,* or the like. Most likely he was doing so splendidly, no one felt obliged to correct him. Really, once you'd got past the stomach-churning bit of leaping from an airplane at thirty-five hun-

dred feet, it was all a bit of a lark. He was starting to feel
assuredly old-hand at it as he floated downwards, the earth
and all its charms sharpening in delineation. He could clearly
make out now the dark E-shape that was Eggescombe Hall
and the pale circle of its forecourt with two roads leading from
it like shoots on a sprouting bean gently winding and disappearing into a thicket of greenery. And there, to the east of the
Hall, on a little hillock, was the famous Eggescombe Labyrinth, intricate and meticulous as if a sky god had pressed his
signet ring into the soil.

Or was it west?

Tom felt himself vaguely disoriented as he circled around,
more quickly now. Yes, the Labyrinth was east. That was
Dartmoor to the north. The transition from lush pasture and
woodland to bleak tableland never seemed so abrupt as it was
from this bird's-eye view. It was as if two worlds had collided
with each other, knitted only by a silver seam that was surely
Eggesbrooke, one of the streams rising on the moor. Westwards he twisted. Was that a stable block? And that the
kitchen garden? That large irregular shape had to be the dower
house. And what was that gorgeous turquoise lozenge glittering so blindingly in the middle of the lawn? He couldn't tell,
he was corkscrewing east again, now able to make out what
had to be the Gatehouse and its forecourt, and there, a little
farther east down a licorice strip of road, a cluster of cottage
roofs and miniature gardens, and one square Norman church
tower—evidence of the tiny village of Abbotswick.

North and westwards again, he noted the irregular mosaic
of parkland and gardens cede to one large lawn, on which
someone—one of Lord Fairhaven's staff presumably—had

chalked a fat Greek cross, white on green. The parachutes beneath him were streaming towards it like obedient geese.

The cross was his destination, too, the place of safe landing. At one arm of the cross was an elevated wind sock, its narrow end stiffened easterly by the west wind blowing off the Atlantic. This was his beacon and guide. He must loop around, steer into the ground wind, as indicated by the sock, and prepare to glide smoothly towards the target to make a soft landing. Like stepping off a step, their instructor had said in his reassuring voice. Tom glanced at the altimeter on his left wrist as Eggescombe Hall and its outbuildings fell behind him and he swooped down towards the expanse of the western lawn, feeling the earth rise to greet him with a sudden and unexpected force. The sweet tranquility of the canopied descent had somehow confounded time's ineluctable passage. He was two hundred feet nearer the ground than he had imagined he was. It was here, at this height, that he was to prepare to land, to "flare," as the instructor had said, to make his final approach in such a fashion as to ensure comfort and safety. It was here, too, that his squawk box was to intrude with voice commands to ease the novice's final descent. *But where is the voice?*

"Hello," he addressed the box, concern giving over to alarm. "Hello? Jumper Number Nine here awaiting instructions . . . *Hello?*"

The thing was mute.

It was then Tom realised something was awry. Something was worryingly, troublingly *not* kosher.

He wasn't being ignored. The radio was dead.

The ground loomed up faster, no pleasant pasture now. The instructor's directives flew, half remembered, into Tom's brain: *Take toggles at shoulders, pull down to breastbone, turn your wrists to your body and push the toggles between your legs in a smooth motion.* Yes, he thought with giddy relief, he would make the target, not go hurtling into a hedgerow or drop onto the gorse-covered, rock-strewn moor. Yes, he was slowing, but now he felt little gentleness in his approach. The solid unforgiving earth seemed poised to open and swallow him. From the corners of his eyes, he could see a few who had already landed, jumpsuited, stopping in the scooping of their nylon canopies, staring up at him, helpless in the face of danger.

And now, heart again surging into his throat, eyes horrified to see individuated blades bloom in the chalky grass, he quickly lifted his legs behind him in the approved manner, then as quickly extended them, set to land first on the balls of his feet, to absorb the shock. But the ground raced to meet him with astonishing fury. As his feet grazed the armour of the soil, he felt only helpless surprise at his contorting, ungovernable body. His landing turned collapse. Something buckled and twisted. He sensed injury before his brain registered it and when it did, it came as the purest, brightest burst of pain.

CHAPTER TWO

"Tom Christmas."

In the corona of light from the tent's open flap the face fell in shadow. But the voice—pleasant, assured, faintly nasal in that North American way—was recognisable. "Jane Allan. How very good to see you again."

"The last time we met you had a black eye."

"I'm not normally accident-prone, I don't think." Tom frowned down the length of his supine form, past the right trouser leg pushed up to his knee, towards his elevated and naked foot. His swollen ankle was encased in a cold compress. "That time"—Tom wiggled his toes absently—"I got in the way of someone's busy elbow." He was referring to a graveside service at Thornford months earlier that had turned into a bit of a melee. "This time—"

"I heard." Jane let the flap fall behind her and stepped farther into the tent's stuffy interior, brushing a few damp strands from her brow. Her features resolved into the warm, reassuring eyes, the delicate but determined jawline, and the lean little apostrophe of a nose that Tom remembered from their last meeting. "I gather your radio didn't work."

"Still, we did take the training and I might have descended to earth with more finesse."

"Your first time?"

"And likely last. I doubt I shall have the opportunity again," he hastened to add, not to appear fainthearted before fair women. He struggled to rise onto his elbows on the narrow cot. In truth he was still suffering a bit of shock. In the second before his frangible body embraced the planet's inflexible surface, he wondered with a strange detachment which bones might crack, which ligaments might tear. But he was, as the St. John Ambulance volunteer told him, very lucky. His feet, not his posterior nor his hands, had met the chalky grass, as prescribed in the training, but his right foot had inverted sharply, taking his full weight as his body careened awkwardly and collapsed in a sideways heap. The pain had been skewering, as if an arrow had pierced him. He couldn't help but cry out and in a thrice Miranda was at his side, tugging and pulling at the nylon that had rolled over him in soft waves. But after being rushed in a van to the St. John Ambulance tent tucked by Eggescombe Hall, he had been diagnosed with that most banal of sports injuries, a sprained ankle.

"Jamie's suggested I take the opportunity sometime— skydiving seems to run in the family a bit." Jane tucked her dark hair behind her ear. "But I've told him I'll wait until our kids are old enough to better cope with being motherless."

"As opposed to fatherless."

Jane smiled. "I've rarely brought ours to these Leaping Lords events, for that very reason. I know the boys do good works, but I'm not sure how popular skydiving really is with wives and girlfriends and mothers." She glanced at the third figure in the tent, an older woman who had silently and efficiently attended Tom earlier. "We camp followers don't always follow."

"But here you are."

"Well, I thought I would like to come down to Devon." She shot Tom an enigmatic glance. "Jamie had an Old Salopian event to attend at Exeter before the Leaping Lords on Saturday, and so Hector and Georgina invited us to stay over a few days. Our two are in Scotland with Jamie's parents. By the way, I met your daughter coming out of the tent just now. She looks well. Settling in okay?"

"Yes, actually. Miranda's quite fiercely independent."

"So is Olivia, my daughter. They'd make a fine pair. And you've met Marguerite, I see." She nodded towards the other woman, who turned and smiled in acknowledgement.

"Marguerite?" Tom glanced at the third in the tent.

"Hector's mother."

"I am sorry. I didn't realise." He had been attended to by the Dowager Countess Marguerite, Lady Fairhaven. Fuzzed with pain, he had rather wondered why the two lime-and-orange-kitted St. John folk had melted from the tent after a few words with the mufti-clad figure.

"I should have introduced myself." Marguerite's voice was resonant, chesty, as if fashioned by ten thousand Gauloises. She was wearing a man's white shirt, tails knotted in front, sleeves rolled up her arms, and loose-fitting white linen trousers. But it was her peerless blue eyes undimmed by age—only the fan of lines from each corner proclaimed the dowager countess surely in her sixties—and her wide sensuous mouth that held Tom's attention. Here was great beauty, not diminished, but somehow refashioned by time. Tom sensed this was a woman much used to lingering glances.

"And I am trained, as is Jane here," Marguerite continued. "If one lives in the country, as I do, the St. John course proves quite useful. Doctors aren't always to hand."

"Marve." Jane turned. "This is the Reverend Tom Christmas, vicar of St. Nicholas's in Thornford Regis."

"Yes, I made that deduction. You wear your dog collar even beneath a jumpsuit. I believe you're the son of Mary Carroll and Iain Christmas. Am I correct?"

Tom nodded.

"I thought so," Marguerite said. "There's something at my cottage I should like to show you."

Tom looked down at his foot helplessly.

"Later, of course," she said briskly. "When the swelling goes down a bit, we'll put your ankle in a compression wrap. There are crutches somewhere in one of the attic rooms. You'll find walking a bit tender. We can try getting you up later." She frowned in thought. "A cast boot, perhaps, though your sprain isn't severe."

Tom made a noise somewhere between a groan and grunt. "Pain returning?"

"No, it's quite numb now. I was thinking how inconvenient this all is. I've plans to drive with my daughter to Exeter this evening to visit my sister-in-law and then go on to London in the morning." *For my birthday celebrations,* he didn't add. "I expect I won't be able to drive the car."

Marguerite tapped his compress with a slim finger. "I have a brilliant idea. Why don't you convalesce here at Eggescombe for a day or two?"

"Lady Fairhaven, I couldn't possibly—"

"Nonsense."

Tom flicked a glance at Jane, who was regarding the older woman with an interest bordering on curiosity.

"I should point out I have my daughter with me—"

"Splendid! She'll be good company for Max, my grandson . . . and I believe your housekeeper is visiting with Hector and Georgie's housekeeper this weekend."

"Well . . . yes, she is," Tom responded, thinking how remarkably informed the dowager countess was. He glanced again at Jane for some kind of adjudicating signal. Jane and her husband, Jamie—Viscount and Viscountess Kirkbride—he had met once, under somewhat fraught circumstances, but they had proved easy and delightful company, and, unprompted, of great service: It had been Jamie who had offered and organised the talents of the Leaping Lords to raise funds for St. Nicholas. The others at any Eggescombe weekend house party, however, would be unknown to him.

Jane flashed Tom a reassuring smile. "Yes, stay over, Tom. It would be good to have your company."

"We're only a few family this weekend," Marguerite continued, "Hector and Georgina and the adorable Max, of course. Georgina's brother will likely leave tomorrow or Monday."

"Oliver." Jane supplied the name.

"And Jane and Jamie. Quite a small party. You won't be overwhelmed."

"But . . ." Tom groped for a kind excuse. He felt very much the interloper. "Clothes!"

"Ah, yes, I hadn't thought of that." Marguerite's doubt lasted only a beat. "But weren't you on your way to London? What were you planning to wear when you got there?"

"Of course! Our luggage is in the boot."

"Then it's settled. I'll have Gaunt fetch your things from your car." Marguerite frowned. "You haven't a service tomorrow?"

"I'm on a fortnight's holiday."

"Good. Now I'll change the ice along your ankle and we'll wheel you out of here. You must keep your feet elevated for a while longer. I asked them to keep you on the trolley, so you could be pushed out onto the lawn. You don't want to miss the show, do you? Jane, pull the tent flap back."

Moments later, Tom emerged semi-upright like a pasha amid a pile of propped-up hospital pillows onto Eggescombe's sleek and sunlit south lawn. A few heads turned, all recognisable. Half of Thornford, it seemed, had motored to Eggescombe Park for the fund-raiser, and a smattering of clapping and cheering—half in good-natured mockery—followed. Faintly mortified, glad Miranda wasn't witness (he couldn't see her), Tom bobbed his head and waved in imitation of a world-weary monarch. He got a laugh.

Eggescombe's grounds were festooned as if for a summer fête. As he was trundled down the gently sloping grounds, the countess and viscountess straining a bit so he wouldn't slip off the trolley and fly over the ha-ha, he noted a few of the traditional amusements for children, the bouncy castle and face-painting stall, among the usual homely carnival distractions. Hector and Georgina, Earl and Countess of Fairhaven, had given over their house and grounds for the day for this chari-table event, for which Tom was most grateful. Cream teas amid the rich foliage of summer with, as backdrop, a rose-pink palace of gables and chimneys twisted into shapes a confectioner would envy was a great enticement to the villagers, especially as the Hall itself, usually closed the first two weeks in August when the family was installed, was open-to-view for the day. Electric carts took people between the Hall and the landing field, so visitors could admire those with the gumption to jump from an airplane, but the pièce de résistance was the Leaping Lords, a pool of peers of the realm who lent their time and talents a few times in the year to worthy causes. Ten lords were on tap this season and they would soon leap into the blue, not from the mingy few thousand feet that Tom and the novices had, but from a gasp-making twenty thousand—Tom shud-dered anew thinking about it—free-falling through the air not only with the greatest of ease but for a heart-stoppingly long time, too, before gravity's inexorable pull obliged them to open their chutes. Formation skydiving was the Leaping Lords' claim to fame, feats of aerobatics and athleticism, the linked peers together shape-shifting in the sky, all of which would be as flying ants if it weren't for closed-circuit television.

"This should do," Marguerite said as she and Jane twisted the trolley around to face a giant television screen set by the ha-ha's stone border.

"Thank you both." Tom studied their distorted reflections in the glossy ebony lozenge. There were three other TVs—

two on the terrace off the drawing room and another farther along the ha-ha—framing the lawn like a set of brackets.

"Shouldn't be long, I don't think." Marguerite glanced at her watch. "Now, however do they do this? Someone wears a camera on his head, I think. Jane?"

"Someone they hire stays in the plane with a camera and films them through the open door. And one of the skydivers wears one on his head, so we get different views of the same thing. I think it's to be Jamie. He's done it before. He says the videographer always . . ." Jane's voice trailed off. Tom noted her eyes slitting as she peered into the middle distance, towards the cluster of striped café umbrellas on the terrace. ". . . always has to be conscious of where he's aiming his head . . . Marve, is that Lucinda?"

Marguerite turned to look, and Tom's eyes followed. What he saw was a tall and slender young woman with fair floating hair and a light diaphanous skirt striding with an assured gait down the terrace steps onto the shimmering lawn, an immense straw hat in one hand. Even at a distance, he could make out the translucent skin, the slim neck rising from the plunging keyhole opening of her simple blouse. He rather wished he wasn't, in his awkward state, stirred by this beauteous vision, but he was.

"Yes, it is Lucinda." Marguerite's tone seemed to contain multiple shades of meaning though her expression gave none away. "I thought she summered in Cap Ferrat. I'll go and say hello, shall I? Georgina's probably in her bedroom with a cold cloth on her forehead."

Tom leaned a little to the left, as Marguerite's moving figure was blocking Eggescombe's newest attraction.

Jane noted the gesture and said, half amused: "She's very beautiful, Lucinda."

"Yes, she is," Tom responded primly, straightening himself against the pillows.

Jane laughed. "Vicar, you're allowed some frailties."

"Am I? All right then. She's quite stunning. Who is she?"

"Georgie and Olly's sister . . . well, half sister. Lady Lucinda fforde-Beckett. Lucy, to family."

"And is he her husband?" He studied the slim, pale man with modishly long fair hair following a step behind and recognised that a little envy had crept into his voice. Jane didn't seem to notice.

"No," she replied. "Lucy's already shucked two husbands, and she's only in her mid-twenties. That's . . . it's a little complicated. That's Dominic fforde-Beckett. He's Lucy's cousin— and Oliver's and Georgina's, too, of course. They're all related on the fforde-Beckett side."

"Doesn't seem too—"

"The complication, Tom, is that Lucinda and Dominic are both cousins *and* half siblings."

"How—?"

"Oliver and Georgina's father, Frederick, late Marquess of Morborne, had two wives. His first wife was my husband's aunt, Christina. Got that so far?"

"Yes."

"His second wife was Charlotte. Charlotte had been married to Frederick's younger brother, Anthony. Charlotte and Anthony produced Dominic."

"Anthony had died?"

"No. Frederick essentially stole his brother's wife—or so gossip has it. Frederick and Charlotte produced Lucy."

"Ah."

"It was a great scandal at the time, Jamie tells me. Brother against brother. House of Morborne torn apart. Custody battles. Libel suits. Shock-horror headlines. I was barely out of diapers living in Canada so I had no idea."

Tom realised he had some idea, but only flotsam and jetsam from Internet sifting for information on St. Nicholas's church roof fund benefactors, the Leaping Lords. He was sure the words *bigamous marriage* and *High Court* had flitted past his tired eyes in Wikipedia's entry on the Marquesses of Morborne. Several scenes of the lengthy melodrama were set in the West Indies. He said, however, "I have no memory of it. I was too young, too, I expect. This must have been—"

"Close to thirty years ago. Charlotte was quite the society beauty then. All the men wanted her."

"So Oliver and Georgina's aunt became their stepmother."

"And Dominic's mother became his aunt—as well as his mother. And not very good in either role, I gather. Of course, I hear all this from the Allan side, where Charlotte, now the Dowager Marchioness of Morborne, is portrayed as ruthless and manipulative and so forth. I've never met the woman, actually."

"It has the makings of Jacobean drama."

Tom glanced towards the terrace to see Lucinda and Dominic slip through the French doors into the shadow of the Hall, ushered by Marguerite. "I don't wish to be intrusive, but would I be correct in thinking that Lucinda's presence wasn't expected this weekend?"

"I don't think so. No one's mentioned it, anyway. I thought she was in the south of France. She usually is this time of year, staying with Charlotte. I doubt she comes down to Eggescombe much at all. Hector and Georgina really only have the place to themselves for two weeks in August and at Christmas and Easter."

Tom regarded her thoughtfully, detecting diplomacy in her response. Jane caught his look and let loose a little puff of laughter. "The fact is—and you may as well be prepared— Hector is not fond of his wife's family. He's been very abrupt with Oliver, who showed up here about the time Jamie and I did—"

"I noticed a bit of an atmosphere between them when we were at the airfield this morning."

"—I think Hector thinks Lucy takes too much after her mother."

"What does Lady Lucinda do?"

"We're not sure. She's sort of a . . . 'party planner' when the mood strikes."

"And Dominic?"

"He's an art consultant and private dealer. He had a handful of very rich clients—and I think he has a share in a gallery in St. James's, too. I don't really know him—or Lucy—that well. You see, there's a sort of division among the siblings—no surprise given their parents' behaviours. Olly and Georgie versus Lucy and Dominic, and we—the Allans—see more of the first pair since their mother is Jamie's aunt." Jane laughed again. "See what you have to look forward to this weekend, Tom? Lucy arriving uninvited likely means some pot is about to be stirred!"

Tom wished he could share the laugh, but now he sensed himself being drawn unwillingly into some family unpleasantness. "It's very kind of Lady Fairhaven to ask Miranda and me to stay, but . . ."

"Yes?"

"Is it her place to do so? Georgina is mistress of Eggescombe, is she not?"

"We argue about that sometimes, Jamie and I."

"You do?"

"I'm joking. Georgie is mistress of Eggescombe and has been since Hector's father died ten years ago. But Marve . . . well, Marguerite lives down here and is very involved in managing the estate, so I think she forgets herself a little when Georgie comes down—which isn't often. Georgie"—Jane frowned a little—"doesn't really care for the country."

"I'm not sure that answers my question. I don't want to put Lady Fairhaven out—Georgina, Lady Fairhaven—by staying here."

"I wouldn't worry. Even though I know Marve gets up Georgie's nose, I think she's not unhappy for Marve to do the organising. Georgie often has migraines—or at least," Jane added dryly, "she does at Eggescombe."

"Migraines? Jane, perhaps I should beg off."

"Oh, don't. Marve loves company, and she is genuinely concerned for your health. Georgina will welcome you to stay. She will, really. She'll be utterly gracious. Very"—Jane slipped from her Canadian accent into poshspeak—"prop*ah*. Perhaps the only fforde-Beckett who is," she added, her tone thoughtful.

At that moment, the black onyx beside them flickered into

a facsimile of life, a bouncy logo—belonging to some smart media production company—rolling grandly across its screen. Music sounded, too. Haydn's *Creation*. Tom recognised the notes of the first movement, "Representation of Chaos." "The Heavens are telling the glory of God," he murmured to himself and glanced into the sky, which held but the glory of a single rook.

"Shouldn't be long now." Jane followed his glance. "I should say I'm glad for myself that you'll stay the weekend. I remembered your saying in an email that your housekeeper thought she had spotted my long-lost brother-in-law on Dartmoor."

"Someone Mrs. Prowse knows, actually."

"I thought—oh, I know it's unlikely—I might have a chance to—"

"Make some enquiries?"

"*Snoop around*, I was going to say, but yours is more elegant. Yes, see if I could at least find some leads to John—Sebastian, as you call him."

The man Tom knew as Sebastian John was the Honourable John Sebastian Hamilton Allan, third son of the Earl of Kinross, Jamie's father. Sebastian had been verger at St. Nicholas's in Thornford Regis, living incognito, in flight from his family, but had vanished from the village fifteen months earlier.

"It's odd that he mightn't be living all that far away from his cousins," Tom remarked.

"But Georgie's hardly here at all. Hector comes down more often on estate business, or constituency business—he's local Conservative Party constituency chairman—but I'm not sure he'd pay much attention to anything other."

"But the dowager countess lives here all year."

"Yes, that's true," Jane murmured speculatively, casting her eyes up the lawn towards the Hall. Tom looked, too, to see Marguerite slip back out onto the terrace, bending to say a word to one of the guests, a large Irish setter loping along in her wake.

"I wonder . . . ," Jane began, then paused, as if she had another thought. "Still, as you described John the last time we met, his appearance is very different. He was a skinny teenager when I first knew him. And I'm not sure the last time Marve would have seen John. Her connection to him, after all, is through her son's marriage to Georgina. Oh." She turned back to the screen, which burst into a shifting panorama of blue and hazy white as the sound of Haydn's *Creation* dropped in volume. "Here we go."

Tom shivered slightly at the next view, a portion of the frame of the very airplane door from which he'd leapt not an hour earlier. A second later the camera beheld the sky again; so gorgeously brilliant was it that it seemed more true than the genuine article. Tom craned his neck towards the pallid rendition hanging over them. No sight, no sound proclaimed the airplane's presence, so high was it over the county. He glanced around for Miranda, but could only trust his daughter had parked herself elsewhere, because a sudden shift in colour on the screen reclaimed his attention, a riot of rich red. Ten men—Tom counted as the camera quickly panned—were standing along the fuselage in a line, arms behind one another's hips like a row of chorus girls, mouths stretched in cheeky grins. Tom laughed, enjoying the echo of laughter elsewhere in the crowd. The men's jumpsuits were identical, the crimson of coronation robes, while the parachute straps crossing their chests were white with rows of black dots, like the very robes' traditional ermine trim. Puzzling was the gold-and-red confection at the top of each helmet.

"What—?" Tom began but Jane anticipated him: "Coronets."

Tom laughed louder. "They really are good sports."

"They really are quite silly." Marguerite had reinserted herself into their company along with the red setter. "But good sports, too, I agree. Lucy and Dominic will be staying over, by the way," she said, addressing Jane. "I asked Mrs. Gaunt to prepare rooms for them. And Tom, you'll be in the Opium Bedroom, on the ground floor. No stairs. And your daughter on the nursery floor, with Max. Smile, Hector, darling." She turned to the screen as others gathered around to watch.

"Olly looks peeved, too," Jane remarked as the camera moved down the line to decorous clapping on the ground, a caption appearing under each man with his name and title.

It was obvious the cameraman was chivvying the two into better humour, for as the camera pulled back HECTOR, EARL OF FAIRHAVEN (said the caption), allowed a tight smile to crease his face behind his visor, though the smile didn't lift to his eyes. Similarly, OLIVER, MARQUESS OF MORBORNE, let a short, sharp smirk shift his cheeks for the grace of a second.

"Ah, Jamie *is* a camera." Jane read out her husband's name and title: "James, Viscount Kirkbride. There it is, strapped to his forehead." The picture on the screen dissolved unexpectedly into a view of a tall man in ordinary dress holding a camera and waving before taking an extravagant bow. The caption read DENNIS PAPNORTH, COMMON AS MUCK. "See," Jane said, as laughter again rippled across the lawn, "Jamie is filming *him*."

"Smoothly done, the transition from one camera to another," Tom remarked. "How—?"

"There's a little man set up in the library with some sort of magical electronic board," Marguerite answered as the lords offered a collective thumbs-up and broke muster, heading for the airplane's open door. "They're off."

Jamie leapt first. The view on the big screen switched from a hazy impression of Devon's chessboard landscape and a startling shot of the earth's very roundedness to a smear of feathery white. Ice blue lasted for a moment, followed in quick succession by flashes of wispy cloud, the underside of the airplane, and finally a jumble of nine men tumbling from the airplane's great maw, each speeding like a crimson bullet towards Jamie's camera. The effect was so vivid, viewers on lawn and terrace—Tom included—gasped and instinctively leaned away. The raucous beat of some rock music replaced the Haydn as—the camera view was from the airplane now—the lords began a kind of aerial ballet, twisting and turning in swift choreographed sequences, grasping and ungrasping one another's limbs to form ever-changing patterns. Rather like watching the formation of giant red snowflakes, Tom decided, as the mesmerising configurations changed again and again. In a quarter at the top of the TV screen, the Jamie-cam view offered a more abstract version of the same sequences, arms and legs and concentrated faces behind plastic visors gliding past as if the troposphere were a lovely place for a swim. Tom was about to voice his wonder at their skill and professionalism when the airplane camera caught a certain wonkiness in the smooth and pleasing patterning. At first he thought the skydivers were all about to break off—they had less than a minute for their free-fall display—and deploy their parachutes, but instead one of them broke from the rhythm of glancing grabs and held on to another man, pulling him close, raising his arm and—as the Jamie-cam made clearer—attempting to drive it towards the other man's stomach. A murmur rose from the crowd, as the two engaged in an aerial ballet of their own, pushing and tugging at each other. *Is this part of the show?* Tom recognised the stupidity of the thought when an arm, now giant on the screen, pushed in between the two figures, as if to peel them apart. Two enormous scowling faces, each behind a plastic shield, turned to the screen.

"It's Hector and Olly." Jane's hand went to her mouth. Somewhere someone screamed. "What are they *doing*?"

"They're fighting like schoolboys. At twenty thousand feet in the air!" Marguerite gasped, adding, "Bonzo!" to quell the barking dog.

The top corner of the screen showed the airplane camera's view. As Hector and Oliver grappled and Jamie struggled to part them, the others abandoned formation. Deploying chutes was now critical, and in a twinkling the whole screen exploded with seven crimson blossoms. Seconds were eternities, and after an eternity Hector and Oliver, figures in the corner screen, broke apart. Instantly, the whole screen again filled with crimson from two blossoming parachutes.

"Oh, thank God!" Jane cried as Jamie's camera picked out the rigging of his open canopy, the suspended figure of the second man drifting by gently in nearby view—Oliver, Tom thought, judging by the slimmer figure. A collective sigh of relief sounded all around them. Then suddenly the sighs turned to perplexed and frightened mutterings. On the TV, cascading from view, as if into a hole in the screen, a figure dangled from the end of a tangle of lines themselves connected to little more than a flapping crimson flag.

"The chute didn't open!" someone cried.

"Oh, God." Jane's hand went again to her face as they watched the figure, growing tinier now, seem to struggle to disentangle the lines.

"Who is it?" Tom muttered, cold with horror.

"I think it's Hector." Marguerite's voice was steely, disbelieving, but Tom noted her knuckles whiten as her hands gripped the edge of his trolley.

"Jamie, turn your camera away. I can't stand this," Jane pleaded. "Just turn all the cameras *off*!"

"Hector, for heaven's sake, deploy the emergency chute." Marguerite stared at the screen. "The emergency chute! He was always such a bloody-minded child."

And they watched in growing horror as the crippled parachute with its human cargo plummeted, fluttering, towards the earth's heartless embrace, disappearing into a tiny red dot.

CHAPTER THREE

"*H*ello. Are you off to a fancy dress party?"

"No," the boy replied fiercely.

Tom regarded the diminutive figure curiously carapaced in well-tailored evening wear: black jacket with shawl collar, low-cut waistcoat, black silk bow tie, and patent-leather Oxfords glinting in the evening sunshine. If there were anyone on the terrace better dressed for a weekend country house party, it was this bright young thing in full formal fig. He was wearing a monocle, too.

"Aren't you a little young to be smoking?"

"They're Turkish cigarettes."

"I'm not sure that answers my question."

The boy placed the cigarette against his lips, affected to take a long drag, then waved his hand away, raising his head to the sky to release a long plume of imagined smoke.

"Where did you get that?" A woman's voice sounded sharply behind the open French doors, startling them both.

"Uncle Olly gave it to me." The boy edged away.

"Yes, and that's precisely how it begins." A moment later a sandaled, tanned foot slipped onto the terrace to the tinkle of ice cubes, followed by the figure of Lady Lucinda fforde-Beckett, pale skin flushed, though not, Tom considered, by the roseate refraction of sunlight on Eggescombe's red brick. She curled her glass against one arm and brandished the other arm at the boy. "Give it to me."

"Darling, have you a light?" The boy put the cigarette again to his lips and waggled one eyebrow in a saucy, come-hither fashion.

"Maximilian!"

"Oh, darling, you *must* have a light."

"Stop it, Maxie." Whatever ill temper Lucinda had brought with her to the terrace now evaporated like mist drenched by sun. A tiny smile twitched at the corners of her mouth, setting a kindling light to her deep blue-violet eyes.

"What do you think? Is it me? Is it *one*, rather?" The boy struck a number of mannequin poses, all with the cigarette in hand.

"It would be, if you weren't eleven years old." She laughed, with a quick confiding glance at Tom. "Now give that to me."

Max ignored her through a couple more poses, then said with exaggerated effect, "Darling, I've run out of cigarettes, why don't you have this one?"

"Thank you, darling," Lucinda responded, now Gertrude Lawrence to Max's Noël Coward, taking the offending item.

"I'm Lucy fforde-Beckett"—she turned to Tom, fixing him with her remarkable eyes—"and this is my nephew Max, who may have a career in theatre."

"And you're the Reverend Tom Christmas," the boy said, offering a hand. "I'm *so* pleased to meet you. I've been having a splendid time entertaining your charming daughter. Don't get up."

"I don't think I'm allowed," Tom replied from his sun lounger, taking the small hand in his own. "Your grandmother is insistent I stay off my feet for a while."

"Mr. Christmas is spending the weekend." Lucinda rolled the cigarette thoughtfully between the fingers of one hand and raised her glass to her lips with the other.

"I say, how wizard! I'm so pleased. I have a theological question I should like to ask you."

"Oh?" Tom replied.

"For instance, if Pater's emergency parachute hadn't opened—"

"But it did open, Maxie."

"If it *hadn't* opened," Max continued, ignoring his aunt, "and he had died, would his soul have gone to hell?"

Tom started. "Well—"

"Maxie, for God's sake, surely you have enough RE at Ampleforth."

"Yes, but I should like to have Mr. Christmas's views." Max adjusted his monocle and explained, "We're Roman Catholic."

"Ah, yes." Tom knew that from a spot of Googling. "I believe the Catholic conception of the afterlife teaches that those who die in unrepentant mortal sin go to, well, hell. But

I'm sure there's no danger of your father . . ." He stopped, troubled at the wave of uncertainty that rippled across Max's features.

"Perhaps Pater was given the wrong kit. Perhaps someone *wanted* him to die."

"Max, don't be horrid." Lucinda contemplated her now empty glass. "Why would you think such a thing?"

"I heard . . . Miranda and I heard," the boy amended, "someone say so."

"The emergency chute opened," Tom said gently. *Though it took a bloody frighteningly long time.* "They almost never fail. Your father made a perfectly safe landing. He's very practised at this, of course. He was an officer in the Parachute Regiment."

"Long before you were born," Lucinda added unnecessarily.

"If Pater died, then I would become eleventh Earl of Fairhaven, wouldn't I."

"Max, darling, buzz off."

The boy flashed his aunt a faltering glance before straightening himself and brushing an invisible dust mote from his jacket. "Yes, I really must see to my guest. I left Miranda in the drawing room."

"Gruesome child," Lucinda laughed when he had disappeared behind the French doors.

" '*Wizard*'?"

"The antique slang, you mean? I suspect his grandmother's influence. Sending him copies of Enid Blyton to read. Or what are those old books about that silly pilot . . . ?"

"*Biggles.*"

"Or perhaps Wodehouse. Saki? I'm not sure. Anyway, he seems to have a healthy dose of the fforde-Beckett gene."

"For . . . theatricality?"

"No, for a certain cold-bloodedness. Look us up. Not *Burke's*. Try the *Daily Mail*. I think I will have this cigarette," she added, placing her empty glass on the balustrade. "Do you have a light?"

"I'm afraid I don't smoke. Do you? You seemed adamantly against it."

"I'm not adamantly against anything, really, but I'd rather my nephew's innocence not be poisoned by my brother."

"Which brother?" Tom asked without thinking.

"Oliver, of course. 'Mad' Morborne, as he likes to call himself. The one who gave Maxie the cigarette." She raised a shapely eyebrow. "Then you know a bit about the twisty twigs on the fforde-Beckett family tree."

"Only a bit. Lady Kirkbride kindly filled me in."

"My two brothers are only halves—to me. A good half and a bad half," she added glumly.

"I expect you could get a light over there." Tom gestured towards the other end of the terrace where a wreath of smoke floated lazily above heads in the evening's luxuriant light. With the boy gone, he allowed himself a more candid appraisal of Lady Lucinda fforde-Beckett, of whom he had only been vouchsafed glimpses through the afternoon from the prison of his sickbed in the middle of the lawn. The simple, creamy frock cut low across the shoulder seemed to hug the curve of her body, an invitation for his eyes to linger then follow as she waded through the human sea of villagers and children, her half brother Dominic, similarly attired in off-white, in tow. There was something alluring, too, in her bearing, with its athletic fluidity and self-confidence, and he realised, as his eyes roved around the lawn in search of her, that he was enduring an uncomfortable spurt of lust.

Now as she looked over towards the group of men at the other end of the terrace, he could behold her more properly. With the earlier flush subsided in her cheeks to tiny strawberry patches, her skin was revealed almost translucent, fine and white, in the Elizabethan ideal, even after months of summer sun in the south of France. There was a fineness, too, to the bones of her face, to the graceful jaw, and to her hair, tousled filaments of gold and auburn. But her eyes trounced all these measures of female delicacy. Heavy-lidded, under high-arched brows, they were immense, remarkable and bold, and somehow managed to seem both challenging and withholding. As she looked towards the knot of casually dressed men, Tom saw those eyes harden with a flashing hint of some strong emotion. At the same time, one of the men, Oliver, distinguishable by his embroidered African-inspired shirt and coloured kufi hat, turned his head, as if inexorably drawn to do so. He was at the centre of the men, a passel of other peers, winding up some story with a burst of chortle and boom, his right eye screwed up against the smoke ascending from the cigarette bobbing on his lips. He scowled, his left eye telegraphing a beam of such contempt that Tom caught himself suppressing a gasp. Brother and sister held each other's gaze for a time longer than was decent. And then Lucinda turned back, her face altered by a thin veil of loathing. She flicked the cigarette over the balustrade.

"Do you have a family, Mr. Christmas? Of course you do.

Maxie is entertaining your daughter. Where then is Mrs. Christmas this weekend?"

"I'm a widower, as it happens."

"Oh?" Doubt shaded her voice as she glanced at his hands.

"I am, truly. Yes, that is a wedding band, but I've put it on my right hand. A little hard to let go completely."

Lucinda regarded him speculatively for a moment. "Have they put you in the bachelors' corridor then?" She smiled. "I expect not. Far too many stairs."

"It's only a light sprain," Tom protested. "Lady Fairhaven has kindly supplied me with a pair of crutches." He gestured to an antique dark oak pair leaning against the brick.

"Marguerite?"

"Your sister, actually, though I think Dowager Lady Fairhaven went looking for them."

"Really? Georgie lifted a finger to help someone?" Lucinda's smile tightened. "I'm sorry. Do go on."

Tom blinked, uncertain whether to pursue the subject of her sister. "Apparently an ancestor of Lord Fairhaven's in the nineteenth century had an accident similar to mine."

"He couldn't possibly have fallen from the sky."

"No, I think he fell rather badly over a croquet hoop. He was an early enthusiast for the game."

"Ah, then you're in the Opium Bedroom on the ground floor. Whoever Hector's ancestor was, he had it redecorated for his short convalescence. It really is the most splendid bedroom in the house. I am sorry about your wife." Lucinda canted her head slightly. "Was it—?"

"Sudden? Yes, very. She was killed."

"How awful." The words were anodyne, but an eyebrow twitched with curiosity.

Tom was used to it. "Murder. By person or persons unknown. We were living in Bristol at the time."

Lucy glanced again down the terrace towards the grouping of men. "At the time," she murmured. "You don't—"

"We live—my daughter and I—live at Thornford Regis now. I'm the vicar of St. Nicholas Church, have been for about the last year and a half."

"Of course. It's your church that today's event was for. But your wife—"

"It will be four years in November."

"Do you get lonely?"

Her candour gave him pause. "From time to time."

"I don't like being alone. I expect that's why I forced Dominic to drive me down from London. Dominic's my good half brother."

"I know. Well, I know at least that he's your half brother."

"They *have* been talking about me."

"No, not really." Tom spoke honestly. All he had sussed was a vague air of concern wrought by her relatives' reactions to her unexpected presence—Jane's warning tone, Marguerite's dash to the terrace, now Oliver's cold glance.

An amused light in Lucinda's extraordinary eyes suggested she didn't believe him. "You don't have a drink."

"I did, a G and T, but someone scooped up the glass."

"The redoubtable Gaunt, I expect. I'll get you another."

He watched her trim figure stride down the terraced steps, the back view as captivating as the front view had been earlier in the day, but he quickly sent his eyes elsewhere, through the falling light, across the dusky expanse of the park, lest he be caught out in an unvicarly oglefest. He noted the borders of the lawn, highlighted against the darker mass of trees, dotted with the detritus of the afternoon's event, the tents and stalls, all waiting for tomorrow's disassembly, soon to disappear into creeping shadow. He shifted his glance nearer, to the drooping bunches of wisteria along the balustrade, mauve in the afternoon, now, he observed, plum purple in evening. But he couldn't help his eyes searching out Lucinda, though she was largely obscured by the stonework and floral array as she busied herself at a drinks table. More visible was Gaunt, Lord Fairhaven's butler-valet, ramrod-stiff in his impeccably neat black suit and white shirt, ministering to a very large gas barbecue—untroubled, judging from his impassive expression, by spurting flames—from which the smell of cooking beef wafted gorgeously into the evening air. The peerage sipping gin on the terrace, however—Tom couldn't help noticing—appeared little distinguishable from those undoubtedly quaffing ale this fine summer evening outside Thornford's Church House Inn, many in short trousers, all in knit shirts, men dressed as boys, in the modern and universal fashion. He looked down at himself, still in clerical shirt, clerical collar, and long dark trousers. He felt out of place.

With his head turned again towards Lucinda, who seemed to have fallen into conversation with one of the lords, he failed to notice the figure bending down towards him until a silver tray dotted with canapés slid under his nose.

"Mr. Christmas?"

"Mrs. Prowse?" Tom glanced at his housekeeper with astonishment. He had never seen her wearing the stiff black skirt and starched white blouse that was the traditional uniform of the housekeeper. And was that a spot of makeup? "Where did you—"

"It's one of Ellen's," she cut in, adding, frowning down at the cinched belt, "It's a bit loose, but it will do."

"Mrs. Prowse, you're meant to have a holiday, too."

"I can't very well sit about when Ellen is run off her feet, can I? The only staff are she and her husband. One of the dailies from the village was to come and help this evening, but there was a death in her family, so . . . Would you care for a nibble?"

"I'm sure the Gaunts can cope." Tom selected something with salmon and crème fraîche. "Supper's only a barbecue, very informal."

"Oh," Madrun murmured. "I thought it all might be a little more grand than this."

"You mean no candlelit table groaning under the weight of crystal and china and silver. No evening dress. No gowns. This *is* the twenty-first century, Mrs. Prowse."

"I do know that, Mr. Christmas."

"And there are hardly any wives present."

"Still, they might have made an effort."

Tom sighed and popped the canapé into his mouth. He understood these Leaping Lords charity events were boys-only weekends for the peers involved. Wives weren't forbidden, they were just discouraged. All the host had to do was crown the event with a slap-up meal of some nature that didn't involve black tie—in Lord Fairhaven's case a sort of slap-up *déjeuner sur l'herbe*—and send the boys on their way, to shoot in Scotland, as Tom overheard some of them say they were doing. He suspected there had to be a sleepover in some circumstances, but he had picked up from snippets of conversation through the afternoon that Lady Fairhaven was averse to company at Eggescombe. She had been, as Jane said she would, perfectly gracious when she had supplied the crutches and gave him directions to the Opium Bedroom, but Tom found her smile thin and fixed, her interest in her guest strained and formal.

"Well, I hope you're enjoying yourself at any rate, Mrs. Prowse," he said, conscious of rising voices down on the lawn. "At least the titles are grand. Do you know that's the Duke of Warwick over there—that very tall one, knobby knees, balding a bit, like Prince William?" He detected a glitter in her eyes as she glanced across the terrace.

"Yes, I saw him on the television."

He couldn't help himself. An opportunity to prick Madrun's balloon was too tempting. "He's an estate agent somewhere in the southeast, you know." *Sic transit gloria,* he thought, amused.

"Nonetheless"—Madrun straightened herself and cast him a withering glance—"it's an ancient title. And anyway, His Grace *owns* several estate agencies in Kent and Sussex and Surrey, and according to the *Sunday Times* Rich List he's the seventy-first wealthiest man in England."

"I am humbled. How do you know this?"

"I used the Google."

"Mrs. Prowse? You and a computer?"

"Your daughter's been showing me. It has its uses, I'll allow."

"Signs and portents!" Tom reached out for another canapé. "We must be at the End Times. Mrs. Prowse?" he pleaded as the tray retreated from his hand, out of reach.

Then he saw that her attention had been distracted by a sudden commotion in the middle distance. He followed her gaze to witness Oliver in the midst of an abrupt exit from his friends and swift descent of the stone steps to the lawn, his features a clot of ferocity as his red hair, worn near Byronically long, caught the sun's rays and flared suddenly like an angry flame. He seemed to lunge in Lucinda's direction. Tom couldn't see properly through the thick balusters. All he could do was hear, and realise he had been hearing the genesis of some unpleasant exchange. Now there was a shriek, a growling incoherence of invective, and an unmerry tinkle of shattering glass.

CHAPTER FOUR

"I seem to recall seeing you pull a rabbit out of a hat at some venue, Camden way, about fifteen years ago." Oliver pulled the cigar from his mouth, enveloping his long, bony face in a cloudy wreath. "Can't think what I was doing there."

It was on the tip of Tom's tongue to say that His Lordship had remarked on that very thing when they'd been introduced that morning at the Plymouth airfield.

He was growing impatient with his own self. His ankle was giving him gyp, his backside was growing numb, and he had been struggling to rise from the sun lounger onto his crutch with Max and Miranda as unhelpful witnesses when Oliver fforde-Beckett, who might have lent a hand but didn't, sidled over, drink in one hand, cigar in the other, whistling for some unaccountable reason.

"I doubt I did the rabbit trick," Tom grunted, balancing awkwardly on the crutch as he tried to recover a little dignity.

Pulling small animals from headgear had largely vanished from his repertoire by his late teens. He glanced at Oliver, whose frown suggested Tom's memory was the faulty one.

"*Were* you a magician, Mr. Christmas?" Max looked up at him brightly.

"Before I entered the priesthood, yes."

"How *spiffing*! Do you—"

"I know." Oliver's drawl cascaded over his nephew along with a cloud of smoke. "You did something with a tie. I remember because the mark was sitting next to me. You snipped it to ribbons then restored it a moment later. Clever. I suppose," he added dismissively.

Max coughed and put his fingers to his neck. "Could you do mine, Mr. Christmas?"

"A tie would be best, but—"

"Untie yours, old man." Oliver addressed his nephew. "An unknotted bow tie would work as well, wouldn't it, Vicar?"

"Don't tell me, Maximilian, that you're wearing one of those pre-tied jobs." Dominic fforde-Beckett had been hovering near, glowering—Tom thought—at his cousin, but he turned to the child and spoke amiably.

Max grimaced. "Mater has a headache, and I couldn't find Pater."

"You should have asked Gaunt." Dominic lifted the tab of Max's collar for examination. "He tied all my ties when I was a boy."

"Yes." Oliver smirked into his drink. "I expect your dear mother was likely too tied up in some other fashion to be of any use."

"Shut up, Olly."

"Why don't you see if you can find a tie for the vicar?" Oliver ignored Dominic and addressed his nephew.

"Oh! Shall I?"

"But—" Tom watched with dismay as Max darted back through the French doors into Eggescombe's interior only to poke his head around a second later and say with a gallant smile to Miranda, "I shan't be long."

Tom, prepared to dissuade Max again, was distracted by his daughter, who had remained silent during the exchange. Usually, she would sigh or groan or roll her eyes in advance of any of his harmless feints of magic, having reached the age of finding her father faintly embarrassing in certain instances, but here she was smiling vacantly after Max, her dark eyes glistening.

"You need some things from your magic kit, don't you, Daddy?" She turned to him.

"I'm afraid so, darling. It may be in the car, unless it was brought up with the luggage. Your grandmother has a notion for me to perform at their church fête when we get to Gravesend, but I suppose I could pull a coin out Maximilian's ear."

"Oh, Daddy." That one bored Miranda beyond measure.

"Speaking of tricks, Oliver," Dominic said. "I've spent much of the last week consulting with Raymond Firbank at Thorpe End about his art collection. You know of Raymond, of course—"

"Yes, he's an old queen with a taste for—"

"Interestingly," Dominic interrupted, "he's recently purchased—privately, but from whom he did not say—a Pissarro, specifically *Church at Dulwich*. I—"

"I had a notion you were in Cap Ferrat with Lucy and that bitch mother of yours." Oliver scratched an eyebrow, dropping cigar ash onto his shirt.

Tom glanced with worry at Miranda then at Dominic, who bared his teeth and snapped:

"I wasn't. As I said, I was with Raymond Firbank."

"Looking at paintings? I'll bet that wasn't all you were up to," Oliver drawled, smirking at Tom.

Dominic shared his cousin's long face, though his jaw was squarer, more taut. Now his face blazed as he raised his voice: "I found it remarkable that Raymond had *Church at Dulwich*, as it has hung in the upstairs hall at Morborne House since I can remember. Pissarro did a number of paintings of the Pont-Neuf and the Louvre and Kew, but he only did *one* of a church in Dulwich."

"How do you know? Perhaps he did two and one's been hiding in some attic somewhere."

"There isn't! I went around to Morborne House last week—"

"What?" Oliver nearly spat the cigar, his languid tone vanished. "I gave Haddon strict instructions—"

"Haddon couldn't reach you on your mobile. And as I am family and told him I only wanted to examine a painting in the course of my work, he let me in. Remarkably, *Church at Dulwich* was hanging where it's always hung."

"Said so, didn't I. There are two."

"Pissarro didn't make exact copies of his own work, you idiot."

"Watch it, you!"

"The one at Morborne House is a forgery, Oliver—a superb forgery, but a forgery nonetheless. I am, as you very well know, an expert in nineteenth- and early-twentieth-century painting."

"Are you?" Tom interjected quickly, hoping to stem the rising acrimony. "How interesting. A Guercino painting disappeared from my church a few years ago. We've had no luck finding it."

"I'm afraid, Vicar, that your Guercino is likely hanging in some vulgar Russian oligarch's bloody ugly bunker," Dominic responded with impatience, turning back to his cousin. "So I examined more of Great-Great-Grandfather's collection. There's a Morisot, a Monet, a Renoir, and a Félix Bracquemond that are clearly fakes."

"Really? I am surprised. Then Great-Great-Grandfather didn't have quite the eye we thought he had."

"Haddon informs me that a number of works have gone out for 'cleaning' or 'reframing' over the past year or so, notably when my mother is absent."

"Your mother is almost always absent from London, Dominic—south of France, California, West Indies. It's ridiculous that she has a life right to the use of Morborne House."

"Those are the terms of the Trust. You can live there, too, if you wish."

"Too right, I can. And I will. *I'm* the bloody Marquess of Morborne. Why am I living in a squat?"

"A *squat*? You mean your mews flat in Belgravia?"

"Dominic, with you it's always been too easy to take the piss."

Dominic's face darkened. "You've never been bothered before about living at Morborne House!"

"I am now! I have my reasons, which"—Oliver pointed his cigar at his cousin—"you will learn in due course. In any case, Charlotte will not be living there if I'm living there. Imagine living with that twat! And Lucy won't be living there, either."

"Which is why you've had the locks changed."

"Precisely."

"You don't have the permission of the Trust."

"Bugger the Trust."

"And you've been selling pictures and putting fakes up on the wall, haven't you, Oliver. I don't need to tell you what an absolute violation of the Trust that is!"

"I said, bugger the Trust. The Trust will do what *I* want! *Le trust, c'est moi!*"

"*Vous parlez français!*" Miranda interjected.

"Only because he's as madly arrogant as the Sun King," Dominic sneered.

"Mad Morborne they call me in the music trade." Oliver waved his hand airily, evidently pleased with himself, the smoke from his cigar trailing in the frail evening light. "And here comes our little Maxie."

"This isn't over, Oliver," Dominic warned.

"Sod off, cousin. Look, Vicar, Max has brought a tie. Over to you."

Max displayed the tie with a flourish.

Tom drew it forwards with his finger to examine it—it was dark blue with discreet yellow and burgundy striping, the sort, he thought, that adorned the necks of millions of men every working day. Oliver glanced at it, then looked away, seeming to lose interest in baiting his cousin, settling again into a kind of off-key, tuneless whistle. Dominic's eyes slid off Oliver, his lip uncurling to turn a kinder face to his cousin's child.

"It's a splendid tie, Maximilian," Tom said, rebalancing himself on his crutch, "and it would be perfect for the trick, but—"

"Daddy needs his magic wand," explained Miranda. "He can't do magic without it."

"In effect," Tom allowed, grateful to his daughter, though it was a bit of a fib. "And my arm on a crutch would make manoeuvring difficult."

"Oh, what a pity." Max regarded the neckwear glumly.

"Here, Max, you'll like this." Dominic took the tie from him and began threading it through the belt loops of his cream trousers, tying it loosely so the ends fell against his hip. "We'd do this at school sometimes. What do you think? Fred Astaire used to wear a tie as a belt on occasion. Very smart in the day."

Max tilted his head as he studied the effect. The monocle fell from his eye. "Who's Fred Astaire?"

"Dominic's tutor at Oxford," Oliver said airily.

"I'm not sure it's proper." Max frowned as he reinserted the monocle.

But attention seemed to drift to the darkening lawn where two silvery silhouettes, ghost-like, glided entwined like lovers towards the terrace. Unable to identify them, Tom looked beyond, towards the distant trees now a ragged crown, dusky against an icy sky shot through with pink and crimson, set with a single jewel, Venus, twinkling on the far southern horizon. The evening seemed suddenly advanced. Well to the west, a corner of the kitchen garden's high brick wall coloured the red of dried blood in the paling sun; to the east, the curved edge of the Eggescombe Labyrinth crouched in shadow like a brooding animal. With summer night conquering day, the stronger light came now from the Hall, a honeyed glow from the open French doors pouring onto the terrace and down the stairs, burnished gold from the ground-floor windows, lemony candle flame setting the table linens aglow; the scarlet burn of Oliver's cigar seemed now to navigate the air like a luminous insect. Turned towards the parkland vistas, Tom sensed through the skin on the back of his neck the massive and intense bulk of Eggescombe, its brick and terracotta radiating the stored heat of the day into the cooling evening. The sound of recorded music wafted from the drawing room into the silky air, which was an amalgam of summer scents, of grass and trees and flowers, tainted by the cruder aroma of cooking meat, the supper they were soon to begin. Somewhere a night bird cried out in alarm. As the figures drew clearer, Tom could see that one was Marguerite in a simple white shift, pale hair piled artlessly on her head. Accompanying her, his hand slipping into hers as they neared the steps, was a young man of uncommon beauty. Little taller than Marguerite, lithe and slimly muscular in a sleeveless white shirt, he glanced their way, hesitating as Marguerite gathered her skirt with her other hand before taking the steps, letting Tom take in the well-formed head, the wide, dark eyes and the dark curly hair half covering his ears.

"This should interest you, *my dear.*" Tom heard the malicious purr in Oliver's murmur and glimpsed Dominic shoot Oliver a hateful glance.

"Marguerite's . . . lodger," Oliver continued, tilting his head to drag on his cigar. "Did you know? The hand-holding, you'll find, is a bit of show. She's his *muse,* don't you know. I think you understand my meaning."

Hector stepped through the French doors at that moment, as if he had seen his mother's approach from the drawing room and felt compelled to greet her. Georgina was in his wake, with Bonzo coming behind. He flicked an unhappy glance at either Dominic or Oliver—Tom couldn't tell which—then moved quickly to the edge of the steps.

"Mother." The word seemed to suppress a world of exasperation.

"Hector, darling, I hope we're not late."

"No, Mummy."

"Roberto was absorbed in his work, so . . ."

Hector smiled thinly at the young man. "Good of you to put something on."

"Roberto is a bit of a . . . naturist." Oliver continued whispering at Dominic. "Can be quite the sensation, I gather. If you fancy that sort of thing."

"Fuck off, Oliver," Dominic spat, though his eyes didn't leave the new visitor.

"Maxie, my darling, don't you look splendid!" Marguerite exclaimed. "Quite like the old days at Eggescombe," she continued, directing a calculated smile at Georgina, who received the implied criticism with a frosty stare. "Everyone dressed resplendently for supper. Do you remember, Hector darling, Nanny bringing you down for presentation, and you doing a little turn in your jimjams?"

"Not really," Hector responded impatiently. "Would you care for a drink? I'll have Gaunt bring something."

"Vodka and tonic."

"Mr. Sica?" Hector's lips drew to a pinch.

"Mineral water." They were the newcomer's first words. He spoke gravely, with a hint of disdain.

"Of course," Hector murmured dryly, removing himself from the scrum.

"I thought I'd like to see how our patient is coming along." Marguerite moved down the terrace. "Tom, you're supposed to be resting, with your feet up," she admonished him, though her eyes were lively with amusement.

"I'm afraid I couldn't bear all the lying about."

"Well, I expect you'll live. I've also found a cast boot for you to wear. I pulled one off St. John Ambulance before they left, so we can fix you up with it tomorrow. And this must be your daughter." Marguerite extended her hand. "Miranda, *enchantée de faire votre connaissance*. Max here has been telling me about you. I'm sorry we didn't meet earlier. I understand you're absolutely wizard—Maxie's favourite word—at French, which unfortunately Max is not doing well in at school. You must give him a lesson."

"Moi de même." Miranda took the dowager countess's hand and smiled up at her shyly.

"If only I'd run up some pretty dress for you to wear. You and Maxie could have been a matched set and put us all to shame."

"You've never 'run up' anything in your life, Mummy." Hector returned, followed by Gaunt with a silver tray and two crystal glasses.

"I learned dressmaking at Mon Fertile, Hector. I've simply never had any need to apply it. But I could sew a dress if I set my mind to it. I'm sure I saw a machine in one of the attic rooms when I was looking for crutches for Mr. Christmas." Marguerite seemed to hesitate over the tray's offerings, which looked alike. Gaunt tilted the tray to indicate the vodka.

"You are joining us for supper, Marguerite, yes?" Georgina spoke.

"If you'll have me, my dear. Please don't let me interrupt you in whatever you were doing. Now," she continued. "Some introductions I think are in order. This is Roberto Sica. Roberto, this is Tom Christmas, who is vicar of St. Nicholas Church in Thornford Regis, for whom today's jump was done, which you missed of course, busy boy. And his daughter, Miranda. I don't think you've met Dominic fforde-Beckett before, have you. Odd you haven't. You're both in the same sort of . . . line of work, I suppose one could say. Georgina's cousin," she added unnecessarily, as the two men shook hands.

"Interesting belt," Roberto remarked.

"Oh, do you think so?"

"I don't," Hector said. "You look a fool, Dominic. What are you trying to—"

"Never mind, Hector. It was only a bit of fun, Christ! Here." Dominic whipped the tie out of his belt loops and dropped it in Max's hands. "Another time, perhaps, Vicar."

"And here," Marguerite pressed on, as another figure stepped forward, "is Lucinda fforde-Beckett, who is . . . well, another fforde-Beckett. We do seem to have rather a lot of fforde-Becketts here this weekend. I wonder if there's one of those amusing collective nouns we might use? 'A tyranny of fforde-Becketts'? What do you think?"

"Really, Mummy, must you . . . ?"

"'An intemperance,' perhaps, Marve," Roberto suggested, lowering his eyes to his glass.

"Yes! Clever! 'An intemperance of fforde-Becketts.'" Marguerite laughed throatily as the fforde-Beckett siblings looked on. "See, Oliver is amused." Oliver had snorted with a wet burst of noise, but Georgina maintained a mask of sufferance, staring off into the middle distance. Dominic and Lucinda kept delighted eyes on the speaker, however, as if the characterisation of the family were mere wordplay. Tom sensed it was not.

"And, of course, this is Oliver, whom—" Marguerite added with a detectable lightness of tone, "I believe you know."

Roberto raised his eyes but refused Oliver's hand, though it was proffered. Rather, he glowered, a corner of his upper lip twitching almost imperceptibly—startling in its effect, Tom thought, until he observed Oliver's startling—and strangely humanising—reaction: a faltering glance, a flash of vulnerability, superciliousness vanished, then as swiftly recovered.

"But Oliver," Dominic began snidely, "you've been at Eggescombe for absolute days and Marguerite hasn't brought her friend to renew your . . . acquaintance?"

"I've been preoccupied with my work." Roberto gave Dominic a level gaze over the rim of his glass, then took a swift, sharp sip.

"What is it you do?" Tom asked.

"He's a sculptor," Marguerite replied in Roberto's stead.

"He has the most wizard studio at the stable block!" Max

enthused. "Mr. Christmas, you and Miranda must come and see."

"Yes, Tom, do." Marguerite shifted her body slightly, as if to exclude the fforde-Becketts from her invitation. "I mentioned those photographs earlier I thought you might find interesting. And Miranda, too, of course. Come for elevenses. That would be a good time to get out the album. And put on that boot I mentioned. Then we can visit the studio."

Some hours earlier, in the late afternoon, as the charity event was winding down, Marguerite had brought out onto the lawn Eggescombe Hall's visitors' book, a compendious volume, wood-covered, embossed with the Fairhaven coronet, and bound with string so new pages could be added when needed. Marguerite licked her finger, flipped quickly back through a number of pages, then with a small grunt of satisfaction passed it to Tom. He was, at first, interested to see scrawled in various styles of penmanship a number of notables of an earlier generation.

"You had Mick Jagger to stay?"

"No. Well, yes, he popped in one afternoon. But that's not why I've brought this book out. Look." She put her finger against a pair of signatures farther down the spread.

"Oh!" Tom felt strangely affected at the sight, as he often did when evidence of his first adoptive parents presented itself. IAIN CHRISTMAS in a neat, rounded, schoolboy script and, below, MARY CARROLL in a flowing, decorative hand. "They were here at Eggescombe?"

"About forty years ago or so, in the summer, I think. What's the date?" She leaned in. "August. Exactly forty years ago. It was the Alice party. My father-in-law adored *Alice's Adventures in Wonderland.* He had a costume party every July, the month *Alice* was published. Can't remember the year. I have photos, I must show you."

"But how—"

"Oh, my late husband had some connections in the music business in those days. And of course your parents were musicians. Anyway, I do remember talking with your mother, with Mary. You see, she had just learned that a baby would be coming their way. You. I expect the adoption had been pre-arranged in some fashion. The girl . . ." She faltered, glancing at Tom. "Do you know . . . ?"

"No, I don't."

"You know nothing about your natural mother?"

"Not really, no."

"You weren't curious?"

"Oh, of course. Very much, at times. But the women who raised me—Iain's sister—and her partner knew very little themselves. Or so I understand. Iain and Mary died, as perhaps you know—"

"Yes, in that awful plane crash."

"—the spring after they adopted me." Tom stared at the signatures. "If they knew any details about my natural parents, they decided, for some reason, to keep it to themselves. And, of course, as you get older, you don't think about it overmuch. Is there something . . . ?"

"Not really. I only recall your mother saying she and your father would be travelling to Liverpool for the adoption. I remember distinctly because my husband had some business to attend to on behalf of the family in that part of the north."

"Liverpool," Tom repeated thoughtfully. "I only know the adoption was a private arrangement of some nature."

"How mysterious!"

"Yes, I've thought that at times."

Marguerite glanced from the date of the Christmases' visit to Eggescombe to Tom. "Then your birthday is this month. Your fortieth, yes?"

"On Monday, as it happens."

"Oh." And then in an altered tone, "Oh! Now I understand your hesitation to stay."

"Well, I expect my family has something planned for me. There's still a chance tomorrow . . ."

Marguerite's brows arched sceptically. "If it had been your *left* ankle, perhaps, you might be able to drive but . . ." She had left the rest unsaid.

Now, recalling his mind to the present, Tom heard Marguerite remark, "Roberto is working on a splendid new commission for Delix Fennis's sculpture garden in Cornwall. You know the one, of Gods and Goddesses. He popped by last month and commissioned one after seeing Roberto working on the sculpture that's in the Labyrinth."

"Sculpture?" Tom recalled no mention of such in the literature about the noted Eggescombe Labyrinth.

"Installed last month," Marguerite explained. "A new feature."

"I believe Roberto works in marble, don't you, Roberto?" Oliver blew a plume of smoke into the air.

"I'm surprised you would know that." Dominic eyed Oliver with disdain.

"Bit quaint, isn't it?" Oliver ignored his cousin. "I thought it was all pickled sheep in vats of formaldehyde these days?"

"I'd very much like to visit your studio, too, while I'm here," Dominic told Roberto.

"If you feel you have the time," Marguerite murmured without enthusiasm.

Roberto added, "I most often work late at night."

"That's when I like to get the job done, too." Oliver smirked.

Roberto's nostrils flared as if he'd smelled something offensive. "Have you seen my work in the Labyrinth, Oliver?"

"I haven't been in that bloody thing in years. Seems like a lot of walking around in circles for no good reason."

"You really are a philistine." Dominic's mouth twisted.

"I insist, Oliver." Roberto spoke more forcefully.

"Why? What's the statue bloody *of* then?"

"BVM."

"What?"

"The Blessed Virgin."

"Oh, for Christ's sake." Oliver threw his cigar over the balustrade. Tom's eyes followed the red glow in its arc, noting the apparently fastidious Gaunt move swiftly to remove the offending thing from the darkening lawn. "I haven't got time for that sort of bollocks. Sorry, Vicar."

"No, Oliver," Marguerite cut in before Tom could respond. "You really must view Roberto's wonderful addition to the Labyrinth. You'll find it extremely compelling, I'm quite certain."

Oliver looked from the older woman to the younger man, his eyes narrowed to a black intensity. "I'll give it," he replied slowly, "some thought."

CHAPTER FIVE

*T*om studied the chimneypiece's timber overmantel, which he'd glimpsed in the late afternoon as he hobbled from the terrace—the whole day seemed to have been spent outdoors—to a loo tucked under a staircase in Eggescombe's labyrinthine interior. Then, with the curtains drawn against the hot sun, the drawing room in cool shadow, the overmantel's elaborate carvings had seemed a squirming abstraction of light and shadow. Now, with evening's fall, with a chandelier switched on and the room aglow, the abstraction resolved into a phantasmagoria of roiling and terrified figures in macabre dance around an imperious skeleton like some Caesar of the underworld risen to destroy the world of the living. Orbless eyes mercilessly scanning the bleak landscape, one hand raising a scythe, the other preparing a sword, the figure trampled on tokens of earthly vanities—sceptres and crowns and coins.

"Not the most welcoming motif, is it?" Jane joined him

where he was steadying himself against the back of a chair set at an angle to the fireplace, unlit on this warm summer evening.

"The Triumph of Death? No." Tom felt a laugh catch in his throat. "The Jacobeans had a taste for moral imagery, I seem to recall. Or perhaps Lord Fairhaven's ancestor was particularly keen on this sort of didactic moral ornament."

"I wonder if it's inherited," Jane murmured, though the chatter in the room masked any need for discretion. "I am fond of him, but Hector can be kind of a scold at times. He's involved with various traditional-values groups and the like."

"Oh?"

"And he's standing for Parliament if he wins the open primary, did you know? The MP stood down over some expenses scandal, so there's to be a by-election this . . . October, I think. Hector's chair of the local Conservative Association, so . . ."

"Did he ever sit in the Lords?"

"Hector? For about two minutes. His father died quite young, but Hector inherited the title about the time the Lords was being reorganised. So he lost his seat along with most of the hereditary peers. There's—what?—about ninety hereditary peers in the Lords these days? And six hundred life peers? Anyway, since hereditary peers may now stand for election and serve in the Commons, Hector's keen to get in. His grandfather and great-grandfather pushed their weight around in government years ago from the Lords." She smiled at him appraisingly. "I'll bet you've never voted Conservative in your life."

"I worked many years in an inner-city ministry so I think, Lady Kirkbride, that you've made a safe bet. And you?"

"Well, Father Christmas, I think . . ." She surveyed the room. "I think you and I may be a party of two here. Promise not to tell my husband?"

"I won't." Tom's eyes stole once again to the overmantel.

"Eggescombe is full of such carvings." Jane followed his glance. "When you're a little more mobile, you can take the tour. There's a Judgement of Solomon over the fireplace in the dining room—judging the quality of the fare maybe. I think Hector and Georgina's bedroom has the Virtues . . . accompanied by the Vices. You're not laughing. Are you okay?"

"I'm fine."

"You don't sound it."

"I expect I'm feeling a bit mortal, spraining my ankle and all."

"Nothing to do with Eggescombe, then."

"What do you mean?"

"Eggescombe can be a sort of gloomy pile in the wrong light. It's been used in films for effect, did you know?"

"Mrs. Prowse mentioned something about an Agatha Christie."

"And an American outfit hired the place for some sort of horror film—along the lines of *Devon Chainsaw Massacre*. Can't remember the real title. Hector held his nose and took the money. I wouldn't let my kids watch it—it was a bit disturbing. The shots of Eggescombe Hall looming out of the murk made me shiver. I'm shivering now, and it's a warm evening! Perhaps"—Jane lowered her voice—"I'm having a . . ."

"Frisson?"

"That's the word. Or perhaps the ghost of Eggescombe is set to walk tonight. There is a full moon."

"Is there a stately home in England without a ghost?"

"Bridgemary, my father-in-law's home in Shropshire, seems to be ghost-free. As far as I know."

"And what does Eggescombe's ghost do?"

"I'm not sure. You should ask Max. He loves all the lore of the place." Jane sighed. "Actually, I think Eggescombe's ghost haunts the park, not the house. Something nasty happened on the grounds five hundred years ago. Anyway, I think ghosts are a crock."

"Me, too."

"Perhaps then the barometric pressure is rising . . . or falling, or whatever it is. Marve was telling me when she and Roberto walked over from the dower house, they could see clouds massing over the moor."

"I'm not sure I'm very susceptible to those sorts of atmospheres."

"More the sorts between people then."

"Possibly."

"You've noticed the fforde-Becketts don't play happy families very well."

"You did warn me." Tom's eye happened to catch Lucinda's at the moment. She was speaking with one of the guests—introduced to Tom at the airfield as Jimmy (James, Baron Pownall, in fact), the shortest of the Leaping Lords—but suddenly she turned her head and cast him a smile of such radiance, he could only respond with his own giddy version. Lucy excused herself to her interlocutor and moved to where Dominic was nursing a gin, his pale features lit by a lamp. Tom turned back to Jane, startled from his thoughts by her appraising glance.

"You're not feeling a bit mortal because you're coming to a certain significant birthday, by any chance?"

"Lady Fairhaven has been talking."

"She happened to mention it."

"I suppose certain birthdays give one pause for reflection. I count my blessings however, and they are many."

"Most of us are much more blessed today than they would have been when that thing was carved." Jane gestured to the overmantel. "When it was installed five centuries ago it must have terrified. People then literally believed in hell. But now . . ." Tom felt her shrewd glance. "Tom, you don't . . . ?"

"Believe in a literal hell? Fire and brimstone? No. The Church views all that as outmoded, though there are some dissenters. 'Separation from God,' I tell my confirmands. But 'hell' can be an apt metaphor, can't it? The hellish things people have done to one another in war or to the world, to the environment. Or people dwelling in a sort of private hell—living some lie, carrying around some corrupting secret. I expect we've all had a moment, a day, a week, a year—or more—in which we live in hell, haven't we?" He turned his attention back to Jane. "I do apologise. I'm being morbid, for some reason."

She laughed. "I told you Eggescombe had an atmosphere. Now you won't be able to sleep."

"Speaking of which." Tom scanned the room. "My child should be getting off to bed before very long. Where is she?"

"Don't worry. The Gaunts are wonderful with Max. I'm sure Mrs. Gaunt has already got her settled. You might," Jane responded as he frowned at his wrapped foot, "find it a bit of a climb to the nursery floor."

"No 'good night' for me then."

"They do grow up. If I phone Olivia now at Tullochbrae to say good night, she'll just groan and say, 'Oh, Mummy, *really!*' Look, what's this?" Jane gestured towards the door at the far end of the room through which Gaunt was pushing a trolley laden with half a dozen bottles and fresh glassware, the gentle tinkle of which pierced the low hubbub of conversation.

"What's this?" Hector's echo sounded sharply behind Tom. He and Georgina had entered the drawing room from the terrace at the same moment, Bonzo following.

Gaunt stopped the trolley by the fire screen and settled one of the wobbling bottles with a gloved hand.

"Lord Morborne's wishes, my lord," he replied, turning as Hector rounded the Hepplewhite sofa.

"Are these from the cellar?"

"No, my lord."

"Good. He can't have brought them from London. Champagne couldn't possibly have survived Oliver's . . ."

"Oliver's what, Hector?" Jane asked as Hector's voice trailed off.

"Oh, nothing." Hector flicked his hand dismissively.

"Lord Morborne asked me to purchase these at the Pilgrims Inn yesterday afternoon," Gaunt explained.

Hector's lower lip protruded in a pout. "He's got a cheek. Do you know any of this, my dear?" He addressed his wife, who had twisted one of the bottles to examine the label.

"Nothing," she replied.

"I hope this isn't on my behalf . . . or St. Nicholas's," Tom amended in a muttered aside to Jane. "Everyone has done so much already."

"I doubt it's on your behalf, Vicar." Hector had evidently

overheard, adding with a swift glance at Tom, "Oliver wouldn't have the consideration."

"Really, darling." Georgina's tone was admonishing.

"Well, he wouldn't! He tried to kill me this afternoon."

"Hector, don't be ridiculous!"

"Lord Morborne says it's to be a surprise." Gaunt's visage, pale and square, showed no emotion, but a nuance in his tone contained a world of disapproval.

"I've had quite sufficient . . . surprises this week," Hector muttered darkly. "Well, where is he then? He's not on the terrace. Georgie and I were the last."

As if everyone shared the same thought, Oliver's name began to percolate through the room. "Olly!" Someone moved to the French doors and shouted onto the shadowy terrace.

"He's not bloody out there!" Hector countered.

"I'm right here, Hector. Keep your hair on." Oliver pushed through the second of two entrances from the corridor to the drawing room, mobile phone in hand, his pique melting into a grin as he crossed to the fireplace.

"What are you up to, Mad Morborne?" one of the guests joshed.

"Wait and find out." Oliver stopped next to the drinks trolley. "Gaunt, start on those bottles, there's a good man." He lifted one of the fluted glasses and pinged it with his mobile. "My lords," he began to little effect. "*My lords,*" he roared to quell the noise. "Thank you." He smiled as silence descended. "My lords, ladies, and gentlemen . . . Vicar," he added, in a faintly mocking tone, to Tom. "As you know, I've honed to a, well, somewhat different path than most of you, I would say, don't you think? No RAC Cirencester and a life as Farmer

Olly for me or being a director of some merchant bank in the City."

"You were in the Paras, Olly," someone remarked. "You can't be all bad."

"A mere idyll, my boy. It pleased Papa, somehow, though we all know he was a wicked old man and not the cynosure of conventionality himself."

"Apples and trees, Olly," someone called.

"Possibly. I wouldn't know. I've always thought myself pure as the driven snow, spending my humble life dedicated to serving the needs of the Great British Public for wholesome entertainment and pleasant venues for conversation and light refreshment."

"You *are* mad!" called another.

"'Though this be madness, yet there is method in't.'"

"Money in't more like, Olly," retorted the same voice. Laughter rippled through the room.

"A comment unworthy of you, unkind sir," Oliver said mockingly as Gaunt peeled the foil on the champagne bottle. "But I must wax serious: There comes a time in every man's life when one begins to take the long view. I thought as I was down in Devon with my family—my sister, my nephew, cousin Jamie, his charming wife . . . my other *kin*." He bared his teeth at the word in the direction of Dominic and Lucinda, who received the apparent slight with cold stares. "And of course you, my friends . . ." He made a sweeping gesture of the room. ". . . that I would make this very important announcement that I'm sure you will all greet with . . . well, some emotion appropriate to the occasion, I'm sure. Especially if you've had enough to drink."

"You're finally having that bloody awful boy band you manage drowned in the Thames," one person suggested.

"You're to be the new judge on *X Factor*," said another.

"You're opening a new club."

"My lords, et cetera, all those may be true, particularly the last one, but unworthy—perhaps—of this toast. In truth, I come before you, to humbly announce that—wait for it; you will be delighted, I guarantee—that I am about to close a life of iniquity by an act of timely repentance, after which it will be as if I had led the most virtuous of lives."

"Oh, hell!" came a voice. "You're not taking up the vicar's line of work?"

"No, you gormless twit. I am shortly to become a married man."

"About bloody time, Morborne!" Someone laughed, breaking the moment of stunned silence.

"And may we know whom you are marrying?" Georgina wore a worried frown.

"Serena Knowlton."

"Serena . . . ? Lord Knowlton's daughter! Olly, she's half your age!"

"And your point would be, Georgie dear?"

"Where did you . . . ?"

"Happened across her at Icarus. Couldn't keep my eyes off. She's been my PA for the last six months."

"Your personal assistant?" Roberto sounded disbelieving.

"Yes, what of it?" Oliver snapped.

"Does Frank Knowlton know?" Georgina asked.

"That she's my PA?"

"No, you pillock," Hector intruded, "does he know that you're intending to marry his daughter?"

"He will." Oliver blasted Hector with his ice-blue eyes. "I thought you at least would be pleased, Georgie."

"I'm not *dis*pleased. I'm . . . startled, that's all. When—"

"Yes, when are the nuptials, Olly?" A male voice crushed Georgina's. "Do tell."

"Soon. Very soon. We are expecting, Serena and I—"

"What, Olly? An appointment from the prime minister."

"No, you young idiot, our first child—"

"Not *your* first child, Olly!" someone said to a chorus of laddish chortles.

"Yes, well"—Oliver's humour appeared to be growing thin—"that's all in the past. More significantly, Serena has had one those test thingies—I can't think what they're called—and I'm very pleased to say—" He paused and turned his head with great deliberation towards Dominic and Lucinda, whose strained smiles, Tom noted, appeared the product of intense effort, then turned back to frown at Gaunt's slow, methodical untwisting of the wire cage around the champagne bottle cork. "—that we're having a male child."

"Excellent news!" a shout came from the back.

"Yes . . . Give me that, Gaunt." Oliver tried without success to snatch the bottle from the butler's hands. "A son and heir."

But the moment brought no further encomiums, for a rich and frothy explosion suddenly ricocheted around the drawing room's gilded paneling. Tom's eyes had travelled helplessly back to Lucinda but it was Dominic, a head above and behind her, who commanded his attention now. The fixed smile had vanished: His lips were pinched to a small mean moue; his eyes were flecked with loathing. But before Tom could give this transformation a moment's thought, a new sound diverted him, a roar of rage intense as a lanced bull's, attended by a barrage of cursing so vile he could only thank God for his daughter's absence. The flying cork had found its target in Oliver's face.

CHAPTER SIX

*T*om prepared to slip between the cool sheets. Someone, Gaunt most likely, had placed on the bed a pair of crisply pressed and folded pajamas as white as a bride's gown, but they weren't his. Tom's own sleepwear was informal—a T-shirt and cotton lounge pants most times—and almost always mismatched, frayed, and inelegant, and he guessed Gaunt had thought him lacking proper sleepwear—or any sleepwear at all—when he had unpacked his bags. The evening held its warmth, the room, too, so he hopped across the room to a daybed and set the pajamas down unmolested, returning to plunk his naked self down on the edge of the bed, an exotic four-poster with scarlet hangings, a japanned and gilded frame, surmounted by a pagoda roof with winged golden dragons at each cornice. His eyes travelled from the dragon's lewdly curling tongue down to the lacquered lattice-backed chairs to the ornate mirror frame over the fireplace to the delicate cream silk wallpaper with foliate motifs. Tom supposed it was all very lovely, if out of character with the rest of the house's Jacobean gloom, but somehow it reminded him more of a high-class tart's boudoir, not that he had ever been in such a place. He eyes fell to the carpet—unadorned and green, like a lawn—and to the terminus of his right leg. *Oh, my poor little foot.* Alice contemplating hers when she'd grown nine feet tall came to his mind. *Will I be able to put a sock and shoe on you tomorrow?*

Not bloody likely.

If his wife were alive, she would be a helpmeet, though it would be a day or two at least before the compression wrap could come off and she could fit him into a shoe. But Lisbeth was gone, lo these several years, he thought wistfully, and a little sleepily. Perhaps this was why he was thinking of Alice: She had ingested something—Was it a piece of cake? A pill? He couldn't remember—that had made her open out like a telescope. He had ingested a sleeping tablet, which was making him shut down like the same instrument. Lady Fairhaven had suggested it for the discomfort he was sure to have sleeping. She herself took fifteen milligrams of zopiclone to sleep. By her tone, it sounded like the done thing at Eggescombe. And as she had taken the trouble to come to his room with it and remained while he fumbled on the bedside table with the water carafe, refusing had seemed impolite. Lady Fairhaven's mother-in-law, the dowager countess, had been the one to lead him to his room earlier, and she had said sweetly, echoing Alice, "You must manage as best you can, but you must be kind to it."

His foot, that is.

So the pill was a kind of kindness, he supposed, though he had managed surreptitiously with his fingernail to break it in half before swallowing. Fifteen milligrams sounded much too much.

Perhaps he might favour his foot with new and unique footwear, like Alice. Sent by carrier. And how odd the directions will look!

TOM'S RIGHT FOOT, ESQ.

HEARTHRUG,

NEAR THE FENDER,

(WITH TOM'S LOVE).

He yawned deeply. The Opium Bedroom contained no hearthrug. His watering eyes roamed up his legs, past his thoroughly bored penis, to the accordion crinkle of his stomach. He absently pinched an inch of flesh. Two inches. More. How dismaying. In less than an hour it would be Christmas Eve, his family members' jokey private name for the day before their birthdays—this year, for him, a milestone birthday that he had been approaching in slithering trepidation with little prayerful increments, like someone sidling up to a woman in a wine bar. Really, another birthday shouldn't matter. He'd given the previous ones little mind. And he did indeed thank the Lord for the gift of life, for the gift of his daughter, his mothers, his friends, for the precious years he'd had with Lisbeth, for all the good things about life in a first-world country. But at forty he was midway through his earthly journey or, if one wanted to come over all peevish about it, he was suddenly, irrevocably, half dead. Being peevish about one's age was not an attractive quality, though he had said nothing to his parishioners about his forthcoming birthday and had laid down the law to Madrun to keep *schtum* on the subject, which was in truth rather peevish of him. "Perhaps a small party when Miranda and I return from Gravesend," he'd allowed, frowning over a much-too-early card from an old friend in London featuring a dinosaur, ha ha, how very droll.

If he hadn't been theologically trained, it might matter less. But he couldn't help but be reminded of the appearances of the number in the Bible. God, the God of order and purpose, had a penchant for things forty: forty days of rain for Noah, forty days of fasting and temptation for Jesus; forty years of exile in the desert of Midian for Moses, forty years of wandering the wilderness for the Israelites. The common theme: tribulation, testing, and trial.

Oh, dear.

He yawned again, so hard this time his jaw ached. He wasn't sure he was quite ready for a bout of tribulation, testing, and trial. Perhaps tomorrow. Yes, tomorrow and tomorrow and tomorrow will be the day of tribulation, testing, and . . . that other thing. He pinched his pudge again. Jesus lived to only thirty-three and odds were He didn't have time to get a pudge. Lot of walking in His ministry, of course—good exercise!—and He didn't have a housekeeper who'd trained at a very good catering college. *I wonder how they managed all those meals,* he wondered as he pulled the sheets down and slipped into the bed, vaguely aware his thoughts were growing gabbled and silly. All that cooking for the Twelve, plus Jesus, and who knew who else. Couldn't do the loaves-and-fishes bit every day!

Must have hired a team of excellent women.
Funny the Bible never mentioned them.
But then men's doings got all the attention, didn't they?
Patriarchy! Lisbeth would have said.
Ha ha. I love you.
He would have laughed.
And she came to him as an angel
As the waters of Lethe
poured over him.

Some time later—not long he thought, though in his woolly state he couldn't be certain—he was jolted to wakefulness, not by some nightmare's trident, he considered after a dull moment, but by light, an unrelenting stream of it training against his eyelids. He had been dreaming a falling dream, the ragged edges of which flittered away in the soft safe certainty he was home in Thornford in bed. But the bed felt oddly out of place. And the furniture, shadowy forms, appeared newly arranged. The window loomed high and strange, a glowing frame pulling his eyes to a full moon suspended in the black, black sky like a mammoth crystal, from which cool rays, like those from a dying sun, streamed into the room, seeking out its remote corners, pooling along the floor, and pouring over the bedclothes. Tom widened his eyes to the transfixing loveliness and in his trance felt himself set on a silver barque on a silver sea. But the trance lasted little time. The fairy dust of moon-light soon settled dim and cold along the room's alien shapes as his night mind sharpened to his surroundings. He knew where he was now. And he knew, too, that it wasn't simply moonlight that had disturbed his sleep. Someone had entered his room.

Eggescombe Hall

Dear Mum,

Lovely station~~aryery~~, don't you think? I am ~~ensconed ensc~~ at Eggescombe at last. All the years I've lived in Devon and never thought to visit even though it's open-to-view most weeks. Remember Hazel Turriff, Mum? Of course you do. Dad's cousin (third?) who I boarded with when I went to Leiths. She'd lived near 50 years in Shepherd's Bush and hadn't seen the Tower of London or the V&A. One day, she said. But she never seemed much wont to leave Tunis Road and I'll wager she never did see them before she died. I expect this happens when you live not far from something so well known. I'm ~~rectu~~ rectifying that! I can now tick Eggescombe off my list! I drove here with Miranda yesterday morning in Mr. Christmas's car, as he went off to the airfield. I could tell he was skittish of jumping from an airplane. He hardly had a bite of my very good breakfast and kept looking at the clock over the

Aga. You'll do yourself an injury, I said to him, and began to think again that perhaps Karla was right, that the traditional ways to raise money for the church are best. And see if she wasn't right! Mr. C. went and sprained his ankle when he landed—not badly, but enough to scotch his plans to drive to London last evening. He and Miranda are staying over at Eggescombe, I'm not sure for how long, which makes me wonder if I should mention his birthday (tomorrow!) to someone, as it seems wretched not to have at least a cake at the ready, but he was quite insistent I "hone to discretion" as he put it. Anyway, Mum, there was much worse than Mr. C.'s spill! Lord Fairhaven's parachute didn't open properly when the lords were jumping. We were watching it all on CCTV as it was happening and everyone was horrified, staring at the TV screen then looking into the sky expecting this poor man to come tearing out of it. What luck he had an emergency parachute, and all was well in the end, but I think something funny was going on. When I was helping serve last evening I overheard someone say Lord Fairhaven's parachute must have been fiddled with! Anyway, Mum, I'm getting ahead of myself! Yesterday Ellen met Miranda and me at the Gatehouse, where she and Mick are staying instead of the Big House, which I thought a bit odd at first. The Gatehouse is quite splendid! A bit like a little castle all by itself, though longer than wide, three storeys high, with those ~~crennel cre~~ *bumpy bits along the roofline and a tower at each end. Apparently Eggescombe's senior managers live in apartments one on each side of the big gate, which they vacate with most of the other estate staff for an August*

holiday while Lord and Lady Fairhaven are in residence.
Ellen and Mick are living in the north apartment, which
is very cosy. My bedroom's at the top of the tower—it has
eight sides! With wonderful views one way down the road
towards Abbotswick and the other towards Eggescombe
Hall and all its chimneys. (No wonder it "played"
Chimneys in the TV version of The Seven Dials Mystery!)
I shall be queen of all I survey, as Miranda said when she
helped with my bag. Ellen looks ~~just the same as~~ *perhaps a*
little plumper than when I saw her last all those years ago.
Do you remember me bringing her home to visit one
weekend when we were at school? Lively thing, she was. I
remember her saying then that the old shack down by the
quay at Thornford could be a super little restaurant if
someone put his mind to it, and now of course it is and she
was right! But I must say she SEEMS *different somehow.*
Well, you would be, after all these years, I suppose, but
there's something gone a bit severe about her, I'm sorry to
say. I don't think she cares much for her employers, for one
thing. Apparently Lady Fairhaven is a bit of a trial, really
doesn't lift a hand, and you have to these days, don't you?
It's not like when Great-Grannie Prowse was
parlourmaid for the Northmores at Thornridge House and
there was nearly a dozen staff. There's only Ellen and
Mick doing everything. Lady Fairhaven is prone to
migraines, Ellen says, though her tone suggested Her
Ladyship finds migraines rather CONVENIENT, *and says*
they live much too informally given their position and
such. She seemed to prefer her last employers, the Arouzis.
Do you know them, Mum? Sometimes Mr. Arouzi is on

telly talking about banking or stocks or the like. He always looks very dignified, like some Arab prince, but they're not Arabs, they're ~~Persi~~ Iranians, and not Muslims, but something else, which I've forgotten. I shall have to ask Mr. Christmas if he knows what it's about. Ellen said they were lovely to work for and had a household staff of seven—very grand, like the old days!—which she and Mick managed, and that the Arouzis had houses in Los Angeles and Switzerland, too, and they would travel there with them sometimes, and it all sounded very posh, so I couldn't help asking why they had left, and she said Mick wanted it. He saw an advert looking for a butler-valet and cook-housekeeper for the Earl and Countess of Fairhaven and thought a change would do them good and they were getting on a bit and maybe should take it easier with a smaller household and suchlike, but as Ellen pointed out, with no other staff, they're working harder than ever before. By the way, Mum, Lord Fairhaven's last butler was that big winner last summer in the National Lottery, the biggest ever, I think, £43 million! Ellen says he and his wife didn't even give Lord Fairhaven notice! Just packed their things and flew to Malta. Haven't been heard of since—well except for the stories in the tabs. Does make you wonder though what Lord and Lady Fairhaven are like to work for, if their staff can't wait to get shot of them?! Ellen hinted she would like to find a new situation, but they are fond of Maximilian, L & L Fairhaven's son. Viscount Boothby, he is, with his courtesy title. He's a funny little boy, but Miranda, I can tell, has taken a shine to him. We met him walking up from the Gatehouse and I

*thought for a second he was a midget got up for some
entertainment at the Fund-raiser or some little chap
wandered away from a wedding in the village. He was
wearing a grey morning coat, if you please, waistcoat,
stripey trousers, all of it. Lovely tailoring, I could tell, and
I did wonder how any mum and dad would afford to keep
a growing boy in such finery, until I was introduced. In
the evening, he changed to full evening dress! Quite the
best-dressed "man" there by a long chalk, I must say!
Really, Mum, most of the Leaping Lords dressed no better
than half the men in the village at the weekend. How
standards have fallen! Still, there wasn't much to dress for.
I thought Lady Fairhaven might have had a glittering
dinner party—but of course there's not the staff, and I even
filled in helping Ellen serve. I gather Lady Fairhaven
doesn't think much of her husband jumping out of
airplanes, and perhaps she really is a migraine sufferer as
she did look very drawn. None of the other wives were
present, either, except for Lady Kirkbride whose husband
organised the event for Mr. Christmas. She's very sweet,
Lady Kirkbride. She asked me all sorts about Thornford R,
but of course, she's still worried about her brother-in-law,
our former verger, who went missing more than a year
ago. I AM rambling. I was going to say that Maximilian
has lovely manners, too, which is nice for Miranda. The
boys in the village her age seem only to want to tease the
girls, if they pay any attention at all. I even had a
moment's fancy of one day Miranda becoming Lady
Boothby, then, in time, Lady Fairhaven, though I am
being a bit previous, aren't I? Anyway, Mum, I was going*

to tell you a bit about Mick. For one thing, he's younger than Ellen, by a few years at least. Ellen Maddick, you old cradlesnatcher, I thought! Quite like something the Ellen of the old days would do! Though I wouldn't say it to her face, of course. Anyway, Mick's name suits him. He is a bit gaunt, a little bit grim, even in private, though he and Ellen seem to rub along together well enough. We had a natter before bedtime and he did unwind a bit, telling us about a proper row between Lord Morborne, another of the Leaping Lords, and his half sister, Lady Lucinda fforde-Beckett. His Lordship is refusing to let Her Ladyship back into Morborne House in Eaton Square, rendering her homeless—well, as homeless as a marquess's daughter is ever likely to get! There was a thrown crystal glass and everything. Shocking bad behaviour, I thought, but I could tell Mick was only sorry that Lord Morborne ducked in time. His eyes fairly glittered when he told the story and he laughed out loud because later a champagne cork flew into Lord Morborne's face—all of which Ellen and I missed as we were in the kitchens loading the dishwashers. Busman's holiday for me, Mum! Mick says Lord Fairhaven thinks his wife Georgina's family—the fforde-Becketts—is a cross to ~~be borne bare~~ bear and here they are all at Eggescombe for the weekend! Oliver, Lord Morborne, Lady Lucinda, and Dominic (no title!) whose brother-sister-cousin connections are enough to make you cross-eyed. (I won't try!) Anyway, Lady Lucinda is very attractive in a ~~cockett cokettish~~ flirty sort of way. Have you read about her in the papers, Mum? I think she ran off and married the stable boy (or something like) when she

was 19, then turned around and married some aging
Italian count, though that's ended, too. She seems very close
to her untitled half brother (and cousin?) Dominic. ~~I
overheard them in the drawing room last night making a
very peculiar wager with each other that I can't bring
myself to write down.~~ Anyway, she cut quite a figure last
evening and I could see she was getting on VERY WELL
with some of ~~their lordships who ought to know better as
they have wives~~ the other guests. I could tell Mr.
Christmas found her attractive, too. They're all so
predictable, men, aren't they, Mum? Even good priests. I
am glad Màiri White is out of the picture. Did I tell you
she's gone to Exeter for proper police training? Perhaps I
did. At any rate, I did worry that something might happen
there, and bring scandal upon us. A priest of Mr.
Christmas's education and the village bobby? I think not!
And no one can accuse me of being a snob. Anyway, Mum,
I best crack on, even though I don't have to, do I? I'm on
holiday! Ellen says I'm not to try and lend a hand, though
I can't help myself. It's my training, I expect. I shall walk
into Abbotswick to post this letter a little later and look at
the ruins of Holne Abbey, and I'll do the famous
Labyrinth, though Ellen thinks it's mostly a bother. I'm
tempted to try and get my head down for another hour or
two. I didn't sleep well. A strange bed perhaps, though I
always sleep well on holiday in Tenerife. I'm certain I
woke to thunder and lightening in the night, but I can't see
any evidence of rain, and then, around dawn, someone
was whistling quite loudly in the forecourt. I did get back
to sleep, but not for long. Anyway, I can hear them shifting

themselves the floor below, so perhaps I'll let them get on their way to the Big House before I go downstairs for some tea and toast. I'd tell you the cats are well, but I don't know, as they have to fend for themselves for the few days I'm here. Plenty of mice in the garden! The Swans have elected their Daniel to look in on Bumble and take him for walks. Hope he does better with dog care than delivering newspapers. Love to Aunt Gwen.

Much love,
Madrun

P.S. Roger did jump! His mother didn't stop him after all. He was quite the sight in a jumpsuit!

CHAPTER SEVEN

Tom's eyes opened to the shadowy underside of a canopy—a pagoda, his synapses crackled fuzzily—brushed by the grainy gleams of first light atop the curtains, which—he shifted his gaze—were now closed, billowing faintly in a breeze. Had he risen in the night to draw them? He pulled one hand from under the bedclothes and flicked grit from the corner of his eye. The moon! Yes, of course, the staring moon had pulled him from some gabble of dreams. He must have struggled from the bed to shut out the abrasive light and return to luscious sleep.

And then his memory fused: He had never left the bed nor been awakened by the moon. Soft footfalls had sounded through the darkness and at first, in consternation, he thought the source an anxious, troubled Miranda, because who else interrupted his monkish slumbers these days? But before he could reach out, whisper his child's name, a silhouette slipped into the window's spill of silver light, no child's, but a woman's. A swift swishing tickled his ears; gossamer tissue floated past his straining eyes to pool on the floor; his heart drummed as, in a trance, he watched the figure glide towards him, moonlight limning the assembly of curves, suppressing a gasp as her hair and eyes and mouth resolved into familiarity. His nose drank in a heated perfume pouring off her as she curled the coverlet back; his skin tensed to a near-forgotten sensation as hers glanced his, pressed his, claimed his. Their lips met.

He was lost in an instant.

He looked now from the sealed curtains to the tangle of bedclothes beside him, grey lumps in the greyer gloom. The scent of Lucinda's hair still clung to the pillow, but the sheets to his probing fingers felt cool. She had vanished as she had arrived, unbidden, as he slept, drawing the curtains on her journey back to her own room. They had exchanged no endearments as lovers would, only grunts and commands, the purest invocations of—he squirmed as the unholy word formed in his mind—lust, as they tangled and arched, united in an urgency of animal need until finally, spent, they had collapsed panting onto the dampened bedclothes, followed swiftly by sleep. Thoughts of those moments came now, willy-nilly, and he felt his body tightening, flouting his censorious superego, unable to deny the elation, the reminder, nearly four years from his wife's death, that his body could be the cause of happiness, to himself, and to another. He felt affirmed: He had not lost *it* in the vale of widowhood. And yet, and yet, as the zopiclone cobwebs faded and his ankle throbbed anew, he felt the batterings of his conscience. Irrational the first thought—and it was irrational: It hit him that he had betrayed

Lisbeth, opening, brazenly, nakedly, as if he had been bent on punishing her in some fashion, for some inexplicable reason. He pressed his palm against his forehead.

What have I done?

"Now the body is not for fornication, but for the Lord." St. Paul's strong words from Corinthians came to him with all the authority of Scripture, and though he hated the selecting of random verses to distort larger truths and justify hurt and hate, still the words were piercing darts. He had not felt *quite* this way before. Before he had discerned a call to ministry, in college, in the days when he had entertained as a magician in clubs, on cruise ships, and such, he had been no tyro in the arts of love, refusing few opportunities to make a fool of himself in one fashion or another in that male eagerness to bed a woman no matter what the circumstance. There had been girlfriends, yes, one with whom he had vaguely entertained the notion of formal commitment, but he had been too restless, too searching, until he bumped into the Lord. As an ordinand, he had made a *volte-face*, priding himself on his continence, until he had bumped into Lisbeth or, rather, she had bumped into him, saving him from sinking like a bloody fool into the Cam in a punting mishap. His trip from a figure soaking wet on the lawn of the Cambridge Backs to her bed had been swift, ridiculously swift, should have been shamefully swift, if he hadn't known deep within his heart that he would be with her all the days of his life—or, as was cruelly the case, all the days of *her* life, her sweet, short life.

And then, until this night, a dry spell. First poleaxed by grief, then hedged by the conventions and obligations of widowhood, single-fatherhood, priesthood, an outsider in a village of a thousand curious eyes and clacking tongues, less interested in his churchmanship than in his personal affairs (for what is a presentable, unwed man of a certain age but someone's project?), he fought shy of romantic entanglement. There were some attractive women in the village, and he could feel their eyes upon him in a speculative way in the pulpit, in the street, in the pub, but only one, Màiri White, the village bobby, held an allure, possibly because her flirtation was so bold, so cheerful, so nonchalant. She made him laugh. Once, last January, he had nearly succumbed to temptation—or at least the temptation to temptation—but he had been deflected by a hellish tragedy, and the moment passed. Màiri was too young anyway, on a career trajectory that would take her to who knew where, evincing little interest in becoming a wife, much less a vicar's wife. Tom flexed his ankle and groaned. Perhaps, he thought, he underestimated the perspicacity of Thornford's village pump: Màiri didn't share his direction, his education, his faith. But, my, she was easy on the eyes.

Tom shunted the coverlet and sheets aside, exposing his naked self, feeling the cool air on his flesh, forcing his attention to his ankle, the bruising a darker shade of shadow in the dark room. However, even the injury returned his mind to Lucinda, as it had proved such little impediment to their lovemaking, and astonishingly so. But he had been eager, she had been adept, wordlessly, tenderly conscious of his deficiency. He could feel his face burn as images of their entwined limbs rioted through his head. An unwelcome twitch turned to arousal. Hastily, he pulled the bedclothes to his neck.

Why had Lady Lucinda come to his bed? What secret trove of need drove her to seek comfort from a virtual stranger?

Or had it all been but some nocturnal amusement, as you might find in a novel of manners about the English upper classes disporting themselves carelessly at a country house weekend party? Had Eggescombe witnessed other nocturnal peregrinations upstairs and down? He groaned again.

A remembered image slipped into his mind. The milky, silky underside of her forearms, stretching forth as she steadied herself on his hips, caught the moonlight, revealing random striae like threads of white ribbed silk. What affliction, he wondered, had driven her to cutting, that strange, awful release of troubled teenage girls? He knew almost nothing of the woman he had a short time earlier had in his embrace. He felt suddenly like doing a flit, snatching Miranda, finding the car, and tearing back to Thornford, left foot on the pedal, if necessary. It was all very thoughtful of Lady Fairhaven—both Ladies Fairhaven—to have him to stay, to convalesce, but he felt more than ever out of his depth, landed in something treacherous. Suddenly the breakfast table loomed. Conversation over the Weetabix seemed an impossible embarrassment. Flight was the fix.

But it wasn't. It was the Sunday-morning impulse of a thousand craven blokes who had bedded a girl on a Saturday night. He was no better than his own self in his own spotty youth.

He struggled with pillows behind his head and pushed himself up against the headboard. Though it was August and avian courting season well over, a few birds outside his window heralded the coming dawn, a little more light crept over the tops of the curtains. He had an idea. He would do the decent thing, join the other guests for breakfast, then depart by noon with many thanks for their kindness. Madrun could drive Miranda and him to the train station at Totnes—it wasn't far—then in London they could get a cab from Paddington to Charing Cross to catch the Gravesend train. He could return the crutches to Lady Fairhaven at some later time. If Lady Lucy chose to speak of their midnight dalliance, it would be well out of his earshot. With any luck he would never see these people again!

But breakfast was some little time off, and vacating this sweating, swinking, fusty, musty chamber of sin and corruption took on a certain urgency. He shifted to the edge of the bed and gingerly tested his bandaged foot on the floor. Pain bloomed, but did not explode. He would dress and hobble outdoors. There was a feature of Eggescombe Park he very much wanted to see before he made a hasty exit. It would be a good place to say his Morning Office. And it would be at a good time, at dawn, when the world was renewed. The hymn came to mind:

Lord, I my vows to Thee renew;
disperse my sins as morning dew;
guard my first springs of thought and will,
and with Thyself my spirit fill.

Access to the Labyrinth began with a pitch-roofed, wood-and-red-brick porch. Tom glanced at the benches on either side, each fit to seat ten pilgrims or more, while framed posters on the walls explained the provenance of labyrinths and the history and construction of the Eggescombe version, the largest hedge labyrinth in England. He hobbled past the signage with little regard. He knew something of labyrinths and mazes, their origins and their meaning, the more outlandish New Age spiritual claims to which he was immune. He had visited the ur-labyrinth at Chartres Cathedral on a trip to France with Dosh and Kate when he was eight and had, his mothers reminded him (though he had forgotten), raced impiously around its sinuous trail until stopped by a kindly priest. Though he was getting the hang of walking aided by his little crutchy friend, there would be no racing this morning, he considered, as he passed through the unlatched gate and on to the pebble apron heralding the single opening in the topiary hedge, the Labyrinth's true starting point.

He lifted his eyes to the vast arrangement of bushes, a grey silhouette against the dawn's vague paling. Only a god's-eye view, he realised—his view from the heavens yesterday—made sense of the Labyrinth's cunning geometry. Here, on the ground, at the entrance, the curving seams of foliage, chest-high, appeared baffling, vaguely threatening. The arrangement was reminiscent of some mythical animal, alive but slumbering. He had a moment's irrational panic, a throb along his veins (had Theseus felt thus on his venture to the heart of Daedalus's labyrinth?), which he quickly suppressed. Bowing his head, he awkwardly clasped his hands through the crutch's frame.

> *Lord, my heart and mind are open to you.*
> *May your gentle presence calm the storms around me,*

And lead me to a place of inner peace
Forgive my foolish ways
Reclothe me in my rightful mind
Breathe through the heat of my desire
Thy coolness and Thy balm,
And let flesh retire

(Well, at least for a goodly interval, he amended.)

Amen

Raising his head, he began his journey, shuffling along a straight path for a few feet. The first bend was a veering left, and he was about to turn when some quick movement, a blur at the corner of his eye, drew his attention to the heart of the Labyrinth. "Hello?" he called out unthinkingly, realising at once that he was violating the Labyrinth's norms of quiet and contemplation, but too surprised that someone else would share his notion for a pilgrimage so early in the morning. And yet he could see nothing, no movement. A head, perhaps? A woman's head, peeking above the hedge wall? But no. As he strained his eyes farther into the thin rays of the new sun, he did indeed discern a shadowy shape, rounded, head-like, and he remembered the previous evening's discussion of a new artwork for the Labyrinth.

Relieved and pleased, for he was savouring the privilege of private access, he continued down the arcing avenues, taking the prescribed turns where they came, keeping his head bowed prayerfully. He had been to Hampton Court Maze once, on a school trip, and with some of his mates had gotten dizzingly lost, nearly panicked, amid green walls much taller than any towering adult. Only the directional shouting of their very cross teacher brought them stumbling, at last, from the exit. But a labyrinth was not a maze. It was designed not for puzzlement and perplexity but for contemplation and tranquility. It had a single exit and entrance and a single path, coiled though it be and mystifying in its seeming meanders. It was life's journey, of course—Dosh had said as much all those years ago at Chartres, though his eight-year-old mind hadn't taken it in. The centre of the labyrinth was the goal. The centre was Jerusalem, enlightenment, Christ consciousness, Atman-Brahman, what-have-you. As you walked the leafy purlieus, you moved tantalizingly close to the centre, then suddenly you veered away, but eventually, always, you arrived at the transfiguring centre.

And then, transfigured yourself, you returned to the world.

Right? Or left? No such decisions were necessary in a labyrinth. Tom walked on, conscious now of the counterpoint of his breath, heartbeat, and scrunching steps along the path, his mind slipping ineluctably to the visitation in the night. Now, away from his stuffy bedroom, away from Eggescombe Hall and its mazy interior and moralistic carvings, in the still, fresh air of pre-dawn twilight, he felt the glimmerings of restoration—that, in the words of Julian of Norwich, "All will be well, and all will be well, and all manner of things will be well."

God made us for joy, had He not? And mightn't there be a grace in an encounter, however fleeting? After all, how are we to understand our embodied existence? Mightn't desire simply be love trying to happen?

Or was he paving the road to hell?

A soft scraping sound interrupted his thoughts, and he lifted his head again, this time towards the quadrant opposite, the apparent source. Was he really not alone? Had a living figure—no statue—been at the centre of the Labyrinth after all? Lucinda? Could it be? Is this why she had left his bed, and where she had come? The notion seemed wild, unlikely. And why would she conceal herself? Unless she shared his discomfiture. Tom pricked up his ears and pressed forward. He had skirted the Labyrinth's centre once on his journey, glanced at the shadowy shape there; now he was doubled back, twisting away from the centre. The sound came again, closer this time. Was one of the children up early and larking about? Or both of them? Max and Miranda's heights, though greater than the hedge's, nevertheless made hunkering down easier, but he knew the game wouldn't endure without one of them giggling or whispering. Only random birdsong interrupted the quietude. He moved ahead, more cautiously, alert now to irregular sounds. If there was someone bent down scuttling along the path, he would run into him or her soon enough. There was only one way out of the Labyrinth: the way you came in.

He returned to his reverie with steely resolve not to be distracted: Or, he began again, was he simply rationalising? Mightn't there be danger, rather than grace, in his encounter with Lucinda, however fleeting?

Or—?

Another scrape, closer still, though, strangely, rather softer. Tom paused again, frowned. He was now on the arc farthest from the centre. On this soft summer morning, with the sun's touch drawing colour from the grey, staining the horizon tender pale pink, he sensed no sinister thing lurking in the Laby-rinth's dark green lanes. Untroubled by concern, he felt more peeved that this sweet opportunity for thought and prayer was being soured by some mischief-maker. Of course, some ani-mal could be the source. He was outdoors, he realised that. However manicured and tamed, these hedges weren't wax-works. As if to confirm his thought, before he could take an-other step forward, an extrusion of whiteness like cotton batting squeezed forth from under the foliage. A rabbit, Tom thought, with a flutter of relief, as the creature hunched on the pebbles. *Where's your waistcoat and watch, old man?* But the light was dim by the bottom of the hedge. It wasn't a rabbit. Those weren't rabbit ears. It was a cat, he realised. A very fat white cat.

The cat, as if hearing Tom's thoughts and highly offended, abruptly scampered across the pebbles and scrambled under the hedge opposite. Tom sighed, adjusted the crutch under his arm, set to continue, but, again, an unexpected noise gave him pause. No pebble scraping this time, but a rustling and thrash-ing, of twigs snapping and leaves tearing, somewhere on the opposite side of the Labyrinth.

A dog?

A rogue sheep?

It was then that Tom felt the first intimation of impending trouble. The crackle of disturbed foliage stopped almost as soon as it started, but the rest of nature seemed to rise up in sympathy. Protesting birds streaked noisily into the sky in a dark plume of distraction, scattering to the trees. A jackdaw sounded its high, squealing distress call. And then, as abruptly, a kind of restorative peace settled on the landscape, but a false one, Tom felt in his bones. Something or someone had surely violated the perfection of the topiary wall. Was he to encounter another creature, a more fearsome one than a cat, on the path to the centre? Or had some more fearsome creature retreated from the Labyrinth and padded silently away? Mind arrested from his own worries, concerned now that misadventure awaited, Tom limped his way more quickly along the coiled intestine of the Labyrinth. Glancing over the top of the penultimate ring, he thought he saw a blemish in the smooth topiary wall of the outermost ring, and when at last he looped around, he saw with sinking heart a dark scattering of leaves and bits of twig along the pale path ahead. In a moment, he was in front of the vandalisation itself, an ugly, ratted gash through the leafy wall. Someone—surely no animal would do this—had burrowed below its tidy trimming to escape. Fear? Panic? A labyrinth was not a maze. There was no reason here for the claustrophobic dread some suffered at Hampton Court.

Or was it a deliberate desecration?

Tom looked over the hedge towards Eggescombe's park, misting faintly as the sun, now half a crimson ball, stirred heat into the air. Here, at the farthest point from the entrance, the Labyrinth revealed its purchase on a soft mound that sloped gently to the lawn below, to the ha-ha, and to the purpled silhouette of majestic trees in the middle distance piercing the shimmering grey sky. Nearer, his eyes settled on an ancient oak the mighty limbs of which embraced a marvellous white tree house that glowed softly in the new light. And nearer still, the pinnacled bulk of Eggescombe Hall, mullions turning to glittering diamonds. It was as magnificently timeless as it had been yesterday. Only unpeopled. Utterly unpeopled. No sound, no motion suggested anyone but himself in this arcadian landscape.

With new concern, he shifted awkwardly on his crutch. Though he had yet again swung to the farthest reaches of the eleven circuits, he had come a good distance. In a few short turns, he knew, he would be ushered into the Labyrinth's sacred heart, where, presumably—according to the most ardent fans of such things—he would experience a kind of rebirth, though the fanciful notion that a minotaur, half man, half beast, lay in waiting crept into his mind. He snorted at the absurdity. The sound was preternaturally loud in his ears. He continued on down the path, alert to other breaches to the peace of the Lord's day, but none came, for which he was grateful.

Around the last bend, the path straightened, resolving into a short corridor into the Labyrinth's green nucleus. A pale silhouette emerged from the black bath of shadow. The head's fine features and slim neck—more discernible now as he pushed forwards—seemed to drink in the dawn light and gleam gently, as if lit from within. The marble face wore none of the mournful piety typical of such statues; the posture suggested nothing of the torment to come. The sculptor—Roberto, presumably—had rendered, with sublime skill, the sweetness of mother and child bound in love. The chubby-limbed child fairly gurgled with bliss; the slim mother, her youthful body draped in classic modesty, rejoiced at her son. Her upturned mouth, her delicate nose, her large, wide-set eyes were so finely rendered that she seemed less a symbolic representation of the feminine than a highly individuated woman, captured in a moment of pure maternal joy. He sighed a little, earlier trepidation vanished, affected not only by the loveliness of this exquisite representation of Madonna and Child, but by a stinging of his own loss. Mary had been his first adoptive mother's name. Had she ever held him like that? And what of his natural mother? Had she? Or had he been torn from her minutes after his birth? Liverpool: Marguerite had slipped him a clue to his natural parentage. Liverpool. How . . . odd.

He put the thought aside and glanced past the statue to the bordering hedge, deeply scalloped here, each cool shadowy lunation embracing a rounded wooden bench, suited to rest after the journey, and to contemplation. He had thought centres of labyrinths ought best be holy absences, places to fill with one's own thoughts, and wondered a little at Lord Fairhaven's conspicuous expression of his Roman Catholicism. Was it even a good marketing strategy in a nation of nominal Protestants? But the sculpture held an irresistible power he was sure others felt. He turned his thoughts to Morning Prayer, the General Confession slipping easily onto his tongue:

> *Almighty and most merciful Father,*
> *We have erred and strayed from Thy ways like lost*
>   *sheep,*
> *We have followed too much the devices and desires of*
>   *our own hearts,*
> *We have offended against Thy holy laws,*
> *We have left undone those things which we ought to*
>   *have done,*

*And we have done those things which we ought not to
have done . . .*

Tom paused in his recitation, the last words sinking like
stones into his soul. *"And we have done those things which we
ought not to have done,"* he intoned again, his voice this time
fallen to a murmur. He shifted his weight on his crutch and
continued:

*And there is no health in us: But Thou, O Lord, have
mercy upon us miserable offenders.*

Tom paused again, the severity of the avowal—*there is no
health in us*—reminding him, with a ridiculous literalness, of
his ankle. Twenty minutes of hobbling with crutches was
wearing. He would sit to finish Morning Prayers.

He made to twist around to move to the nearest bench,
one behind him, which sat in the deepest shadow. Six luna-
tions, he counted as his eyes circled past, a rosette pattern.
What delightful symmetry! His eyes fell first on a torch left
on the ground, switched on still, its feeble light casting a pallid
arc no match for the rising sun's. And then his gaze travelled
to what seemed at first glance a large grey heap marring the
perfection of the scene. Puzzled, fears rekindled that some
creature had indeed penetrated the Labyrinth by defiling its
boundary, he moved closer, steeling himself for some sort of
unpleasant confrontation, and peered into the gloom at the
base of the bench. It was no animal, but a man. Oliver, he realised with a shock when he peered closer, noting the rumple
of red hair, the idiosyncratic needlework at the neck of his

shirt. One arm was wedged against the base of the bench, the other flopped forwards, the kufi hat just beyond the reach of clawed fingers. Tom gazed upon the sight unbelievingly for the time it took another jackdaw to sound his alarm, battling a wave of nausea. Oliver fforde-Beckett, seventh Marquess of Morborne, wasn't sacked out, sleeping off some night of drunken debauchery. No snores, no guttural snorts, competed with the bird's call. Lord Morborne wasn't asleep at all.

CHAPTER EIGHT

"Jane!"

"'Morning, Tom!" Lady Kirkbride's arm lifted in a cheery wave as she jogged along the lawn, Bonzo loping in her wake.

"Jane!" Tom shouted again, urgently. She had disappeared behind a grove of trees and would soon vanish down the road to the Gatehouse and the village if she were not diverted. "Would you come over here?"

For a second he thought she hadn't heard, or was ignoring him, but she rounded the trees in short order and continued her run across the grass towards the Labyrinth.

"You're up early," she called, stopping near the Labyrinth gate, gasping a little as she caught her breath. Even at fifty feet, Tom could see her cheeks pink with exertion.

"Jane, there's been a . . ." He hesitated. He needed to raise his voice to be heard, but he feared frightening anyone unnecessarily in the Hall, though sound had little chance against Eggescombe's thick walls.

"... an accident."

"An ...? Oh, God. Are you all right, Tom?"

"It isn't me. It's—" He glanced again towards the Hall. "You'd better come here. But leave Bonzo outside the gate," he added as an afterthought. "And close it behind you."

Jane seemed to hesitate, but did as instructed. After a moment, she was moving quickly along one arc of the Labyrinth's path, then turning down another, as Tom had earlier, swinging by the centre, then swinging away from it. "This is maddening!" she called as she took the next turn at a run. "I'll be forever!"

"You're coming to a straight bit in a second. I'll meet you on the other side of it." Tom hobbled out of the centre and found Jane waiting across the width of the hedge, anxiety stamped on her face as she searched his.

"What is it? What's happened?"

"It's Lord Morborne ... Oliver—"

"Oh, no! What is it? He's *here*? Is he hurt badly?"

Tom slumped along the crutch. "No, Jane. It's much worse. I'm sorry I have to tell you ... that Lord Morborne is dead."

Her lips parted to form a strangulated *how*.

"I'm not quite sure. I'd only barely found him when I saw you passing by. You don't happen to have your mobile with you?"

"No, I ..." She glanced in the Madonna's direction. "I've got to get over this damned hedge."

"Are you sure? You could—"

"If it were only a simple fence . . ."

"If you push in a bit, I think I can reach you and lift you over." Tom studied the foliage. It was the girth of the hedge, rather more than its height, that made scaling it difficult. Jane had a petite figure. He judged her about five foot three. But even a man six foot one, as he was, would have no success vaulting over it, with or without a bandaged ankle. Her advantage to him was that she couldn't weigh more than eight stone.

"But your foot!"

"I'll be fine," he lied.

Jane raised a doubting eyebrow but pushed into the hedge, grimacing as the foliage stabbed at her bare legs.

"Does it hurt?"

"Not bad. Sweatpants would have been a better choice, if I'd known. It *is* dense. Hector won't be happy if I make a mess of his hedge."

"There's worse, I'm afraid." Tom leaned in as close as he could and put his arm under Jane's back. "Now, if you can . . ." He suppressed a wince. ". . . lean back and elevate your feet a little while I've got hold of you. Quickly as you can so—"

"I see. Okay."

He could hear her legs thrashing through the foliage with sufficient momentum that he was able to thrust his other arm under her legs and lift her over. The sensation felt odd, tender: like carrying Lisbeth over the threshold of their first shared flat.

"Are you sure you're all right, Tom?" Jane brushed at her running shorts as he settled her on the path.

"My ankle will heal at any rate."

She gave him a wan smile and together they moved into the heart of the Labyrinth.

"Oh, Olly, how on earth . . ." Tom could hear the catch in Jane's throat as they gazed down on the lifeless form of Lord Morborne. "That poor woman, Serena Knowlton, the one he's engaged to. And Georgie! Oh, and his mother!"

"Where is . . . Lady . . . ?"

"She's Mrs. Quintero now. She lives in Panama. Her second husband is in shipping and hotels." She paused. "A heart attack, then? Is that . . . ?" She faltered, looked at him with anxious eyes.

Tom shook his head. "Jane, it's not a heart attack . . . or an accident. You can't really see well in this shade—" It would be hours, he realised, before the summer sun moved through the skies to illuminate this particular petal in the rosette. "—but . . . Jane, Jane!" he added with haste as she moved to bend for a closer examination. "It's not very pleasant. You don't want to—"

She ignored him, falling to her knees on the damp grass. "He's been strangled," she murmured in a tone of astonishment after a moment's examination.

He looked down on her vulnerable neck where her dark hair parted. He had not found probable cause quite so quickly, but he had been nursing the hope that the only violence done had been Oliver's body failing itself somehow: an aneurysm, a heart attack, a fatal stroke. But when he let his crutch drop and crouched by the body for a closer study, he could see even in the imperfect light the marked congestion of Oliver's face, the glazed, half-opened eyes red with blood, the tiny hemorrhages along his lids. A ribbon of blood oozed from his nostrils, coiled onto the grass, gleamed blackly. What violence could cause this? His answer came swiftly from a glance at Oliver's neck above his open collar: a demarcating raw redness. Revulsion battling pity, with slender hope, he had rested two fingers at the neck where a pulse should be, and wasn't.

"He can't be long dead." Jane rose shakily. "The blood hasn't dried completely."

Tom flicked a curious glance at her as he steadied her with his arm.

"When I was in service," she responded, "before I met Jamie . . . well, even at the time I met Jamie, I found myself involved in some puzzling deaths . . ." She trailed off, turning from Tom to look around the patch of shadowed lawn.

"I was doing a recce myself when I saw you running by," Tom said, making an inference from her gestures. "I couldn't see anything that looked a likely . . ." The word was sickening to say. ". . . ligature."

Jane folded her arms across her chest as if she were suddenly cold. "I feel like the earth has shifted in its orbit," she murmured, then straightened, as if finding a new resolve. "I'll tell Georgie and Hector. Hector can make the call to the police, I guess. Or I can. Will you—"

"I'll stay here. I'd like to say a short prayer."

"Of course. Let me join you, then you can help me back over the hedge."

"Actually, there is another way out, a quicker one. I should have thought of it earlier when you arrived."

Tom watched Jane emerge from the chrysalis of the hedge onto the adjoining lawn.

"Whoever made this breach," she said rising from a crouch and picking scrubby tangle from her hair and T-shirt, "has got to have a mark on him somewhere, don't you think? I do. Look." She twisted the underside of her forearm to reveal a thin red scratch.

"Yes, quite possibly." Or on *her*, he thought, if indeed it was a woman's head he'd seen earlier—if he'd seen a head at all, other than the Madonna's. The memory seemed long ago and like a dream now. He watched Jane veer to the right and break into a jog. She whistled. Bonzo joined her with joyous barking and together they disappeared down the mound.

Nature being indifferent to human tragedy, the morning swiftly restored itself to tranquility. Tom girded himself to return to the sad task of holding vigil over Lord Morborne's body, but his eyes were caught by the field of tiny diamonds scintillating before his eyes. The sun, now a lemony ball on the southeastern horizon, sent its rays glancing prettily off the drenching of dew on the tract of grass that glided down from the Labyrinth knoll, and for a moment—only a moment— Tom experienced a tiny unexpected fillip of joy. *Lord, I my vows to Thee renew*—the words of the hymn came to him like a gift—*disperse my sins as morning dew, grant my first springs of thought and will, and with Thyself my spirit fill.*

He glanced again at the sparkling and immaculate carpet when he noticed a blemish, a darkening of the lawn by the hedge itself. He realised quickly Jane was the cause. She had trampled the grass emerging from the hedge and ghosted a trail that disappeared northwest towards the Hall. But the sun, he noted, highlighted another track, this one running directly south, down the dew-covered mound. No, that wasn't quite right. At the bottom, he could clearly see the trail split in two: one path twisted west, vanishing into the growing brightness of Eggescombe's south lawn; the other travelled east, towards a copse of trees, roughly in the direction of Abbotswick. Tom pressed the side of his hand to his brow and squinted at the sun, a golden ball now. Another hot day in the offing. Soon the dew would burn away and the trails vanish. He pinched his lips in indecision. These weren't paths trod by early-rising gardeners. This was the Lord's day. Gardeners were having a lie-in.

What he was about to do, he knew, was transgression of what would soon be declared a crime scene, but the opportunity would not come again. Tom tossed his crutch over the hedge, listened to the dull thump on the grass beyond, then bent to crawl through the breach in the hedge, as Jane had done, and, if the dew paths did not fib, two others, too, in recent hours. He poked his head into the scrubby tangle of branches, had a moment's self-doubt, then shouldered through on hands and knees, elevating his painful ankle so it didn't catch, pushing at the more resistant branches to protect his face. Emerging, feeling assailed, he brushed the few leaves and twigs that adhered, checked his shirt for tears, and retrieved his crutch. Gentle as the slope was, he narrowly avoided slipping and half skidded to the bottom where the trail diverged.

Which way, which way? Both tracks looked the same. Each was little more than a progression of iridescent skid marks along the grass. But the direction of the tracks was more expressive. The eastwards track suggested a connection to the world beyond Eggescombe Park, to an intruder, perhaps, from Abbotswick or elsewhere, a stranger to Oliver. Someone deranged? Someone with some base motive? Had Oliver, for instance, been strangled for the contents of his pocketbook?

Tom turned his head to the west. A nasty shiver travelled his spine: The westwards track led to the peopled heart of the estate, to Eggescombe Hall, where no one was a stranger to Lord Morborne.

He turned west. He told himself it was likely the shorter route, that by following it he might be rewarded with some useful nugget to present to investigators. He pushed from his mind the possibility that someone close to home, someone in Oliver's orbit, might have taken his life.

He traced the scuffings along the shorn grass, feeling the cool dampness of the dew on the skin of his unshod foot, passing the oak with the tree house and crossing the south lawn where yesterday half of Thornford had made merry. The confection of fanciful gables, towers and turrets, flaring an intense rose-pink, seemed yesterday a welcoming backdrop, exalted by the centuries, a mellow manifestation of an England timeless and unchanging. This morning it loomed over him, a lone figure in the landscape, as a spiky bulk, massive and intense, shut to the world, animated only by the hard diamond glitter of sunshine on the window mullions as he passed. He knew what manner of men had built this great thing—ambitious, fierce, restless, and unscrupulous men.

The dew path did not meander. Soon it took Tom around to the shaded west façade of Eggescombe Hall, down to a walled yard with stacked outdoor tables, folded chairs and café umbrellas, and potted trees corralled to one side. The servants' and tradesmen's entrance of old, he surmised, but now refurbished, decorated, and signed to indicate the Eggescombe tearoom, of which the yard was the outdoor patio, public lavatories, and souvenir shop within. His eyes went to the fresh stains, darkly wet on the dry grey stone steps. The shape of a shoe was now discernible. A woman's shoe, he was certain, noting the marks grow less distinct as he followed the trail across the yard to a glass-fronted door set into the far corner. It was slightly ajar, which startled him a little. Who had risen and been to this part of the house so early in the morning? Or had the door been left unlatched and unlocked all night? Surely Eggescombe was alarmed? And yet he himself had exited by the front entrance with no trouble.

Tom pushed through the door and found himself in a tiled vestibule, dim and grey without benefit of electric light. To his right, he could see through another glass-fronted door into the souvenir shop, the china and the books slumbering in neat display. Over his right shoulder he glimpsed the tearoom, similarly grey and lifeless. More interesting, though, was the passage straight ahead where a tracing of wet footprints vanished into shadow. He noted door frames, two on the left side of the passage, but no welcoming light streamed forth onto the tiles from an open door. With trepidation, wondering what he would find if he burst in, he tried the knob of the nearest one, but it resisted turning. He looked down the passage to the next door, some ten feet away. A fresh green leaf caught his eye, squashed in a smear of damp on the floor between the two doors. He stepped around it and tried the next door. It, too, was locked or bolted. He glanced again at the leaf, set in the last of the footprints, puzzled at the abrupt termination of the trail. No stride could have taken a man or woman to this second door. Whoever had come this way had to be behind the first door, surely.

He moved to knock this time, but was arrested by a sudden dazzling burst of light. He blinked to see a woman in a navy button-front tunic with a white apron around her waist standing in the doorway to the tearoom, chairs upturned on tables behind her, stripped of their covering cloths, naked and ugly in bright overhead lamps. She was, ludicrously, brandishing a rolling pin.

"Oh! It's you, Mr. Christmas." Ellen Gaunt cast him a severe frown. She was a plump woman with a full, high bust, and a deportment that seemed almost military.

"Mrs. Gaunt, I'm sorry to startle you. I—"

"We had a stranger wander in here last week so—"

"A man?"

"Yes."

"Oh." Tom frowned. "You haven't seen someone else here this morning? A woman, perhaps?"

"No, but I've been in the kitchen. I only came into the

tearoom to fetch one of the larger coffeemakers, when I thought I saw someone lurking in the passage."

"How long have you been here, if I might ask?"

Ellen didn't answer immediately. Small, sharp eyes seemed to assess him in some fashion. Then she turned to the watch on her wrist, affecting to study it. "Not more than an hour, I shouldn't think."

"That's very early."

Her lips formed into a thin line. "I like to make an early start. There's breakfast, but I have a lunch to prepare, too."

Tom couldn't help his eyes darting to her sensible black shoes. It was impossible these footprints along the corridor belonged to her. The trail would have led to the kitchen, which the rooms at this end evidently were not. And unless she was lying about her time in the Big House, the footprints would have dried and vanished. But to reassure himself, he asked:

"And you arrived by way of . . . ?"

"Along the drive from the Gatehouse." She regarded him frostily and added, "Of course."

"Of course." Tom pinched his lips. "You didn't see anyone on the grounds?"

Ellen seemed to hesitate. "Lord Fairhaven, I think. He often goes out for a run early mornings. The light was poor, though."

"Which direction?"

"Well . . . in the other direction from me. There are many paths. Why—?"

"I'm sorry, Mrs. Gaunt. You must be wondering why I'm asking these sorts of questions." He drew a cleansing breath. "I'm afraid someone has died. Lord Morborne."

Ellen responded with sharp breath.

"And it appears not to have been natural causes," Tom continued. "I found him—"

He stopped, fascinated to see the rolling pin slip from her grasp along the fabric of her apron, hit the floor with a nasty crack, and clatter along the tiles in a crazy progress towards his feet.

"I found him . . ." He adjusted his crutch and stooped to retrieve the thing as it rolled by his foot. ". . . in the Labyrinth, and I wondered if perhaps on your way here you had seen—"

"An accident?" Ellen's voice came to his ears as a croak, as if the words strained her voice.

Tom raised his head sharply and stared at her. A shadow had crossed her features. She seemed to struggle to maintain her composure.

"No, Mrs. Gaunt," he replied cautiously. "Not an accident. Not an accident at all."

CHAPTER NINE

om couldn't help but pause in his worried thoughts to consider the comic spectacle of an individual tearing around the Labyrinth at top speed. Hector—he was certain it was Hector, though he was yet too distant to be absolutely sure—appeared as a disembodied head-and-shoulders going back and forth and back and forth, sometimes nearer, sometimes farther, rather like a marble on a marble run. So concentrated was Lord Fairhaven on reaching the centre, he didn't appear to notice Tom as he struggled back up the slope nor hear him as he pushed—with some discomfort—his way through the breach in the hedge. By the time Tom climbed to his feet within the Labyrinth, Hector had rounded the final arc and was on the straight path to the Labyrinth's heart. Tom hurried to catch him up, returned again to worry. Had someone been lurking behind one of the locked doors while he talked with Ellen Gaunt? They opened to Eggescombe's estate offices, she explained when he knocked on one of them and received no response; the former butler's pantry and footmen's room, she assumed, though this was her and her husband's first stay at Eggescombe as staff.

Or had the damp leaf left by the wall been nothing more than the souvenir of someone removing her shoes and tiptoeing up the stairs at the end of the passage in stocking feet? Where did these stairs lead? To a corridor that linked to the great hall, Ellen answered, one of several sets connecting the disparate worlds of servant and master in an earlier age.

Tom stepped into the Labyrinth centre, his eyes flicking from the Madonna to a swathe of fluffy white brilliant against the shadow along the ground—Hector's terry-cloth robe open and flared like a cape as Hector himself bent over Oliver's body, in a pose almost of supplication but for the busy movements of his arms. At first, Tom's mind refused to countenance what he was witnessing, and when it did, he snapped unthinkingly:

"Lord Fairhaven!"

The effect was to spur Hector into a final flurry of furtive motions before he scrambled off his knees and gathered his robe together. Damp-haired, he appeared to be a man who had recently stepped out of the shower. Naked, almost hairless, calves showed below the hem of the robe, but he was wearing a pair of crimson bedroom slippers.

"Ah, Vicar, where did you spring from?" Hector turned, gripping the folds of his robe around him like a vestal but not before Tom glimpsed purple bruising along the top of his chest. The man's breath came hard and fast; the sun caught the planes of his broad face and high forehead, flaring them

the red of embarrassment, though his eyes regarded him
coolly.

"It looked like you were—" Tom began indignantly, noting
that the robe's belt was missing before Hector interrupted
him:

"I was looking for Oliver's mobile, his iPhone. To call the
police. I forgot to bring mine when I dashed from the house.
Awful business this!"

"And did you find it?"

"What?"

"His mobile?"

"No . . . no. I . . . odd he didn't have it. He would check the
bloody thing every five minutes, it would seem. Oh, good,
here's Jane and James now. Did you ring through?" He shouted
over the rows of hedge towards the two figures advancing into
the Labyrinth. "I seem to have forgotten my mobile."

"Yes, Hector, I said I would," Jane called back. "Apparently
a police constable lives in the village. He'll be along shortly."

"Widger. He's a bit dim," Hector muttered not unhappily,
running a hand through his crimped, damp hair. "You were up
early, Vicar," he added. The conversational gambit seemed ab-
surd with the enormity of the horror sprawled at their feet.

"Yes, well, I . . ." Caught off guard, Tom groped for an excuse. "I couldn't sleep."

"The ankle? Thunder and lightning woke me at some
point. It appears we didn't get any rain, though."

Lord Fairhaven eyed the landscape vaguely. Tom looked
again at Oliver's corpse, flinched, then looked away. "I'm so
very sorry for your loss," he said to Hector, aware the words
were anodyne, but unable to conjure a suitable phrasing. The

last twenty-four hours had suggested little love lost between the brothers-in-law.

Hector regarded him uncertainly, his fleshy lower lip pushed forwards. A quick, hard smile followed. "Thank you, Vicar. It will be a great shock to my wife. No, she doesn't know," he added when Tom opened his mouth to interject. "I thought it best not to wake her until . . . until we were certain."

Of what? Tom thought. Did Lord Fairhaven think neither he nor Jane could ascertain the absence of life in a man's body?

Jamie reached the other side of the hedge in advance of his wife. He looked like he had been ripped from slumber, his fair hair shambolic, his normally bright blue eyes opaque. "This is absolutely shocking. Jane's given me the details." He turned to his wife and took her hand as she stepped up beside him. "Where's Olly been all night? Apparently his bed's not been slept in."

"I thought I'd look in his room," Jane explained.

"He's wearing what he wore yesterday," Tom added, noting again the embroidered shirt.

"Perhaps he spent the night at the Pilgrims Inn," Hector offered.

"So he wouldn't have to look at you across the breakfast table, I daresay."

"Jamie!" Jane's tone was cautionary.

"I'm sorry, Hector, I've been knocked for six. But you will allow the two of you have been at each other for days."

Hector's face was thunder. "Are you suggesting I had something to do with this, this . . . ?" He gestured impatiently to the body.

"Of course not. Really, Hector, I am sorry. I was asleep two minutes ago."

". . . the last time I saw Oliver was when he went off to the village with the others last night. I *fully* expected to see him at breakfast, along with the rest of my wife's bloody family. I don't mean you, James. Or Jane," Lord Fairhaven hastened to add. "Someone's come down off the moor or in from the village and done this, of course. Mrs. Gaunt said there'd been an intruder the other day, didn't she. There you go then."

"If it were this intruder, Hector, he would have to be insane, don't you think?" Jamie craned his head in an effort to see over the hedge. "Otherwise, why would he kill Olly?"

"Then . . . he wasn't a stranger, at least to Oliver. You can't say Oliver didn't put people off, can you?" Hector shot Jamie a quelling glance. Jamie opened his mouth to respond, then winced. Tom noticed Jane squeeze her husband's hand.

"Didn't Mrs. Gaunt talk to the police about the intruder?" she interjected.

"I don't think so." Hector frowned.

"But there was a policeman here. We passed one when we were driving up from the Gatehouse, didn't we, Jamie, when we arrived on Thursday? He gave us a little salute. This PC from the village perhaps? I'd meant to ask you, Hector, but forgot."

"Oh, it was just someone from the local constabulary wondering about a police presence at next week's nomination meeting, nothing dire." Hector shrugged and tightened his robe around his chest. "If Mrs. Gaunt did report anything to the authorities, I'm sure Gaunt would have told me."

"Look, is there anything one can do?" Jamie looked beseechingly at Tom.

Tom shook his head. "There's nothing any of us can do. Not in these circumstances. I might suggest that I stay behind and meet with PC Widger as I was the one who found Lord Morborne's body."

"And the rest of us go?" Jamie grimaced.

"I think that's a good idea." Hector glanced at his apparel as if seeing it for the first time. "Thank you, Vicar. I do need to change into something decent. And," he added, his lips forming an unhappy slit, "I do need to tell Georgie."

"Yes, Tom's right. Let's go, Jamie. There really shouldn't be a crowd." Jane cast Tom a meaningful glance. "We might be making things more difficult for the authorities if we stand around . . . contaminating the scene."

"Say a prayer for my cousin, will you, Tom?" Jamie added, his face very pale.

"Of course."

Tom glanced at his wrist where a watch would be if he had thought to put it on earlier. Really, the police response time was rather slow. Apparently being a peer of the realm buttered no parsnips with the local constabulary, which, on the other hand, was perhaps a good thing: We're all as one in the great democracy of poor service.

It had to be well more than an hour since he had risen that morning, before five thirty, twenty minutes since Hector, Jane, and Jamie had returned to the house. He had had sufficient time to pray for Oliver and for all who would be affected by this tragedy before his mind moved, as minds do, to matters more mundane: For instance, he was not, he thought now, going to be able to make a swift and gracious exit from Eggescombe anytime soon. There would be police questions, an investigation; likely no one would be allowed to leave the estate for some little time. (What a good thing he and Miranda had packed for a week.) So much for spending his birthday in Gravesend with his mothers. And he would find himself yet more in the company of the alluring and troubling Lady Lucinda fforde-Beckett. Could she possibly be the woman the back of whose head he thought he glimpsed in this very centre of the Labyrinth? She wasn't in his bed when he woke up. A sordid and outrageous notion emerged into his consciousness: She had perpetrated this appalling act. Had she not run her half brother to ground at Eggescombe with a festering grievance? Was this its awful climax? Lord knows, he had witnessed her efficient passion in another arena.

It was too fanciful, too horrible. He couldn't possibly have slept with a murderer. Besides, a woman couldn't strangle a man. Oh, surely. He glanced again at Oliver's lifeless body. He was not a big man, but he had to be taller than Lucinda by five inches and heavier by four stone. He was more than fifteen years older than his half sister, though, and despite this parachuting lark didn't appear exceptionally fit. A bit of pale podge escaped from his midsection where his shirt had lifted free of his trousers. His forearms showed no generous sinew. Lucinda was a fit lass. Lord, yes, she was fit. Tom pushed certain riotous images from his mind and concentrated on the mechanics of strangulation. The woman would have to be strong, the man weak. The woman focused, prepared, aided by the benefit of surprise. The man dulled by drink or drugs, distracted, utterly surprised. The bench—the bench would lend leverage. You could crouch on the bench in the shadow and pounce on your taller, heavier victim. That might give you the edge.

It appeared Oliver had not gone down without some struggle. There looked to be a little scratching along the bottom of the neck that was visible, as if Oliver had tried to pull the ligature away. (And there was a mark on his face, but that, Tom realised, was the consequence of last evening's rocketing champagne cork.)

Perhaps a woman couldn't have done this.

Tom was pulled from these thoughts by the soft thud of someone approaching along the drive at a fast run. He looked up to see a figure burst past a stand of trees and tear towards Eggescombe Hall, a blur of black and white. The police, at last.

"Over here!" he shouted and waved at the figure. "Over here!"

"Bloody car wouldn't start!" The constable's voice came as a loud gasp as he nearly collapsed at the border of the hedge. He was capless, his tie loose, his white shirt above his duty belt even from Tom's distance looking like it had been pulled from the laundry hamper. His wrist wore a large thick ring. "How do I get in?"

"Through the gate, over to the left," Tom called, gesturing.

The constable found his way in, made the first turn down one green avenue, then made the switchback to the next one. He stopped in the middle. "Will I ever get to where you are?"

"Keep going a few more feet, you'll come to a straight bit, then take the first left after that and you'll be opposite me."

"I can't get over this hedge." He looked blankly at Tom when he reached the destination. He looked very young, almost beardless, and not so much dim, as Lord Fairhaven had said, as green and clearly anxious.

"If you really want to come into the centre, you're going to have to go all around all the rows."

"How long's that going to take?"

"A while."

"I could push through, I suppose." He regarded the hedge doubtfully.

"Best not. Your superiors might not think it a good idea. And Lord Fairhaven is rather keen on his hedges staying all tidy and trim. Listen, Police Constable Widger—it is Widger, isn't it?—why don't I stand here and you stand there and I'll give you the basics and you jot them down in your notebook. I think that's part of the usual procedure. There's probably been more people here at the centre of the Labyrinth this morning than is going to make your superiors happy. What have you been told so far?"

"That someone was found dead in the Eggescombe Labyrinth."

"Have you a notebook?"

"But I'm to see there are no signs of life." PC Widger fumbled in the pocket of his trousers.

"I can assure you there are no signs of life."

"Are you sure?" PC Widger stood on tiptoe and leaned in for a better view. He wasn't as tall as Jamie Allan. Doubt played on his face. "I can't see a body."

"There is a body. Really."

"Well, if you say so. I've never seen a dead body. Here, can you hold this?" He passed a spool of blue-and-white police caution tape over the hedge, assessing it as he did so. "Blimey, there's not enough tape to go around this great thing!"

"I think you only need to cordon off the entrance. There's only one way in and out of the Labyrinth." *Not completely true,* Tom thought, *but never mind now.*

"That entrance?" PC Widger pointed to the opening to the Labyrinth's heart near where Tom stood.

"No, the one you came through, with the gate. That should be sufficient. Not . . ."

"Not?"

"Nothing." He wanted to say, *Not that Eggescombe Labyrinth early on a Sunday morning is Oxford Circus on a Saturday afternoon.* There really wasn't anyone to keep out.

"Actually, they showed us a dead body at the morgue one day, as part of our training like. I've just never seen one, you know, in this sort of situation . . ."

"New, are you?"

He nodded. "I live with my girlfriend in the village—well, with her mum and dad, so it's . . ." He made a face, pulled a biro from his pocket and licked the tip, settling his features into a grave expression. "Now, um, let's see."

Tom noted the uncertain look in the man's eyes. Gently, he said, "You'll want to know, for instance, who the deceased is."

"Yes, that's right. Can you tell me who the deceased is, sir?"

"Yes, I can. His name is Oliver fforde-Beckett—double *f* and it's lowercase for some reason. Beckett is uppercase. Two *t*'s. Hyphenated." He watched PC Widger scribble, hesitate, cross something out, and scribble some more. "He's the Marquess of Morborne."

PC Widger mouthed the title as he wrote. He looked up from his pad, his long face an exclamation mark. "Not Mad Morborne?"

"Well—"

"Who puts on all those big concerts and owns Icarus—the famous club in London—and all?"

"Apparently. It's not something I follow, I'm afraid."

"Blimey!" PC Widger regarded him goggle-eyed.

"And you'll want to know who I am."

"Right. And who might you be, sir?"

"I'm Tom Christmas. I'm the vicar of St. Nicholas Church in Thornford Regis."

A smile twitched at the corners of PC Widger's mouth. "You're Father—!"

"I'm not. You can call me Tom or you can call me Mr. Christmas or you can call me Vicar Tom."

"I see. And you found the dead man, did you, Father . . . Vicar, sir?"

"Yes."

Tom furnished him with a basic sketch of his early-morning movements, excluding his own excursion across the south lawn to the servants' entrance. Best, he thought, leave the finer details to brighter minds. "But I'm staying here at Eggescombe for the next . . . little while, I expect," he added after giving the constable his contact details. "Now, if we're done, I'll join the others. Here's your caution tape. I can help you secure it, if you like."

"You've a long walk ahead of you, sir."

"Yes, I suppose I have."

The breach in the outer hedge was an option he could no longer entertain.

". . . call the minister."

"Georgie, darling, it's simply not a Home Office matter."

"You could, if you wanted."

"I can't be seen to be throwing my weight about. Not now with the by-election so soon. The local force is adequate to the task. If they're not, then . . . we'll see."

"I hope I'm not intruding," Tom said, hobbling into the breakfast room. He could hear Hector and Georgina contending with each other down the hall as he approached. It was less the anguish in Lady Fairhaven's tone than the exasperation in her husband's that caught his attention.

"Not at all, Vicar." Hector held Tom's eyes momentarily, then turned to the newspaper in front of him, coffee cup in one hand. Jane and Jamie sat nearby, each worrying a bit of toast. "I'm afraid it's catch as catch can." Lord Fairhaven nodded to the elaborately carved sideboard, which supported several silver chafing dishes heated with spirit lamps and a brace of plates and cups, next to which Georgina stood, dressed with care, despite the very recent tragedy, in black trousers and a white shirt, her hair drawn back in a severe chignon. She glanced at Tom with surprise, as if she had forgotten he was a houseguest.

"Lady Fairhaven, I'm so very sorry for your loss," Tom said. Her expression was one of sullen grief, her eyes puffy.

"Thank you. Hector tells me . . . tells me you found my brother."

"Yes, I'm sorry to say."

She stared at him as if trying to formulate a question. "How—?" she began, but Hector cut her off:

"You really should eat something, darling."

"I'm not hungry."

"Or have a lie-down."

"I only just got up, Hector! I'm not an invalid. I was going," Georgina continued with some vehemence, eyes snapping at her husband, "to ask Mr. Christmas how Olly died, as none of you seems to know or wants to say. And if it wasn't something natural like Daddy's heart attack—"

"Darling, do let's leave all this to the police."

Tom could feel three sets of supplicating eyes from the table trained on him. "That's probably wisest." He addressed Lady Fairhaven though puzzled at the others' circumspection.

"You're all conspiring against me!"

"We're not, darling. We don't really know for certain, do we?" Hector dropped the paper he was halfheartedly reading and glanced around at the others. "And we want to spare you any—"

"You want me to read about it in the newspapers? And why are you reading a newspaper at breakfast when my brother has *died*?"

Hector blinked. "Darling, I always read the paper at breakfast."

Tom watched Jane move to put her hand on Hector's. The two looked at each other, a certain intelligence seeming to pass between them.

"Georgie," Jane said. "Hector's right. We don't know for certain, but—" She paused and bit her lip. "—it appears as though Olly was . . . strangled."

Georgina staggered against the sideboard and released a short piercing animal cry. Jane pushed back her chair, as if to run to her, but Georgina raised one arm as if to ward off any attempts at comforting, her handsome immobile face resuming its mask of gentility. "I'm all right, I'm all right, really." She looked unseeingly at the fare on the sideboard. "Who would want to do this thing?"

Hector's eyes slinked to his newspaper. Jane regarded him speculatively, then turned to her husband, as if prompting him.

"Georgie, I'm sure whoever it was will be found out before very long," Jamie offered. "Some stranger. Some . . ." He shrugged. "Perhaps Olly had an argument with someone in the village last night."

"But the Labyrinth . . . why . . . ?" Lady Fairhaven trailed off, staring at Tom, seeming to see through him, then suddenly registering his presence. "Mr. Christmas, Tom, you must come and have something. I'm sure *you* must be hungry after your ordeal."

Her odd emphasis on the personal pronoun seemed to suggest that as a stranger he shared neither her nor her family's absence of appetite over this tragedy. In truth, he was ravenous. It seemed a lifetime since he'd awoken.

"There's ham, bacon and sausage, and coddled eggs and

scrambled, too, I think, porridge . . ." Georgina trailed off, reaching for a cup. "Hector enjoys kedgeree, so there's that." She pointed to one of the silver domed dishes. "Mrs. Gaunt has outdone herself, as usual." She frowned, as if disapproving.

"I'm wondering, Hector, if you shouldn't consider hiring some private security," he heard Jamie say behind his back as he took a plate and lifted the lid of the first dish.

"Why?"

"So you're not bothered by reporters, and there's bound to be rubberneckers come along. Am I right, Tom? You had something in your village."

"There was a tragic death about a year and a half ago in Thornford, which I'm sorry to say did seem to attract unhealthy interest. The victim was a young woman whose father had a certain celebrity at one time—well, in roughly the same business as Lord Morborne—music. Colm Parry, if you remember the name. He's St. Nicholas's music director now. Lord Morborne visited Colm only last week, in fact," he added as an afterthought. "To coax him out of retirement for some concert in London next year." He glanced at Lady Fairhaven, who responded hollowly,

"Yes, something at the O2 Arena. He was often on his mobile about it. He—"

"We can close the gate at the Gatehouse." Hector interrupted his wife with an annoyed frown. "I'll put Gaunt on guard."

"Hector, Eggescombe Park is hardly inaccessible." Jamie looked over his coffee cup. "There are lanes to the farms, off the moor, footpaths . . . You had the trespasser only last week."

"Damn Oliver!" Hector exploded. "This is not the sort of

attention I want or need. It's going to turn into a bloody media circus."

"My, who's a grumpy bear this morning?" Lucinda came sleepily into the breakfast room. "I hope you'll forgive me for coming down in my dressing gown, Georgie. Good morning, everyone." She cast them a radiant smile, gripped the top of the nearest chair, and did an allongé, extending her fetching legs behind her, first one then the other. Tom's eyes went help-lessly to her décolletage accentuated by the embroidered material at the bust and felt a rush of panic that she might single him out with a sudden suggestive word or gesture. He turned back to the offerings on the sideboard.

"You needn't stop talking because I'm in the room," Lucinda added with a sudden touch of pique, frowning and step-ping towards the sideboard near Tom. "Did you sleep well, Vicar?" Her eyes didn't meet his. Heart racing, he managed to match her unaffected tone with a simple "Yes, thank you," as she lifted the silver domes one by one to examine their contents. "Kedgeree, heavenly. And Hector didn't eat it all! I'm starved."

Lucinda glanced over her shoulder as she reached for one of the breakfast plates. "Whatever is the matter?" she enquired, running her eyes over everyone at the table, as if counting heads. "No Oliver this morning?"

It was the invitation to break the ghastly silence. Tom's eyes went to Hector, the host, the paterfamilias, the oldest man in the room. So did everyone else's. The room seemed to lie in waiting as Hector rubbed his hands absently in an agi-tated gesture. Finally, as Lucinda pivoted back to the sideboard with a sigh of boredom and dipped a serving spoon into the kedgeree, Hector cleared his throat and said,

"No Oliver, Lucy, I'm afraid. Oliver is dead."

His tone was gruff, uncompromising, as if it were a fact unworthy of embellishment. Lucinda paused almost imperceptibly in her movements, then resumed the rhythm of spooning onto her plate the rice, egg, and fish concoction. Returning the dome to the dish with a metallic scrape, she turned to the others, catching Tom's eye as she did. In hers, he thought he saw a distasteful admixture of triumph and sly satisfaction. Everyone seemed to be waiting breathlessly for her response, and when it came, it sent a tremor through the room:

"I'm surprised someone didn't kill him earlier."

Over Georgina's gasp, Jane asked: "What makes you think Olly was killed?"

"Well, wasn't he?"

"Seems a leap in logic, Lucy." Jamie's voice was stern.

"Not really. He was a complete bastard to me, to my mother, to . . ." She paused. "He's a bastard in business—ask anyone whose worked for him. God knows what else he's got up to in his sordid life. His lifestyle"—she laced the word with sarcasm—"wouldn't kill him. Unlike Daddy, he's the sort who can drink and smoke and take drugs and whore around and live forever, so presuming that *someone* killed him, Jamie, is *not* a leap in logic."

Their stunned silence was their assent.

"Besides," Lucinda said, her tone lightening, almost amused, "I happened to glance out the window when I was coming downstairs and spied a little man off in the Labyrinth who looked a lot like a policeman. So when you told me Oliver was dead, I made a *link* in logic—not, I might add, a leap."

"Lucinda, you're behaving abominably." Lady Fairhaven seemed to recover some spirit.

"Georgie, Oliver and I did not get on, never have, so I'm not going to parade great sadness."

"You might try parading a little decorum, Lucy," Hector snapped.

"You didn't care for him any more than I did, Hector, so don't play the grieving brother-in-law for my benefit. I arrived in time yesterday to see your little exchange of blows high in the sky. What *was* that all about?"

"It was nothing, and anyway it's entirely private, Lucinda, and has nothing to do with you or with anybody . . . or anything."

Lucinda snorted. "If Oliver was murdered, Hector, I expect the police won't think it so private."

"Why don't you sit down," Hector snapped again. "Your food's getting cold."

Lucinda glanced at her plate, then at the others. She lifted an eyebrow. "How . . ." She drew out the word. ". . . how did Oliver die?"

Tom watched the others exchange another round of cautious glances, sensing a subtext known only to the family. Finally, Jamie spoke:

"It appears, Lucy, that Olly was strangled."

Sundry emotions flicked in Lady Lucinda's lovely face, none of them horror: surprise, curiosity, acceptance. Finally, her attention shifted to Georgina, evincing for her half sister at least a bit of pity. "Oh," she said, as if conceding a point. "I am sorry." She paused, took a few steps towards the table, tilted her head. "Might we know what he was strangled with?"

"Really, Lucinda, does it matter?" Lord Fairhaven's drawl was dismissive. He darted a glance at his wife.

"Nothing appears to be in evidence." Jane seemed to choose her words with care.

Lucinda's finely plucked eyebrows went up a notch, but her expression turned hooded. She hovered by the breakfast table holding her plate as if expecting someone to pull a chair out for her, and Tom, in gentlemanly knee-jerk reaction, twisted painfully in a move to do so, but he could see her attention had shifted to something or someone out of his sight line.

"Ah," she said, leaning over the back of the chair and dropping the plate on the table. She almost skipped to the door of the breakfast room, outside of which a voice, a light baritone, Dominic's, could be heard brightly hailing her,

"Good morning, Lucy, darling."

Tom watched with astonishment as Lucy dropped into a curtsy of balletic grace and athleticism and responded in a tone silvery with laughter,

"Good morning, my lord."

CHAPTER TEN

"*G*eorgina lost a child to strangulation, you see," Jane ex-plained to Tom once the children had moved from earshot.

They were on foot along the curving gravel path west of Eggescombe Hall, the dower house, Eggescombe Lodge, their destination. Max and Miranda had scrambled on ahead, Max eager to show Miranda something.

"It was . . . a freak accident, though the word *freak* seems so . . ."

"Indecent?" Tom supplied.

"Yes, indecent. And unfair. Max was born a twin, you see. He had a sister, Arabella, who choked on—of all things—the border of a baby shawl when she was not many months old. The border had become detached and twisted in some fashion."

"How absolutely devastating."

"The shawl was an old thing that Hector had been swad-dled in, and his father before that, I think. Amazing a baby blanket could last for so long. There was no one to blame, really, though poor Georgie did blame herself—and Hector, too, I suppose: I think she does in some way hold Hector responsible because it was his family heirloom. The nanny had the afternoon off, so they couldn't find fault with her."

"Faultfinding should come with a sell-by date," Tom murmured, watching as the children veered off the main path.

"I agree." Jane followed his eyes. "Where are those two off to? Marve's is over . . . oh, I know. Let's follow them. Is it too much with the crutch? Marve wasn't expecting you—or us—at any particular time and we're not even sure if she's at home."

Roberto had answered the telephone in the dower house when Hector had called earlier from Eggescombe Hall's morning room, where some of the adults had repaired after breakfast, entering, though hardly aware of it, that strange suspended state of agonised waiting that follows a family death. Hector's call was intended to inform his mother of Oliver's death and to say he was sending the children over to remove them for the time being from the disturbing atmosphere. Tom had watched His Lordship's face pucker with disapproval during the brief conversation; he'd dropped the phone into its cradle with barely disguised contempt.

"'Have them come anyway.'" Hector reported Roberto's response with a sceptical rise of the eyebrow. "Mummy's probably still out riding somewhere." He had glanced at his watch, as if the time—it was past nine thirty—proved she couldn't possibly be out on a horse. "Shall I try her mobile? Perhaps she's still at the stables." The question was rhetorical. He dialed but received no response, and left no message. Hector, Tom noted, omitted any word of Oliver's murder to Roberto.

"Anyway," Jane continued, as they turned down a fresh path through a phalanx of topiary bushes past a sign that read ALICE'S GARDEN, "Hector and Georgina were here in Devon at the time when Arabella died. In August, as it happens, which explains in part why Georgie seems to only endure these two weeks she and Hector are in residence here in the summer. But Hector insists—it is his ancestral home and country seat. And Max"—she flashed a smile at Tom—"loves it down here. Well, kids do. There's so much to explore. Even if one of them is dressed in a suit."

They both looked ahead to see Max leading Miranda past a pair of stone gates. Earlier, when the family had been at breakfast, he had come in with Miranda (who had eschewed her overalls for a light summer dress) to the breakfast room wearing a sort of Jazz Age summer suit, beige with white stripes, and white shoes, and carrying a boater, looking for all the world like he had stepped out of a musical comedy. They had already breakfasted in the kitchens, with the Gaunts, which struck Tom as odd: the formally dressed boy eschewing the formal surroundings of the breakfast room.

"I say, Pater, there's a policeman in the garden," Maximilian said airily.

"You've been outdoors then." Hector had cast his son a weary glance.

"Miranda saw the ghost of Sir Edward on the south lawn last night. We went to look."

"I can't think ghosts leave evidence of their presence." Dominic looked up from his plate.

"Well, no." Max's aplomb faltered a moment. "Anyway, I escorted Miranda up into the tree house—"

"I see," Hector murmured, his eyes returned to his newspaper.

"—and we saw a man wrapping tape around the Labyrinth."

"Wrapping tape?" Hector rose from his chair and moved to the window, almost stumbling over Bonzo. He pulled aside the sheers and craned his neck in the direction of the Labyrinth.

"POLICE. DO NOT CROSS, it said. We offered to help, but he didn't have enough tape to go around. He wouldn't tell us why he was wrapping the Labyrinth, though. However—" Max paused and looked about the room in a bid to capture everyone's attention. "—Miranda and I have a theory, don't we, Miranda?"

Miranda nodded, exchanging a knowing glance with Tom, who gave a passing thought to Mrs. Gaunt saying nothing to the children of the morning's tragedy.

"We think—" Max began grandly with a sweeping gesture of one hand.

"Maximilian, come here," Hector commanded, not unkindly.

"Don't you want to hear what we think?" Max moved obediently down the room.

"Max, there's been a death."

"That's what *we* thought!" Max squealed excitedly.

"Your uncle Oliver has died."

"Oh." The carapace cracked. Max appeared doubtful for a moment, his lower lip slipping forward in the same pout his father affected. "Is this true, Mater?" He turned to the stricken Georgina.

"It's true, Max." Hector answered for his wife. "In the Labyrinth, as it happens."

As the room fell into an uncomfortable silence, Max looked to Miranda, who seemed to take a cue. In a bright voice, she asked, "Was he murdered?"

There was a perceptible intake of breath around the table, followed by a short, sharp laugh—Lucinda's—quelled by a warning glare from Hector. Coming as it did from a child and voiced for the first time, the word *murdered* seemed to fall like cold rain upon the adults of the room. Tom saw Hector glance at Miranda with a flicker of contempt, which sent him hurtling to her defence.

"We don't know," Tom had lied, inviting her with a protective arm to be hugged.

"How interesting!" Max had enthused.

"Max!" Georgina spoke sharply.

"How?" Max ignored her. "*How* was Uncle Olly murdered?"

"Never mind!" Hector's volume evoked a regimental sergeant major's. "You're upsetting your mother!"

Max flinched, his eyes widened, but he held his ground. He looked around the table, very much the cynosure of everyone's attention now.

"No one, I daresay," he said, "really liked Uncle Oliver very much, did they?"

"He's an unusual boy, Max," Tom remarked, his thoughts returned to the present.

"Very bright. His father could be more attentive to him.

Georgie seemed in many ways to withdraw from motherhood, with the death of Arabella, I'm sorry to say. Marve is the one who really mothers him. Phones and texts him at Ampleforth. Writes long letters—yes, letters. Remember letters? Telling him all about what's going on here at Eggescombe and so forth. And the Gaunts are very good with him."

"Would you say . . ." Tom hesitated to voice a passing thought.

"Would I say what?"

"Would you say Max was perceptive?" asked Tom.

"You're referring to that remark of his at breakfast about Oliver not being liked."

"Yes. Out of the mouths of babes."

A silence of more than several beats had followed Max's remark at the breakfast table. Was it shock at the boy's manners? Or shock at his candour? Into the breach, not even crossed by the boy's mother, Jane had supplied the gentle admonishment: "Max, that's unfair."

"I think Max has picked up on some of the atmosphere here this week," Jane said now after a minute. "Hector and Oliver have never got on, as far as I know. They each have their tribe's sort of fearless, arrogant authority, but—"

"Tribe?"

"You know, the upper class." Jane drawled the last word. "They all seem to have this unthinking self-confidence. It's useful in many ways, but there are moments . . . and when you're a simple Mountie's daughter like me . . ." She laughed. ". . . well, I feel like *her*." Jane pointed to the first of the figure topiaries past the boundary wall. The subject matter of the garden was self-evident. Greeting them was a six-foot-high figure of a girl remarkably rendered in boxwood with certain details, the face, for instance, cast in painted clay, the Peter Pan collar a band of small white flowers. Beyond, where Max and Miranda had travelled, were shrubberies trimmed into other recognisable *Wonderland* shapes: a waistcoated rabbit, a hookah-smoking caterpillar on a mushroom, a flamingo-wielding queen at croquet, a grinning Cheshire cat, even a cluttered tea table with the Mad Hatter and the March Hare at one end.

"I've felt a sense of social displacement myself this weekend," Tom remarked, marvelling at the masterful sculptures.

"I often feel that way." Jane laughed again, as if her life were as fantastical as the garden before them. "But then I married above my social station."

And I've sinned above mine. Tom pushed the thought from his head. "This is brilliant," he said.

"To open next summer. Not even in the brochures yet. There's some fine-tuning to do, I gather. Hector's . . . great-grandfather, perhaps? . . . had this designed originally for his own pleasure, and Hector's father used to have an annual Alice party, but it went wild in later years. Some of Hector's staff have spent the last several years restoring it." Jane ran her hand along the puffy dress sleeve of the Alice figure. "I think the estate managers thought Eggescombe Park needed another attraction for visitors, particularly kids."

"The Labyrinth being for visitors with more serious intent."

"Yes. Hector prefers Eggescombe be more a place of pilgrimage. There's the abbey ruins near the village, for instance. But of course, these great estates have to pay their way now, don't they? So he's permitted a bit of whimsy. Anyway." Jane cast an eye towards the children, who had set themselves down on the empty seats at the Mad Hatter's herbaceous tea party. "I was saying"—she dropped her voice—"that Max may well be picking up on the atmosphere, which has been thickened by Lucy's and Dominic's unexpected presence. Oliver has always loathed his stepmother—Lucy's mother—and has resented Lucy, I think, for simply being born. And now this trouble about Morborne House and who has the right to live there. I'm not sure why Dominic has tagged along."

"Oh."

"What?"

"I think I do." He told Jane about Dominic's contention that Oliver was committing a fraud against the Morborne family trust by selling its priceless works of art, pocketing the money, and hanging fakes in their place. "I didn't intend to overhear. They argued right in front of me—and Miranda—on the terrace last night, and being somewhat immobilised I couldn't easily get out of the way."

"Good Lord, I had no idea. What would Olly need the extra money for?"

"I'm not sure the music business is as lucrative as it once was."

"I did read he's planning to expand the Icarus club idea to other cities," Jane mused. "Maybe this is why Oliver came down to Devon days before the parachute jump—unusual for him to spend much time lingering in the countryside—to avoid Lucy and Dominic. Although," she added as they moved on to the Cheshire cat topiary, "I don't think Olly has ever had much problem with confrontation. His self-confidence isn't only unthinking—it's colossal. I don't think he's the type who ever questions his motives or feels guilty about the way he's behaved."

Tom looked at her sharply. "Really? That makes him seem rather like a—"

"I know what you're going to say. I've made Olly sound more like a . . . madman, but I didn't intend to. I only mean that he's always had a *very* large dollop of ego. I've heard he can be quite ruthless at business. But lots *like* him, I'm sure—and that's what I meant at breakfast when I contradicted Max, who half the time only sees his uncle during family rows. Olly seems to get on well enough with the others in the Leaping Lords. I think he thrives on that sort of masculine company. He was in the Paras after school, after all. He and Georgina are close—though I don't know how much they see of each other. And there's Serena Knowlton. I've met her. She's lovely, I mean as a person, which makes me wonder what . . ."

"The attraction is?"

"Yes, actually. Olly's been through quite a few women along the way, which I don't think makes him the best marriage prospect in the world." She added after a moment, "He's likely made enemies in business . . ." She trailed off, then shrugged. "His death is stunning, really."

"And you?" Tom ventured. "What are your views on the late Lord Morborne?"

"Me? I'm not sure, really. Jamie and I had little to do with him. Not out of . . . disaffection, you understand. Our daughter Olivia's named for him, after all, but that was more family tradition. Really, Tom, our paths rarely cross. Oliver moved in different circles. I think he's only ever thought of me as this peculiar colonial his cousin decided to marry." She shrugged.

"I suppose Jamie finds . . . found him tolerable. Oliver lived with Jamie's family in Shropshire for a time when he was in his early-mid teens and his parents were going through their horrendous divorce. I think he was a handful. Getting into trouble at school and the like. 'Scrapes,' my father-in-law calls them."

She glanced again at Max and Miranda and murmured, "I'm so glad we didn't bring the children on this trip. I'm sorry, what am I thinking?" she amended quickly, giving her head a little shake. "Here I am saying that, and there's your child . . . and Hector and Georgina's."

"I don't think they're in any danger . . ." But giving the notion voice suddenly made him uncertain.

"Maybe. But the atmosphere now . . ."

"It's hard to know the effect on them. Miranda seems to take everything in her stride, remarkably so—though now it seems she's seeing ghosts, which is quite unlike her. We've had more than one unhappy incident in the village. Of course, I first met you in Thornford after our music director's daughter was murdered. And there was another one in the village the past winter."

"I'm sorry."

Tom looked at Jane as she studied the next topiary. He felt an un-Christian desire to divorce himself from the troubles of this privileged extended family, give his evidence to the police, and quit Eggescombe as soon as it was permissible. But he owed a debt of thanks to Lord Fairhaven for lending his home for a charity event. And he felt a pang of concern for this likable young woman whose husband had helped organise the Leaping Lords for St. Nicholas's benefit and whose family had not been untouched by violent death: one brother-in-law murdered a dozen years ago, another imprisoned, and now her husband's cousin, strangled to death.

"You said before that you'd become involved yourself in the past in certain . . . investigations."

"Still do, from time to time. I have a little agency in Kingly Street that I involve myself in between running my children to their various extracurricular activities. When I was on staff in the Royal Household years ago, before I was married, there were a few incidents in which I was of some help. I can't really talk about them, you understand."

"Of course, and I'm glad of that. I'm glad that you value discretion."

She regarded him curiously. "What is it?"

He hesitated, but felt the need to voice his qualms. "I'm wondering now if I'm being indiscreet, but . . . I feel in need of an ally, of sorts. Someone close to the fforde-Beckett and the Strickland families, but removed a little, like you. Someone with a vigilant eye."

"Now you're frightening me, Tom. This doesn't have any-thing to do with the kids, does it?"

"No, I really can't imagine harm coming to them, but—"

"You don't think it's some stranger, this trespasser that's been troubling Mrs. Gaunt, for instance, who's responsible for Olly's death."

"No."

Jane sighed audibly. "Nor do I. It might be better for all if a stranger does turn out to be the case. I'm sure that's what everyone back at the Hall is thinking. Or nearly everyone," she added ominously. "But murder is rarely random. And this is a murder."

Tom glanced at the topiary queen, whose severe frown had been well rendered. "Shortly after you left the Labyrinth earlier this morning, I happened to notice a dew path in the grass. Well, two dew paths. One moved towards the Hall, the other more or less towards the village. I had to choose one before they both evaporated in the heat, so I chose the one leading to the Hall."

He explained glimpsing a woman's head in the faint light of sunrise, the sound of the hedge being defoliated, then his following the trail over the damp lawn towards the former servants' entrance.

"And the footprints vanished," Jane murmured, echoing his last remark.

"Then Mrs. Gaunt appeared. She said she hadn't seen a soul. I did tell her Lord Morborne had met with death. She expressed shock, of course. Oh, and she must have kept the news from Miranda and Max, when they went to the kitchens later for breakfast. That was the best thing to do." Tom rubbed his fingers absently over the queen's leafy dress. "Anyway, I'm sorry to say it, but it does rather link Lord Morborne's death with Eggescombe Hall and its inhabitants."

"There was the other dew path." Jane raised her eyebrows. "Or am I simply refusing to face the truth?"

"You can't have risen much later than I this morning. Did you hear—?"

"Not a thing. The house was as quiet as a . . ."

"Tomb?"

Jane nodded. "I saw nothing, either. No, that's only true for the house. Once I was on the drive, I could see a figure well down towards the Gatehouse who looked to be coming in my direction. It looked like Gaunt, but then you called out to me and . . ."

"There's something else."

"Oh, dear. What?"

"When I returned to the Labyrinth a little later, after my conversation with Mrs. Gaunt, I happened to witness our host—" Tom frowned in memory. "—going through Lord Morborne's pockets."

"Oh, God."

"He claimed he was looking for Oliver's mobile to phone the police, as he had forgotten his."

"But *I* phoned the police, as I told Hector I would. He'd come out of the shower when I got to his room. When I told him what had happened, he raced out in his bathrobe and slippers. I called after him that I'd make the call, since he seemed in such a terrible hurry."

"I remember you saying so when you and Jamie arrived at the Labyrinth. Hector's taken something. I don't know what."

"Nor do I."

As the four of them turned off the main drive into a lane bounded by flowering hedgerows, a Range Rover crawled the gravel behind them, a figure silhouetted in the windscreen. As they parted to make way, a pale arm, copper bracelet slipping, emerged in greeting from the driver's-side window. A hundred yards down the drive, where the apron nestled in the shadow of a large chestnut tree, Dowager Lady Fairhaven stepped out dressed in a grey jumper, sleeves pushed to the elbow, and blue jeans pressed into black riding boots. Behind her, the dower house glowed a mellow pink in the midmorning sun. It was, Tom thought, a diminutive foretaste of Eggescombe Hall itself with its red brick and stone quoins, corner turrets and fanciful chimney pots.

"Hulloooo," she called, opening the car's rear door. "How is everyone this morning?"

"Roberto thought you were out riding," Jane said when they came up to her.

"Oh?" Marguerite bent down as Max removed his boater and proffered his cheek for a kiss, setting his lips in a little moue. She stepped back to admire him. "Don't you look splendid!

"And Miranda. It wouldn't be fair to miss you." Marguerite gave her a dainty peck. "You look splendid, too. And Tom, how is your ankle? I have the cast boot for you. You slept well?" She held his eyes for the moment rather than glance at his foot, a swift appraisal that seemed to sift his soul. He felt guiltily that she could smell the whiff of sex on him, though after breakfast he had showered and shaved and changed into mufti. The sensation vanished. "Yes, I slept well," he replied. "And my ankle feels remarkably better."

"We phoned over . . . well, Hector did," Jane continued, "and Roberto answered. I'm afraid we—"

"I thought I wouldn't ride this morning." Marguerite bent into the car's interior. "I had an errand in the village." She pulled a bulging carrier bag from the backseat. "The Sundays." She lifted the bag and smiled. "Coffee? When you rise as early as I do, elevenses come at ten o'clock. Come through." She pushed through the dower house's great oak front door. "I have my old albums out for you, Tom."

"I say, Grandmama," Max began as they passed into a cool dark hall, his voice rich with import. "I have some astonishing news."

"Oh, do you."

"Max!" Jane's voice contained a world of warning, but the boy could not be stopped. He darted around his grandmother as she entered a bright reception room first. He did a little jig around her as she dropped the bag on top of a pile of books on a large ottoman.

"Uncle Olly's gone and snuffed it."

Miranda giggled.

"Miranda!" Tom cautioned.

"Sorry, Daddy." She turned her head to look back up at him, but she didn't appear remorseful.

Vexed with his daughter, he almost missed Marguerite's response or, rather, lack of it. She half turned, her handsome profile accentuated by the light from a high window.

"You don't say."

"I *do* say."

Lady Fairhaven gazed gravely at her grandson for a moment, then turned a slightly cocked eyebrow to the other adults in the room.

"It's true, I'm afraid, Marve," Jane said.

"He was *murdered,* Grandmama." Max plucked a sweet from a bowl of dolly mixture on a side table, then offered the dish to Miranda. "But we're not to know how. We're *children*, don't-you-know. Bonbon, Miranda?"

"Why don't you two go and visit the chickens?"

"But I want to look at the pictures, Grandmama." Max pushed his lower lip out.

"Then you make a start. The albums are there." Marguerite pointed to a pile tucked against the arm of a couch. "I'm going to take Jane and Mr. Christmas into the kitchen for a moment, for some *adult* conversation."

"Oh, all right. If you must. Don't be long."

Whereas the drawing room, despite its considerable clutter of *objets* and chintz, had been showroom-tidy, perhaps little used, the kitchen showed strong evidence of being the stage for the dower house's day-to-day life. If in earlier times it had been a warren of drab kitchen, spartan scullery and formless pantries, which Tom guessed it had been from the architectural irregularities, all had been knocked together into one commodious common room, bright with a wash of creamy yellow on the walls, brighter still by the sun slanting through low windows overlooking a back garden. A fireplace, unlit, filled with logs, flanked by two Windsor chairs, occupied one wall, while a long oak dresser shelving a hodgepodge of plates and bowls, cups and saucers, occupied the other. In a far corner, next to a rank of book-laden shelves, which might once have been a butler's cupboard, sat a roll-top desk, top up, its surface laden with papers, pens, books, phone, clock, a teacup, evidence of work interrupted. In another corner, almost a discordant note, a large flat-screen television perched on an oak refectory table faced towards a many-pillowed couch and a newish kitchen island with jutting sink faucet and cooker knobs, above which blackened beams teemed with gleaming copper pans. The TV screen was black, but strains of a radio switched on sounded under the scrape of their shoes along the stone floor.

"Strangled, Marve," Jane said as Marguerite moved deeper into the room and reached for a kettle.

"Ah." Marguerite turned, her composure little affected, but for a slight lift of her brow. "How is Georgina?"

"In shock, but bearing up, I think." Jane looked to Tom for agreement as Marguerite poured water into the kettle. "But it does have an awful echo of eleven years ago."

A play of emotions crossed Marguerite's face—sorrow, pity, exasperation—but none settled. Finally, she sighed, put the kettle on the hob and said simply, "I'll make coffee, shall I?"

Not waiting for their assent, she moved around the island to a length of cupboards over a long counter against the wall, removing a bean grinder. Tom's eyes went to the long pine table, which anchored the room, large enough to seat ten. At one end, half hidden by a bowl of summer blooms, was the remains of breakfast: An old wooden cutting board with a loaf of whole-meal bread sat in a dusting of crumbs, several pots of jam and marmalade, opened, with sticky spoons left on their tops, another glued in a sticky puddle on the well-scrubbed surface itself, filmy glassware next to a carton of orange juice, coffee mugs, cream jug, and cafetière, the last drained but for a puddle of coffee grounds. Jane lifted it.

"Do you need this cafetière?"

"No, I have others," Marguerite called over her shoulder.

"Let me clear."

"Oh, would you? How kind." Marguerite's head turned

sharply as she moved to the refrigerator. She stared at the table, as if momentarily disconcerted. "Roberto must have made himself at home."

"Tom found Oliver," Jane remarked as she loaded the lengths of both arms with plates, then said to Tom, who had openly admired her skill, "I've done this before. I waited tables at a lobster restaurant in Charlottetown, Prince Edward Island, when I was a teenager."

"I was going to ask where." Marguerite popped the lip from a canister and spooned coffee beans into the grinder.

"Where I grew up?"

"No, where Oliver was found."

"I found him in the Labyrinth, Lady Fairhaven." Tom hobbled into the room out of Jane's way, feeling inept before these competent women. The door into an adjacent mudroom was open; so, too, was the top half of a Dutch door that led onto the garden. Pegged along a rack against one wall between the doors he glimpsed the usual array of outerwear—waxed jackets, quilted jackets, a riding coat, assorted tweed caps and felt hats—all in country drab, but for one red hoodie crested with an ARSENAL FC logo. He had a notion who that might belong to and gave a passing thought to the nature of Marguerite and Roberto's living arrangements.

"When?"

Tom turned from his glance at the footwear under the mudroom bench, walking sticks and other paraphernalia to respond: "Very early this morning. The sun was barely nudging the horizon."

"Then no one else was about?"

Tom hesitated. The metallic shriek of beans being pulverised gave him leave to consider his reply. Had it been a trick of the light or, rather, a trick of the shadow? Had he truly seen the back of someone's head? And why did he think it was a woman's? Something about the shape, the sense of hair longer than most men wore these days? Lucinda remained worryingly in his mind. But now, unhappily, not wishing to acknowledge the terrible possibility, he studied the back of the dowager countess's head as she bent to her task, at the cut of her silvery blond hair, conscious that Her Ladyship was an early riser (she had said so moments earlier in the forecourt), conscious, too, that though she was a woman in her sixties, she exhibited the agility and vigor of a woman a decade or more younger. But to be capable of strangling a man? Then beetling off into the shrubbery? And for what possible reason? It was all too ridiculous.

And yet there was something watchful in her eyes when she turned and met his, clearly expecting an answer to her seemingly nonchalant question. Her eyes dipped as she removed the top of the grinder and the moment was lost.

"There wouldn't have been enough light for me to know for sure if there was." He chose his words with care as he watched Marguerite spoon the ground coffee into the cafetière. ". . . anyone about," he added, noting Jane transfer a curious doubting frown from the used coffee mugs she was carrying to him.

"And you heard nothing?" she asked, depositing the china on the island near Marguerite.

"I can say for certain I heard a cat. And saw one. And I'm pretty sure I heard some noises in the shrubbery."

The kettle's hiss turned to a shriek at that moment, severing conversation. Marguerite lifted it from the hob and they waited in silence for the water to cool slightly, the murmur of the muted radio and the ticking of the wall-mounted clock now the ascendant sounds. Tom glanced at the two women, each of whose face reposed in private thought.

"Someone must have been *very* angry with Oliver." Jane broke the silence as Marguerite poured a little hot water over the grounds and swirled the cafetière around. After a few seconds, she tipped the kettle to pour in the rest.

"Perhaps." A plume of steam obscured Marguerite's face momentarily. "Well, yes," she said, as if conceding the point. She flicked a glance at Tom. "What with? Do you know?"

"If you mean the . . . instrument of death, I don't know," Tom replied, taking the liberty of sitting down. "Nothing was in evidence that I could see. I expect when the scene of crime experts are through something will come to light."

"We're going to have the whole spectacle of the police and the law upon us, aren't we?" Marguerite pressed the plunger into the cafetière. "I can't think this will go very well for Hector. Jane, fresh mugs are on the dresser."

"Because the police will learn that Hector and Olly had been fighting?" Jane lifted three mugs off their hooks.

"In part. If Hector's determined to stand for Parliament, any breath of scandal will do him no good. The prime minister's very hot on propriety of all sorts these days."

"Marve, do you have *any* idea why they were at each other yesterday?"

"Not at all. I asked Hector yesterday and he stubbornly refused to tell me. There wasn't much point in asking Oliver, as he never gives . . . gave, rather, you a straight answer about anything." Marguerite carried the cafetière to the table. "I suppose all one can say to the police is that Hector and Olly never got on, so that yesterday's incident is simply another in a long line." She flicked a glance down at Tom. "I can read the 'why' in your face, Vicar."

"Oh, dear. And I thought I was doing well looking blank."

Marguerite laughed and continued: "They've never really rubbed along, Hector and Olly. There's no point in not saying these things. If I read detective novels correctly, we're all in for a bout of living in each other's pockets." She settled the cafetière next to the cream jug Jane had left on the table. "I think it's simply . . . well, sometimes you meet someone and you simply can't bear them from the moment you shake their paw. Biscuit, anyone? Mrs. Gaunt sent over some lovely baking the other day. She's a superb cook, she really is, but I do find her a little severe." Marguerite glanced about. "There it is!" She walked over and lifted a tin from the counter under the window. "Now what was I saying?"

"Hector and Olly not getting on," Jane prompted.

"Right, yes, well, I think there was some incident when they were in the Parachute Regiment. I don't really know. I'm not sure if it's important now." Marguerite opened the lid and placed the tin on the table. "Plates, Jane, if you please. Anyway, the Stricklands and the fforde-Becketts are rather chalk and cheese. Unlike the fforde-Becketts, the Stricklands have managed to weather the chop and change of the last century. Perhaps it's having remained resolutely Catholic through the Reformation and the Civil War. It's made the Stricklands wilier. I've just thought of that. I'm not sure it's true. But it is true that the fforde-Becketts threw most of it away on the horses, women, bad investments—that foolish scheme in the West Indies of Olly's father. By the way, Tom, you should get Maxie to show you and your daughter the priest holes at the Hall and such. He adores the intrigue." Marguerite glanced at her watch as she sat down and bid Jane do the same. "I wonder . . ."

"Wonder what?"

"I don't usually go, even on Sunday. Sorry, I'm thinking out loud. Father Downes, Jane. You must have met him while you've been here. He comes up to Eggescombe from Ivybridge every morning when Hector's in residence to say Mass in the chapel. A retired priest." Marve turned to Tom. "Quite the amateur architectural historian. Loves Eggescombe." She laughed. "And last Sunday, he stayed on for lunch, Mrs. Gaunt's cooking being the attraction. I can't say I blame him. She is a little treasure."

"Shall I be mother?" Jane's hand brushed the cafetière's handle. "Black or white?"

Both Tom and Marguerite opted for black coffee.

"But you are coming for Sunday lunch, Marve."

"Oh, of course. I'm simply wondering if I should go to Mass. I'm a convert, you understand," she said to Tom, adding obliquely, "it was the price of admission. Dare I bring Roberto?" She smiled knowingly at Jane.

"To lunch? Hector didn't say." Jane flicked a glance at Tom as she poured the coffee.

Marguerite snorted. "Roberto's too busy working anyway."

She pinched her lips in thought, then said in a somewhat reluctant tone, "I suppose I could take you over to the stables when we're done here so you could see what he's doing."

"I'd like that," Tom said, considering the excursion another way to keep the children preoccupied.

"He won't be terribly communicative, though." Marguerite looked as though she regretted the invitation. She glanced at Tom then lifted a biscuit from the tin. "I've had a thought—Dominic!" She bit into it. "Was he terribly pleased?"

"Marve!" Jane looked up from the cream she was pouring into her mug.

"Was he, Tom?"

"I couldn't say." In truth he couldn't, though he had a qualm. When Lucinda had dipped into her deep curtsy and addressed her half brother with the honorific, Tom, later than the others, had realised the implication. With Oliver possessed of no legitimate male heir of his body, the marquessate passed automatically to his late father's late brother's son—his cousin, Dominic fforde-Beckett.

Dominic had received Lucinda's gesture with an expression of bemusement. He was wearing cream-coloured khakis and a fresh white shirt, the sleeves of which he was rolling to his elbows as he responded:

"I feel like I've stumbled into Act Two of some Regency farce—or is it Jacobean melodrama?—and haven't the foggiest what the play is about. What *is* the play about? Is that kedgeree I smell? Good morning, all." He pushed his long, slightly damp hair behind his ears.

"The gods have smiled upon you this morning, brother dear."

"Lucy, that's *quite* enough out of you," Hector barked. "Oliver has died, Dominic.."

"What do you mean, died?"

"Died. Ceased to be." Hector sounded the exasperation of a man fed up. "Died!" he said again.

"I take your point, Hector, but *how* did he die? He certainly looked hale yesterday. Liver failure? Sorry, Georgie, I didn't mean to sound cavalier."

"No, Oliver's been killed—well, murdered, I suppose." Hector glanced at Miranda.

"Oh, don't be silly."

"Somebody else tell him."

"It's true, Dominic." Jamie spoke. "Oliver's body is in the Labyrinth. We're waiting for the police, well, more police."

"Good God."

It fell to Hector to explain the events of the morning, which he did briefly and gracelessly—in a growing bad temper.

"It's unbelievable," Dominic said, turning to his cousin. "Really, Georgie, I am so very sorry." He addressed her with further expressions of condolence, yet, somehow, to Tom's ears, the words were formulaic and the tone practised—more a facsimile of sympathy than sympathy itself—though he knew from his pastoral work how oddly shock could shape words and affect people.

"Inheriting the marquessate and all wasn't alluded to again," Tom said to Marguerite now, his thoughts returned to the present. "So no, I couldn't really tell you what Dominic's feelings might be."

"Not that there's much left in the kitty, I shouldn't think."

Marguerite looked over the table. "There's still the house in Eaton Square. At least now Charlotte and Lucinda won't be homeless, not that Charlotte's much in London, I'm given to understand. Oh, Jane, you don't have a spoon." She rose quickly.

"Marve, it doesn't matter," Jane called after her.

But Marve, having reached the counter, held up a warning finger, her other hand adjusting the knob of the radio so the familiar strains of BBC Radio Devon's news summary filled the room. Belinda Dixon's practised voice followed:

> *The headlines: Police are reporting the death of one of Britain's leading entertainment entrepreneurs this morning. Oliver fforde-Beckett, the Marquess of Morborne, founder of London's Icarus club and of the Daedalus Group, manager of such bands as Lovebox and Heir of the Dog, and organiser of last year's Child-Aid benefit at Wembley Stadium, was found dead early this morning at Eggescombe Park, the Devon estate of his brother-in-law, the Earl of Fairhaven. His death is being treated by police as suspicious. In other news, more than seventy organisations have expressed concern about the government's plans to overhaul the benefits system—*

Marguerite snapped the radio off. Tom could see the rise, then the fall, of Marguerite's bosom under the shirt she wore as she released a deep sigh. She turned to them, her face somber.

"Why," she asked, as a burst of childish laughter, perversely timed, came from down the hall, "does hearing it on the radio make it seem that much more *real?*"

CHAPTER ELEVEN

"My plan . . . or rather, *the* plan," Marguerite said, as if it were necessary to make the distinction, "is to convert much of the stable block into artists' studios—or studio and accommodation, in some instances. One of them is finished, for display." She gestured to the back of the large central yard. "And I'll still keep a few horses—there." Her hand moved to the left from whence came a scuff of hooves and the thump of great weight against a stall, the animals' response to their mistress's voice. "So it can be put to good use."

"Pater thinks it's a rum idea. I heard him tell Mater."

"And what do you think, poppet?" Marguerite smiled at Maximilian indulgently.

"I think it's wizard. When I'm earl I shall do all sorts."

"Good boy. Eggescombe needs single-minded attention and lots of imagination, if it's going to survive."

Tom and Jane exchanged glances. Poor Hector, Tom

thought: damned all but in name. In a battle of wills, he suspected the dowager countess would easily vanquish her son.

"The notion"—Marguerite shielded her eyes against the high sun beaming into the central courtyard—"is that the artists can display and sell their wares, in this courtyard, in good weather, or in a shop that will be over there." She indicated a complex of arched door wells at the far end of the stable block. "Once we remove the old box stalls, of course. And there'll be a tearoom next to it for light refreshments. There's an old kitchen and scullery in that corner, so the conversion shouldn't be too, too difficult.

"An all-season attraction, I explained to Hector." Marguerite glanced down. A hefty white cat had darted from seemingly nowhere and curled around her legs. "Visitors don't want to tramp around the Labyrinth—or Alice's Garden when it's finished—in wet weather. So they can come here in February. People can watch the painters and sculptors and potters at work. We'll have exhibits and openings and the like. Event planning, they call it."

"Great larks, Grandmama. Here, puss."

"One of the village cats, I think, but it's become quite attached to Roberto." Marguerite pushed it gently away with her foot. "It will mean some extra winter employment for the village. There'll be more people rattling around here than just me and the estate manager and his wife, so Eggescombe Park won't seem such a museum. It will promote artists from the southwest, or London, or wherever. There'll be increased revenues . . . eventually, of course. I think it's a winner. And," she added *sotto voce,* as Max and Miranda wandered towards the source of horse noises, "the other directors of Eggescombe Enterprises agreed with me. Ha!

"Come, you two." Marguerite amplified her voice. "Let's see what Mr. Sica is up to this morning. How's the cast boot, Tom?"

"Splendid."

It was. Quite the contraption, the boot hugged most of his lower leg and foot in a shell of plastic held together by a fiesta of Velcro straps. He had tried it out as the five of them had walked from the dower house towards the stable block, down a private path, marvelling at the relative comfort, grateful that he could—almost literally—throw away his crutches. (He left them in the dower house mudroom instead.) Intermittent birdsong and whispering trees slowly gave precedence to a steady manufactured rhythm as they drew closer to the stables, the whir and whine of a machine, more evident still where the path joined the drive and they passed through the arched entrance beneath the clock tower. "Georgian," Marguerite had remarked apropos of very little as Tom glanced about, noting the classical detailing. "Built nearly two centuries after the house and my little cottage. Catholics couldn't own more than one horse at one time. They were weapons of war during the Reformation. Rather like owning a tank today."

Now the mechanical sound from within the stables seemed to stall and start as they approached the pair of great wooden doors, one of which rested on its hinge, open a crack and allowing the cat egress. Tom could feel the courtyard bricks below the naked toes of his right foot radiate with the day's growing heat and he felt sweat bloom under his arms.

"Roberto's been a bit the canary in the coal mine in this venture. But having him here at Eggescombe has proved that resident artists can work well. Roberto," she called, tugging at the heavy door and peeking in, "I hope we're not intruding. Roberto?"

The hinge squealed in protest as Marguerite pushed and Tom, awkwardly, pulled. The sun sent an angle of honey-yellow light spilling several feet into the dark interior, scintillating the mote-heavy air into a blurring scrim. But it was his nose, not his impaired eyes, that was first assailed by the peculiarities of the studio. A washhouse dampness pervaded, a stale smell of wet clay, yet, oddly, blunted by a kind of dust, so desiccating that Tom's eyes watered as he fought to prevent a sneeze. Through his teeming eyes, he glimpsed a cavernous room, the full two storeys of the stable block, lying in half shadow, a jumble of vague shapes obscuring its perimeters. The spill of sunshine surrendered to the blue-white brilliance of two floodlights on stands directed towards a cleared space near the centre of the room where more fine powder fanned out in silky plumes, whitening the air. The person wielding the machine—some sort of sander, Tom presumed—was obscured by the artwork's massing, but the sound of grit upon stone was not. An almost satisfying shrill, it filled the space. Tom sneezed loudly, then sneezed again with greater force, but his echoing blasts (to Tom's ears) provoked no reaction. Wiping his eyes, he glimpsed, through a curving limb in the statuary, a frightening mask with gleaming eyes and a snout like a metal pig's, then another glimpse, this of a flowing head-dress, like the white keffiyeh of an Arab. No one watching moved. Tom sensed them all transfixed by the artist in the act of creation, and when Roberto backed around the statue with the sander, a figure streaked with white, no one, at least not Tom, noticed for a moment that he wore nothing below his neck save for dust-covered trainers and gardening gloves. Jolted, feeling as if he were intruding on a very private act, Tom glanced away, then glanced at Miranda, who was staring with open-eyed surprise.

"Roberto!" Marguerite shouted, moving towards the man, who seemed now to sense that he was no longer alone in the room. A flick of the hand and the mechanical noise died away; a murmuring radio in the background filled the void. Roberto twisted his torso around. Tom glimpsed a gladiator reimagined in a filter mask and powder armour, and his hands went unthinkingly to shield Miranda's eyes, feeling as he completed the act silly and prudish.

"Roberto," Marguerite began again, in an exasperated tone, "put something on, would you? You have guests."

Obediently, Roberto placed the sander on a nearby bench and peeled back the filter mask and goggles, handing them to Marguerite. The head covering he tugged off, revealed as a pair of old white rugby shorts, which he stepped into, snapping the band against his slim waist. Roberto regarded them with faint hostility, as if he had been pulled from a sound sleep. He offered no apology for his dishabille, but Tom realised, as Miranda pushed away his hands, that it was they who had intruded upon his realm. He sensed a new tension in the atmosphere.

"I thought I would show Tom and his daughter the stable

conversion." Marguerite dropped the mask on a nearby table and fetched what looked like a strip of linen. "You met last evening."

"Yes. I remember." Roberto flicked him a disinterested glance and took the cloth from Marguerite, wiping the perspiration first from his forehead and around his eyes, then in long, firm strokes across his torso, pushing the layer of fine white powder to the dusty brick. Tom noted the powerful sinews of his forearms rippling beneath the skin and tautness of the pectorals—the benefit of labouring over a lump of stone with a cold chisel—but he noted, too, bruising and cuts, fresh-looking ones, in the same areas—the result, he presumed, of labouring over stone with no protective clothing, though the sanding looked harmless to bare skin.

"What are you working on?" Jane asked with forced cheer, stepping into the penumbra of light.

"The commission for Delix Fennis I mentioned last evening." Roberto's eyes ranged over his work, his mouth turned down with a hint of critical dissatisfaction.

Joining them, Tom's eyes were at first dazzled by the ethereal, luminous quality of the marble, as if the moon shone from within its compressed form. Two figures emerged from the stone, limbs entwined, as if struggling for release, he thought for a second, before realising the figures were male and female locked together in an embrace, their naked forms writhing and twisting. His eyes darted to the faces, to their frozen features modelling passion—or perhaps pain—as if it were suddenly imperative to find in the finely wrought details the living models. Absurdly—he was conscious he was driven by pure guilt—he looked for his own face and for Lucinda's, as if Roberto had been witness to their tryst and had rushed to replicate it in marble. He could feel himself blush with relief that it was not. The faces of the man and woman, unlike the face of Mary in the Labyrinth, were idealised, as beautiful as the statues of the gods of antiquity. A little troubled at the mature theme of the sculpture, he glanced at the children. Max's face wore the studied frown of an art connoisseur at a gallery. Disturbingly, Miranda's attention fell to the artist, not the art. She seemed to be studying him in a way that pierced a father's heart. He followed her gaze. The sculptor himself would offer a worthy subject: the high forehead, the deeply set eyes, the sensitive mouth, a Cupid's bow, but Tom didn't give a damn. He shuffled forward to block Miranda's view, saying the first banal thing that came to his head:

"Remarkable."

"Yes," Jane and Marguerite murmured as one as if mesmerised by the artwork's erotic power, but not daring voice it.

"Dionysus I'm guessing from the vines and grape clusters." Jane gestured to the renderings ornamenting the male figure. "But who is the female?"

"Ariadne." Roberto dropped the cloth on the bench.

Jane frowned.

"One of Dionysus's consorts," Marguerite responded.

"I would hope so!" Jane laughed. "But she's not familiar to me. I associate Dionysus with Aphrodite."

"Ariadne helped Theseus slay her monstrous half brother—" Roberto began.

"The Minotaur," Tom interrupted, uncomfortably reminded of the slaying of a half brother at Eggescombe this very morning. "Theseus and Ariadne were to wed after, but Theseus abandoned her, I think."

"Yes." Roberto regarded him with some annoyance. "But Dionysus came to the rescue."

"And they all lived happily ever after," Marguerite summed up with a throaty laugh. She caught Tom's eye, then returned to scrutinising the artwork. "You've made great progress."

"I've been at it all night."

"Not all night, surely." Her gaze seemed to command his assent.

He blinked. "No. Not *all* night."

Tom frowned as he watched Roberto turn to switch off the floodlights. The words of their exchange were commonplace, but the tone was oddly freighted. He glanced over to a far wall, to a cot in half shadow, rumpled with bed linen. It looked slept in, but—on the other hand—nothing about Roberto suggested the boarding-school diligence of making up a bed every morning. The cot might have been rumpled for days or weeks. *Where did Roberto sleep? Were he and Lady Fairhaven really cohabiting?*

And did it matter?

The rest of the studio fallen now to a kind of chiaroscuro seemed a maze of things: Drawings, diagrams, and photographs partially covered the exposed-brick walls; much the same covered worktables, themselves arrayed in no particular order. Several large pieces in various stages of creation sat on wheelie tables here and there along with rolls of plastic sheeting, ladders, various manual and electrical tools, and industrial lighting snaking with cords. Small completed works lined one shelf while casts and studies in clay sat beside strips of linen piled on a table by a basin of water near a slop sink. It was towards these that Max and Miranda moved, intrigued perhaps by their potential for play. The cat followed.

"Mind the water on the floor by the sink!" Roberto called. "That drain's still not working properly." He glanced at Marguerite. "And don't touch the sculptures!" he snapped as Max turned a linen strip into a neck scarf.

"Maxie, darling," Marguerite said, "why don't you show Miranda the horses."

"Yes, let's!" Miranda enthused, leading the way towards the bar of buttery sunshine at the door. "Come, puss." She turned with a coaxing gesture. "What's its name?"

Roberto shrugged. The cat didn't obey.

"Let's call him Fred Astaire," Max said, following Miranda. "Come, Mr. Astaire."

When the children had gone, Roberto cast them a dark look. "I've heard some news." He gestured to the radio, an old brown Bakelite model, resting on a shelf near the sink. "But of course you would know already."

"You left Radio Devon on in the kitchen." Marguerite seemed to watch him carefully. "Jane and Tom told me earlier."

"Hector might have said on the phone."

"Would it have mattered?" Marguerite asked.

"No." Roberto's nostrils flared. "Although knowing a few hours earlier that someone had topped that shit might have gladdened my heart more."

"Perhaps *not* a wise thing to say, Roberto, darling. Not at this time."

"I'm not going to make some polite display, Marguerite—"

"That's not what I meant." She murmured as the cat leapt onto the table nearest them, deftly missing knocking over a small clay sculpture. "How did you know Oliver had been . . . as you say, 'topped'?"

"The newsreader said his death is being treated as suspicious. What else could it be?"

"Of course." A little cloud seemed to lift from Marguerite's face. "Yes, that's right, she did."

"Obviously," Roberto carried on heedless, his voice bitter, "I'm not the only person in the world who wanted to see him got rid of."

"Then why"—Tom found the words flying from his mouth before he had time to think—"did you?"

"Because, mate," Roberto threw the crusty gloves against the table with force, sending the cat flying to the tiles. "He killed my sister. He did, Marguerite," he added darkly, as if expecting her to contradict him.

"Roberto, there's no—"

"Of course there isn't. Why would there be? Some crap island police force, corruptible, corrupted—or just plain bloody stupid—kowtowing to an English lord?"

Tom looked to Jane, to a new alertness in her eyes.

"Alessandra Sica was your sister?" she said in a wondering voice. "Sica, of course. I knew it sounded familiar. I should have made the—"

"Yes. Was. *Was* my sister," Roberto interrupted. He intoned, as if he had stated the facts a hundred times: "My sister drowned off a boat on Baissé—it's one of the Grenadines—six years ago. She was twenty-two. There were bruises on her neck and a cocktail of drugs in her blood—at least we got *that* information out of the filth that accounts for the police on Baissé—and my father got the boat captain to admit Alessa and his bloody lordship had quarreled—but nothing! *Nothing!* An accident! Bah!"

Tom felt the full force of the man's anger wash over him like a powerful tide. He looked to the two silent and shocked women and struggled for a response. "I know injustice is difficult to bear—" he began.

"Yeah? And how would you know that, posh vicar?"

"Because"—he took a sharp breath, labouring for an even tone—"I see it daily and I bear my own."

Something in Tom's fixed look quelled the man, for Roberto flinched and shifted his attention to the cat winding around his legs. Like a storm waning, his body slackened. He reached down for the cat—an albino, surely, the thought passed through Tom's mind as he noted the cold pink glittering eyes—and tucked it into the crook of his arm. But he wasn't done. It was as if he had to trump Tom.

"And . . . *and* she was carrying a child—that man's child. Morborne's."

The tone was one of disgust choked back; the look on Roberto's face barely disguised hatred. Such an oppressive, distorting emotion, Tom knew, giving a passing thought to his own feelings in the wake of his wife's death, though he then had—and still had—no individual, man or woman, to attach them to. He glanced away, to take in the kinder vision of the plump purring cat content as a baby in a mother's arms, but as he did a terrible thought suddenly possessed him.

CHAPTER TWELVE

"*I* never made the connection before."

"What connection is that, my love?" Jamie Allan glanced up absently. He had been browsing the newspapers and magazines on the library table.

"You remember that awful incident six years ago or so when Oliver was winding up his father's affairs on Baissé? There was a woman Oliver took with him who drowned."

"I think it's the only time I've ever seen a chink in Olly's armour."

Jane looked at Tom, then at her husband. "Really? I thought it was the only time I've ever seen Oliver in love."

"What? You never said at the time."

"Didn't I? I'm sure I did. You just don't remember."

"Oliver fforde-Beckett in love—what a mad idea."

"He must be in love with Serena, Jamie. Or must have *been*," Jane amended.

"Oh, do you think? Another of Olly's dollies, I would have said."

"Yes, Jamie, but he was prepared to *marry* this one."

"True. Well, Serena's suitable. Frank Knowlton had investments in television and film, I think. A good alliance from Olly's point of view. Fair bit of money there, too." He lifted a copy of *The Sunday Telegraph,* pulling out the flyer and assorted rubbish from between the folds. "What's this to do with that girl? Worked in a sandwich shop or something, didn't she? Did we meet her?"

"No. Her picture was in the papers, though. Afterwards, of course, with all the press coverage. Very beautiful." Jane tapped her fingers along the cover of the book she was holding. "Anyway, her father owned a string of sandwich shops in London. She happened to be working in one, in Wigmore Street, near Oliver's offices, when Oliver popped in—well, for a sandwich, I presume. I think he was between personal assistants at the time. Anyway, she was involved in music somehow herself, but more practically—studying music therapy, I think. Olly lured her away. She was very young and I suppose what Olly does— did—made him attractive. She became his PA. Well, I guess that's the polite term."

Jamie gave an unhappy grunt and settled into a chair opposite his wife. "What makes you think Olly was in love with her?"

"Something he said to me later, when it had all blown over. Do you remember? My mother was visiting. We'd taken her to see some play in the West End. I can't remember the play, but I remember we were having our drinks in the street at intermission and Olly was doing the same at the theatre across the lane. On Shaftsbury. Do you recall?"

"Vaguely."

"Some protégé of his was in some musical." Jane frowned in recollection. "Anyway, I think you'd gone to the loo and my mother had wandered off. Olly and I had a few moments alone together and I told him I didn't think he looked well, though he was very tanned from being on Baissé. He said he was having trouble coming to terms with Alessa's death. Alessa—that was the PA's name. He said he'd never again find someone like her."

"As a PA, he meant, presumably."

"No, Jamie, as a woman. I'm right! Don't frown at me like that. It was the look in his eyes—*and* they misted up!"

"I can hardly imagine it."

"Probably not something he would reveal to you men."

"No. I expect not." Jamie's eyes fell to the newspaper on his lap. "Still, you mentioned a connection. What connection?"

"She was Roberto's sister. Roberto *Sica*? The girl was Alessandra Sica—Alessa."

Jamie looked up. "Small world." He glanced from Jane to Tom with suspicion. "What is it, you two? It was an accident on Baissé, wasn't it? Misadventure, whatever you call it."

"Mr. Sica doesn't think so," Tom said, glancing around the Eggescombe library, hundreds of feet of mellow morocco bindings and richly shining shelves. He had had half a hope the "magical electronic board," as Marguerite had called it, that had mixed the filming of the Leaping Lords, might be in evidence, but it wasn't.

"He's really *very* angry," Jane added. "Thinks the police were inept or corrupted or something."

"Do you mean to say he thinks Olly . . . killed this girl, this Alessa?"

"In so many words."

"Deliberately? Malice aforethought? In cold blood. Et cetera."

"I'm not sure about that." Jane looked to Tom for confirmation.

"He thinks your cousin had a hand in it—and I'm not being funny," he said.

"Apparently there was considerable bruising around Alessa's neck," Jane continued. "I remembered some of the details from the press reports at the time. Unexplained bruising. And there was no one else on the boat but the captain."

"But that's outrageous. Olly's many things—and not all of them good, I'm sure—but he's not the sort to, you know . . . how do you know all this?"

"From the horse's mouth," Jane replied. "We paid a call on Roberto at his studio in the stables this morning. Marve filled us in on a few more details when we walked back for lunch."

Jamie scowled. "Are you suggesting that Roberto has somehow contrived to be at Eggescombe intending to—"

"No," Jane interrupted. "Well, I don't think so. According to Marve, he had no idea that Georgie was Olly's sister. And really, if he were set on a plan of revenge all these years . . ." She looked to Tom.

"It would make more sense to do so in London, where your cousin lived and worked," Tom supplied.

"Olly never spends any time here, Jamie," Jane pointed out. "Georgie is rarely here, so there's no reason for Olly to come down. When Hector comes on business, he arrives alone and usually stays with Marve, at hers. No Olly, no opportunity, you see."

"There has been these last few days, since Olly arrived," Jamie countered.

"Well, I'll grant you that."

"Seems a bit of a fluke, each being at Eggescombe at the same time."

"Flukes happen, Jamie. But I don't think Oliver had run into Roberto, until last evening when he and Marve arrived together. We hadn't seen hide nor hare of Roberto, either. He's in his studio all the time."

"Where did he come from? Mr. Sica, I mean."

"Marve told me she met him at some arts do at Falmouth. She's a trustee of University College. She's had this scheme to turn the stable block into artists' studios, found his artwork to her liking, and invited him to be the first artist in residence."

"Found more than his art to her liking, I daresay," Jamie murmured.

Jane raised a book and flung it at her husband. He caught it deftly.

"First cricket eleven at my school." He grinned at Tom, then glanced at the title. *The Heath Government: 1970–1974: A Reappraisal,*" he recited, grin turned grimace. "Looks like heavy wading. Hector does read some wretched stuff."

Jamie proffered the book to Jane, who shook her head and indicated a side table. "What do you think *is* the relationship between Roberto and Marve? Are they, you know . . . ?"

"Is it important?" Jane asked.

"No, I expect not. It does seem a bit . . . unnatural."

"Says Farmer Jamie." Jane regarded her husband wryly. "And if the shoe were on the other foot, on the *male* foot, what would you say?"

"I would say, lucky old male foot."

"Double standard."

"Help me out, Tom," Jamie moaned. "Men with younger women—it has history. But women with younger men—much younger—well, it's not really the done thing, is it?"

Tom felt a blush creeping up his neck, a riotous reimagining of his own nighttime coupling with a younger woman, more than a decade younger. "I think I should keep well out of this discussion."

Jamie grunted. "Dominic thinks he's gay."

"Roberto?" Jane frowned, rising from her chair and moving towards the library table. "I don't think so. Tom?"

Tom shrugged. "Oliver hinted as much to Dominic. I happened to overhear. But—"

"Wishful thinking on Dominic's part, I expect. Where is Hector? We were going to look at his plans for a micro-hydro system for the estate. Perhaps he's still in the dining room." Jamie glanced towards the door to the corridor. His face fell. "That was a bit of a cheerless gathering, wasn't it? The nosh was very good, though. Yet again. We've had some wonderful meals here, haven't we, Jane? Georgie's certainly struck lucky with Mrs. Gaunt." He paused. "That *is* your housekeeper, isn't it, Tom? Serving last night on the terrace? I glimpsed her through the door to the dining room this lunch."

"She went to cookery school in London with Ellen Gaunt. She's here for a visit."

"More a busman's holiday, I should think."

"Oh, Mrs. Prowse is in her element, very much enjoying herself."

"I wish I could say the same." Jamie's face fell. "I was thinking at lunch that of the three great friends at school, at Shrewsbury, all are gone well before their time—Boysie, my brother," he clarified for Tom, "Kamran Arouzi, who died—by his own hand—just before our wedding, remember, Jane? The three of them had that scheme to open a nightclub in Villiers Street then. Icarus. Still there, isn't it?"

"You can tell we don't get out much, darling. Icarus is the most popular dance club in London—has been for a dozen years. And Olly was planning to expand—didn't you know? It was in the news. Versions in Berlin and Amsterdam and New York and such."

"Sorry, yes, Olly did mention some business scheme when we lunched at the Pilgrims on Friday. The Icarii. Seemed awfully ambitious in this economic climate, I thought. It's not easy getting the banks to loan you money for anything." Jamie turned to look at his wife. "That won't come to pass with Oliver gone. It's all terribly sad."

"Yes, it is," Jane agreed, sifting through the literature on the library table.

"You seem a bit restless, darling."

"Do I? It's just the waiting, I suppose. A death in the family seems to suspend time."

"And speaking of family, there's my parents to consider."

"Jamie, you haven't phoned Tullochbrae yet?"

"You wouldn't care to, would you? My father's having a slow recovery from his stroke," Jamie explained to Tom. "This will be a bit of a blow."

"Probably best coming from you, Jamie. Your mother can tell your father. She won't know what's happened here yet, I'm sure. She'll have the TV and radio off and the kids' computers under lock and key—particularly on Sunday. My mother-in-law is a fresh-air fiend," Jane added for Tom's benefit. "Particularly at Tullochbrae. But, Jamie, better let her know before she hears it from one of the staff."

"It may be a while before we can rescue our little darlings." Jamie rose from the chair and reached into his pocket, pulling out his mobile.

"Wait! Before you go . . ." Jane glanced up from the newspaper on the table before her. "At Tullochbrae years ago, when I first knew you, wasn't there a boy named David who was mentally challenged?"

"Yes, David Corlett, the land agent's son. Why?"

"Oh, Corlett." Jane's disappointment was audible. "Never mind. I was just glancing at this story. What is this paper?" She turned back a page. "Local. *South Devon Herald.* There's a story about an inquest next week into the death of a David Phillips who shared a cottage in Abbotswick with his sister, Anna. Hit and run. Near Buckfastleigh. According to this, he was mentally challenged. Lived in a Steiner community."

Jamie turned back. "Does it give an age?"

Jane glanced at the paper. "Twenty-seven."

"That would be . . . about right, I think. Photo?"

"No."

Jamie moved to look over Jane's shoulder. "But the sister's Christian name isn't right, either. David's sister was Ree to us. Ree Corlett. Attractive girl. Very bright. Had to be mother to the boy, really. Her own mother died years earlier, of what I'm not sure. I was too young to remember." He frowned. "Not quite the lead one would like, do you think, darling?"

"Just a minute." Jane's voice grew excited. "Look at this, Jamie. It mentions Anna's partner—John!"

Jamie leaned down as Jane held up the paper for his scrutiny. "It says 'John Phillips.'"

"But isn't that odd? Don't you think so, Jamie? If he's her partner—not her husband—why would they have the same last name? And if John and Anna are a married couple, her brother's unlikely to share her husband's last name, yes?"

Jamie was silent a moment. "Perhaps . . . though, honestly, darling, *John* is an awfully common name, and so is *Phillips*, come to that. They might be disparate Phillipses that somehow came together."

"Jamie!"

"I'm sorry, Jane. I simply don't wish to have my hopes dashed again. It all seems too much of a coincidence."

"Tom?" Jane lowered the newspaper and cast him beseeching eyes.

"Well, I think things that seem like coincidence are often more . . . oh, how can I put it? . . . more often confluences of shared circumstances and shared interests and shared people and the like. Quite natural in a way, so—"

"Yes!" Jane interrupted. "Jamie, I remember you telling me that John was always very kind to David, who wasn't easy to handle. And mightn't John have been attracted to Ree? Isn't it possible? Teenagers? Around the same age? They would have at least known each other. And don't forget that Tom said in an email last year that his housekeeper saw John on Dartmoor."

"It was a woman in the village who *thought* she saw him," Tom reminded her, "and told Mrs. Prowse who told me—"

"It's all a bit straw-grasping, darling," Jamie interrupted. "We're still faced with the fact that this woman's name is Anna."

Jane looked unconvinced. "But it's reasonable. John—Sebastian, as Tom knows him—disappeared from Thornford over a year ago when that poor girl was found dead in that Japanese drum. He could have gone anywhere—"

"I can't think how!" Jamie interjected. "He seems to have no passport, no driving licence, no bank cards. And don't think we haven't looked into it." He glanced meaningfully at Tom.

"But the point, my darling, is that John may not have gone far. Not if he knew someone nearby, someone who could help him—Anna! Though why she'd change her name . . ." Jane trailed off, frowning. "Mr. Corlett died, didn't he? Around the time of John's trial."

"Heart attack, much too young. Tragedy all around in those months. Ree and David left Tullochbrae soon after. Too much a place of sorrow, I expect. I have no idea where they pitched up."

"In Abbotswick!"

"Darling, really."

"What seems like coincidence, isn't. It's a natural . . . Tom?"

"Confluence."

"More of a miracle, I would say." Jamie glanced at his watch. "And I thought those went out with loaves and fishes."

"Oh, ye of little faith." Tom raised an eyebrow.

"We've got to talk to this Anna Phillips, Jamie."

"Wouldn't we be intruding on her grief?"

"I think you'll have a time getting into Abbotswick," Tom said. "The police wouldn't let Father Downes in, and they're not going to let anyone leave, at least for some while."

When Tom returned to Eggescombe Hall from the stables with Jane, Marguerite, and the children, the police were already a palpable presence on the estate. Various specialist vehicles were visible at a distance hugging the edge of the drive nearest the Labyrinth, with assorted uniformed people in purposeful movement. With a little dismay, he noted behind the other vehicles in the circular sweep of gravel in front of the Hall a familiar red Astra, glinting fiercely in the noon sun. As he approached, the equally familiar figures of Detective Inspector Derek Bliss and Detective Sergeant Colin Blessing of Totnes CID emerged, ushered forth by Gaunt, immaculate in his suit, his face in the open door's half shadow unreadable. DI Bliss stepped into the sunshine and waggled a finger at Tom as the others slipped back into the Hall.

"I understood you'd dropped in," he barked without apparent irony, casting him a baleful glance. DS Blessing looked at his cast boot.

"As long as I'm not dropped *in* it," Tom countered, struggling for levity. Bliss and Blessing, he'd discovered through previous encounters, were always a bit of rough sailing. Bliss, the younger of the pair, though senior in rank, was a twitchy sort, seemingly uncomfortable in his own skin, while Blessing had skin that was uncomfortable, at least to look at, as the man had a face battered—Tom figured—from a virulent case of teenage acne.

Bliss grunted at Tom's *bon mot,* ascertained that Tom had

indeed, as PC Widger had already informed him, found Lord Morborne's body in the Labyrinth. Their conversation was perfunctory: Tom gave them a précis of the sunrise circumstances, including his dew path excursion, for which he received a ticking-off for disturbing a crime scene, and was invited in no uncertain terms to remain as Lord Fairhaven's guest for the time being. He wasn't completely forthcoming with the inspector about the morning, however. Two things about those early hours in the Labyrinth disturbed him, but he didn't want to say anything unless he determined himself they were consequential.

"I can't bear having to stay put when John may be somewhere on the other side of the Gatehouse," Jane said now. "I wonder if the police would let me—"

"I think they would sense a wild goose chase in the offing," Jamie interrupted.

"It's neither 'wild' nor 'goose.'"

"Gander, then. I'm going to root Hector out. I can sense your little grey cells on the march, darling. Better I get out of the way. Try not to be a nuisance to the vicar."

"Don't forget to phone your mother," Jane called after him, adding to Tom: "My husband is very sweet, but he can be a bit incurious. I do know he's more affected by Oliver's death than he's letting on, though." She paused. "I guess you'll have to make other arrangements, too."

"I had thought Miranda and I might get to London by train this afternoon and leave the car with Mrs. Prowse, but I guess that's off. I'll have to phone my mothers shortly, as well."

"By the way," Jane began in a low voice, after the sound of Jamie's footfalls along the corridor had faded, "did you tell the inspector what you told me about Hector? About your finding him looking for something on Oliver's body?"

Tom shook his head. He had crossed Hector's path outside Eggescombe's great hall after his brief exchange with Bliss and Blessing and received a glance that he could only describe as wary. An attempt to enter into dialogue was rebuffed: Hector claimed important work to attend to.

"No, I didn't think it fair to say anything," he replied to Jane's question. "I must speak to Hector privately first."

"That's very fair."

"Jane . . ." He had another thought.

She glanced at him expectantly.

"Jane," he began again, "had you walked the Labyrinth before?"

"You mean before this morning? Yes, Jamie and I walked it the evening of the day we arrived."

"And did you get a good look at the statue of Mary?"

"Yes. Well, sort of. It's very good."

"And had you met Roberto before?"

"Only when you did—last evening when Marve brought him to the barbecue. He works all the time, as I mentioned earlier, and I'm sure he's figured out that Hector doesn't approve of him." She refolded the newspaper in front of her. "May I ask where this is leading?"

"I'm not entirely sure. It may be nothing, but last evening Roberto seemed quite insistent that Oliver view his creation, view the statue at the centre of the Labyrinth, almost as if . . ." He hesitated. ". . . almost as if he were enticing, tempting, challenging?—I'm not certain which word would do—Oliver in some fashion."

"Setting him up, in a way."

"Yes—ugly as that sounds."

A shadow crossed Jane's face. "Marve chimed in a bit, didn't she."

"The face of the Virgin is exquisite, finely wrought. When I studied it this morning I thought how highly individuated the features were, how distinctive the brow, the nose, the chin. And then, later this morning, when we were with Roberto in his studio, something about his features, his—"

"Of course!" Jane interrupted. "There's a resemblance. It's like—"

"A feminine version of Roberto's face. A smaller chin, a less robust nose, but—"

"But not Roberto feminised."

"No, not some narcissistic replication. The statue has a living model—had, rather. I'm sure it's Roberto's sister, Alessa, idealised as the Virgin Mother."

"Recognisable to anyone who knew Alessa well—like Oliver."

"But there's more, Jane. That white cat, Fred Astaire—very much the wrong name for such a fat cat—that has attached itself to Roberto—"

"That Marve says follows him around, yes."

"It crossed my path in the Labyrinth this morning."

Eggescombe Hall

Dear Mum,

I can't remember writing twice in one day before, but what a difference a few hours can make! I'm just returned to the Gatehouse from the Hall, having helped poor Ellen and Mick with Sunday lunch for Lord Fairhaven and his guests, and I can see police cars and all sorts in the gardens if I look out my west window and people standing about in the forecourt of the Gatehouse if I look out my east. And the big gate itself has been shut. A PC was pushing it across the entrance when I was returning from the Hall just now and it sounded so ~~ominious~~ ominous as it rolled across the track! It made me feel we were soon to repel a Norman invasion, but the PC, who had trouble latching the gate (I showed him how!), said it was to keep out the riffraff while there's a criminal investigation. You must know what I'm talking about, as it will be all over the

papers and TV by the time you get this. One of the
Leaping Lords was found dead in the Labyrinth early this
morning. Mr. Christmas came across him, as it happens.
Poor Mr. C. He's already gone and sprained his ankle, and
now this! He and Miranda won't be going up to London
this weekend, I'm sure. Mum, I met the Marquess of
Morborne yesterday! The one who died. I should have said
earlier. Hard to believe he's gone today. He cut quite the
figure, now I think on it. Not a big man, but dressed in a
fancy shirt and wearing a funny cap which made him
stand out. I was serving the nibbles on the terrace last
night and he was telling some roaring joke when I passed
by with the tray. Wish I could remember what it was now.
I had to keep my po face on, of course, but afterwards I had
to laugh. He seemed like good company, but then I
remembered things I've read in the papers about him.
Done the dirty on business partners. And all those women!
Some of them other men's wives, too! But then I think the
~~For~~ fforde-Becketts have been ~~cock~~ cuckholds and ~~rooays~~
roues and blaggards and such forever. Look what his father
did—divorce his wife and steal his brother's. You could cut
the atmosphere with a knife here, what with all the ~~For~~
fforde-Becketts down for the weekend. Not much love lost,
I must say! And didn't the father—the VERY *late Lord*
Morborne, not the recently late—lose pots of money on
some casino hotel scheme in the West Indies before he died
playing tennis? And the grandfather was shot dead in
Kenya because he was misbehaving with someone's wife, I
think. And then there was that scandal a few years ago

when that girl who was the recently late L. Morborne's
girlfriend drowned. It's all ~~very exciting interesting~~ quite
shocking! I won't go on. I'm sure the Mail or the Mirror is
dredging it all up and you reading it this very minute.
Anyway, I knew none of what was going on for the longest
time this morning. After I finished my first letter to you, I
went down for a bite. Ellen and Mick had gone up to the
Big House, but as I was eating I could see out the window
this young man tearing up the road on foot half dressed as
a policeman and I did wonder. But as it's a holiday, I
thought I'd go into Abbotswick and post your letter (though
there is a letter box built into the wall right by the
Gatehouse—so handy!—though I wonder if anyone will
let me out to post THIS letter?) and view the Holne Abbey
ruin and go to the Morning Service at St. Swithun's. The
ruin is quite nice, but it did look much more romantic in
that Tess of the ~~Derby~~ D'Urbervilles series on telly a few
years ago—do you remember? Where the hero places Tess
in an empty stone coffin then nods off? Anyway, there
wasn't much doing in the village. I saw Dowager Lady
Fairhaven pop out of one of the cottages (doing good
works?) and I attended the service, which was a bit down
the candle, I must say (the sermon was VERY dull), but
when I got back to the Gatehouse, I could sense something
was off. I could see a lot of vans up the drive towards the
house, for one. And then when I went into the Gatehouse I
could hear someone making the oddest noises above me,
which I thought peculiar as I expected Ellen and Mick to
be at the Big House most of the day. I was a bit unnerved,

*but ~~intrepdily~~ intrepidly I followed the sound up to Ellen
and Mick's to find Mick rummaging around in a drawer
in the bureau in their bedroom, but absolutely convulsed in
sobs as if some ~~damn~~ dam had burst. I was quite rooted to
the spot for all of a moment it was so disturbing, but then I
thought—Lord God, something has happened to Ellen! I
went to him, and oh dear, I did surprise the poor man and
he tried to cover, as they do. You know what men are like.
But it took a very anxious moment (for me!) before he
could speak and tell me that it wasn't Ellen, but Lord
Morborne. I was quite surprised that he would take His
Lordship's death so hard. I couldn't think they would know
each other, though I do remember Ellen saying that she and
Mick, in their early days together, were staff to Lord
Morborne's uncle, Lord Anthony fforde-Beckett, the
younger one who lost his wife to his older brother. Anyway,
everyone reacts differently to death, and of course this is a
murder, so it makes it all the more worrying. I thought I
might lend a hand to Ellen in this troubled time and said
so, so I left Mick to recover his sensibilities while I went up
to the Hall to help her with Sunday lunch. Poor Ellen, she
was suffering in her own way. Gone all white and stiff.
"Say your prayers when meeting a red-haired man, since
he is not to be trusted," she said which startled me a bit as
Lord Morborne was the victim and I said so, but Ellen
wasn't having any of it. She said he used to hang about
when she and Mick were in service to the Arouzis and she
didn't trust him then and she didn't trust him now, though
she didn't really say why other than to disapprove of the*

way he dressed. And of course the Arouzi boy took his own life some years ago and that was the last Ellen and Mick saw of Lord Morborne until this weekend. As ye sew, so shall ye reap, she went on a bit. Sometimes I feel that the Ellen I knew at Leiths has gone missing, but I was able to jolly her out of her mood a bit, recalling the time when we were cooking partners at school and she made me ~~evizera~~ debone a duck as she was too squeamish. She's quite capable of all that now, of course. We cooked roast chicken with courgettes for lunch and served for pudding an apple and marmalade tart. (The same recipe we learned at Leiths!) Quite like the old days, I thought, as we worked together. Eggescombe has a brilliant modern kitchen, carved out of the old servants' hall. However, Mum, I think I know now why Ellen really went all funny this morning—and why we lost touch—and it's so very tragic, really. Years ago, about 25 years or so (hard to imagine!), her younger sister Kimberly was killed by some wretch. All of 15 she was, interfered with in the woodland on The Wrekin. And she was strangled, like Lord Morborne! So that's brought it all back for Ellen, poor woman. When her sister was killed, she couldn't bear to write about it to any of her friends, hence the silence. (I can't think what I was doing 25 years ago that I didn't see it in the papers!) Oddly enough, in a roundabout way, it was Kimberly's death that brought Ellen and Mick together. Ellen was putting flowers on her sister's grave in the churchyard at Telford and Mick was doing the same for his mother. Love among the gravestones, it turns out. Married 20 years next year, Ellen said. No kiddies, though. I haven't liked to ask. Well,

I must crack on, Mum. I don't know what the next hours will bring. I thought I might look at the gardens, as the Labyrinth is sealed off as a crime scene, or walk up onto the moor, as it's such a nice day, but perhaps I best hang about. Love to Aunt Gwen! (I already said that once today!)

Much love,
Madrun

CHAPTER THIRTEEN

"*D*idn't you bring swimming trunks, Vicar?" Lucinda slipped her sunglasses down her nose and squinted up at him from the sun lounger.

"I didn't expect to be staying."

"Nor I, really. But I found something of Georgie's that fit. Can't imagine her ever wearing this, though!" She shifted slightly in the chair, which had a cantilevering effect on her breasts encased in the scrap of costume. "Well, sort of." A smile twitched at the corners of her mouth as she plucked a tube of sun cream from a raffia bag next to her. "Wonderful of Hector to fill the pool."

Tom glanced at the translucent water—the tiny turquoise lozenge he had seen from on high the day before—and at the sun-dazzled ripples, which might have transfixed him on another day, a day set aside for relaxation, if he wasn't otherwise troubled. At luncheon, Lucy had declared for an afternoon at the pool, which met varied shadings of opprobrium from much of her family, none of which deterred her, he'd noted from his bedroom window, on his mobile, trying (unsuccessfully) to reach his mothers in Gravesend. A gauzy white kimono jacket fluttered around the tops of her bare legs as she moved with self-possession over the south lawn. Reattaching his cast boot, he had hobbled through Eggescombe Hall and out the terrace after her, joining a path that branched from the one leading to the walled kitchen-garden-*cum*-garden-centre, through a topiary hedge corridor, to a gate marked STRICTLY PRIVATE. The pool, once he'd manoeuvred the latch and climbed down a few steps, seemed a world apart, protected from the wind and curious eyes by a high stone wall and a curtain of trees. In a climate of uncertain sunniness, it was an extravagance, as much a folly as the adjoining Gaze Tower, a giant's pencil of stone purposelessly piercing the sky.

"I understood at lunch that Lord Fairhaven's intent was to fill the pool *in*."

"Perhaps." Lucinda twiddled the tip of the tube, adding, as if in explanation, "Hector's in a foul mood."

"Understandably so, yes?"

Lucinda's response was to squirt a dollop of white cream onto her fingers. "Although I suppose this patch really could be put to better use." She glanced over the rims of her glasses around the enclosure, almost shimmering in the hot imperturbable calm of August. "A petting zoo, perhaps? A paintball arena?" Her tone contained no irony. "Can't imagine what Hector's grandfather was thinking putting a swimming pool in? Turning Eggescombe into a country house hotel, likely. I expect someone came along with a different view." She smoothed the cream into her upper arm. Tom noted the faint white souvenirs of cutting on the lower. "Clever old Georgie.

"Marrying Hector," she added, as Tom frowned at the non sequitur. "The Stricklands have—oh, what's the word?—*husbanded* their resources well. My grandfather, on the other hand, sold off the family seat while he was living in Kenya. Riseley Castle. In Cambridgeshire. Do you know it?"

"Vaguely."

"*It's* a country house hotel. And then there was Kilmore in County Armagh, which my grandfather also sold. It's now the headquarters of a potato crisp manufacturer. And then, of course, there's my father's—our father's, Oliver and Georgie's and mine . . . have you thoroughly plumbed the fforde-Beckett line . . . ?"

"As I indicated, I was given a scorecard earlier."

". . . our father's disastrous investment on Baissé in the West Indies, where I was born, incidentally." She paused in her application of cream. "Why don't you sit down? You're casting a shadow. Pull that sun lounger over here."

Tom chose instead a deck chair, which seemed less louche. Like his hosts, he judged sunbathing—or even the appearance of sunbathing—in the circumstances of family tragedy ill considered. With his free hand, he dragged the chair across the tiles, wood scraping paving stone, sensing her eyes resting on him rather like a cat's on a mouse. He felt uncommonly uncomfortable.

"I take it you're here to talk to me," Lucinda said as Tom settled himself into the chair. "Not take in the sun."

"Yes."

"*About last night,*" she murmured throatily, resuming the application of sun cream.

"About the early morning."

"The early morning? Oh, do tell."

Tom took a cleansing breath. "You know, don't you, that I was the one who found your brother's—"

"Half brother."

"—half brother's . . . body—"

"Yes."

"—in the centre of the Labyrinth. Well, in the short time before that I thought I saw—"

Lucinda looked at him expectantly. "Yes . . . ?"

Tom had paused. "You haven't had a conversation with the CID yet, have you?"

"No. I wasn't expecting to."

Tom raised an eyebrow. *Can she be so ingenuous?* "I don't doubt we'll all be interviewed by them before very long—helping them with their enquiries, as the saying goes."

"I can't think there's much I can tell them." Lucinda affected to stifle a yawn.

"Unfortunately, there are one or two things I may need to tell them."

"Really?" she drawled, popping her sunglasses in place over her eyes.

"One of them," Tom persisted, "has to do with what I saw when I entered the Labyrinth—"

"*Thought* you saw, you said."

"Yes, all right, 'thought.' It was a head, the back of one, at any rate."

"Perhaps it was Eggescombe's famous ghost."

"I'm told Eggescombe's ghost is male," Tom responded, glancing at his own vexed reflection in her sunglasses. "I'm fairly sure I saw the back of a woman's head."

"A woman's." Lucinda pushed the glasses down her nose. "Do you mean like mine?" She twisted on the sun lounger, exposing the mane of reddish blond hair parting gently to reveal a few wispy hairs on her neck.

Momentarily distracted—there was something so vulnerable about the back of a woman's neck—Tom could only murmur, "It was very early, the light was poor—"

"You think it may have been me." Lucinda twisted her body back round. "You must or you wouldn't have bothered to come all this way."

"I'm not saying that at all. I'm merely saying that I saw a woman."

"*Thought* you saw a woman."

"In either case, I feel duty-bound to say so, which means the police may ask certain . . . questions—awkward questions—of the women at Eggescombe. Well," Tom amended, "of all of us, really."

Lucinda lifted an editorial eyebrow. "Well, it couldn't have been me. I took a cup of coffee on the terrace about eleven and that was the first time I was out of doors today."

Tom found himself fidgeting with his wedding ring with rising embarrassment. It occurred to him that in the midst of His innumerable concerns, God had paused to lend an interested ear. Helplessly, he glanced up at the sky, past the Gaze Tower, as if expecting the divine auricle to manifest itself among the wisps of clouds over Dartmoor, and saw only a lean figure—possibly Dominic from the white of his costume—leaning out of the tower's window looking their way. It didn't matter that Dominic lacked God's omniaudient attribute; Tom was made to feel uncomfortable anyway. He returned his eyes to Lucinda and said the words before he had any more time to think:

"When did you leave my bed?"

Her lips parted in the beginning of a smile. "When? Why, Vicar, I haven't the foggiest. It was dark."

"And you returned to your room?"

"Ah, a trick question! But Jane has already told me she went looking for me early this morning and couldn't find me. I'll tell you what I told her—I was in Dominic's room." She pushed the sunglasses back up the bridge of her nose. "I took a nightcap with me to Dominic's room after the party last night and fell asleep on the daybed in his room. And then, later, after we, you know . . . I returned to his room."

"Why?"

"Why?" The question seemed to catch her unawares.

"You might have stayed with me."

"Is that something you would have wanted?"

Tom could feel a blush creep up his throat. Yes, damn it, he very much liked to wake up with a woman, but he felt absurdly as if doing so breached some country house weekend etiquette.

"It occurred to me," she continued when he didn't reply, "that . . . well, that you might not want your daughter to find us together. Children are known to barge into their parents' bedrooms, are they not?"

"Yes," he said, though he sensed she was improvising. He

wasn't sure Miranda would know how to find the Opium Bedroom without a trail of bread crumbs.

"Anyway, you mustn't worry, Tom. I shall swear I was with Dominic all night—should I have to, of course. Your secret is safe with me. Now, would you be a lamb and rub some cream on my back?"

"No," Tom responded more vehemently than he intended.

"No? How *very* unkind."

"I meant, you must be forthright with the police." Though he realised his response lacked honesty—he didn't at all look forward to anyone knowing.

"Must I?"

"If you want your brother's—your half brother's killer found."

"I'm not sure I do. Or care, really. A lot less Olly in the world is purely beneficial as far as I can see."

"You can't mean that."

"But I do."

"A human life has been snatched away," Tom protested. "He was to marry. He is expecting a child!"

"I meant beneficial to *me,* Vicar." Her mouth twisted unevenly. "Olly has dominated and bullied the family Trust in the years since our father died and mismanaged what's left of the estate terribly. Georgie has no idea what's been going on. She likes to keep her head in the sand, but then in marrying Hector she has the wherewithal to do so. Olly's been selling properties like mad without any discussion, looting Morborne House while my mother and I have been away—and, Dominic told me this weekend, putting up fake pictures in their place. Dom thinks he's been doing it for years! Then Olly said he was going to sell the house itself, claiming the Trust can't afford the costs of maintaining it and the money is best placed elsewhere. But what he really wanted was the house to himself and Serena, who needs to have her head examined for assenting to marry him. 'It's a Trust decision,' he always said." She popped her glasses down her nose again and fixed him with her gaze. "I shouldn't bore you with this, because it is *such* a bore! But I got back from visiting mother in Cap Ferrat on Friday to find the locks on the house had been changed. He claimed to me yesterday we had received notice to vacate the house by August first. We received no such notice. My mother has a life right to the use of Morborne House, according to the terms of Daddy's will, and that only changes if she remarries."

"Is she? Remarrying?"

Lucinda looked away. "No. Well, not yet. Anyway, I've only the clothes in my suitcases, you know. Everything else is in Morborne House. Olly's rendered me homeless. And worse . . . !" She paused. "I suppose all this could constitute motive, couldn't it? I might be a character in one of those country house murder-mystery weekend thingies—which I shouldn't be surprised is on offer at Riseley Castle." She held out her hands. "But for these." She wiggled her slim fingernails tipped with the faintest pink varnish. "I don't think these could strangle a man, do you?"

Twitching with the memory of those hands running down his back, Tom failed to respond immediately. Her hands were not flaccid mittens. They were strong hands; Lucinda was fit, gym-toned. But her hands were a woman's hands, and besides . . .

"Well, do you?" She broke into his thoughts.

"Lord Morborne was strangled with a ligature of some nature," he said dumbly, still remembering her hands.

"Really? I didn't know." Lucinda shifted on the sun lounger. "What exactly?"

"It's not clear."

"You mean whatever was used hasn't been found?"

"Not that I'm aware of."

Lucinda's lips formed a thoughtful moue. Then she flicked her head suddenly, as if alerted by a movement in her peripheral vision. She put her hand to her brow to shield her eyes and stared up to the Gaze Tower. "Is that Dominic?"

"I believe so. He's been up there awhile."

"Dominic!" Lucinda called and waved. "Come down from there! Come here!"

Tom watched as Dominic leaned from the opening, his hand cupping his ear. Lucinda shouted again, but Dominic shook his head.

"He can't hear me. Pity. I'd have him put sun cream on my back." She flicked Tom a sardonic glance.

Tom watched her take up the sun cream once again and continue her toilette, spreading the white liquid along her legs in strong strokes. The front of her was now almost unashamedly glistening with sun cream—a sunblocking SPF 90, he noted, wondering at the point of lying in the sun if you didn't wish to encourage a bit of a tan. An aroma of coconut and Bounty bars wafted in the tepid breeze to his nostrils, redolent of bucket-and-spade holidays on the Isle of Wight with his mothers. One summer they had gone to the south of France, when he was about Miranda's age. Not Cap Ferrat, though. Somewhere much less grand.

"What might be worse than homelessness?" he asked, his mind returned to their earlier conversation.

"A philosophical question?"

"No, earlier, when you said your . . . half brother had rendered you basically homeless, you alluded to a worse condition."

"Oh." She regarded him steadily, arrested in her movements. "There's something about you that makes me want to tell secrets. What is it?"

"I've been told I have a kindly face." Tom laughed for the first time that day. "Or that people think priests are of necessity discreet."

"Aren't they?"

"I am."

"Well, then . . ." She restored the cap to the bottle. "Illegitimacy is worse. Oliver had it in his fat melon that our father did not properly divorce *his* mother, thereby making our father's marriage to *my* mother bigamous and illegal. Which in turn would make me a bastard. From there, he could challenge my right—and my mother's—as beneficiaries of the Trust, and deny us our titles."

"That seems malicious."

"That is precisely Oliver fforde-Beckett. I'm sure that as a child he pulled the wings off flies."

"Is there any foundation to his belief? I would have to say that when I glanced at an entry on the Morborne marquessate on the Internet a few weeks ago, my eyes did pass the words *bigamous marriage.*"

"It's absolute nonsense. Uncle Anthony—Dominic's father—made the accusation years ago, at the time of the trials, but there was no proof. Anthony insisted that our father—Olly and Georgie's and mine—married my mother *before* he was properly divorced from Olly and Georgie's mother, Christina—that there had been a secret wedding on Baissé and so on. The High Court dismissed it. Oliver claims now that he had been rummaging recently through some of Daddy's old papers he'd collected when he was wrapping up our father's affairs in Baissé six years ago and found something that proves Uncle Anthony's claim, which is rubbish. Anyway—he chose to spring this on me some weeks ago, before I joined Mummy in Cap Ferrat. He was gleeful! It was a bloody *assault*! Mummy was properly outraged when I told her. It's one of the reasons I returned from France when I did. I wanted to know what Olly's been up to."

"But surely, others . . ." Tom cast about for an explanation. "Oliver's mother, for instance, wouldn't she have knowledge of this?"

"Pooh! Christina had already ingratiated herself with the richest man in Central America and was set to marry him. He has absolute brimming *pots* of money. She wasn't that bothered by divorcing Daddy, and I don't think she would be at all pleased with Olly's recent busywork. But then Olly loathed his mother's remarriage as much as he loathed his father's. For someone who's spread himself about and lived so immoderately, he can . . . could be surprisingly middle-class in his conventions. The hypocrisy of it all. He's treated me all my life—and Dominic, too—as if somehow his parents' estrangement was our fault. All the nonsense with Daddy's divorce from Christina happened before I was born!" She looked towards the Gaze Tower, its summit now empty. "It's Dominic who suffered the most. His father went to bits when our mother left to marry his own brother. Before he was packed off to boarding school, his nanny and the Gaunts were mother and father and whatever. There's Gaunt now."

"The Gaunts?" Tom asked as they both looked past the brick wall to where Dominic and Gaunt appeared to be in conversation at the base of the tower.

"Funny they should be working for Georgie and Hector now, but then it is awfully hard to find good help. Uncle Tony, Dominic's father, you see, retained custody of Dominic. He had enough pluck to do that, at least, before he descended into drink. He drowned, you know, in the Indian Ocean. They really shouldn't let an alcoholic sail around the world alone."

"Then surely your mother would have then taken over your brother's care."

"Dominic's? Oh, nominally. He was at boarding school for most of the year, of course, and came to us in London or Baissé on holidays. I adore Mummy, I do, but really, a bitch sow would be better at mothering. She never quite got the hang of it." She smiled. "Now I've told you much too much about the fforde-Becketts. Of course, I know in the circumstances you'll be discreet. As—" She paused and narrowed her eyes. "—shall I."

Her meaning was not lost on Tom. She would not embarrass him about their assignation, if he did not air the fforde-Becketts' dirty laundry. He moved to leave, uncertain if he had spent the time usefully, when Lucinda interrupted: "Whatever can they be talking about? Dominic!" she called again as the two men began walking away from the base of the Gaze Tower. Dominic heard this time. He waved in her direction absently and the two men disappeared past a row of trees.

"Oh, well." Lucinda sighed. "Are you sure you won't take a dip, Tom? You don't really need a bathing costume, you know. I shan't really be surprised by anything, shall I?"

"I have no towel," Tom pointed out, growing a little tired of her flirtation. "And the water probably wouldn't do the bandage good." He gripped the ends of the chair preparatory to heaving himself up, casting about for a polite excuse to make his exit, when Dominic pushed through the gate in the wall and strode towards them.

"According to Gaunt, we are to assemble in the great hall at four thirty," he announced without preliminaries. "Hullo, Vicar."

"We? Me and thee?" Lucinda searched Dominic's face. With his eyes covered by sunglasses, he appeared expressionless.

"Thee, me . . . he." Dominic gestured at Tom. "All of us, except Maximilian and . . ."

"Miranda," Tom supplied.

"Marve and Roberto?" Lucinda continued to search his face.

"Apparently."

"I suppose it's the police who want us at this assembly."

Dominic nodded.

"A summons, then. I'm not sure I care to be summoned." Lucinda lifted her watch and frowned at it. "I had planned to stay here well into the cocktail hour." She glanced to the summer sky, scrimmed by a few high white clouds, and sighed. "I should never have left Cap Ferrat."

Dominic lifted his sunglasses to his forehead and regarded her thoughtfully. "No, perhaps you shouldn't have."

"Do you have my fifty pounds? I forgot to ask . . . earlier."

"You'll get it when we get back to town, Lucy."

"It's ridiculous to place bets in a cashless society, don't you think, Vicar?"

"I didn't think you were serious . . . about the money, I mean," Dominic responded instead.

"I was. With Oliver bullying the Trust, I expected to be cut off from funds any minute. Of course, that's all changed now that—"

"Don't go on about it, Lucy."

"Dominic and I had a little wager yesterday." Lucinda smiled at Tom.

"Lucy." Dominic's tone was warning.

"On the horses?" Tom asked out of politeness.

Lucinda canted her head at him. Her smile broadened. "In a way. We each chose a different . . . steed."

Tom suppressed a sigh. Arch conversation made him weary. "Who won?"

"I believe I'm the one requesting the fifty pounds."

"Lucy." Dominic threw her a disgusted look. *"Shut up!"*

"If you insist, darling." Lucinda granted her half brother a tight smile. "What were you doing up the Gaze Tower?"

"Gazing, of course, darling. What else is there to do? The country really is rather a bore. Do you not find the country boring, Vicar?"

"Not at all."

"I do."

"What a good thing Riseley Castle and Kilmore went for back taxes. No demesnes for you, darling. No tenants and sheep and land agents and day-trippers and point-to-points and dog trials and God knows what else." Lucinda picked up the sun cream once again. "Moths have got to the ermine, I should tell you. I was looking for something up in the attic rooms in the spring at Morborne House and found the robes in a trunk. If Her Majesty pops her clogs anytime soon, you'll be in for a new kit for the Coronation. The coronet could use some repair, too."

Dominic seemed lost in thought, looking over the turquoise waters.

"I'm not sure Dominic is looking forwards to his new responsibilities," Lucinda stage-whispered to Tom.

"Lucy, do shut up."

"I've been telling the vicar our family secrets."

"Have you," Dominic responded dryly. He seemed to rally. A thin smile parted his lips. "Nothing too outrageous, I hope."

"Nothing that hasn't been in *The Daily Mail* or *The Sun* or the late unlamented *News of the World.*"

"I'm going to take a swim. It's ridiculously hot."

"You didn't bring a bathing costume, either?"

"Either?"

Lucinda gestured to Tom.

"Joining me, Vicar?" Dominic moved around Lucinda's sun lounger and began to unbutton his shirt.

"No, thank you." Tom pointed to his cast boot.

"Gaunt is bringing towels."

"Good old Gaunt." Lucinda reopened the sun cream tube.

Dominic stripped off his shirt and folded it over another of the deck chairs. Tom glanced at the man's lean, smooth torso, noting a bruising where the right pectoral met the shoulder muscles and a light, but still visible, scratch along his upper arm.

"Yes?" Dominic shot him an ambiguous look.

"I didn't mean to stare." Tom realised that is what he had been doing. "But you look as if you've had some sort of misadventure."

"I'm a fruit, I bruise easily," Dominic responded, peeking at his chest as he tugged at the belt of his trousers.

Lucinda glanced up sharply and struggled to look over the back of the sun lounger. "I was going to have you do my back," she addressed the air, waggling the tube of sun cream.

"It will have to wait." Dominic dropped his trousers to the tiles. His pants followed. He stepped out of them with brisk, urgent movements and turned to toss them onto the chair. Tom cast his eyes to the sky where a loop of inky black birds circled over the Gaze Tower, thinking how peculiar it was that nudity could endow someone with a social advantage. Clothed, he felt oddly defenceless. He dropped his eyes to glimpse Dominic's eel figure slice the water in a perfect arc and pull himself down the pool's length in strong, smooth strokes.

"He tripped over my slippers last night and fell into the wardrobe," Lucinda said.

"I don't understand." Her remark drew Tom from envious contemplation of Dominic's prowess. He had never learned to swim.

"The bruising."

"I see." There seemed little point now in remaining by the pool. Dominic continued his methodical harrowing of the water's surface; Lucinda remained motionless, Ingres's odalisque simmering in the sun, the carapace-black lenses of her glasses tilted to the sky. He moved to rise from his chair, but again he was arrested, this time by the children coming through the gate. Miranda, nearly obscured by a tower of towels, was led by Max topped by a checked tweed hat, the flaps of which were tied at the crown by a jaunty ribbon. No Inverness, however. A simple white collared shirt and pale trousers were likely concession to the heat.

"Over there, I should think," the boy commanded. Miranda dropped her burden on the chair that held Dominic's shirt.

"Where's your spyglass?" Tom asked the boy, one troubled eye on the unclothed figure gliding through the pool. His daughter had seen one too many unclothed males in a single day. It was all getting a little too sybaritic.

"Dash it! I don't have one," Max replied. "And I did look *everywhere.*"

Lucinda twitched, seemingly roused, and lowered her frames to examine her nephew. "A deerstalker? Maxie, you'll boil your head in that thing."

"But, Aunt, we're looking for clues."

"To what?"

"To the mystery of the murdered marquess."

Lucinda's laugh set the birds on the wall to scattering.

"Strangled, I mean," Max amended.

"How did you know that?" Tom asked sharply.

"My dear Mr. Christmas, we listened at the door at Grand-

mama's," Max said imperiously. "And we also know that
the . . . the . . ." He snapped his fingers. "Miss Christmas?"

"Ligature."

"Precisely! That the ligature hasn't been found. Miranda
and self are helping the police with their enquiries."

Lucinda smiled. "Do the police know that?"

"Ours, dear Aunt, is an independent enquiry."

When Miranda asked, "What's the matter, Daddy?" Tom
realised his growing unhappiness that the cavalier turn of conversation had telegraphed itself to, at least, his daughter.

"I think," he said, fingers drumming along the arm of the
chair, "we all need to keep in mind that a man has died, he's
died in his prime, and he's died in a cruel and painful fashion."

"But, Daddy, no one really liked him very much." Miranda
echoed Max's words of the morning.

Perhaps it was the enervating heat of the afternoon, perhaps it was the vexation of a twisted ankle, or perhaps it was
the folly of his moments with Lucinda, but Tom sensed an
unaccustomed and uncomfortable lick of anger curling up
within, tempered only by the reminder that children could be
artless creatures. He said, reining in his temper but aware that
he presented a spectacle of severity to his young audience:

"Whether the late Lord Morborne was liked or disliked by
anyone should have no effect on our attitude towards him in
death. Whatever his sins, he is loved and forgiven by God,
and on earth the crime against his person demands justice.
This is not some parlour game. The process of finding Lord
Morborne's killer and bringing that person to earthly judgement deserves and commands our respect. Do you understand?"

"Yes, Daddy." Miranda's head bent to her shoes.

"Yes, headmaster." Lucinda suppressed a laugh.

Max tilted his head and crooked his arm on his hip regarding him coolly, as if this were a debate, not a dressing-down. "I say, Mr. Christmas, you may have something there. One must put aside one's feelings if one is to be a proper detective. Reason must rule passion. Mr. Holmes would approve."

"Reason must rule what?" came Dominic's voice from the edge of the pool. Tom glared down at the slicked-back hair, at the wet planes of a face sharpened by the sun, with a silent warning that he oughtn't even *think* about hauling himself from the water in his state of undress.

"Passion," Max repeated.

"Very wise." Dominic fingered some residual moisture from his forehead.

"Were you wanting a towel, Cousin Dominic?"

Dominic caught Tom's eye. "No, I'll soak here for the time being. If you're Sherlock Holmesing, Maximilian—*love* the hat—you might find a clue in the Gaze Tower."

"Might I?"

"If I were Moriarty I would leave one there."

Max regarded his cousin with uncertainty. "A villain wouldn't deliberately leave a clue."

"Only if he wanted to be caught," Lucinda pointed out dryly.

"A villain, Maximilian," Dominic corrected, "might *in*advertently leave a clue."

"Yes. I read somewhere—in a Beano comic, I think—that a murderer always takes something away and leaves something behind."

"You couldn't possibly have read that in a Beano comic."

"But why the tower, Cousin Dominic?"

"The only thing to do is go and find out."

"By George, you're right." Max adjusted his deerstalker. "We must eliminate all possibilities. Come along, Miss Christmas."

"You were eager to get rid," Lucinda remarked to Dominic when Max and Miranda had disappeared past the gate.

"Only because the water, dear Lucy, is absolutely bloody freezing if you're not moving through it." He scrambled onto the pool's ledge behind Lucinda, darted for the nearby chair in a cascade of dripping water, and snatched a towel. Even at a distance, Tom could see gooseflesh.

"And *is* there a clue in the Gaze Tower?" Lucinda called to be heard behind her, as Dominic wrapped one towel around his hips and another one across his chest.

"Don't be silly. Of course there isn't."

"You used to play awful tricks on me. I followed him around like a puppy at holidays on Baissé," Lucinda said in a confiding tone to Tom. "I was besotted by my older brother . . . cousin, whatever you are, Dominic. I think your daughter is rather taken with Maxie, don't you, Vicar?"

Tom emitted a feeble noise of agreement.

"They're much too young, and nothing would come of it anyway." Dominic pulled the chair over and sat down, splaying his white legs.

"Yes, true." Lucinda waggled the sun cream in his face and shifted in her lounge chair. "Back."

"What time is it? Is there time?"

Tom glanced at his watch. "Three twenty."

"Is it worth it?" Dominic frowned as he took the bottle from her. "We have this . . . this summons to the great hall. You'll get oil all over the Louis Quinze."

"Back!" Lucinda commanded again, turning fully. Tom's eyes went helplessly to her curvaceous backside, then felt Dominic's smirking glance upon him. He wiggled the bottle invitingly. Tom responded with a shake of the head.

"You're the eighth Marquess of Morborne." Lucinda's voice echoed against the tiles she looked to be addressing. "Where will the ninth come from?"

"I believe that's a non sequitur, Lucy dear."

"Not really. Answer the question."

"Shut up."

"Maximilian will be the eleventh Earl of Fairhaven when Hector dies. Where will the twelfth come from?"

"Don't be so bloody obtuse."

"I'm merely reconsidering your remark that nothing would come of Maxie and darling Miranda. Your daughter *is* darling, Vicar."

"Thank you," Tom said evenly.

"You will have to perform your feudal duty, Dominic," Lucinda continued.

"For the sake of passing on moth-eaten ermine and a tarnished coronet?" Dominic grunted and popped the top of the bottle.

"Morborne House? Four Paul Cézanne, three Paul Gauguin, two Claude Monet, and Renoir's painting of a pear tree?"

"But are they real or are they forgeries?" Dominic squeezed a dollop of cream onto his fingers. "Anyway, as Maximilian stands to inherit all of this—Eggescombe and the rest of it—and needs must pass it on, I'm sure one day he will put his mind to his duty."

"Well, Hector did." Lucinda's laugh eased into a sigh as Dominic's hands pressed into her back.

Dominic smiled at Tom, who realised his expression must have betrayed the curiosity he felt. "I think you'll find, Vicar, that with Max the apple hasn't fallen far from the tree."

CHAPTER FOURTEEN

$\mathcal{G}$eorgina arrived at the great hall next to last. She hesitated in a swift, sweeping assessment of the assembled, and clacked across the floor in low heels to the long oak draw-table where Ellen Gaunt had laid out tea and stood ready to serve. Tom thought Lady Fairhaven's eyes rested for a fraction of a second longer over her mother-in-law, the dowager countess, who had assumed earlier a red wing chair to the right of the fireplace, matched throne to the wing chair to the fireplace's left, which accommodated Hector in slumped repose, one ankle over the other. Each had a familiar: Roberto rested on a hard cane-backed chair next to Marguerite, arms folded over his chest, eyes directed to the chimneypiece, as elaborately carved as the screen above the door; Gaunt stood stiffly by Hector, arms by sides, eyes alert to the needs of those in the room. Bonzo was slumbering at his master's feet.

"Darling, take a seat, why don't you?" Hector spoke impatiently to his wife as she received a cup of tea from Mrs. Gaunt.

"Georgie, have this one," Marguerite said, though she made no effort to move.

"I'm all right to stand for a moment." Georgina took a tentative sip. "There's room on the sofa with Jamie and Jane. Lucy, what on earth are you wearing?" she added, her cup hitting its saucer with an elegant scrape.

"A dressing gown, can't you tell? I've been by the pool and have sun cream all over me."

Lady Fairhaven's lips disappeared into a disapproving moue. "And what are you drinking?"

"I had Gaunt make me a *blanc-cassis*. I don't feel like tea."

Tom glanced from Lucinda, who was seated beside him in an upholstered chair, into the milky stew of his own half-finished cup. He didn't much feel like tea, either, though the great hall, with its north face, its white marble floors, and its soaring plasterwork ceiling, seemed to cling to the chill of a spring months past. In late-medieval times when the hall was built, it would have been the heart and hearth of Eggescombe, crackling with fire and life. Now its wintry resplendence served only to impress. Tom suspected that in Hector's choosing the great hall to receive the police detectives, he wished to make plain that this was his house; possibly he hoped to intimidate them. If so, he wasn't certain the strategy was wise. He felt vaguely apprehensive, as if he were about to sit exams, and he expected the others, as evinced by Lucinda's snappish remark, were too. The atmosphere was sour with a tension that might have been soothed in the relatively homely surroundings of the sunny drawing room. He exchanged a glance with Madrun, who stood with Ellen at the draw-table, but he could discern no particular sentiment behind the reflective glass of her cat's-eye spectacles. It was as if she had taken on the impersonal mien of a servant, though he was certain her mind was coursing wonderfully over this scene. Whatever would old Mrs. Prowse be treated to in the next letter!

Porcelain tapped porcelain, a throat cleared, fabric shushed along fabric as legs crossed and uncrossed: The waiting seemed interminable, though—Tom let his eyes fall surreptitiously to his watch—the detectives were not late. Finally, though Tom heard no heralding sound, Gaunt squared his back, glanced at Hector, then at Dominic, who sat bolt-upright in a cane-backed chair near Hector, and slipped out of the hall. A moment later, heads turned to the two blocky figures in dark suits Gaunt ushered into the room. Hector rose from his seat and indicated two chairs that had been placed in front of the fireplace, closing the straggling ring of family, guests, and staff, and introduced them.

"Some of you, I believe," Hector continued, his voice controlled and plummy, "have already spoken with Detective Inspector Blessing and Detective Sergeant Bliss—"

"Detective Inspector Bliss, Your Lordship," Bliss corrected. "He's Blessing." He flicked his thumb to his partner, who sat himself on the spindly chair and pulled a notebook from his jacket pocket.

"Quite." Irritation flickered on Hector's face. "Detective Inspector Bliss and Detective Sergeant Blessing asked to see us as a group to . . . to—"

"To try and get a picture of Lord Morborne's activities and

movements here since he arrived at Eggescombe. We'll also be speaking with you separately, later, of course."

"Why don't you sit down, Detective Inspector," Hector said, dropping into his own chair. "Would you care for tea?"

"I'll stand for the time being, if you don't mind." Bliss squared his feet along the marble tiles. "And thank you, no."

"Darling"—Hector, nettled, turned his attention to his wife— "do sit down."

"You're all welcome to sit," Bliss said as Georgina tucked her skirt behind her legs and took the end cushion of the couch next to Jane.

"We'll stand, Inspector." Gaunt looked to his wife and Madrun. Tom glanced around the sparsely furnished room. There were no other chairs. Gaunt had intended staff to stand.

"Suit yourselves."

"I should point out, Inspector"—Lucinda lifted her lips from her glass— "that some of us only arrived yesterday."

"I'm aware of your arrival times," Bliss responded evenly. "Lord Morborne arrived Wednesday afternoon, for instance, having driven down from London—alone, I might add."

Hector frowned. "Is there some significance to his coming down alone?"

"I understand that Lord Morborne announced his engagement last evening to a Serena Knowlton of Knightsbridge, London. It seemed to me if you'd got engaged you might bring your fiancée down to meet your family."

"He was down for a charity event, you know," Hector said.

"Has anyone spoken with Serena?" Marguerite interrupted. "We discussed doing so at luncheon."

"Marve, no one has a number." Georgina lifted her teacup.

"Nonsense. Frank Knowlton is hardly ex-directory. He has a business empire. Hector, you must have a number for him. Or couldn't someone have simply looked on Oliver's mobile?" Marve looked to Gaunt. "Besides, mightn't she have phoned *here*? It's all over television. I looked."

"No, my lady," Gaunt replied.

"We've shut off the switchboard, Mother," Hector explained. "You can understand why."

"*I* spoke with her," Bliss interrupted. "When she couldn't get through here, she was patched through to me."

"Well, I hope she doesn't think you all callous," Marguerite murmured.

Bliss cleared his throat noisily as Hector opened his mouth to protest. "The Honourable Serena Knowlton told me that Lord Morborne did not tell her he planned to be in Devon other than for the jump yesterday. He texted her when he arrived here Wednesday saying he had business in the area. What, she didn't know."

"I might be able to help you there, Inspector," Tom said. "Lord Morborne paid a visit to my church's music director, Colm Parry—whom you know from Thornford Regis. I understand Lord Morborne was trying to coax him from retirement to perform at some musical event next year in London."

"But, Tom"—Jamie leaned forward to address him—"Mr. Parry was among the party that came with you to the airstrip at Plymouth for the charity jump. I remember because it was such fun to meet the guy who sang 'Bank Holiday.'"

"That's true. They could have spoken anytime before or after the jump," Tom reflected.

"Maybe Oliver just wanted a few days out of London," Jane said, though Tom could hear the doubt in her voice.

"It's true he can be impulsive," her husband added.

"Then I take it, Lady Fairhaven"—Bliss turned his attention to Georgina—"that you hadn't expected your brother to arrive when he did."

"Well, no." Georgina looked to her husband. "But of course he was very welcome to come and stay, with or without notice. There's plenty of room—usually," she amended.

"And how did he spend his time here those few days before yesterday's jump?" Blessing looked up from his notebook, speaking for the first time.

"On his bloody mobile," Jamie laughed. "Talking or texting. Doing business. He wasn't a relaxed sort of fellow, Olly. I took Friday lunch with him at the Pilgrims Inn at Abbotswick and the thing was going off all the time until I wrenched it from his hands and switched it off."

"Lord Morborne's fondness for his mobile has arisen several times in our investigation." Bliss frowned. "And yet there is no evidence of it. Anyone explain that? No? We may need to search the house, Lord Fairhaven."

"Of course, if you must."

"You might want to consider reinforcements, Inspector," Dominic remarked. "Eggescombe isn't exactly a suburban semi."

"What did you talk about with Lord Morborne?" Blessing addressed Jamie before Bliss could apply a snappy comeback.

"Oh, gosh, nothing that seems memorable. The jump the

next day. Cricket, business . . ." Jamie shrugged. "We had a bit of a family catch-up . . ."

"Did he seem different in any way?"

"Different?"

"Worried? Frightened? Threatened? Anxious? I ask this of all of you," Blessing added, his biro hovering over his pad.

Lucinda made a rude noise. "Oliver fforde-Beckett? Don't be ridiculous."

"He seemed quite himself, Detective Inspector." Jamie directed an annoyed frown at Lucinda. "I don't see my cousin often, usually at family gatherings or at the Leaping Lords events we do a few times a year. We travel in different circles on the whole. Anyone else think him a bit off these last days?" He looked around at the others encouragingly, but received only noncommittal shrugs.

"And he remained on the estate the whole time?" Bliss picked up the questioning.

"Except for our lunch in the village, as far as I know," Jamie responded. "And, of course, the trip to Plymouth, to the airfield, yesterday morning."

"Then did anyone visit him here?"

"I wouldn't think so." Hector replied. "Gaunt?"

"No, my lord. Not that I was made aware of."

"We prefer a quiet life when we're down here in August, you see, Inspector. We entertain few visitors. I do a little constituency business. The Leaping Lords fund-raiser was a rare exception, which we were pleased to do," he added, nodding at Tom, "but most of the estate staff, except for a few of the gardeners from the village to keep the weeds at bay, have a fortnight's holiday when Lady Fairhaven and our son are in residence. Oh, and a daily girl or two comes in. So, you see, Inspector"—Hector seemed to be losing his train of thought—"life's quite uneventful, really, down here."

"*Was* quite uneventful, Hector, darling," Marguerite said.

"Thank you, Mummy," Hector responded evenly.

"My lord, there was the trespasser . . ." Gaunt prompted Hector *sotto voce.*

"Yes! Thank you, Gaunt. Inspector, we have been troubled a few times by a trespasser. I believe he's . . . importuned Mrs. Gaunt when she's been working in the kitchens. Is that not correct?" He glanced at Ellen, who nodded in the affirmative. "Perhaps you should be concentrating your efforts in that direction, Inspector."

"Anything you tell me will be given due consideration," Bliss responded impassively, glancing down at his colleague's notebook. "So, despite Lord Morborne's unannounced appearance Wednesday, nothing happened that you would say was out of the ordinary."

"There was that policeman, Hector," Jane remarked.

"Yes," Jamie chimed in. "You were seeing him off when we arrived Thursday."

"Oh, yes." Hector frowned. "I can't think what he wanted."

"You told me it was about the police presence at the nomination meeting next weekend," Jane said.

"Yes, that was it."

"PC Widger, sir?" Blessing turned a page in his notebook.

"I believe so, yes. Yes, it was. New to the village."

"Are you sure he wasn't here examining the vehicles on the estate, Lord Fairhaven? There's an ongoing investigation into a recent hit and run in the area."

"Oh! Yes, you're quite right. That's why Widger was here. I'd forgotten. I told him he was welcome to look around. There was only mine and Oliver's in the front drive anyway. Gaunt, you had parked the van next to the stable block. Mother?"

"Yes, he looked at mine, too."

"I'm surprised he didn't drive down in that ridiculous pink Cadillac he spends ten thousand pounds a year to garage in London," Dominic remarked.

"How do you know he spends ten thousand?" Jamie looked faintly aghast.

"It's a guess."

"Well, as it happens, Olly started out in his Cadillac," Jamie continued. "He told me at lunch in the pub. But it had engine problems near Salisbury, so he hired a car."

"Olly in a nasty little hire car, imagine!"

"Is any of this relevant?" Lord Fairhaven sighed, appealing to the inspector.

"I would like to move on," Bliss said evenly, placing his hands behind his back. "Yesterday evening, Lord Morborne left Eggescombe Park around . . ."

"Around ten thirty, sir." Blessing looked up from his notebook.

"Yes." Hector picked up the story. "That would be correct. You see, Inspector, despite the size of this house, we don't really have the facilities to have large parties to stay, so I arranged for those who wished it, to stay overnight at the Pilgrims Inn. Several did. So Oliver went off with them . . . to continue drinking, I expect."

"And none of you joined him."

"It had been a rather long day, Inspector. Leaping Lords events usually have an early start."

"Olly's a bit of a night owl." Jamie sipped his tea. "Wouldn't you say, Georgie? Part of his job, really."

"Who saw him last?" Bliss asked.

"I haven't the faintest," Hector replied peevishly, looking around. "Does it matter? Gaunt, I think. Didn't you go after them with a torch?"

"It was quite dark, my lord, despite a full moon."

"You were expecting him back, then," Bliss continued. "He would need a light to walk back in the dark."

"I had no idea he hadn't returned until Lady Kirkbride informed me that his bed didn't appear to have been slept in. He didn't tell you he had other plans, did he, Georgie?" Hector addressed his wife. "Oliver knew the security code to get in. I asked Gaunt not to bolt the doors so Oliver could return without having to make a fuss and wake up the household."

"Then, Detective Inspector," Marguerite said, placing her cup on a table next to her, "where was Oliver most of the night?"

"Sergeant?" Bliss prompted his deputy.

Blessing flipped through his notebook. "The Duke of Warwick and Baron Pownall were the last to see him, around one in the morning, before they went to their rooms in the—"

"And then—what?—he vanished?"

"I was coming to that, Your Lordship. According to the bar manager, Lord Morborne left the Pilgrims Inn with a Miss Janice Sclanders, a barmaid, at about one thirty." He glanced up from his notebook. "We have contacted Miss Sclanders. She lives with her parents in a cottage in the village, but as it happens her parents are away in Cumbria to attend to the birth of a grandchild so—"

"What an impossible *pig*!" Lucinda lifted her glass to her mouth.

"You mean, he was with this woman?" Hector thundered.

"Hector, don't be obtuse." Dominic crossed his legs. "My question is why he left this woman's cottage so early. It had to be early for the vicar to find him at—what was it?" He flicked a glance at Tom. "Sunrise? He could have had a very nice lie-in." He smirked and dropped his voice theatrically. "Don't tell me our Olly had some regard for the proprieties?"

"I doubt he got much sleep." Lucinda drained her glass.

"Have the decency to shut up, would you? The pair of you!" Hector glared. Bonzo raised his head and yawned.

Bliss waited a beat until tempers had simmered. "Miss Sclanders says they were awakened by thunder—around four thirty, is her reckoning. There was quite a lot of thunder and lightning over southeast Dartmoor last night—not surprising, given the heat we've been having. It even woke me in Totnes. Lightning almost continuous, too, according to the Met."

"You mean, Inspector"—Dominic's voice was laced with sarcasm—"that Olly forgot his brolly and had to make a dash for home."

"No." Blessing responded for his superior. "In fact, what very little rain there was fell only on that patch of the moor, not on the surrounding countryside."

"Are you sure it didn't fall on a plain, in Spain, Inspector?"

"Have you been drinking?" Hector leveled his gaze at Dominic.

"Tea, Hector. I'm drinking tea." He held up the cup. "Then perhaps Oliver did have some regard for proprieties."

Bliss twitched and shifted his body. "I'm afraid I have no idea of Lord Morborne's regard for proprieties. According to Miss Sclanders, he spent some few minutes texting—"

"At four thirty in the morning?" Jamie interrupted.

"California. Then he told Miss Sclanders that . . ." He looked to Blessing. "What was it exactly?"

Blessing licked his thumb and flipped back several pages, "That he had—and I quote—'a rendezvous with'"—he looked up from his notebook—"'a lady.'"

The word fell on the assembled like fine rain. All except Lucinda, who ran her finger absently around the lip of her empty glass. "Then he was a pig twice over. Imagine leaving some woman's bed with the announcement you're expected at another's."

"I'm not sure Miss Sclanders is the type to care. She wasn't expecting to become Lady Morborne," Bliss remarked. "She barely knew who Lord Morborne was."

"She does now, I daresay." Marguerite spoke impatiently. "But I think you're missing the inspector's point, Lucy. Are you certain"—she turned her attention to Bliss—"he didn't say 'woman'?"

"No, my lady, she was quite certain Lord Morborne said 'lady.'"

"In any case," Blessing added, "the word *woman* would only expand the numbers in the category slightly."

"You can't possibly mean—" Lucinda began. Tom felt her stiffen with a new alertness. But Jane interrupted:

"The word is also generic, Inspector. It can refer to any adult female."

"Yes," Bliss conceded blandly, "that's true. But I need to consider any information given me. Lord Morborne left Miss Sclanders's cottage in the direction of Eggescombe Park and he was found in the Eggescombe Park's Labyrinth. I'm sure of the six women present at Eggescombe—and present here this afternoon—all of you are ladies." He smiled thinly. "But four of you are *Ladies*, you understand." He nodded to each in turn. "Dowager Lady Fairhaven, Lady Fairhaven, Lady Kirkbride, and you, Lady Lucinda."

"But that's nonsense! What would my wife, my mother . . ." Hector spluttered. ". . . be doing wandering around the grounds in the middle of the night?"

"I don't know, my lord. That's what I would like to find out."

"*Rendezvous?* The word is outrageous! These woman are *family*, for God's sake!"

"*Rendezvous* does not mean 'assignation,'" Blessing muttered into his pad, but Hector heard him:

"I should bloody hope it doesn't!"

Tom exchanged a glance with Jane. He sensed they shared a thought born of an earlier discussion: There were five, not four, Ladies at Eggescombe.

"Inspector," Tom began, mulling the words over in his mind so as not to unnecessarily shine a light on anyone, "Lord Morborne's remark about having a rendezvous with a lady may have another meaning—and it may explain why he was in the Labyrinth at such an early hour. You've noticed, I'm sure, the sculpture at the Labyrinth's centre. It's the Virgin

Mary, of course. The Virgin is sometimes referred to as the Lady. We have Lady chapels in our churches, for instance. Lord Morborne's remark may simply have been ironic."

Bliss appeared to digest this, while Blessing looked up from his pad and asked, "But why rendezvous with this 'lady' at all? And why at that particular hour?"

Tom not only felt Jane's eyes upon him, but sensed a sharpened interest in the others. Keeping his focus on Blessing, whose brow was beginning a familiar furrowing, he said truthfully—for the words were true: "I really couldn't say."

Blessing opened his mouth as if to pursue another enquiry, but Bliss, shifting his stance, interrupted with a bark: "Well, statues can't shift themselves, so I'm afraid I must ask you all—lords, ladies, and gentlemen—about your movements between the hours of midnight and six this morning."

"What movements, Inspector?" Hector snapped. "We were all asleep, of course."

"None of you was disturbed by the thunder and lightning on the moor? Lord Morborne was. PC Widger, apparently, too, and a number of others in Abbotswick. It would have been the talk of the village but for . . ." Bliss cleared his throat.

"The noise and light woke me," Jane answered. "I'm not sure of the time. I went to the window, thinking I should pull the window shut against any rain, but I saw nothing worth noting, other than the grounds and gardens suddenly flashing with light."

"I slept through it," Jamie said. "Jump days are usually long days. They tend to take it out of one."

"My husband would sleep through Armageddon," Jane added.

"I'm the same as Jamie," Hector said. "Slept like a top."

"I take medication to sleep, Detective Inspector." Georgina looked grave. "I wasn't aware of any storm. Or anything else, for that matter."

"No one awoke?" Bliss's tone was testy. "No one, but for Lady Kirkbride, went to the window to look out? No one nipped down to the kitchen to get a cup of cocoa to get them back to sleep and ran into someone in a corridor or on the stairs. No one—"

"Are you suggesting that someone from this household is responsible for Oliver's death?"

"No, my—"

"Because surely the solution is that someone followed Oliver from the village in the early hours of the morning, someone with some . . . *animus* against him—and God knows he's offended enough people in his life—and . . . well, you know . . ."

"My lord, I am conducting an investigation and am making no accusations. I am only interested at this time in people's possible movements during the night. Those people could be here in the Hall or over in the village."

"Well, I was with my wife," Hector continued gruffly. "I heard nothing until Jane knocked me up about six thirtyish. I had just come out of the shower."

"I was with mine," Jamie added.

"Your Ladyship?" Bliss turned to Lucinda.

Tom's eyes rose, above Bliss's head, to the massive overmantel and its elaborate alabaster carving of the Wise and Foolish Virgins. He waited with dread while Lucinda hesitated over her answer. Was she delaying to taunt him?

"Your Ladyship?" Bliss prompted.

"I was with Dominic."

Blessing looked up from his notebook, instantly alert. "The entire night?"

"I joined my *brother*," Lucinda replied with hauteur, "for conversation after the party and fell asleep on the daybed in his room. I'm not sure how well I slept—I had drunk a little more than I should—and perhaps the thunder did disturb me. I can't recall."

"I slept through it all," Dominic said.

"Lady Fairhaven?" Bliss turned to Marguerite.

"I'm at the dower house, Inspector, some distance from here." She favoured him with a charming smile. "So I can't really help you. And Mr. Sica was with me."

Her tone, her emphasis on the final word, suggested a relationship less sexual and more maternal—Tom watched both Bliss and Blessing's stony features struggle to suppress bemusement—and designed to nobble further enquiry. Surely, he thought, Marve was being economical with the truth. He recalled their freighted exchange in the stable block: Marve had been keen to remind Roberto he had not been working in his studio *all* night. Jane had heard this exchange, too. He could see her regarding the dowager countess with frank curiosity. Indeed, everyone regarded Marguerite with some varied emotion—distaste, admiration, amusement.

"You're an artist, I understand," Bliss addressed Roberto.

"A sculptor," he replied tonelessly. "Lady Fairhaven is my patron."

Bliss blinked. Tom suspected the inspector found the descriptor little clarifying. He seemed to heave a world-weary sigh as he turned to Gaunt.

"The Gatehouse—"

"We heard and saw nothing, Inspector," Gaunt was quick to reply. He glanced past the draw-table to his wife.

"You rise early, yes?" Bliss pressed. "I'm sure you have things to ready before the household gets up."

"Indeed," Gaunt replied, "Mrs. Gaunt gets up before I do, as she has the morning meal to prepare and usually makes a start on dishes for other meals."

"Then, Mrs. Gaunt"—Blessing took up the enquiry—"you would have walked near to the Labyrinth early this morning on your way here. About what time?"

"About five thirty."

"Still fairly dark."

"I saw nothing nor heard anything out of the ordinary." Ellen trained her eyes on the detective sergeant.

Startled, Tom wondered at her choice of words, supposing *out of the ordinary* precluded mentioning Hector's very ordinary early-morning run.

"Lord Morborne would—presumably—have walked through the Gatehouse gate on his return to Eggescombe," Blessing continued.

"Sergeant," Hector said with a hint of asperity, "Gaunt has said he and Mrs. Gaunt saw and heard nothing."

Bliss stepped in. "Mrs. Prowse?"

Tom regarded his housekeeper. Madrun ran a smoothing hand over her skirt and adjusted her spectacles on the bridge of her nose, as if she were preparing for a longish disquisition to a rapt audience. "Well, Detective Inspector, as it happens, I was troubled by noises in the night. Thunder, of course, but then I was awoken by some rather loud whistling."

"That had to be Olly," Jamie interrupted. "He's a champion whistler. Usually sort of jaunty and vaguely baroque sounding."

"Yes. That's it precisely!"

"Never knew what the tune was. He always seemed to whistle it when he'd completed something to his satisfaction."

"James, really!" Georgina frowned.

"What? What have I said?"

"Jamie," Jane said, "consider where Oliver had been earlier."

"Sorry, Georgie, I didn't intend—"

"I always thought," Lucinda interposed, "Olly whistled when he was looking *forwards* to something."

"Whatever do you mean?" Hector demanded.

"A rendezvous with a lady?" Lucinda's tone was arch.

Bliss ignored Lucinda. "Can you recall what time you heard the whistling, Mrs. Prowse?"

Madrun reflected. "No, I can't. Not precisely, no. I neglected to bring my travel clock and I left my watch on the dressing table. After the thunder, as I said, but before dawn, though the sky was beginning to lighten a bit. I believe. Then I heard my hosts rise—my bedroom is above theirs—though I may have fallen back to sleep in between."

Bliss appeared to absorb this as Blessing continued with his scribbling. Tom sensed a fruitlessness to this strand of the enquiry. It *had* been dark. Everyone *had* been in his or her bed—or at least each could make such claim, because each had an ally—a spouse, a lover, a sibling. Lucinda had been economical with the truth. So, too, Tom suspected, had Marguerite. Madrun had no one to vouch for her, but she had been forthright with her pinch of information. He had no one to vouch for him, though. And yet he did, for at least a part of the night. *But what part and how large?* He sensed Bliss awakening from his brief reverie, about to turn his large head to him, the last of those assembled in the great hall to be questioned about the night.

He had once been in an automobile accident with his mother Kate, who, as an American, never really accommodated herself to the narrow lanes and congestion of the small island she made her home. He had been fourteen, Kate speeding him to a football match, when abruptly the car ahead on the A227 stopped—to avoid hitting a dog, it turned out. Kate had taken her eyes off the road in the few seconds it took to light her fag off the lighter of their Volvo. But Tom, staring through the windscreen, could only watch helplessly as the hood sped relentlessly forwards to the inevitable collision. Long after, his memory was not of screaming tires and crushing metal, but of the remarkable sense of time slowing, as in a film, and of himself, growing strangely detached, as the back of the car ahead filled his vision. Only on impact did time snap back and trigger alarm. He felt like that now as he watched Bliss's heavy lids slide up his eyes and his head slowly begin an arc that would shift his attention to him, Tom.

And now the thoughts followed on one another like the waves of an incoming tide: his rebuke to Lucinda by the pool, clearly obviated, to be forthright with the police, his felt need to reclaim forthrightness, by contradicting her—and, oh, what that would mean: how the fact of the matter would startle everyone, surprise some, appall a few—and shame him, very much, before these not unkind people, before his housekeeper, the vigilant minder of his days, and spread like a stain to touch his daughter, the village, the Church in ways predictable and unpredictable, dreadful to contemplate. He met Bliss's disinterested gaze, his slightly red-rimmed, grey eyes—*not enough sleep, Detective Inspector?*—and then, as if out of a dream, a bell sounded and sounded again, urgently, demandingly, and that gaze veered, deflected towards the source of this irritant. It was Blessing's phone. A trespasser had been apprehended by the kitchen garden claiming to have vital and urgent information about Lord Morborne's death.

Bliss excused himself.

There is a God and, Tom thought with provisional gratitude, *He uses mobile telephones His wonders to perform.*

CHAPTER FIFTEEN

"*I* might as well be playing with a flamingo," Tom remarked to Jane as he hobbled a few steps across the croquet lawn with his mallet. "And that," he gestured to his orange ball, which had failed to clear the wicket, "might as well be a hedgehog."

"At least it's not crawling away."

"Our team will lose with me playing."

"Your daughter is very good." They both looked up the sun-dappled lawn to Miranda, who was studying Max as he stalked his blue ball, mallet in hand.

"We found a wonderful old croquet set under the stairs at the vicarage last summer, so croquet has become all the rage at ours. Miranda has grown quite skilled at it." He paused as Max aligned his feet before his ball and considered the scene, the manicured lawn, the neatly trimmed boundary hedge, the undulating roof of Eggescombe Hall peeking above the trees.

"It's lovely to have a garden where she can play games. In Bristol, our back garden was a postage stamp."

"Oh, bad luck," Jane murmured as Maximillian's blue ball stalled in front of the wicket.

"Worse luck," Tom added in a lower voice after a moment when Miranda's red ball, a dead cert to bash Max's and push on through the wicket, tiddled feebly across the short grass to a sad halt an inch in front of the blue ball. "She seems to have gone off her game suddenly."

"Dominic!" Lucinda called across the lawn, diverting their attention to the silhouetted figure under a tree conversing with Gaunt, who had earlier arrived with a drinks trolley. "Your turn."

Dominic waved a dismissive hand and continued talking to Gaunt as the latter shook a cocktail shaker.

"I'm told the Gaunts were once staff to Dominic's father," Tom said in a low voice as they waited. He glanced at Marguerite in a wicker sun chair some few feet away from Dominic and Gaunt. She appeared to be sleeping behind a pair of sunglasses.

Jane swung her mallet idly. "Yes, Georgie mentioned that to me. I think she was a little reluctant to employ them because of their association with the family during an unhappier time, but, well, you know the old saw . . ."

"Yes—*It's so hard to find good help these days.*"

"Don't laugh. It is sometimes. But the Gaunts had excellent references from the Arouzis and of course with Hector's previous staff having run off to Malta with their lottery winnings, he and Georgie were pretty much up against it." Jane stopped in her mallet swinging. "Tom?"

"Yes?"

"I've been thinking about something else: DI Bliss's remark that Oliver's mobile is missing."

"I'd been having the same thought: If Oliver's phone has gone walkabout, and if Hector really did remove something from Oliver's pockets this morning, as I suspect he did, then isn't it logical that Hector took his phone? Unless Oliver left it at that barmaid's cottage."

"You haven't spoken about this to the police yet?"

"No, as I said before, I'd prefer to have a quiet word with Hector first. At least now I've a better idea *what* he may have taken."

"Hector's in hot water anyway, I think." Jane glanced over the croquet lawn towards Dominic. "Well, I suppose it would have come out before very long in any case. Someone would have mentioned it."

"Most likely," Tom murmured, though he thought Dominic needn't have made quite such a show of it—It being a video clip of Hector and Oliver's sky-high punch-up, which had slipped through the sluice gates of social media with the usual unseemly haste. When DI Bliss had exited to attend to the matter of the demanding intruder, Blessing had remained, a damper to ordinary conversation. In the awkward pause, Dominic had pulled his mobile from his pocket, and Tom had watched his face shift from detachment to curiosity to amusement as his fingers danced over the screen.

"Look at this, Hector," he'd said, passing the instrument, "you've come a cropper on YouTube. Thirty thousand views and it's not yet five in the afternoon."

Lord Fairhaven's face suffused with blood and his nostrils

flared as his eyes held steady to the instrument, provoking his wife to a tentative enquiry as to his health.

"This is an outrage!" Hector thrust the phone back into Dominic's hands. "It's CCTV—*closed-circuit* television. How could it possibly—"

"Easy enough to copy and upload, Hector," Dominic said with a shrug. "Hector and Olly's bout of fisticuffs *up there*," he announced to everyone, gesturing with his thumb, "is now on-line."

"You needn't take quite so much pleasure in it, Dominic," Jamie said.

"I am *not* taking pleasure."

"You are."

"I'm simply preparing Hector for the coming brouhaha. It will be on television next. Are you still intending to stand for Parliament, Hector?"

"Perhaps you can have it pulled off the Internet somehow," Jamie addressed Hector, who appeared mute with anger.

"Not bloody likely," Dominic muttered as everyone, as if pulled by invisible strings, turned to DS Blessing to gauge his reaction to this episode. He looked up from his notebook, as if the same string had yanked at him. The Grand Guignol smile he cast them actually softened his homeliness.

"And what were Your Lordships fighting about?" he asked.

"None of your bloody business," Hector snarled.

But Tom thought now, as they waited for the match to resume, it very well *was* their bloody business.

"Dominic," Lucinda called again.

"Play through!"

"You can't 'play through' in croquet! Where did he get 'play through'?" Lucinda appealed to Tom and Jane. She had a mallet in one hand and a glass of something pink in the other. "This isn't golf!"

"You hit it then."

"My dear chap, that is not on," Max shouted.

Dominic stepped quickly across the lawn, mallet in hand. Using a quick side-style swing, he sent his black ball rocketing towards the boundary hedge before returning to Gaunt, who was pouring some liquid into a tall glass.

"Perhaps we stand a chance after all," Tom remarked to Jane, as Max groaned in disgust. "Your turn."

He watched Lady Kirkbride position her mallet and send her yellow ball trailing over the short grass, hitting Lucinda's green ball with a satisfying click, sending them both scooting through the wicket.

"A roquet," Jane said, gripping her mallet, "two bonus shots! I'm afraid I have you now, Lucy fforde-Beckett," she added with evident relish, resting her shod foot on her ball and sending Lucinda's boundary-bound with a quick flash of her mallet. The ball came to rest under the hedge.

"What a shit you are, darling Jane Allan," Lucy said without malice, raising her cocktail to her lips.

"Croquet is a metaphor for life," Jane declared, lining up her next shot. "It occupies a middle ground between sophistication and savagery. Like the upper classes," she whispered to Tom, then raised her voice: "I read that somewhere."

"Then I am in the slough of despond." Lucinda took another sip. "But—ha!" She laughed as Jane's stroke failed to send the ball through the next wicket. "Tables may turn."

"Tables may," Jane responded with light humour as Lucinda handed her glass to Max and glided over the grass to claim her ball.

"Everyone is lying . . . or maybe *dissembling* is the word." Jane presented a furrowed brow to Tom as she resumed their earlier conversation. "Even me. Maybe I've lived in England too many years. You English are all great dissemblers, you know. Putting on false appearances, concealing facts or intentions or feelings under some pretense or other."

"One of my mothers is American. That lets me half off the hook, perhaps." Tom smiled. "Then what *are* you dissembling about?"

"I did see something from my bedroom window, Tom. Or at least I think I did. The thunder woke me from a dream, so wisps of the dream may have been clinging to me, but I thought I saw a figure down on the lawn near the parked cars. There's a motion-sensor light there."

"Your bedroom faces north?"

"Yes, towards the moor."

"Did you recognise the figure?"

Jane lowered her voice to a near whisper. "Not at the time. I looked down and thought, oh, someone is checking the drainpipes—the kind of dopey thing you think when you're half asleep. I remember seeing my father do it once, when I was girl, and we had a fierce storm in the middle of the night. But our house was tiny, and Eggescombe is huge—I have no idea how water drains, and the staff are on holiday anyway and wouldn't check drains at night in any case."

"Then . . . ?"

"Hector. I'd forgotten what I saw, as you do when you awaken in the middle of the night, but then when Jamie and I came across him in the Labyrinth in that white robe, I suddenly remembered what I thought I'd seen."

"What will you do?"

"I don't know. Is it anything meaningful?" Jane swung her mallet absently. "What I thought I saw—if I really saw anything at all—might have been some time before Olly returned to Eggescombe. I didn't look at a clock—"

"The Met might have times for the storm activity on the moor."

"—and I'm loath to drop Hector in the soup. He's part of my husband's family and they've had more than their share of trouble. Georgie's baby strangled; Georgie, Oliver, and Lucy's father falling and hitting his head playing tennis; Dominic's father drowning on that insane solo round-the-world sailing venture; now Olly murdered. They're not a family for dying in their beds. My husband's a sweetheart, but my detecting efforts make him a little cross sometimes. He's a bit old-fashioned when it comes to women's careers, but my failure to be of any use over his brother's murder years ago, when I had had successes elsewhere, I think has put him off my sticking my nose in."

They paused to watch Lucinda's shot, which ably took her green ball almost the width of the court and—amazingly—through the next wicket at a challenging angle.

"Ha! I told you tables would turn," she called to Tom and Jane, taking her glass from Max for a quick sip before addressing the ball to take her bonus shot.

"And," Jane frowned, "I find Lucinda's story about spending the entire night with Dominic not entirely convincing, don't you?"

Tom started. "Well . . ."

"She wasn't in her room when I went looking for her this morning, but her bed had been slept in at some point. Besides, I know the room Dominic was assigned. It's in what they used to call the bachelors' corridor. The bed isn't large, and there's no daybed, as far as I can remember. They might have spent some time in his room after the party last night, I suppose, but all of it?" She shrugged. "They're really thick as thieves, the two of them. Which is fascinating since Charlotte essentially abandoned Dominic's father—and Dominic—to marry his brother. You'd think resentment would have thrived like weeds. Anyway, they were probably in Dominic's room hatching a scheme of some nature." A look of horror flashed across Jane's face. "I didn't mean—"

"I know."

"Your turn, Tom," Jane said as Lucinda's ball failed to achieve further glory.

Gingerly, Tom planted his feet into a straddle before his ball, thinking that his ankle really did feel much healed. The shooting pains had almost vanished. But somehow the cast boot made his play awkward.

"Don't put too much pressure on it yet," Marguerite cautioned from the sideline.

"I thought Marve was having a pre-dinner nap," Jane muttered, as Tom scored the wicket, but achieved nothing on the next. His orange ball piddled to a rest in the middle of nowhere.

"I used to be half decent at sport," he said, as Max called from up the court, "Poor show, Mr. Christmas."

"I'm not sure this is a sport," Jane commented. "More a game."

They watched Maximilian ably smack the ball through the wicket and claim a bonus shot.

"That's better," Jane observed of the boy's play.

Miranda was next. Her ball missed the wicket.

"Oh!" Tom exclaimed, disappointed. "That's not my girl."

"She's usually much better?"

"Much."

"Where *do* we learn to do this?" Jane sighed.

"Learn to do what?"

"I think your daughter's letting Max win."

"Perhaps she's simply being a gracious guest."

"Perhaps. But have you considered that she may be developing an interest in boys?"

"May I keep my head firmly rooted in the sand?"

Dominic now returned to the court after retrieving his black ball from the hedge where it had earlier landed. His shot sent Miranda's ball out of bounds.

"I remember letting a boy beat me at badminton when I was thirteen," Jane mused. "My mother told me to never give less than my best. So I did, and boys were still interested anyway, so it was good advice."

"Moments like this when I miss her mother."

"Shall I say something to her? I could even say it *en français*. Few of them understand a word of French, even though some of them summer in France."

"You're too kind. But I'll have a word."

"I'm up." Jane moved a few feet up the lawn and took a stroke. Her ball hit the upright, trapping itself in the jaws of the wicket. "Oh, damn.

"As well," she continued, glancing back to Marguerite, her

mind seemingly tethered to their earlier conversation. "Something's not square at the dower house. I think we both caught Marve's . . ."

"Dissembling?"

"Yes, I think so—her dissembling about Roberto being with her last night, though he said at his studio this morning that he had worked all night on his sculpture."

"Not *all* night."

"No, Marve was insistent it wasn't *all* night." Her eyebrows shot up. "I don't know what that means. But there's something else, Tom. You recall I cleared the table in Marve's kitchen?"

"Yes."

"I cleared three place settings, not two. I don't know if you noticed."

"I noticed you noticing something."

"There were plates and cups and cutlery for *three*. Marve suggested Roberto had breakfasted alone, after she'd gone into the village, which may be true. If so, who was the person Marve breakfasted with? Who else might have been at the dower house this morning? Who else was in Eggescombe Park so early in the morning?"

"One could ask."

Jane flicked a worried glance at the dowager countess. "Marve is the last person I want to believe has any connection to this terrible death. It would be like finding out my mother-in-law is a cat burglar. I adore my mother-in-law. She's the only one in Jamie's family possessed of pure common sense. But," she added after a pause, "she is highly protective of those she—"

"Come on, you two," Lucy broke in, "pay attention. It's your shot, Vicar."

Tom glanced down the court to see Lucinda's ball inches from the fourth wicket. He regarded his hedgehog, but his flamingo wasn't up to the task. His orange ball veered pointlessly to one side.

"Oh, Daddy!" Miranda called.

"Sorry, darling, I'm not in top form today. Perhaps," he murmured to Jane, "I should ask Lady Fairhaven to take my place."

"She may have the same idea," Jane remarked, gesturing with her head towards the boundary line where Marguerite was pushing herself out of her chair. But the dowager countess instead walked over to Gaunt and the drinks trolley to return an empty glass.

"And what of the Gaunts? Dissembling?" Tom asked as Max bungled his shot, stamped his feet, and shouted, "Oh, applesauce!"

"I don't know them well enough and they seem good at blending into the woodwork. Your housekeeper is more readable, but of course she can't have anything to do with this. And then there's you, of course." Jane cast him an enigmatic glance. "Women can read body language better than men, I think."

"I'm not sure I—"

"Marve, are you joining us?" Jane interrupted.

"Tom," Marguerite said, "you looked so uncomfortable, I thought I'd give you the chance to be spectator."

Phrased that way, Tom felt he had no choice but to retreat from the field of battle and settle into one of the wicker chairs on the sideline. The advantage was that non-players—with the evident exception of Lucinda—were invited to a drink by Gaunt. Tom's eyes lingered over Lucinda as she moved across the dappled greensward and pondered Jane's words. He felt vaguely caught out.

"Thank you," he responded vaguely as a silver tray entered his field of vision. He lifted the glass fizzing with fresh tonic and glanced at Gaunt as the tray disappeared to the man's side. He found himself curious about the man. It was true that he, Tom, had in Mrs. Prowse, his housekeeper, staff of sorts, but it was more in name than in reality. Madrun had her own income, derived from a considerable inheritance from a previous incumbent in the vicarage, occupied the entire top floor of the vicarage, and managed the household down to menu choices, with little reference to him. She did everything without a hint of deference—not that he expected any. "Mrs. Danvers with a Hoover," his sister-in-law Julia, who had once lived in Thornford, had quipped. That was in a moment of pique—Madrun was nothing so formidable—but some small grain of truth held. There were times when Tom felt a little like the second Mrs. de Winter, never quite getting the hang of life at Manderley, convinced he'd violated some local custom or expression. Certainly Madrun never hovered with an expression of proper, impersonal charm, the way Gaunt was doing now, as if balancing his own dignity with the readiness to oblige was a skill learned long ago. You most often knew what Madrun was thinking, particularly when something engaged her lively curiosity.

"Where did you train, if I might ask," he said conversationally. "A school in London?"

"My father was butler to the Earl of Rossell," Gaunt replied.

"Then you more or less learned at your father's knee," Tom commented when the man failed to elaborate. "I didn't think those opportunities existed much anymore."

"They are few," Gaunt allowed. "Most of my colleagues train in schools in London, as you say, or near; a few abroad."

"I associate the Earls of Rossell with Shropshire, I think. Or is it Staffordshire? One of them was a botanist, an early champion of Darwin in the nineteenth century, if I remember my school lessons correctly."

"Shropshire."

"You grew up on Lord Rossell's estate, I presume."

"Longwood, yes."

Tom sipped his gin. The conversation was getting a bit teeth-pull-y. He searched his mind for some sparkling badinage, but came up empty. He smiled weakly at Gaunt, who took this as a signal to withdraw.

"May I be of any other service?" he asked.

"Thank you, no."

Gaunt slipped down to the drinks trolley. Tom returned his eye to the croquet court, to the figures moving about on the sun-streaked lawn like errant chess pieces, to the pleasant clicking sound of wooden balls kissing, and considered as the first of the gin entered his veins how elysian this would be in any circumstances but those of the last twelve hours. His mind flickered with images of those he knew who had died unkind deaths, but, sharpening as they were, he couldn't stop his eyelids sinking—*I am tired!*—and sensing himself sailing through calm waters towards the sweet shores of the land of Nod.

But for a sudden shout of dismay.

The shoreline vanished. Something red and streaking met his startled eyes. It was a ball speeding over the lawn towards him. Reflexively, Tom leaned over his chair and caught the ball neatly in his hand. The others continued to play as Miranda trudged over, hair flopping against her shoulders, to retrieve her ball.

"Rough go, darling?" he said, running his hands over the smooth surface.

"I'm okay," she replied, though her voice belied a little uncertainty.

"You're sure? It would be nice if we were on our way to London. I'm sure this will all be resolved soon enough."

He realised he was repeating the assurances of midmorning when he'd had a few moments alone with Miranda, before Maximilian and Jane assembled and they'd walked to the dower house. He had been disturbed in the breakfast room by Miranda's blunt response to Lord Morborne's death—"Was he murdered?"—worried that his little girl, whom he had removed to bucolic Devon from big bad Bristol after her mother's slaying, was becoming inured to sudden and inexplicable death in close circumstances, as if such things were a fact of her new life. But she had evinced more curiosity than qualm over Lord Morborne's death then, and now she seemed to be silently ruminating over something. But what? Miranda leaned toward him and whispered:

"Max says one of us strangled his uncle."

He had his answer. The words jolted nonetheless. "Not you or me," Tom protested. "Nor Mrs. Prowse, of course. And of course not Maximilian. Or Lady Kirkbride. Or Lord Kirk-bride, I'm certain." But his failure to tick others off the list with equal alacrity seemed only to cement the boy's hypothesis. Miranda regarded him with solemn eyes.

"I'm sure there's some other explanation."

"Oh, Daddy!" she said witheringly.

"Que dirait Alice Roy?" Tom tried his feeble French.

"Qu'il n'y a pas d'autre explication, bien sûr."

Alice Roy was the detective-heroine of a series of gallicised Nancy Drew novels, to which Miranda was devoted and to which Tom felt a sudden disaffection. Damn Alice Roy! It sprang to his lips to ask Miranda if she felt safe at Eggescombe, but to ask was to acknowledge malevolence behind the noble façade and plant a seed of doubt. He felt a sudden yearning to get his daughter away from here, to home, safe and sound, or to Gravesend, safe and sound with Dosh and Kate. How odd it was to watch the tableaux vivants before him, of figures in modern costume, moving about a greensward as if nothing weighed heavy upon the day. He reached out and hugged his daughter in silent collaboration.

"Daddy," she said, pulling away slightly, "why do ghosts wear clothes?"

Tom rolled the croquet ball around in his hands. It wasn't a matter that had ever entered his mind. "What a very good question. Why *do* ghosts wear clothes? They can hardly be suffering chill. Let's see, ghosts are supposedly manifestations of human spirit energy or the like, yes? But their clothes can't be, can they? Of course not. Cloth has no soul. Therefore I conclude that ghosts are figments of people's imaginations and they prefer their figments in costume. Does this concern the ghost you said you saw?"

"Max says I saw the ghost of Sir Edward Strickland. He showed me a picture of him that hangs in the Long Gallery. In the picture he's wearing a collar that looks like a plate—"

"A ruff."

"—and puffy pants—"

"Breeches. Outerwear, really. An Elizabethan fellow. One of Lord Fairhaven's ancestors presumably."

"But I couldn't have seen Sir Edward's ghost, Daddy, even though Max says I'm the lucky one to see him. I don't think the ghost I saw was wearing very much."

"Very much?" Tom asked, suddenly alert.

Miranda squirmed. *"Pas beaucoup."*

"Trousers? Short trousers, perhaps?"

"Peut-être."

"Pants?"

"Peut-être."

"Nothing?"

Miranda squirmed again.

"A robe of some nature?" Tom persisted. "A dressing gown?"

Miranda shrugged. *"Pas de* ruff *ou* breeches. *Blanc. Tout blanc."*

Tom bit his lip. "Darling, you don't really believe in ghosts, do you?"

"Max says they exist."

"But what do *you* believe?"

"I don't believe in ghosts, Daddy. Alice wouldn't. *Les fantômes ne sont pas autorisés dans les romans policiers."*

"Or allowed in life, either," Tom added. "Except in fun."

"This isn't fun, is it?"

"No, it isn't," Tom agreed. "And what will you say to Max? About ghosts?"

"What I said to you."

"Good. You mustn't hide your light under a bushel, you know, my darling girl."

"What does that mean?"

"It's a parable from Matthew's Gospel. It may be interpreted several ways, but in your instance it means you shouldn't conceal your talents or abilities. Who is the best croquet player in Thornford Regis?"

"Me?"

"Of course you. Now here's your ball, and it's your turn again. Listen to Daddy, *regardes-moi:* Don't hide your light under a bushel."

Eggescombe Hall

8 August

Dear Mum,

I hope your sleep was better than mine. I had the worst nightmare. In the one I can remember, I was being chased around and around a ~~labia~~ labyrinth in my nightie only there weren't the nice bordering hedges they have here—it was all twisting chimney pots and towers and turrets instead, like the ones on the roof of Eggescombe Hall, looming and lurching towards me and trying to block me, which they didn't do, though as much as I ran I never got to the centre. I only kept running and running in a panic! I couldn't see who was chasing me either as it was nearly dark, but I sensed who it was, the way you do in dreams. It was DS Blessing, who I've mentioned before. I went to school with his older sister Sandra. He was nearly upon me like some great awful dog (not like Bumble) when I seemed to burst out of the dream and found myself in my bed in the Gatehouse, heart pounding, quite relieved, but very

vexed with DS Blessing. I couldn't think why he was
being so disagreeable. His sister was always perfectly nice
to me. I can't think what the dream means, Mum. I'd ask
Mr. Christmas, but at breakfast in the past when I've told
him about a haunting dream, he always looks at me very
seriously and says it means Thornford Regis shall have 7
years of plenty and 7 years of famine which is silly. Joseph
told that to ~~Faroh~~ ~~Phar~~ the king of Egypt in the Bible, of
course, but at least there were 7 things in the king's dream
so it was easy-peasy for Joseph to work out. I have said
before to Mr. C. that in the Bible, God likes to use dreams
when He fancies a natter with one of His creation, but
Mr. C. says as far as he knows God's rather gone off that
practice now, which I suppose is true, as anyone ~~whom~~
~~who~~ whom God talks to in his dreams these days is usually
thought completely daft. Anyway, the bad dreams and poor
sleep are probably because there's a bit of an atmosphere
here at Eggescombe, including at the Gatehouse. You
wouldn't credit it, what with all the sun we've been
having, but a kind of woe has settled over the place. At
least the children don't seem to be too bothered, which I
suppose is ~~good~~ all right. Miranda and Maximilian, Lord
Boothby, are having a grand time doing their own
investigation. Maximilian even has a deerstalker hat,
though it doesn't fit properly. Mum, you wouldn't believe
how many times a day he changes clothes! He is a bit of a
show-off. The only thing that doesn't seem to be in his
wardrobe at the minute is an Inverness cape, but I expect
that's coming now that he and Miranda are "on the case,"

so to speak. We see a fair amount of the two of them "below stairs" as it were. Ellen and Mick have been staff to Lord and Lady Fairhaven less than a year, but Maximilian seems to have very much taken to them. Poor lad is shunted off to boarding school most of the year, of course. His father is gruff with him and Lady Fairhaven as distant as a stone. Ellen's gone a bit stern and stout, as I've said, but she does pay mind to the lad's witterings, and Mick goes all soft for children. He's quite the proper butler-valet to the household, but below stairs he can be quite the comedian, really. It's almost as if he and Maximilian are in a conspiracy together. Perhaps Maximilian reminds Mick of Dominic fforde-Beckett when he was a boy. They're a bit alike. (I think I told you Ellen and Mick worked for the Anthony fforde-Becketts. I'm including a rough family tree with this letter. Should help.) Anyway, I'm writing all this in aid of what's happened since yesterday afternoon's letter—which by the way I was able to post, as the nice PC let me out the gate. (Some journo ran up to me and asked what I could tell them about Lord Morborne's murder. "No comment," I said, smart as you please.) As I said, it's all gone a bit gloomy here. The police ~~assmembled~~ assembled the household at teatime yesterday and asked some very pointed questions about what we'd all been up to in the wee hours of Sunday morning, which made me think that THEY *think that one of us had something to do with Lord Morborne's death. Anyway, it's put everyone off their feed* AND *their good manners. Supper was cold beef, a sorrel, leek, and mushroom tart, and a tomato, corn, and avocado* salad, which Ellen put out on the sideboard in the dining room for self-service, but half of everybody took their food off to their rooms or somewhere else in the Hall with some excuse, but really so as not to have to talk to one another. Maximilian brought Miranda with him to eat with us in the kitchen, the warm heart of a home, I always say, even at grand Eggescombe, but the kitchen wasn't last evening. Mum, something dreadful has happened between Ellen and Mick but I haven't a clue what. After we'd cleared the tea things, Ellen said she was going to the kitchen garden to gather some tomatoes only she was gone a very long time and then stumbled into the kitchen where I was making the pastry for the tart looking like her world had collapsed. "Madrun," she said, "I've learned something awful." Oh, my heart went out to her, but she wouldn't tell me a blessed thing! Thank heaven it was a simple supper we were preparing as I don't think she could have got through anything fussy. When her back was turned into the fridge I saw Mick across the corridor nip into the wash-house— which still serves as a laundry room—so I went to have some words with him as it is usually husbands that make wives unhappy but I could tell instantly that he was in a state, too. White as a sheet he was, had the big iron out, his jacket off, and had started into cleaning and pressing His Lordship's shirt, trousers, tie, and handkerchiefs, etc. etc. in advance of some Conservative Association meeting next weekend, which seemed a bit far-off, but I expect he finds work calming as I do. He wouldn't tell me anything either, used quite strong language in fact that I won't record here, and so as you might imagine, Mum, supper with the

Gaunts and the children was a bit strained, to say the least, but I got them, the kids at least, onto the details of their croquet game, which Miranda's team won by a squeak. She's awfully good. The rest of the evening went a bit flat, really. Ellen and I were to walk around the grounds, as the weather is so pleasant, but she begged off, and so I went on my own, and nearly jumped out of my skin when a large man in a dark suit jumped out from behind a tree. Well, I'm done for, I thought—here's Lord Morborne's murderer. But it seems Lord Fairhaven has already put a few private security in place to keep out all the nosy folk, including the media, although I think he's hired them mostly to appease his wife. I can't think how successful that will be. It's not as if there's a wall topped with razor wire around Eggescombe Park, and there's lots of secret paths, according to Max. When I returned to the Gatehouse, Mick was nowhere about and Ellen had already gone to bed. ~~I know it's silly, but my bedroom door doesn't lock, so I put a chair up against the knob.~~ You mustn't worry, Mum. I'm quite safe here really. There's police about and private security, as I said ~~and if one of the weekend guests really is a murderer, he won't be after little me!~~ Anyway, I was going to say when I started this letter that when I woke from my nightmare, I could hear Ellen and Mick's voices raised in the sitting room downstairs, but ~~as the chair was against the door~~ as I was tucked up in bed I thought better of opening the door a hair to see if I could hear anything. ~~I'm so worried.~~ I'm very worried about them. I can't imagine what the day will bring. Poor Mr. Christmas. It's his 40th birthday today and he was

*meant to be in Gravesend with his family, and then there's
his poor ankle. I thought to suggest to Ellen yesterday
afternoon that we bake a cake, but then it seemed not the
best idea in the circumstances. I'm sure he'll soldier on. He
always seems to. Which reminds me—our Mr. C.'s eyes
have been roving once too often in Lady Lucinda
fforde-Beckett's ~~dreiction~~ direction, if you ask me, especially
when the CID were ~~grilling~~ interviewing us in the great
hall. I can't think what he's thinking. She's been married
and divorced twice. "Manifold sins and wickedness" there
as the BCP would say, I venture, though now I'm
sounding a bit like Ellen! Anyway, it makes me think that
we in the village must find him a wife soon, as who knows
what he might get up to. It won't do! Not in his instance.
I've just looked out the window, Mum. There's more light
now, and I can see one of those television vans with one of
those big dishes on the roof parked in the forecourt. ITV
West Country News, I can read on the side. Surely Lord
Fairhaven can have it removed. I thought Abbotswick was
part of the Eggescombe estate, but perhaps I'm wrong. I
must sign off, Mum. ~~I could murder a cup of tea~~. If only I
had my trusty Teasmade with me, but I'll have to go down
to the kitchen and put the kettle on if I'm to be refreshed. I
do hope Ellen and Mick have patched things up, otherwise
I shall have to put up with an "atmosphere." It makes me
wonder if I shouldn't ask Mr. C. to talk with them, as he is
so good at ~~consilly~~ pouring oil on troubled waters.*

*Much love,
Madrun*

P.S. For a while yesterday we thought Lord Morborne's murder solved! DI Bliss was called away when everyone was helping him with his enquiries in the great hall. A man who last week had been found wandering the grounds and frightening Ellen in the kitchens confessed to the crime! Poor man was barmy, of course. DI Bliss was not best pleased!

CHAPTER SIXTEEN

"*I* didn't mean to wake you," Tom said to Lord Fairhaven, feeling the pew's silky wood beneath his fingers. It was a lie, but not an extravagant one. He was a little surprised to find Hector in slumber, and in Eggescombe's chapel, of all places. It wasn't yet midmorning. But on second reckoning he suspected His Lordship had suffered a disturbed sleep.

As had he.

The evening before, an uneasiness seemed to settle over the great mansion as the August sun sank below the low hills and evening shadows stole across the lawns to stain Eggescombe's red brick black and swallow the great pile into the night. The library, where Tom had retreated with a few of the other guests, took on a fortress glow, a sanctuary, in which they affected to keep up an appearance of Sunday-evening languor, though the air simmered with tension and unspoken thoughts. Tom partnered with Jane against her husband and Dominic in a near-wordless hand of bridge while Max and Miranda grappled on the library table, out of earshot, with a Ouija board. Lord and Lady Fairhaven had each found an excuse—paperwork in the estate office, a migraine, respectively—to absent themselves. Lucinda, after flipping through a magazine, retreated through doors to the adjacent music room, bringing Tom a modicum of relief, for he found her presence unsettling. Moments later the melancholy throb of the piano sounded through the half-opened door—Rachmaninoff's "Vocalise," Tom realised as his mind drifted towards the languid tempo, drawn to its tinge of regret. Her rendering of the familiar piece seemed skilled and heartfelt, and he found himself mellowing in his harsher assessment of her—and himself—until the Rachmaninoff tipped into Chopin's Funeral March interpreted as a frenzied boogie-woogie.

"She's remarkably good, isn't she," Dominic had murmured over his hand of cards.

"She's in remarkably poor taste," Jamie snapped, slapping his cards to the baize and pushing his chair back. But he was stopped in his movements at the sound of a piano lid crashing and the clacking retreat of shoes along the floor. The outburst did nothing so much as acknowledge their cheerlessness. The children were shooed to bed. Shortly after, the card game ended, none keen for another rubber—or any other diversion.

Tom had told Miranda to take her night things to his room. He didn't think himself an unduly cautious parent—he wasn't fond of the fashion for a helicoptering involvement in a child's life—but the unease the day had wrought had been inflamed for him by his troubling conversation with Miranda about ghosts. Most adults would dismiss a child's witterings about a paranormal sighting, but some certain adult, one among those at Eggescombe this weekend, who possessed a terrible secret, who listened attentively to her description of the ghost—wearing *pas beaucoup* or *tout blanc*—might have reason to be fearful. Who wore *pas beaucoup*? Who wore *tout blanc*? Who might shine with ghostly sheen in a burst of lightning or passing through a motion-sensor light? Roberto stripped and wreathed in marble dust? Pallid Dominic in cream trousers and shirt? Perhaps Hector in his terry-cloth robe, witnessed too (perhaps) by Jane Allan. Or that maligned intruder who had made a false confession? What might he wear at night? Too late Tom realised he had sent Miranda back onto the croquet court armed with a counterargument to Maximilian's assertion that the manifestation on the lawn was of Sir Edward Strickland. Would it spread? Would someone seek to do her harm?

When he got to his room, Miranda had been already tucked up on one side of the four-poster, eyes drooping with sleep, head nodding over her copy of *Alice au manoir hanté*. The door he could only leave as he had found it, unsecured—there was a lock, but he had been given no key. He craved a cool breeze in the room, but he lowered and locked the window instead. Miranda perked up as he readied himself for bed. Striving for light conversation he solicited the wisdom of the Ouija board.

"We asked who strangled Max's uncle." Miranda yawned and readjusted the book on her lap.

"Really, darling, I don't want to harp on this but there is something very serious and sobering about a man's death—any human being's death."

"I know, Daddy. But it was Max who wanted to ask Ouija the question." She rubbed her eyes and yawned again.

Tom undressed behind a Chinese screen in silence, but he could feel the question rising in his mind like a bubble. Finally, despite his best intentions, he couldn't help himself: "Well, what did it say, then? The Ouija."

"It spelled *LUCY*."

Occult twaddle! "Max was pushing the whatsit, the planchette, wasn't he," Tom said as he removed his cast boot. "The way Grannie Kate does when you play in Gravesend."

"No."

"Well, it's nonsense anyway."

"Why couldn't it be her?"

"Lady Lucinda fforde-Beckett? Well, because . . ." Tom could feel a blush rising from his neck, which he fought to suppress. *Because she had been disporting with your shameful father on this very bed.* "Because . . . she's a woman."

"That's not a reason."

"What I mean is, I don't think she would be strong enough to . . . you know."

"I'm going to be strong when I grow up." Miranda affected a biceps pose. "I'll beat any boy. You said not to hide my light under a bushel, Daddy. And I didn't. I won at croquet. Max didn't really mind, though."

"Well done, you."

"All us girls in Year Four think women should be able to do anything men do."

Tom decided for the pajamas Gaunt had left out the night before. "But is it really an advance for women if they behave as badly as men—who can behave very badly indeed."

"Shouldn't women have the right to have the chance to?"

Clever child. "Yes, you're right, of course," he sighed, tying the string of the pajama bottoms. "But Ouija boards aren't . . . right, I mean. They're silly."

Very silly, he'd thought as Miranda fell quickly into sleep and his mind instead roiled over the day's events. The moon followed much the same path as the night before, silvering the bedspread, reminding him of his weakness, though his thoughts were not unalloyed with memory of the pleasure. A near hour of sleeplessness later, he had stooped to the strategy of sliding a chair under the doorknob, to stop intruders or at least wake him if an attempt were made. Was he being paranoid, he thought, and what sort of intruder was he barring? A strangler or a scarlet woman? The jabber of anxious dreams, transmuted vicarishly, punctuated his restless sleep when he finally tumbled into it: He had prepared no sermon, he was late to church, he was in the pulpit with no underpants. When he awoke, the sun was in his room. He wiped the sleep from his eyes, looked around. His heart lurched.

No Miranda.

The chair was returned to its place, the door open a crack. His mind raced over labyrinthine Eggescombe Hall, its myriad rooms, staircases, corridors, and crannies, almost all of them unexplored by him, alarmed as to where she might be. He flung back the bedspread and snatched up his dressing gown from the bedside chair. One arm into one sleeve later and Miranda's head was poking through the door.

"Daddy, go back to bed."

"Why?" he replied, suppressing a gasp of relief, wrapping the gown around himself.

"Because I said."

"Are you coming in?" He perched on the edge of the bed, puzzled, vaguely conscious that standing earlier had not brought a burst of pain from his ankle.

"Close your eyes."

A scraping sound in the hall signaled her intent. He closed his eyes, smiled in expectation (and a little relief), the acrid odour of sulphur penetrating his nostrils as she drew near and the words to "Bonne Fête" came to his ears.

"Happy Birthday, Daddy! You can open your eyes now."

"Wherever did you get that?" Tom feigned surprise at the plate containing four petit fours, each with one tiny twisty candle flickering with yellow flame.

"From Mrs. Gaunt, down in the kitchen. It's left over from Saturday." She frowned at it. "And my present's in the car. I forgot it there, sorry."

"Doesn't matter. This is lovely. Thank you. You've made my birthday memorable—in a very nice way," he added.

"Make a wish, Daddy. What did you wish for?" she asked after he'd blown out the candles.

"That you'll be with me for every birthday of my life, darling. Come here." She sat on the bed and he hugged her, smelling her hair. "I hope you'll have some of this?"

Miranda reached into her dressing gown pocket and pulled out two forks. She grinned.

After a moment's quiet dining, she asked, "Will we be able to leave soon?"

"I shouldn't think much longer. There's little that we can contribute, you and I, I don't think."

"Then we can go to Gravesend?"

"Of course. Grannies are waiting! We won't be able to stop and stay with Aunt Julia, though." He paused in thought, then heaved himself off the edge of the bed. "I wonder . . . ," he muttered, gingerly moving behind the screen to pull his mobile from his trouser pocket.

"Wonder what, Daddy? Oh! Your foot seems much better."

"If Dosh or Kate has called back." He kept the ringer on vibrate most of the time. He scrolled through the received calls in the last twelve hours: His sister-in-law Julia had called in the evening as had a number of folk from Thornford, prompted, he expected, by the news of the death at Eggescombe. "I left a message yesterday explaining what's happened to us, though of course they'll have heard it on the radio or seen it on TV. Ah, they have called. Shall we call them back or is it too early?"

"Not too early," Miranda said slyly.

Breakfast had been a cheerless affair, though mercifully absent the drama of the morning before. Hector passed Tom and Miranda on his way out, turning to announce to those remaining—Georgina, Jane, Jamie—that he would be in the chapel, his tone a warning: Woe to him who dared disturb. But after a decent interval of toast and coffee and conversation tempered by respect for Georgina's evident suffering, Tom made his way to Eggescombe's private chapel, his heart laden but his mind bent nevertheless on disturbing a man at prayer. But Hector was not at prayer.

Gripping the ring of the door handle, Tom had sent the

inside latch shooting up with a noisy clank. Entering, he'd pushed the oak door creaking on iron hinges. He'd shambled down the shadowed nave along the blue-and-white-checkered marble, soon realising from the set of Hector's head and shoulders along the front pew that his was the posture of sleep, not devotion. Bonzo, on the pew next to his master, raised his head a little, blinked, and settled back to his own rest. He'd taken a few moments to glance around at the exuberant use of marble, an indication that the chapel was clearly post-Reformation, a later renovation to Eggescombe Hall, before noisily clearing his throat and setting Lord Fairhaven's eyelids to flutter open.

"I was resting my eyes." He focused blearily on Tom, though his sleep-thickened voice betrayed him.

"I thought I might pay the chapel a visit, while I had the chance," Tom lied, adding another: "I thought you might have left by the time I arrived."

"Have you a ticket?" Hector's smile stopped short of his eyes.

"I must have left it in my other trousers."

Hector grunted at the riposte and straightened his posture. "The chapel sees mostly day-trippers now. Part of the package for some, with the Labyrinth." He flicked an uncertain glance at Tom, as if remembering their encounter there, before looking away, to the sanctuary lamp burning before the altar.

"Built in 1836 by my several-times-great-grandfather," he continued. "Of course, in earlier times the Mass had to be celebrated in the attic because, well . . ." He trailed off, patting the dog's head.

"Lord Fairhaven—"

"Yes."

"There's something I want to speak to you about."

Hector regarded him sulkily. "I thought there might be."

Tom settled into the pew across the nave from Hector. Stained glass fetching a bit of light from the sky cast dancing shadows over pews. "I'm sorry if this sounds like an accusation, but I don't believe I'm wrong in thinking that in the Labyrinth yesterday morning you removed something from Lord Morborne's pockets." When Hector didn't respond, he continued. "By all accounts, Lord Morborne was wedded to his mobile—I noted it myself at the Plymouth airfield—but the device seems to be missing. I'm deducing, I don't think unfairly, that you took it."

Hector's lower lip slipped from its mooring. He regarded Tom with barely concealed displeasure. "Have you mentioned this to anyone?"

"If you mean the police, no. I have, however, discussed it with Lady Kirkbride. Perhaps I shouldn't have, but I think she's of very good character and has your best interests at heart."

"And what would my best interests be, Vicar?"

"In being forthright."

"I'm not sure that would be in my best interests." Hector glanced away.

"Much depends on whether your interests lie with God or mammon."

Hector didn't respond. He shifted in his seat to face forwards. Finally, he said, as if addressing the altar, "I've been sitting here since breakfast wrestling with my conscience, Vicar. I do have one, you know. I realise people think that if you have any association with party politics, then your morals and ethics and what-have-you are suspect. But, you see, it's so often a question of efficacy. How might one get things done—good, worthwhile things—if one must constantly worry about the minutiae of some moral equation or consider every single possible consequence. Sometimes one must push on."

"Ends, not means, in other words."

Hector turned his head and shot him a cold glance. In the moment he took studying Tom's face, Tom could see a beginning crack in the façade of hauteur. "I did take Oliver's mobile—his iPhone," he said finally.

"I see. I assume you believe you had a good reason."

"Apparently, it contains some . . . information that could be damaging. Oliver said so and I . . . could find no reason not to believe him."

"Information damaging to you."

"Yes."

"Might the information implicate you in some fashion in Lord Morborne's death?"

Hector didn't respond to the question. Instead, he said with rising anger: "Do you know they've barred Father Downes from Eggescombe for the time being? It's an outrage."

"You take Communion daily?"

"Yes. Here, and in London."

"I'm sorry I can't be of use."

Hector cast troubled eyes on him for the first time. "Will you go to those idiot detectives?"

"My lord, you've told me that the information on Lord

Morborne's mobile could damage you in some fashion. That suggests a motive. How can I not tell the police what I know? A man has been murdered. Am I to protect his killer?"

"If I'd killed Oliver, why wouldn't I have taken his mobile at that moment rather than later?"

"Because you were disturbed in the act? Because you were in a terrible emotional state? Because you didn't think about the phone until later? I'm sorry to be so blunt, but there might be a number of reasons."

"Well, I *didn't*. Much as I detested my brother-in-law, I wouldn't wish him dead."

"You were seen at a run on the grounds around dawn yesterday."

"I often take exercise early in the morning. What of it?"

"You didn't mention it to the police at our interview in the great hall yesterday."

"I didn't want to complicate matters. It's a routine activity. How do you know anyway? Mrs. Gaunt, I suspect," Hector continued when Tom hesitated. "She's an early riser."

"She claimed to the DI that she had seen nothing 'out of the ordinary.'"

Hector shrugged. "And so it was, quite ordinary."

Tom tried a new tack: "I couldn't help notice that the belt on your robe was absent in the Labyrinth."

"What!"

"Lord Fairhaven, the police are also looking for a weapon, as well as a motive. Lord Morborne was strangled, as you know."

Hector's face coloured dangerously. "But that's outrageous! You're suggesting—"

"I'm simply pointing out that you're in somewhat of an invidious position."

"Then the bloody belt slipped out of the loops somehow. I don't know. The redoubtable Gaunt laundered that robe yesterday. It had grass stains on it. You'll have to ask him. There was a belt on it this morning. You're being ridiculous."

"What then of the mobile?" Tom felt the full force of Hector's anger, which dissipated slowly, like air from a balloon, until after a minute pallor was restored to his face. He said,

"I'm not accustomed to including virtual strangers in what I regard as purely private business."

"Can it be private any longer in these circumstances, Lord Fairhaven? *Should* it be private?"

"Yes, it bloody should be private!"

"I see." Tom struggled to rise from his pew. "I was only seeking you out—"

"Then you weren't simply playing the tourist."

"No, I suppose I wasn't. Despite the size of this house, privacy isn't always guaranteed, and I didn't expect anyone else to come into the chapel."

"An indictment of the state of the Faith, I daresay."

"Possibly. Anyway, I only came to let you know, as a courtesy, that I feel duty-bound to tell the police what I saw. The nature of your conflict with Lord Morborne is not my business. But you must be aware that whatever information happens to be on Lord Morborne's device is also likely to be in another computer somewhere or on a server or in a 'cloud.' If needs must, the police will eventually find it."

Hector, who had set his head in one hand, stared at him through splayed fingers. "Sit back down, Vicar. I have something I might as well confess to you. If Father Downes were here, I would talk to him. But I guess you'll have to do in the circumstances."

"Confess?" Tom hesitated over the word. "I can't offer you what your own priest would offer you, Lord Fairhaven. We're of different churches. I can't give you absolution. Nor, in any case, would I offer absolution unless you were willing to meet certain conditions, going to the police being one of them. Do you see?"

Hector shifted his arms to cross them over his chest. "I said I had been wrestling with my conscience. I didn't say a winner had been declared." He flicked a glance at Tom. "Perhaps you are my dress rehearsal."

"Telling the police is not telling the public. If the police think your information is irrelevant to their investigation, I'm sure it would go no farther."

"I think you may be naïve, Vicar."

Tom waited as Hector appeared to gather his thoughts. Finally, he took an audible breath, as if he were to plunge into a frigid pool, and said: "Oliver apparently had evidence that I . . ." He paused. ". . . that I hired the services of a . . . certain young man." His eyes slewed towards Tom's. "You're not—"

"Shocked? No. Human frailty isn't unknown to me."

"Of course." Hector frowned. "I doubt others shall be so forgiving."

"I'm not sure I'm being forgiving, Lord Fairhaven. I'm trying to be understanding. I gather, however, that your brother-in-law was in the mood for neither."

"No. I wouldn't credit Oliver with finer feeling."

"Why was Lord Morborne bringing this . . . information up to you now? It is true, I presume."

Hector nodded. "The young man in question was a member of some third-rate 'boy band' that Oliver managed some few years ago, one that failed to capture the public imagination, apparently. It broke up and some of its members have found little success since. One is particularly low on funds."

"And he's . . . entered the sex trade?"

"No, no. He was in the sex trade—as you call it—*before* Oliver plucked him and others out of some bar or off the street and did his Svengali bit on them. I'm not sure how much he really was in the sex trade, this boy, but for a time he was . . . available, shall we say."

"Through some website, I presume?"

Hector nodded vaguely. "I only . . . saw him a few times and, as I said, this is some few years ago. I don't have a terribly vivid memory of him."

"There have been others?"

Hector's face flushed, but he didn't reply. "This boy seems to remember me, at least according to Oliver. This is what I was trying to glean from his mobile. Oliver claimed he had compromising photos—I can't imagine how photos would have come about at all!—and some diary entries that suggest—"

"But if this boy is bent on blackmail, why wouldn't he approach you himself? Why would he have Lord Morborne act as . . . intercessor?"

Hector shrugged. "I suspect Oliver has known about this for some time—"

"In other words"—Tom's mind raced ahead—"this boy, this young man, may not even be aware that you were one of his . . . clients. That Oliver had his own reasons—"

"I don't know! That's why I wanted to see what was on his mobile. Yes, it's true, I was with this . . . young man, but is there proof?"

"Why would Lord Morborne choose to reveal to you his knowledge of such a . . . well, ominous secret at this time?" Tom was finding this all very puzzling.

"To ruin my political success, of course," Hector snapped. "I'm one of three on a short list for the open primary the Conservative Association is running in this constituency. You must know about this, of course."

"I've been told," Tom said dryly. Rural Devon was such a redoubt of Tory England, its politics so uncontested, he only ever gave it a passing thought. But he was aware that the MP for South Central Devon constituency had stood down over some dubious financial mismanagement, triggering a by-election, scheduled for late autumn. Rather than have a candidate selected by the local Tory nobs, as usual, the Conservative Association had short-listed three suitable candidates, one of which local Conservatives would select by postal ballot.

"I believe my chances are very good," Hector continued. "I've chaired the local Conservative Association. People remember my father, who sat in the Lords, until Blair buggered with the Upper House. I shouldn't be surprised if I wasn't offered a place in the cabinet after the next general election. And now this intrudes! After Mr. Horsham disgraced himself, you can imagine the prime minister will have no toleration for other misconduct from this quarter. I'm to join the other two candidates at an open primary on Saturday. If this story is likely to become known, I had better withdraw my candidacy, lest I embarrass the PM. But I don't want to withdraw." His lip slipped out in a pout.

"I think these days people are rather more fascinated with politicians' private lives than their public policies," Tom said, musing that Hector's conduct might squeak by with a grovelling apology in the metropolis, where his conduct could hardly be unknown (Lucinda and Dominic had smirking knowledge), but never in the deep countryside. "Even a breath of—"

"We sacrifice our time and our energies," Hector interrupted, "and the minute anyone finds we're a little bit human, a little bit fallible, then apparently we can go swing for our credibility."

Tom glanced at Bonzo, who had raised his heavy head to regard his master. He sometimes thought—though he would not give this voice within the Church—that the sale of sex might just as well be legalised and monitored, much as the Dutch had done to salutary effect. But this would give no quarter in the case of Hector Strickland, Lord Fairhaven, husband, family man, and devout Roman Catholic. Revelation of his dangerous double life (if indeed rentboys were a habit) would embarrass more than the PM and some Tory grandees. It would deeply humiliate his wife, whom he had betrayed in violation of his wedding vows. Had he no concern for her? Her name had not entered their conversation.

"What I find repellent," Tom began, wishing to abandon

the topic of politics, "is that if Lord Morborne went ahead with threats to make your story public, he would bring great suffering to his sister—your wife. That seems beyond the pale. Why would he want to do that?"

Hector regarded him warily. "Because Oliver fforde-Beckett was a shit, that's why."

"That's not really an answer."

"Isn't it? Oliver has always behaved as a complete cad as long as I've known him."

"And you've known him how long?"

"It's a small world, ours, Vicar. Our fathers knew each other from various involvements. I think I first met Oliver at a shoot in Scotland, at Tullochbrae. We were each in the Parachute Regiment, of course, though at slightly different times. It was Oliver who introduced me to my wife, at a dinner given by the Indian high commissioner, though I can't think now why Oliver had been invited. And of course we each belong to the Leaping Lords, although Oliver has always been spotty in his attendance." He paused and seemed to study Tom's face. "What does a Christian do if he absolutely despises someone?"

"Do good to them who hate you. You know this, Lord Fairhaven." Tom frowned. "This incident on Saturday. You were at blows over this threat of revelation, yes?"

"Yes."

"Then what of the parachute—*your* parachute—not opening as it should have? Did Lord Morborne tamper with it?"

"The parachute was tampered with, yes."

Something in Hector's syntax gave Tom pause. "I'm not sure I understand."

"It was tampered with. *I* tampered with it. But, stupidly, I ended up wearing the bloody thing."

"You mean"—Tom was aghast—"you intended to have Lord Morborne die in this cruel fashion?"

"Of course not! Oliver knows what he's doing in a parachute. If it gets tangled, you pull the emergency chute. Simple! My intent was to give him a . . . a little fright."

"If I may say so, how very childish. You scared the daylights out of everyone on the ground, including your mother."

Hector glowered. "Then it's a day they shan't forget anytime soon."

"It will likely be on YouTube, too, you know."

"Will it?" Hector reflected: "It will show me in a good light, don't you think?—fortitude under pressure."

"Sounds like spin to me. The truth is less flattering."

"Only if you choose to reveal it."

Tom paused, then said with reluctance: "You can rely on my discretion. I can't think this episode has relevance to Lord Morborne's death.

"However, Lord Fairhaven, what I still don't quite understand is why, if Lord Morborne has been, for some time, in possession of information damaging to your reputation, he chose this moment, this past week, of all weeks, to threaten you with it?"

Hector looked away. "I really have no idea."

He's lying, Tom thought, reading the stubborn closing of his lips. "Some pressure from this boy?"

"I don't know."

Tom looked to the elaborate cross behind the altar. "Has your conscience declared a winner yet?"

"Again, I don't know. What will you do?"

"As regards Detectives Bliss and Blessing? Only what I witnessed, not what you've told me."

"Could you be persuaded to keep *schtum*?"

"My lord, I'm a priest." Tom instinctively raised his hand to his neck to indicate his clerical collar, but of course it wasn't there. He had put on casual clothes this third day of his holidays.

"I said earlier I thought you might be being naïve."

"You did, but I can't see why any of this would go any farther officially, if you are innocent of Lord Morborne's death. Reconciling yourself with Lady Fairhaven, with your conscience, with God, are entirely private matters."

Hector's face seemed to sag. He looked suddenly exhausted. "When I say you may be being naïve, I mean this: Oliver claims the boy was . . . underage at the time I met him. He may well have been, if his birthday on the Internet is correct. I didn't know. I—"

"Oh, God, Hector." Tom couldn't suppress his dismay. "How could you?"

Indignation flashed in Hector's eyes as a new and dangerous colour returned to his cheeks. "Don't you come the virtuous man to me, Mr. Christmas! I was in the north corridor in the small hours Sunday morning and saw Lucy, in moonlight from the window, tripping merrily up the grand staircase, coming, it would seem, from the ground floor, where the Opium Bedroom is located. I'm quite aware of my sister-in-law's appetites, and they aren't for a nice warm milky drink in the middle of the night. I can't think who else in the house might better satisfy her . . . enthusiasms. I can see from your expression that my deduction is not misplaced."

Tom had tried to compose his face in what he thought was imperturbability, but felt nonetheless the beating of blood along his cheeks. The words caught at his throat: "I didn't intend to cast the first stone, my lord."

CHAPTER SEVENTEEN

"Aptly named, I suppose," Tom said.

"Smallest room in the house, I'll wager," DI Bliss responded gruffly, glancing around the linen-fold paneling.

"Not *quite* the smallest, sir." DS Blessing tapped his notebook against his thigh.

Bliss scowled at his junior and refrained from comment. Tom, seated on a richly carved high-back chair that dug uncomfortably into his spine, looked from one to the other wondering, not for the first time, about the nature of their relationship and their lives. Why, for instance, was the senior officer junior in age? DI Bliss was perhaps early forties while DS Blessing had to near fifty. Blessing's sister, he knew, had gone to school with Mrs. Prowse—which must make her an *older* sister—and his wife attended St. Mary's in Totnes. Bliss's wife liked theatre, and dragged her husband to plays. That was the extent of his knowledge, other than Blessing's confiding remark that Bliss was cursed with an irritable bowel, the goad to Blessing's remark.

"I'm not sure why you think it's aptly named, either." Bliss addressed Tom's earlier remark. "The missus and I did the tour of Eggescombe on an open day a few years ago. I don't recall coming in here."

"It's very plain, sir."

"I expect the local felons were tried here in centuries past, as there was likely no proper court," Tom said. "That's why it's called the Justice Room."

"I do know that." Bliss's tone was testy. "I'm wondering why you think it's apt *now*."

"Because you two"—he gestured with his finger—"are the instruments of justice in this instance, are you not? Lord Fairhaven, I expect, is displaying a sense of decorum."

Or humour, he thought, though Hector seemed cursed with a lack of it.

Or irony.

The Justice Room, adjacent to the great hall, was a comparative closet of a room, bare in decoration, spare in furniture—plain, as DS Blessing said—containing only a single table, oval, with an added leaf, richer in colour than the other sun-bleached boards, and several chairs identical to the one Tom sat on. The smell of warm dust pervaded, though none was evident; the room felt reopened after a very long period. Perhaps, Tom thought, the privilege of maintaining the king's peace had slipped from Eggescombe as Hector's ancestors stuck by their Roman faith, making the room redundant.

"More likely His Lordship doesn't want us mucking up his posh rooms," Bliss muttered.

"Perhaps you won't need this as your incident room for long," Tom said, noting the room was absent of the sort of crime-solving paraphernalia he recalled from the detectives' installation in Thornford's Old School Room during a murder investigation a year earlier. "Anyway, how may I be of assistance?"

Gaunt, who seemed to have a sixth sense of everyone's whereabouts, had waylaid Tom the minute he'd exited the chapel. He'd ushered him past a congeries of rooms and staircases to the Justice Room where Bliss and Blessing had parked themselves.

"I'm also wondering," Tom continued when an immediate reply wasn't forthcoming, "when my daughter and I might be permitted to leave Eggescombe? We were scheduled to leave for London late Saturday, to visit relatives."

"I can't really say, now can I, Mr. Christmas? Much depends on folk cooperating with us."

"But surely once you've interviewed everyone, those of us who don't live here can go. You can always find us later. I'm not intending to flee the country."

"No second home in Cap Ferrat then, Mr. Christmas?"

"No," Tom replied, guessing that Lady Lucinda had entertained recently in this chamber.

Bliss grunted. "We didn't really get on to you yesterday when we were next door." He nodded towards the great hall, adjacent. "That nutter confessing to a crime he didn't commit put a bit of a spanner into the works." He frowned. "You gave us an outline yesterday morning outside on the drive of what you found in the Labyrinth. What was it, Sergeant?"

Blessing flipped back through his notebook and read the relevant entry.

"Have we left anything out?" Bliss asked.

"No . . ." Tom hesitated. "But I'm afraid I've left something out. I neglected to tell you that when I returned to the Labyrinth after my exploration along the dew path yesterday morning, I . . . found Lord Fairhaven in the centre removing something—I thought—from Lord Morborne's person."

Bliss's eyebrows rose imperceptibly. "What exactly?"

Tom glanced at a series of carved figures along the wall. "You must ask Lord Fairhaven. I didn't say anything earlier because I wasn't certain what I saw. I am now. I've discussed this with His Lordship, but I can't in good conscience give you the details— or at least what details I know. The three of you must have a conversation."

"Fear not, Vicar, we will. Anything else your . . . conscience has kept you from?"

"Will you be interviewing the children—Max and my daughter?"

"Only if we think it necessary, and under supervision, of course. Why?"

Tom hesitated again. His experience of the police interviewing Miranda, even under supervision, after her mother had died had left him with a sour taste. "Perhaps I might report something that my daughter saw in the small hours of Sunday morning—a ghost."

Blessing looked up. "My cousin Barry saw a UFO on Exmoor last year."

"I'm not having a laugh," Tom said.

"Nor am I. Turns out it was a police drone. Rational explanation."

"I take your point, Sergeant. Young Max—who seems to

have a fanciful streak—insists that what my daughter saw was the ghost of Sir Edward Strickland who is said to wander the property during full moons, but Miranda is, well, less certain."

"Then what was this ghost?" Bliss asked.

"She's not sure. Nor am I."

"Or you don't want to say, perhaps."

"Inspector, though I can't help but be mindful that a man has been killed, I don't—"

"Want to grass anyone up."

"In a nutshell."

"You lack confidence in our abilities?"

"No," Tom fibbed. His wife's killer had yet to be found and the case was as cold as a tomb. "But bear in mind that what Miranda saw, she saw from the nursery floor in a burst of lightning over the moor—some little distance away."

"Time?" Blessing scribbled in his notebook.

"Miranda's not certain. Anyway, what she saw was not in Tudor costume. The figure was in modern dress . . . or perhaps no dress—or at least in little dress. Pale, white . . . male."

Interest flickered across Bliss's face. He exchanged a glance with his sergeant. "Whereabouts?" he asked Tom.

"I believe the nursery floor overlooks the south lawn."

"Any other details?"

"None, I'm afraid. As I said, Miranda only had a glimpse. Perhaps it's not important."

"We'll be the judge of that, sir."

"If you are going to talk with Miranda, you will of course include me."

"It's mandatory, sir."

"Good. Now is there anything else I can help you with?"

Bliss frowned down at Blessing, who flipped through pages in his notebook and shrugged:

"You told us you retired a little before midnight Saturday and woke about five thirty."

"That's true." Tom's heart began a tattoo.

"Any bumps in the night?" Bliss enquired.

"No." How swiftly the lie came to his lips. How cowardly he was!

"You weren't awoken by distant thunder?"

"No." That was at least true. Thunder had not awoken him.

Bliss's mouth widened to emit another question when a knock on the door interrupted. The door opened a crack and a man's head peeked through, followed by a uniformed arm. Bliss took the paper proffered, nodded a thanks to the departing figure, and studied the document a moment, his mouth parting with the beginning of a smile. He glanced at Tom as if wondering why he was still in the room.

"Thank you, Vicar," he said, handing the paper to Blessing. "I think that will be all . . . for the minute."

Tom understood he wouldn't be leaving Eggescombe anytime soon.

"To get a decent egg, I really think you need to keep your own hens."

"Yes, I expect that's true." Tom regarded askance the congregation of frisky poultry, snowy white and reddish brown, mobbing the dowager countess's legs and tried to imagine the effect in the vicarage garden. A brief one, he thought: pure carnage. Powell and Gloria, the vicarage cats, weren't awfully interested in eggs.

His eyes went up to the top of the high brick wall. He doubted even the most athletic fox could scale it.

"There's wire netting dug nearly two feet into the ground." Dowager Lady Fairhaven seemed to guess his thoughts. "I've only lost one and that's because Roberto's cat—I think of it as Roberto's; Fred Astaire, as Max calls him—snuck through the gate after him."

It was all a bit *Hameau de la Reine,* the rustic henhouse, the tidy fencing, the pretty chickens, the wicker basket at her feet. Lady Fairhaven in a muslin dress and a straw hat *comme* Marie Antoinette would have capped the scene quite nicely, but, as she had on Saturday when he'd first met her, she was dressed in practical fashion in jeans and an old shirt and looked, as her sobriquet suggested, marvellous—authentic, very much in her milieu.

He had only happened upon the chicken run, drawn by a sudden collective shriek that startled him as he limped along a track near the dower house, gingerly giving his healing ankle in its cast boot a little exercise. He had left the detectives, choosing a path that took him into a wood and along a grassy bank of the Eggesbrooke to sit for a time under a huge willow that leaned over the water, trailing its branches on the surface, making ripples in the flow. Walking back, the noise he'd heard was unmistakably that of poultry under provocation, but by what, he'd wondered—vermin? He skirted the high wall past the rhododendron shrubs to investigate. No, he'd quickly seen, peeking through a wooden gate, the poultry had been aroused by the dowager countess who was tossing corn from what appeared to be an antique biscuit tin. She invited him to join her.

"Have you been keeping chickens long?" he asked.

"Some few years. You look a little bemused."

"You mentioned chickens to the children yesterday, but I didn't think—"

"My mother was very fond of chickens. She even wrote a book about them, a sort of memoir, with poultry. *Three French Hens.* My mother was Nancy, Lady Moncrieff."

"Oh!" The name pinged a bell. "I didn't realise you were—"

"One of those Moncrieffs, yes. I'm the quiet one, so-called—the youngest." She threw another handful of corn on the ground, sending the chickens scattering. "My brothers and sister were the tearaways, really. Certainly by comparison." She smiled with her piercing blue eyes.

Tom had a vague notion—largely from television interviews and book reviews, as the Moncrieffs had become prolific published diarists—of the siblings as cynosures of Swinging London in the years before he was born, then later falling into various forms of darkness. One brother, he believed, had died of a drug overdose, but the others had lived to . . . Did one join the Baader-Meinhof in Germany? Oh, surely not. And didn't another defect to the Soviet Union? Had he been a spy?

"Which is how in a way," Marguerite continued, "your parents came to a party here and where they learned they would be adopting you. I had met them at a gallery opening in London, though my husband had already met your father in some business situation. He more or less managed your mother's all-too-short career, I think. Didn't I say this when we were looking at the photos yesterday? Interesting days, I must say." She threw another handful of corn over the yard. "But they didn't last. My father-in-law died quite young, as did my husband—there's a congenital heart condition among the Strickland males, which is one reason I do wish Hector would stop jumping from airplanes—so we had to devote our attentions to this estate and the other businesses.

"Anyway." She paused. "What were we talking about? Chickens! We were talking about chickens. My mother kept them. She found tending to them soothing, oddly enough. As do I, though when they're flocked about me as they are now"— she looked down—"I feel rather like I'm at the Women's Institute about to give a little talk."

Tom laughed. "You must come to ours then."

"Thornford? Oh, I think I have been in the past. But that was before the chickens. I could come again and talk about poultry management. Usually people have me talk about my family or the sixties. Were you out for a walk? I wasn't expecting to see you until teatime."

"I thought I might take some air. I had a short interview with the police, which was a bit . . . cheerless."

"Oh?" She regarded him curiously. "I talked with them yesterday evening after they'd sorted out that poor deranged man who confessed. I told them," she added, her voice growing cross as she reached into the biscuit tin, "I'm not trotting back and forth to the Hall at your whim. If you want to talk to me, you can get it over and done with at my cottage.'" She scattered the corn. "They're a pair, aren't they?"

"Those two hens?" Tom had been admiring a pair with coppery hackles jostling and pecking each other.

"No, those two CID—Bliss and Blessing. Not quite Morse and Lewis, are they?"

"They're . . . adequate to the task, I think, on the whole."

"Oh, you've met before?"

"There have been some unhappy incidents in Thornford."

"Of course, that poor girl in that drum!"

"How did you know?"

"I . . . must have read it in the papers," she replied, handing him the biscuit tin. She swiftly and expertly scooped up a hen, tempted by a new handful of corn, and tucked it under her arm. "You must take some eggs away with you when you leave."

"That's very kind." Tom felt absurdly as though he were addressing the hen, whose beady glassy eye fixed him with alarm. "I'm not sure when that will be, though."

"After tea, at the earliest," Marguerite said firmly. "It's a birthday tea. Happy birthday, by the way. So, you see, you really mustn't leave." She released the hen and picked up the wicker basket. "Did Bliss and Blessing—what peculiar names they have—say anything that would lead you to believe they had . . ." She seemed to search for the words. ". . . focused their enquiries?"

Tom reflected. "Not really. My interview was brief. We weren't long in it when a constable interrupted us with some paper or other and they dismissed me."

"But you said the interview was cheerless."

"I can't help thinking that anything I say could send them haring down the wrong garden path."

"You have a kind heart, I think."

"I don't think I'm unusual in wanting redress, but I don't really want to see someone innocent troubled along the way—which I suppose is a fair bit of wishful thinking." To the flash of curiosity in her gaze, he explained. "When my wife was murdered—"

"Of course."

Tom hesitated over her brief acknowledgement as Marguerite turned towards the henhouse and began plucking eggs from the nesting boxes. "Did you know?"

"Yes . . ." She plopped an egg in her basket. "I did, and I'm very sorry. I can't imagine anything more dreadful."

"You're remarkably well informed, Lady Fairhaven—"

"I'm pottered down here in Devon most of the year. One . . . hears things. Anyway, you were saying . . . ?"

Tom continued as Marguerite gathered eggs: "When my wife was murdered—we lived in Bristol at the time—the police held me under suspicion for a time. It's routine of them, I suppose, to suspect the nearest and dearest, but it's the most awful feeling, dealing with your own grief, your child's, too, and having them on at you all the time. You start to wonder if you *did* do it and lost your mind somehow."

"And the murderer's not been found? I believe I know that."

"I'm afraid not."

Marguerite closed the coop. As she shooed the chickens past the fence and closed the gate, she murmured, "I'm not certain I want Oliver's murderer found."

"Lady Fairhaven, surely not."

"Do call me Marguerite at least, Tom, and you can leave the tin here." She shifted the wicker basket to her other hand and closed the latch. "I know I'm being blunt, but Oliver—and I'm sure others have remarked on this to you in one fashion or another—could be quite a dreadful man."

"I do know about Mr. Sica's sister, Marguerite, but—"

"Oliver's offended more people than Roberto. The fforde-Becketts are a troubling lot, really. At least my brothers and sister, however wrongheaded they were with their politics, had some little notion of something larger than themselves, but the fforde-Becketts have an enormous streak of debauchery and selfishness. With the exception of Georgina, I suppose. Hector's father and I weren't pleased with his choice of Georgina for a wife. We didn't know how . . . fforde-Becketty she might become. She was quite vivacious when she was younger, but she's become terribly conventional. I'm afraid my son's made a very dull marriage, and in the end there's nothing more unthinkable than a dull marriage."

"Lady Fairhaven has had a tragedy."

"Then you've been told. I sympathise with my daughter-in-law. I do, utterly. I would so adore to have had another grandchild, but it's been ten years since Arabella died so tragically. I find myself thinking—perhaps unkindly, but I can't help myself—that Georgie with her migraines and her helplessness has only found a way different from her brother and half sister of claiming everyone's attention." She paused. "Yes, I know I'm being harsh. I can be an awful mother-in-law at times!" Her blue eyes flashed. "I just want to poke Georgina with a stick some days. I know I'm contradicting myself, but sometimes I wish she would show a bit of Oliver and Lucinda and Dominic's spark." She laughed. "And here I am telling you family secrets and I barely know you."

"I'm much in favour of discretion, so you can rely on it."

"I sensed that. The vicar in Abbotswick—do you know him—?"

"No, I can't say I do, though I've probably met him at some church affair."

"—is an awful gossipy old woman, and he's a man." She laughed again, then grew serious. "Tom, I do want to explain something: I don't mean to say that I don't want Oliver's murderer found because I think Oliver somehow deserved what he got. It was your phrase *nearest and dearest*. I felt a weight lift when that deranged man made his claim, but since then—well, I think we both know that someone near and dear has most likely taken Oliver's life. I suppose I'd rather not know who."

Tom felt the weight fall on him. "Marguerite," he began as they stepped through an iron gate into the dower house's walled back garden, "in that regard, there is something I do feel I should tell you—"

"Oh, dear, what?"

"—so you might be . . . prepared. The police of course asked me for any information that might help them with their enquiries, so I didn't think I could *not* tell them about . . ."

"Idiot boy!" Marguerite retorted when Tom finished telling of Hector's machinations over Oliver's corpse. "Whatever can he have been thinking? And you talked to Hector before talking to the CID, so you must know why he would—"

"Marguerite, you wouldn't want me to behave like Abbots-wick's vicar."

The dowager countess's mouth pressed to a thin line. "No, I suppose not. I know he and Oliver have been having a go at each other, but Hector's mostly bluster—which is why he's perfect for Parliament. Oh, hello."

Marguerite addressed a young woman perched on the edge of a stone bench by a garden of pinks and roses. She was wearing a striped T-shirt and pale blue jeans.

"Lady Fairhaven." The woman rose. Her tone was apologetic, faintly tentative.

"I wasn't expecting you today."

"I thought I would come in any case."

"Were you let in?" Tom couldn't help asking. Between the police and Hector's private security Eggescombe Park was, he thought, made impenetrable to outsiders.

"Forgive me," Marguerite interrupted. "Tom, this is Anna Phillips. She lives in the village. Anna, this is the Reverend Tom Christmas, who . . . has been staying with us this week-end."

Anna's eyes darted between him and the dowager countess as he took her hand. Tom sensed a strained atmosphere between the two women, a guarding of words that would have been voiced but for his presence. He looked more keenly at her face, a pale oval, delicately boned and eloquent, small ears exposed by her fair hair loosely tied at the back.

"I clean for Lady Fairhaven," Anna dropped his hand, "and at the Hall, too, as part of—"

"I know your name," Tom responded. "You recently lost

your brother. It was in the local newspaper. I'm so sorry for your loss. I certainly hope the driver of the car is found very soon and some justice is had, although"—he found himself stumbling over the familiar encomium, unnerved by the stoical misery in her eyes—"I know of course that won't bring back—"

"Rough justice may have already prevailed, Mr. Christmas," Anna interrupted.

Startled, Tom opened his mouth to respond, but as if regretting her words, Anna swiftly turned her attention to Lady Fairhaven. "I thought I'd prefer to keep busy."

"Of course, my dear. I quite understand."

"I wasn't seen."

"Ah, good." Marguerite smiled thinly. "Anna knows many of Eggescombe's less frequented paths," she explained to Tom. "Have you been in the house?"

"No," Anna replied. "I've only arrived."

"Come along, then." Marguerite led the way down the grassy path between the borders of flowers. Tom fell in beside Anna.

"I hope you don't think me rude or abrupt," he began, "but I must ask you if you ever lived in the Highlands, on an estate named Tullochbrae?"

Tom noted Marguerite's shoulders stiffen. Anna glanced, too, at the dowager countess's back. She didn't answer immediately. When she did she turned watchful eyes to Tom and said simply, "Yes, I did."

"Then you are—or at least once were—Ree Corlett."

"Yes."

"Jane Allan—Lady Kirkbride—guessed you might be she

after reading the story in the paper yesterday. Of course," he added, gesturing towards the silent Marguerite, "it's nobody's business why—"

"It's all right. Lady Fairhaven knows. When I moved down south, with my brother, I took my mother's maiden name, Phillips. My mother had me christened Rhiannon. She was Welsh and had a certain romantic streak." She cast Tom a tentative smile. "Everyone at Tullochbrae called me Ree, but when I left I decided to call myself for one of the other syllables."

"Why, if I may ask? You've altered your accent, too, have you not?"

"It . . . it felt the right thing to do." Anna's hand brushed a drooping peony as they passed, setting petals scattering to the lawn. "Did Lady Kirkbride tell you my father was land agent at Tullochbrae?"

"Yes. I understand he died a few weeks before her wedding to Jamie."

"I had turned eighteen the month before. David was thirteen. Our mother, you may have been told, had died well before our father. It was my father who raised us, really. As well as he could in the circumstances. Although the other staff at Tullochbrae were very kind."

"I expect you did more than your share in raising your brother." Tom glanced at her pensive profile, impatient with a new question.

Anna turned her head to acknowledge his remark with a small smile. "I'm not certain that's true. As I'm sure the newspaper said, my brother was mentally handicapped. During the week, he was boarded at a Steiner school near Aberdeen.

Weekends, he was with us at Tullochbrae." She paused. "I left Tullochbrae not long after the Allan wedding. There was really nothing for me to do there, although Lord Kinross—Jamie's father—offered to help me, which was very considerate, especially given . . . the terrible ordeal he was going through—the whole Allan family was going through."

"You mean the death of Jamie's older brother, William—Boysie, as they called him. Did that have anything to do with your leaving?"

As they turned towards the brick courtyard adjoining the dower house, sunlight caught Anna's face and played along her high cheekbones. She looked to the sky, as if some memory could be captured from the air. "I left because that's what eighteen-year-olds do, if they're able. I had reached my majority. My father's insurance paid out a very good sum. And Tullochbrae had become a place of grief . . . grief of many kinds," she added, glancing back to him. "David and I left and moved to Bournemouth. I was able to get him a weekly boarding placement at a sister Steiner school nearby. I bought a flat in town, and David would join me at weekends. I . . . I suppose I should have taken some training in something—it's what my father would have expected—but I took a temp job for a cleaning service and found it . . . satisfying. I still do."

"Then it was at Bournemouth you modified your name—and your brother's."

"I wish I could give you a good explanation why," she responded, casting him an uneasy glance as the three of them stepped onto the brick. "As I said, it felt very much like the right thing to do. A new life, a new town, I suppose was part of it. David and I had no real family that would mind. Both our parents were only children; we had no cousins, for instance."

Tom voiced his perplexity: "I believe there's more, if you don't think me unkind for saying so."

Anna glanced at Marguerite, who had stopped by the boot scraper, before replying, "I won't say I have second sight. I don't, I'm sure. My mother did, according to my father. She apparently foresaw her own death. But"—she hesitated in her movements—"perhaps a little rubbed off. I had a strong feeling that if I altered my identity, I would draw a ring of protection around David and me—that if no one knew who we once were, or where we had once lived, then we would be safe."

"And were you?" Tom asked.

She glanced at him. A shadow crossed her face. "For a time." She slipped from his attentions, towards the back door, as if she regretted her candour.

"Perhaps it's best," Marguerite murmured to him as she ran her boots over the scraper, "not to mention seeing Anna here when you're back at the Hall. We wouldn't," she added with a conspiratorial glance, "want the police to know their *cordon sanitaire* has been broken.

"Do step in a minute." Her normal timbre resumed. "I want you to take some eggs up to the Hall. I'll get you a box."

Together the three passed from the sunny yard into the cool of the mudroom, Marguerite handing her basket of eggs to Tom while she removed her boots. Following her into the kitchen, Tom placed the eggs on the counter and studied Anna as she crossed past a bright window to a selection of aprons on hooks along the wall. Something half remembered teased at him. *What was it?* But the sensation vanished as quickly as it arrived. He wanted to probe Anna's remark about "rough justice," but a more urgent concern pressed upon him:

"Lady Kirkbride was very excited to read that you shared your cottage with a man named John. She can't help wondering if it might be her brother-in-law, John Allan, who's had no communication with his family for years."

"No." Anna's hand hesitated over a green apron. "My man's John Phillips."

"Oh," Tom responded, disappointed, wishing she'd turn so he could read her eyes. "Jane thought because you're unmarried and share the same last name . . ."

"A happenchance, Mr. Christmas, that's all."

"Tom, please. I also wonder—" He stopped, his ears pricked suddenly to a rumble of male voices deeper in the house's interior.

"Do you have company?"

Marguerite was washing her hands over the kitchen sink. She half turned. "No, why do you ask?"

"Voices, coming from your front rooms, I think."

She turned off the taps. "Yes, I hear it now." She glanced at Anna who, arrested in tying her pinny, seemed to shrink against the wall. Wiping her hands on a towel, she moved quickly across the tiles and pushed through the door into the corridor before Tom could caution her.

"Marguerite," he called, following swiftly, his mind cringing with images of intruders. "You don't know who it might be."

Tom entered the drawing room in time to see Bliss and Blessing, who had apparently been lounging on a chintz-covered settee, snap to their feet.

"I believe you're to have some sort of warrant to enter my home," Marguerite said in a deliberate, almost regal drawl, regarding the two men as though they were something crawling up her garden wall. "Am I not correct?"

"You are, Your Ladyship." Blessing spoke first. "But Mr. Sica asked us to wait for him here while he . . . cleaned himself up."

"With a view to doing what, exactly?"

"To coming with us to Totnes station to help us with our enquiries."

"I know what that means." The dowager countess's face hardened. "And it's ridiculous. You can't possibly believe—"

"Marguerite, it's all right." Roberto had slipped quietly into the room, his dark hair damp, wearing fresh khakis, buttoning his cuffs. "I'm going voluntarily. I don't expect to be very long."

"Roberto, you have no idea how long you'll be. You don't know what these two have planned. You'll need a solicitor. I have a man in Totnes. I'll ring him and he'll join you there."

"You're certainly within your rights to do so." Bliss spoke this time. To Tom's ears, the suggestion sounded ominous. Evidently it did, too, to Marguerite, for she said, again in her imperious voice:

"I have told you, Inspector, that Roberto has an alibi for Sunday morning. Me."

Bliss favoured her with a feeble smile before flicking a glance at Tom that struck him—to his dismay and confusion—as conspiratorial. He felt Roberto's eyes fall upon him.

"Your Ladyship," Bliss continued, "I can only repeat that Mr. Sica is helping us with our enquiries. There's nothing more I can tell you, I'm afraid. I'm sure you understand Sergeant Blessing and I—" He nodded to his partner as the three men moved into the vestibule. "—are only doing our job."

"Marguerite, don't worry," Roberto called over his shoulder as she moved to follow, "I'm innocent of this. I'll be back before long. Stay with the vicar."

Tom suddenly felt a sting of misgiving as he watched Marguerite lift the curtain of the front window. He could see over her shoulder past the rhododendrons to the unhappy scene of the two detectives and two uniformed officers hovering near Roberto as he bent into a police car.

"Lady Fairhaven," Tom began. Addressing her as Marguerite seemed suddenly presumptuous. "I may bear some responsibility for this, and I'm very sorry."

Distracted by the detectives returning to their Astra and the whole convoy moving down the drive, Marguerite took a moment to respond. When she did, turning from the window, her expression suggested neither consternation nor anger. Rather it was worry and distraction that clouded her eyes. "What were you saying?"

"My daughter woke in the night and thought she saw a ghost on the lawn in a flash of lightning. Of course, she didn't see a ghost. She saw a man. The police may have interpreted it to be Mr. Sica."

"I see."

"I'm very sorry," Tom said again.

"Don't be. Tom, I haven't been wholly truthful—to the police. Roberto was with me for some hours Saturday night, Sunday morning, but I know he left me at some time. I'm not sure when. It's not unusual for him to go to his studio or . . ."

"I'm so very sorry."

Marguerite made a vague dismissive gesture. "I'm not sure it's what your daughter saw that has excited them—Bliss and Blessing."

"What would it be?"

"Something more tangible, surely."

"Yes, most likely."

"When they were interviewing me here yesterday evening—well, in the kitchen—they took an interest in a certain piece of clothing, and they asked to take it for examination. I couldn't say no, of course."

"What was it?"

"A red jacket. A hoodie, as they call them these days."

CHAPTER EIGHTEEN

"'Exploring,' I believe Maximilian said." Ellen Gaunt seemed to search her mind. She brushed absently at the front of her pristine apron as if flour had fallen on it. "He was wearing his pith helmet. I think he was going to show your daughter the priest's room, Mr. Christmas."

"Oh." Tom hoped the disappointment didn't sound in his voice. He'd been hoping for such an opportunity himself, but it seemed ill mannered in the circumstances to expect his host to supply a tour, as though he were some day-tripper. Eggescombe's priest's room and priest hole weren't listed in the brochure as being on offer anyway.

"Let's go up and see if we can find them, if you think your foot can handle it," Jane suggested. "I think I remember how to access the priest hole. Hector showed me on an earlier visit. We'll need a torch or two, though."

"You'll find extras in that drawer, Your Ladyship." Mrs.

Gaunt gestured to a large cupboard by the kitchen door. Tom noted her darkly shrouded eyes and pallid skin. She looked like a woman who'd slept poorly.

Jane reached in a drawer and handed him a torch. "I think Jamie's in the estate office. I'll let him know what we're doing." She popped out of the kitchen. Tom could make out the timbre of a male voice down the passage, the rumble and pause of a man on the telephone.

"Another wonderful meal, Mrs. Gaunt," Tom said, groping for conversation as Ellen stood stiffly in attendance. "The chilled cucumber soup was splendid. You and Mrs. Prowse could have your own cookery program on TV."

"Thank you, Mr. Christmas." Ellen's throat caught on his name. Her distress passed through him like an invisible wave and he felt the helplessness of the bystander, able to offer only the inoffensive words,

"I'm sure this incident will be resolved soon."

She nodded but said nothing. He sensed her composing herself at considerable cost and was relieved when Jane fetched him forthwith.

"Mrs. Gaunt seems troubled," Tom remarked when the two of them were out of earshot along the passage leading into the interior of the Hall.

Jane flicked him a glance as they passed through a recessed door in the wall that opened onto the grand staircase. "Yes, I thought so, too. I guess we're all being affected one way or another, aren't we? Georgie having her lunch on a tray in her room isn't a good sign, for one."

The news that Roberto Sica had been removed to Totnes was the midday meal's chief diversion. It was Jane herself who had seen the car with the Battenberg markings drive past while she was out walking and recognised the head in the backseat. By the time Tom returned to the Hall from the dower house and could confirm events, speculation had grown invidious.

"Poor Marve," Lucinda reacted with a hint of *schadenfreude* as she poured herself a second vermouth from the drawing room's drinks table. "I'm sure she'll miss him terribly."

"He hasn't been arrested or charged," Tom insisted as Gaunt poured him a whisky. "Helping the police with their enquiries is not tantamount to guilt."

"Tom is correct, of course." Jamie glared over his gin at Lucinda, who made a rude noise at him over her drink. "I doubt he'll be detained for very long."

Jane frowned into her mineral water, saying nothing. Dominic, with a dry sherry, retreated to the French windows to look out over the terrace, as if he wished to distance himself from his half sister. Hector flicked uninterpretable glances at Tom between sips of sherry. Had, Tom wondered, Lord Fairhaven met with Bliss and Blessing while he had visited the dowager countess? And what had been disclosed?

"It's that brooding quality they have," Lucinda continued when they were seated for luncheon.

"Who is *they*?" Jamie unfolded a napkin on his lap.

"Italians."

"If you're referring to Roberto, I understood he was born in London."

"Doesn't matter. They *brood*," Lucinda drew out the word, then grazed the air with a kiss. "Ever so sexy, don't you think, Dominic, darling?"

"Shut up, Lucy. You've had too much to drink."

"And then they *explode*!" she continued, ignoring him. "Boom! And they find their hands are around someone's neck and—"

"Lucy! Gaunt, remove the wine," Hector barked to his butler.

"Oh, Hector, I'm simply trying to—"

"For heaven's sake, Lucy," Jane cut in, "you can't attribute this to a Mediterranean temperament. It's ridiculous. From what little I've seen, Roberto's been a gentleman. Has anyone seen an instance of temper? Hector? You come down to Eggescombe during the year and stay with Marve. Have you . . . ?"

"Well, he's only been Mother's guest a little over a year and he keeps out of my way when I'm down, but . . ." Hector's tone conveyed regret more than concurrence. "No, he doesn't seem particularly . . . murderous."

"'Countess's Toyboy in Killing Spree.'" Lucinda's arm shot out in illustration of an imaginary tabloid headline, almost hitting Gaunt in the process of taking the wine carafe from the table. "Gaunt, don't you dare touch that wine."

"Lucy," Hector thundered, "if the police hadn't supplanted me as master of my own house, I would ask you to leave. At once!"

"Hector, don't be such a bore!"

"And now you've spilled wine on yourself, you stupid girl. And a single individual does not constitute a 'spree'!"

Luncheon—in addition to chilled cucumber soup, a crab salad with lemon and caper, and crusty French bread, with a raspberry soufflé for afters—had continued in a similarly fraught vein until Hector, evidently disgusted, excused himself for some work in the estate office, with an invitation to Jamie to join him in due course. Lucy opted for another afternoon by the pool, as did Dominic. Tom, still concerned for Miranda's welfare, followed in the same direction shortly after, his destination the kitchen where the children were ensconced. Jane joined him. Her idea was that they should take Miranda and Max on a nature walk but, of course, they were too late.

Now, as they stepped off the grand staircase and into the bright, mullion-windowed Long Gallery, which ran the length of the house, Jane said, "When I was out walking before lunch, I saw one of Hector's private security hustle Andrew Macgreevy away off the property. Do you remember him?"

"Yes," Tom murmured. He was distracted by the plaster vaulted ceiling carved in coils of honeysuckle and the rankings of family portraits along panelling that glowed like silk in the afternoon sun. "He was that reporter snooping around Thornford after Colm Parry's daughter was found murdered last year. He was very interested in your brother-in-law Sebastian . . . John, I mean. Did he see you?"

"No, I don't think so. I don't suppose it matters. He's just doing his job. But he has sort of got in the way at other critical times in my life." Jane stopped at a door past a large hanging tapestry presenting the Fall of Man. "Jamie says he's my nemesis."

"You managed to rein him in last time, I recall, when I met you for the first time last year."

"I'm afraid I expended all my capital then. I can't call in any favours this time."

"Will you have to?"

"I don't know." Jane opened the door and ushered Tom to another staircase, smaller and cruder in material and execution. "Did you look at the papers this morning?"

"Glanced at a few Gaunt must have placed on the library table. I noticed Hector kept them out of the morning room. The tabloids were predictably obnoxious. I feel very sorry for that woman Oliver was engaged to."

"I know. I'm sure she wasn't aware of some of the family history they dredged up." Jane puffed a little. The stairs were steeper here, curving, with a couple of short landings leading to doors that went who knew where.

Talk of newspapers recalled to Tom his encounter earlier with Anna Phillips. "Good heavens," he muttered unthinkingly, an idea coming to him diamond-bright.

"What?"

"That woman."

"What woman?"

Tom could no more take back his words than he could put toothpaste back in its tube. "The woman I thought I glimpsed in the Labyrinth yesterday morning. I think it's Anna Phillips!"

"Anna . . . ? The local woman whose brother was killed? How—"

"I met her."

"Oh, Tom! You didn't! Why didn't you say earlier? Is John—my John, our John—her partner? Did you ask?"

Tom felt moved by her excitement and hated to dash her hopes. "She's Ree Corlett, all right. She said so."

"Wait till I tell my husband!"

"But she said her partner is John Phillips and it's simply chance they share a surname."

"I don't believe it."

"You're disappointed, of course."

"No, I mean I don't believe it. I don't believe *her*. Where did you meet her?"

"At Marguerite's. This morning. She's Marguerite's daily. She found a back route onto the estate." Tom outlined the encounter. "I had an odd sensation when I was looking at her, as if we'd met before. The way the light caught her when we were in the kitchen. And now I know why, or think I do."

"Then *she* made the dew path across the south lawn—the one you followed?"

"The other one, more likely, I would think," Tom reflected. "The one path leading towards Abbotswick. She lives in the village after all."

Jane glanced over her shoulder at him. "Is it possible she . . . ?"

"I . . . I don't know." Tom's impulse was to exempt the fair sex from brutal displays of physicality, but strong emotion he was certain could trump any physical disadvantage. "She was, I could sense, under strain, but of course she's only just lost her brother. I don't think she was happy to see me with Marguerite, however.

"And she said the oddest thing, Jane. When I offered my condolences and expressed the hope that she would receive some justice, she said, 'Rough justice may have already prevailed.'"

"*Rough* justice," Jane repeated. She had reached the top of the stairs and turned to him. "That's provocative."

"She certainly looked alarmed when we heard the voices coming from the drawing room, and after Roberto was taken away and I went back to the kitchen with Marguerite to fetch some eggs to bring back to the Hall, she had vanished." Tom joined Jane on the small landing. "'Likes to start her cleaning in the upstairs rooms,' Marguerite said."

"I wonder if we should be concerned?"

"For Marguerite's well-being? I don't know. Oddly, Marguerite asked me to keep my having seen Anna to myself—which, obviously, I've dishonoured."

"For good reason, perhaps, Tom."

"There was some . . . undercurrent between the two women, but not, I don't think, a fraught one. I suppose I could be wrong."

"Marve knows everyone in the village. I'm sure if she thought this Anna posed some sort of danger, she wouldn't be passive about it."

"Yes, I expect so."

Jane glanced at her watch. "We're having tea at the dower house later this afternoon. We can press Marve for details then. And I strongly hope Anna will still be there. I have questions for her! You didn't ask her for a description of this John Phillips, by any chance?"

"That would have implied I didn't believe her."

"I suppose that's true," Jane sighed. "Well, here we are. This is it."

Tom observed a wall of brick. "There's nothing."

"Not really." Jane groped along the wall until she found what looked to be an iron handle well concealed among the projecting bricks, seizing it with one hand and pushing. A portion of the wall began to give inwards, making a dull grating noise as it moved.

"Cunning," Tom remarked as they slipped into what was a small garret room, with a low arch-braced roof, a plain unvarnished oak floor, and a deeply recessed double lancet window.

"The priest's room, so called," Jane said. "And that slab of wood under the window was the altar, according to Hector, though it looks very unfinished."

"And appropriately east facing, too." Tom went to look out the window. He could see the edge of the Labyrinth, below, and the police tape surrounding it. Evidently PC Widger had secured it sufficient.

"Now, let's see," said Jane behind him. "Oh, the kids have been here. Look."

Tom turned from the window. One of the timber beams in the plaster wall was pivoted outwards; secreted in the brickwork behind was a cavity large enough for a man to crawl into. Tom flashed his torch along it and shuddered with horror imagining a priest lying with racing heart in that black recess, the beam closed behind him, as the pursuivants, the king's men, ransacked the house. Who knew how long one would lie there, cramped and sore, half starved, barely daring to draw breath.

"Apparently, there's a way of shutting yourself in from the inside, but Hector had it removed—just in case. And somewhere in this wainscoting are tiny holes for tubing to pass through to deliver water or refreshment. Can you imagine? It would be like hiding in a coffin."

Tom peered at the wood, too, and ran his hand over its silky texture, unable to detect any openings. "Ingenious the workmanship, horrible the need for it. But where are Miranda and Max?"

"Wait!" Jane held up a cautionary finger. "This room has other secrets. I'll bet they've gone down the hidden staircase."

"Miranda will be in her element. *Alice au manoir hanté* is one of her favourite Alice Roys. It has hidden staircases galore." Tom looked around the plain room. "Clearly, the one here is very hidden."

"Very." Jane crouched and plucked at several of the floor nails in succession. "It's one of these," she said, shuffling to a new set of floor nails along the wide slats.

"Can I help?"

"Try tugging at the nails where you are. Several of them are loose, if you can get your fingers under just so. If you find one, you'll see what happens."

But it was Jane who first succeeded. "Here we go," she exclaimed, pulling a nail fully out, and gesturing to Tom. "Try the one on that board, and then the one on the board next to that."

Tom did. The nails were pivots and the heavy oak slats revolved around them to reveal a narrow but artfully constructed staircase descending into darkness. An aroma of must flew up to meet his nostrils.

"They have been here." Jane let her torchlight run down to what appeared to be a small landing about six feet below. "You can see the dust's been disturbed."

Tom shivered. "I'm not sure I'm happy about Miranda wandering down there unsupervised."

"Hector has seen to the safety of these hidden passages. I think he's considering opening them up to the public as an added attraction."

Tom grunted, not entirely satisfied. "Have you travelled them yourself?"

"Yes, on a previous visit. It's quite the journey. Shall we? Do you think your foot can stand it?"

"Why not? This boot is working very well."

"I'll lead the way."

"Where does it end?" Tom watched Jane tread carefully on the steep, narrow steps, the beam of her torch dancing along the wooden walls of the narrow chute.

"I'll let you be surprised."

From the small landing crowding the two of them, she pushed through a narrow door into blackness revealed by the light to be a constricted passageway lined with rough brick and mortar and heavy with the scent of damp and dust. The beam of light disappeared into darkness and for a moment a kind of animal dread clutched at Tom's heart, as if doom in some fashion waited somewhere off in the very near distance.

Noticing his hesitation, Jane said, "It's not so claustrophobic as it seems. You'll see in a minute. You'll have to bend your head a bit—you're taller than the average Tudor."

They were, Tom realised—ducking under the sill and pulling a cobweb from his hair—about to move through the vast thickness of Eggescombe Hall's walls. The dust was more evident here under the beam of his torch, and the aroma stuffy, yet the atmosphere was not so suffocating, nor the darkness so Stygian, as he had dreaded, and after a moment following Jane he understood why. Here and there, the brick flushed with pinprick radiance, like a star-scattered night sky. Light and air seeped through tiny openings into the walls of adjacent rooms, no doubt, Tom thought, well concealed in the highly decorated plasterwork.

"Careful," Jane said, casting a narrow puddle of illumination from her torch onto another set of narrow steps. They turned a corner, and then another, followed by more narrow steps downward. Before long, Tom's sense of direction had vanished. The pinholes were too small to permit a passing glimpse of the rooms, but there were no forks in this fusty passage to further befuddle. Eggescombe's secret passage was not a maze offering choices at every turn; it was a labyrinth leading to a single destination, whatever that may be.

"Look through here." Jane flashed her light on a chink in the brick.

Tom squinted. "The great hall!" He could see the ornate minstrel's gallery opposite glowing in the light and felt an odd sense of vertigo. The passage they were walking was about halfway up the interior wall of the room. "What am I looking through that wouldn't have been noticed by pursuivants on the other side?"

Jane laughed. "You're looking between the legs of one of the hundreds of figures on the ornamental screen."

"Ah, no eyeball would be detected that way." Tom felt the tips of his eyelashes brush the opening. "Look, there's Hector crossing the room. At top speed, I might add. Should I say something? I feel like a Peeping Tom."

"You're a Tom at any rate, but I doubt Hector would hear anything more than a muffled noise even if you shouted."

They continued on, around, and ever downward. Before long, Tom detected a greater movement of air along his face, a faintly sweeter, yet drier aroma suggesting perhaps some egress to the out of doors. And yet the blackness did not recede. Soon they were down a short set of stairs, stone, these ones, and—the twin beams of their torches revealed—in a narrow, barrel-vaulted room not much wider than the stairs, the walls brick.

"Do you know where we are?" Tom asked, turning his light

towards the source of the cooler air, flowing stronger now. He noted a new set of stone stairs leading to a brick-lined passage that sloped gently downwards and curved out of sight.

"Near the old servants' quarters. I think this might be the old wine cellar."

"Then that"—Tom kept his light on the sloping floor—"must be a tunnel."

"Yes. Would you like to see where it goes?"

"Very much. The alternative is climbing our way back up to the garret, yes? And surely Miranda and Max have come this way."

"I think actually there are some concealed entrances into other rooms in the Hall, but I haven't a clue where they are. I've only had the tour once."

"You've done well to remember this."

They stepped down to the passage, Tom noting a new sound, the crunch of gravel under their feet, but they'd barely turned the corner into the tunnel proper when they saw two beams of amber light flickering over the bricks and heard the approach of excited voices.

"Daddy!" Miranda's torch dazzled Tom's eyes as it passed over his face. He felt an unexpected surge of relief to hear her excited voice in this dank place and the scrunch on gravel intensify as she and Max broke into a run towards them.

"Have you been exploring?" he asked.

"We've been treasure hunting, my dear chap," Max's voice came out of the gloom. Tom flashed his torch on the boy and noted the pith helmet and khaki trousers and shirt. He looked like a miniature edition of Lord Carnarvon exiting the tomb of Tutankhamen.

"And did you find King John's missing jewels or the Holy Grail?"

"I believe King John's jewels are in the Wash and the Holy Grail is at Glastonbury, at least according to legend."

"Yes, apparently." Tom reflected that the boy could be a trifle ponderous.

"Then did you find any treasure?" Jane asked.

"Regrettably, no."

"We found something, though," Miranda insisted. "*Un indice, peut-être, Papa.*"

"*Vraiment?*" Jane responded in his stead. "*Comme Alice Roy?*"

"*Oui.*"

"*Un indice de trésor?*"

"*Non, désolé. Pas de trésor.*" Doubt inflected Miranda's tone.

"I say, all this French is giving me *mal de mer.*" Max marched ahead, out of the penumbra of torches into darkness. "*Do* let's go inside."

There seemed no other course than to follow his fading footsteps, but when the rest of them regained the tunnel entrance, Tom was intrigued by what had seemed improbable before in the sealed blackness of the chamber: A sliver of light shimmering against the lower wall of the barrel-vaulted space swelled by degrees into a rectangle so dazzling it hurt his dark-adapted eyes, until relief came in the form of a pith-helmeted silhouette.

"Come through," Max commanded, his face turned to them in the frame of light. "It's really very simple," he continued, anticipating questions. "There's a lever there." He pointed, and Tom aimed his torch behind a wine rack where a bottle had been. "Which one pulls and what-do-you-say, the bally thing causes this door to open. Wizard, what? Come through, come through."

Miranda easily passed through the opening, but Jane and Tom were obliged to bend low to enter into the bright corridor. Blinking against the dazzling light, he saw plainly he had stepped into a familiar passage in the old servants' quarters. There was the old kitchen, now tearoom, to the left, past Jane's head. There was the sign to the Eggescombe souvenir shop next to Miranda. He turned to see Max pushing shut on well-oiled hinges—so silent was the movement—what appeared to be a section of the wainscoting. He bent to examine the wood. The light in the passage really wasn't so strong after all, once one's eyes had adjusted, so Tom ran his hand over the patterning of the oak.

"Remarkable!" he couldn't help saying. He could detect no seam. "A jib door. But how do you open the door at this end, should you want to go *in*to the tunnel?"

"Thus," Max said, moving to lift a floorboard cleverly fitted with hidden hinges. As the floorboard rose, the door opened in rhythm.

"Who knows about this?" Tom asked.

Max pushed back his helmet. "Well, I do. And there's Pater and Mater, of course. Grandmama . . ."

"Anyone else? Staff?"

Jane, who had put her hands on Max's shoulders, flicked Tom a frowning glance.

"I do believe I told Gaunt and Mrs. Gaunt." Max tapped his chin. "I'm not certain who else . . ."

"Why, Daddy?" Miranda interrupted.

"Oh, simple curiosity." Tom made his voice light as he gently urged Miranda forwards down the passage towards the door to the yard.

"What was that all about?" Jane murmured as the children scrambled ahead.

"You remember me talking about following a dew path yesterday morning?" Tom dropped his voice to a whisper. "Well, the footprints ended at this part of the wall where the opening is. I thought the wet had simply dried at that point, or that whomever I thought I saw had gone up the stairs and into the Hall." He watched Miranda and Max to ensure they weren't listening. "Where does the tunnel end? And do I still need to be surprised?"

Jane made a face. "The stable block."

"Oh." The word came as a groan.

"Yes," Jane said. It was as if they were possessed by the same unhappy thought: proximity of the stable block and the dower house and what that might mean.

"But the stable block was built in the eighteenth century after restrictions on Catholics were eased," Tom said. "The tunnel is from Elizabeth's reign or James the First's."

"I understand the present stable block was built on the site of whatever building preceded it. They incorporated the entrance to the tunnel into the new building." Jane frowned. "Where once the tunnel was useful to protect priests and recusants, in late-Victorian and Edwardian times it became the way for the servants to come and go, so their masters wouldn't have to see or hear them.

"*Quel suppose indice as-tu trouvé, Miranda?*" Jane took a seat at one of the outdoor tables.

"Max has it. Max?"

Max had wandered away. "What?"

"In your pocket. Top one, right."

"Oh, that." Max pushed his hand past the flap of his jacket pocket. "I say, this could be like a magic trick. What do you think, Mr. Christmas? Perhaps a rabbit will appear. Or a dove!"

"Judging from the size of the bulge, I'd say more likely a sparrow." *And a dead one at that.*

"If only one had a wand." Max's hand continued to brush his pocket tantalisingly. "Hocus, pocus—"

"Mocus, focus, autumn crocus."

"I say, that *is* good."

"Doris, doubtless, Douglas, drabness," Tom improvised. "Fire burn and caldroun's blackness."

"Oh, for a drumroll!"

"And a surrey with the fringe on top," Tom ended quickly, tapping a tattoo on the tabletop.

Max's hand dove in the pocket. "Ta-*dah*!"

He pulled out a roll of cloth and gave it a flick; Tom and Jane watched it unravel from his fingers with the practised look of expectation wise adults were to show clever children.

"Oh." Tom tried to keep disappointment from his voice. "It's a tie."

"It looks like . . . a school tie." Jane took it from Max's hands and gave it a shake. Tiny particles of stone descended to the yard's cobbles. "Actually, it looks like a Shrewsbury tie. But . . ."

She paused, her expression suddenly grave. Tom caught

Miranda's studied gaze at the strip of cloth before she turned to him, her eyes alert; in that moment he realised his little girl had galloped ahead of his thinking. His eyes darted with a new horror to Jane's hands, to the commonplace item of haberdashery draping over her fingers. *Is it possible?* He looked to her face and saw his horror reflected in her eyes, then as swiftly suppressed. She rose from her seat and said with studied calm:

"Let's go have a chat with Jamie. He might still be in the estate office. He was waiting for your father earlier, Max."

"Is it cousin Jamie's tie, do you think?" Max asked.

"I don't know." Jane led the way back across the cobbles.

Jamie looked up from papers splayed over Hector's desk when they entered the office. A map of the estate covered one wall, but two of the others were lined with glass-fronted cabinets suggesting this was once the butler's pantry, files and papers having replaced the silver and crystal of old.

"Hello, darling, what are you doing with my tie?"

"Is it your tie?" Jane asked.

"Isn't it my tie? It rather looks as though it is." Faint puzzlement lit Jamie's features as they crowded into the room. "Although I suppose school ties have a certain similarity." He smiled upon them as though they were an amusing delegation from a foreign country.

"The kids found it in the tunnel," Jane said, holding it up.

"Where's Pater?" Max interjected, squeezing farther into the room between Jane and Tom.

"I'm here!" Lord Fairhaven's voice snapped behind them, adding with evident breathlessness, "What are you all doing in my office?"

"More to the point: What have you been doing, Hector, chopping wood?" Jamie's knitted brow alerted them to Hector's altered appearance, the damp, rubicund face.

"I've been out for a run, obviously." He gestured to his short trousers and damp T-shirt. "I missed doing so before breakfast."

"Mad dogs and Englishmen," Jamie remarked as Hector came around the desk. "You're sweating like a horse, old man."

Hector dismissed the remark with a wave of his hand. His eyes fell on the tie, still in Jane's hand. "What—?"

"Max and Miranda found it in the tunnel," Jane repeated. "Hector, are you sure you're okay?"

"Max"—Hector recovered his sergeant-major voice—"I've asked you *not* to play in the tunnel. It makes your mother worry when you do."

"But Mater doesn't know."

"Nonetheless!"

"Very peculiar," Jamie interrupted, "I can't imagine how my tie would get in the tunnel." He frowned. "I'm certain I saw it rolled in a drawer this morning when I was dressing." He stepped around the desk, took the strip of fabric in his hand, turned it over, fingered the back label, then unfurled it to full length. He shrugged. "Oh, well, as the old hymn says, it once was lost and now is found. Darling, why don't you put it . . ." His smile dropped as his eyes moved between his wife and Tom. "Is it important?"

No one leapt to an answer and in the silence the ominous march of sensible shoes on tiles was a not unwelcome diversion. Ellen Gaunt stepped into the room, a large butler's tray in both hands. She evinced no surprise at the numbers who jostled to make room for her, expertly slid the tray onto a stand next to the desk, and turned to make a bland announcement of tea. Before the words fell from her mouth, her eyes landed on the article in Jamie's fingers. Tom saw her start, then quickly recompose her features. But he wasn't alone in noting the transformation. Hector's eyes narrowed. Blandly he enquired, "Mrs. Gaunt, you wouldn't happen to know how Lord Kirkbride's tie might have found its way into the tunnel?"

"The tunnel, my lord?"

"Yes, there's a very old one between the Hall and the stable block. Perhaps I failed to mention—"

"I told you about it, Mrs. Gaunt," Max insisted.

"Yes, of course you did." She struggled to smile at the boy. "I am aware of the tunnel, my lord, but I'm sorry to say I know nothing of Lord Kirkbride's tie."

"It mightn't be my tie, I suppose. It does look a bit stretched." Jamie's voice conveyed a certain exasperation. "Although who else here attended Shrewsbury? Ampleforth for you two." He gestured to Hector and Max. "And Dominic was at Winchester, was he not?"

"Oliver went to Shrewsbury," Jane pointed out.

"But he wouldn't have any reason to bring an old school tie with him." Jamie frowned. "Then it must be mine, although I can't think how it could go walkabout."

"Ow!" Max interjected, jerking away. "That hurt!"

"Miranda," Tom gently cautioned his daughter, having witnessed the rib poking.

"Dash it all, I suppose I shall have to make a confession." Max pushed out his lower lip.

"You put my tie in the tunnel?"

"No. But I did borrow it. Sorry, cousin Jamie, I didn't tell you—"

"That's all right. It's only a tie."

"Mr. Christmas wanted one for a magic trick Saturday when we were on the terrace—"

"Of course!" Tom exclaimed. "I'd forgotten. But I needed some of my kit to complete the trick, so—"

"Isn't this rather a lot of fuss over a tie?" Jamie frowned.

"I should say." Hector gave the thing a wary glance.

"The two of you," Jane sighed, "are as thick as two planks. Where exactly, Max, did you and Miranda find it?"

"The bally thing was tucked behind a loose brick, wasn't it, Miranda?"

"When we were looking for treasure. You couldn't help see it once the brick was removed."

"Someone"—Jane turned her attention back to her husband and Hector—"tried deliberately to conceal this tie."

"Bloody hell," Jamie intoned, looking at the thing in his hand with new eyes. He dropped it on Hector's desk, while Hector pushed himself on his chair a polite distance. "But . . ." Jamie paused, as if gathering his thoughts. "How . . . I mean, what happened to it, Max, after you . . . borrowed it?"

"I brought it out onto the terrace. Mr. Sica and Grand-mama and cousin Dominic—and you, Pater, were there, re-member? Cousin Dominic made it into a belt."

"A *belt*? I think I'd moved away to talk to someone else by then."

"No, you hadn't. You said Dominic looked a fool in it.

Dominic said his tutor at Oxford, Fred Astaire, used to wear men's ties as belts."

"Preposterous."

"It's superb, Pater. Quite stylish."

"Do you mean"—Jane seemed to be thinking out loud—"Dominic removed the tie and you put it on? Or you tried the effect later, with a different tie?"

"Cousin Dominic only wore it for a moment." Max removed his pith helmet and smoothed his hair. "I was going to return it to cousin Jamie's room, but I thought to try it on when I was in the drawing room."

"And?" Jamie prompted.

"Well, it didn't really work with evening dress. No belt loops."

"What did you do with it?"

Max's features fell into a series of gestures—a moue, an accordion forehead, narrowed eyes as he probed his memory. "No idea. I might have left it on a sofa or one of the tables. I remember Gaunt bringing me a cocktail. Well, orange squash. Perhaps Bonzo took it."

"Mrs. Gaunt." Hector turned to his housekeeper. "Do you recall finding a tie next day in the drawing room?"

"I'm sorry, my lord, I did not."

Tom's eyes went from Ellen's peculiarly fixed gaze to the tie, coiled now on the desk. So did everyone else's. They stared at it as if it were a slumbering snake about to raise its head and strike. Jamie broke the silence after a moment:

"I must say, however, I'm very certain I clapped eyes on my tie this morning. I remember distinctly, as I was looking for pants, and there it was, rolled up to one side of the drawer."

"Is that where you placed it when you arrived at Eggescombe last week?" Tom asked.

"No. I stuffed it in my pocket when I got out of the car."

"And where did you find it?" Tom addressed Max.

"From cousin Jamie's suit pocket. I saw him put it there when he arrived. That's what I always do with my school ties."

"Was it in the drawer yesterday morning? Sunday?" Tom asked Jamie.

Jamie frowned. "I'm not sure. We were all in shock yesterday morning, weren't we? But I *think* I saw it *this* morning. And when I did, I assumed my wife had been tidying. She does that."

"You might be tidier if you had boarded at Shrewsbury after all." Jane's smile was brief. "But in this instance, I'm blameless. I didn't touch your tie."

"I say, this is a rummy affair," Max remarked.

"Quite, old chap," Jamie added in mild mockery. "However, I think we might have a bit of clarity if I go upstairs and have a recce in my bedroom. Jane?"

Jane exchanged a glance with Tom.

"I think," she replied, "it might be useful to tour the tunnel to its very end. It's one way, at any rate, of getting to Marve's for tea.

"And by the way, ye of little faith." Jane turned to her husband, "Anna Phillips *is* Ree Corlett."

CHAPTER NINETEEN

A scurrying graze across his exposed toes brought Tom's torch in a swift downward arc, exposing for an eyeblink a panicked rodent before it hurried into the void. Involuntary disgust shot up his spine, and he cast his light over the tunnel's rough brick walls and earth floor, seeking its nasty little mates. Creatures great were generally preferable to creatures small—rodents among them. Even if the Lord God did make them all, He wasn't obliged to share propinquity, as humans were. He—the Lord God—never awoke in bed of a morning to the unpleasantness of a dead mouse nestled in the folds of His duvet, courtesy of vicarage cats.

Nasty little mousy mates there appeared to be none, mercifully, and the others—Jane, Miranda, and Max, who walked ahead of him—evinced no awareness of other commuters. Still, Tom anticipated journey's end. Scarcely higher than he was tall, room abreast for only two at a time, red-brick walls flaming and flickering with monstrous shadows in the flare of four passing torches, the tunnel brought to the edge of consciousness primal fears—entrapment, suffocation, death—which no prayer seemed powerful enough to allay. The damp-ish, earthy smell amplified the oppressive feeling, and he pitied the servants obliged to make their way by candle lamp. Water glistened in shallow poolings here and there, and glimmered in spots along the walls. The subterranean labyrinth, twisting like an intestine under Eggescombe's grounds, seemed ram-shackle, faintly dangerous despite its centuries of use, but Hector assured them a recent engineer's report declared it sound: He had been reviewing developing the tunnel as an additional visitor attraction to cement Eggescombe Park PLC as the very model of a modern manor house attraction.

"Here." Max's voice echoed preternaturally loud in the tight space. He aimed his torchlight low along the wall where a few pieces of brick jutted as though squeezed by a great weight. Below those were black gaps in the wall, and on the floor directly beneath a small midden of cracked bricks.

"Then it wasn't simply lying here on the floor, as if it had been dropped," Tom said, guessing the answer. The brick midden appeared disturbed.

"No, Daddy," Miranda responded. "One of the bricks looked put back, so we pulled at it—"

"Thinking there might be *trésor*?" Jane asked.

"And," Max said, "blow me if there wasn't a tie!"

"Someone had to have known the tunnel well enough," Jane murmured.

"And be carrying a torch," Tom added.

"Onwards and upwards?" Max didn't wait for an answer.

After several moments they reached the bottom of a set of stone steps which travelled up into darkness, a thin line of light testifying to an opening of some nature at the top. Tom groaned inwardly at the thought of manoeuvring more stairs, but hobbled ahead nevertheless. Max pushed through a door in the thickness of the wall that led them into a scintillation of dust-moted light. From the evidence of racks of saddles and horse trappings hanging in shadow, Tom recognised a tack room. He took a deep breath, glad for healthier, pungent air redolent of leather and linseed oil and saddle soap. Had whoever come this way early Sunday morning felt the same relief? Or had open air brought fear of exposure? And where might he or she have travelled from here? He glanced at Jane, noting her pensive expression, guessing she shared his worried thoughts.

"What say you, Mr. Christmas? Do you think Uncle Oliver's murderer came this way?" Max tilted his pith helmet back on his head.

"I suppose it's possible," Tom replied reluctantly, unwilling to voice in front of the boy the question that rose in his head: Who at Eggescombe Park lived nearest this tunnel exit? Dowager Lady Fairhaven, Max's beloved grandmother, did—with her protégé Roberto Sica, a man with no affection for Oliver fforde-Beckett. The thought was discouraging.

"Perhaps there are clues here, Daddy." Miranda bent to lift the lid of a wooden trunk.

"Perhaps. But we're best leaving the work to the police." Tom hobbled forward. "Shall we . . . ?"

"To your grandmother's?" Jane addressed Max, who was eyeballing the space. "We're expected for tea before very long."

"Oh, look, maybe that's a clue." Max gestured to a corner of the room.

"I think that's a person," Miranda corrected. They all peered through the shadow at a figure reclining on what looked to be a pile of horse blankets assembled on the floor.

"Oh, bother, it's only Anna." Max sounded disappointed.

"Anna?" Jane glanced sharply at Tom.

"Anna . . . Phillips, I think," Max answered unnecessarily. "Nice girl. She cleans for Grandmama."

But Jane had already advanced to the figure who, evidently, was no longer asleep, if indeed she had been. "I'm sorry if we disturbed you."

"We met this morning." Tom stepped forward, noting the girl's hesitation as she rose to greet them. "This is Jane Allan," he added by way of introduction. "And my daughter, Miranda."

But Anna had eyes only for Jane—who, studying her with frowning intensity, said:

"We've met before."

But Miranda interrupted, "Are you hiding?"

The question seemed to startle Anna. "I'm keeping out of the way."

"Why don't you two," Tom interceded, noting Miranda's furrowed brow, "go on to Lady Fairhaven's and help her sort out the tea."

"Isn't it appalling"—Max turned to Miranda—"how adults try to fob us off, as if we were six-year-olds? Really, Mr. Christmas, cousin Jane, if you wish to speak to Anna in private you have only to say so. Miss Christmas and I can entertain ourselves quite adequately."

"You could give the horses their tea," Jane suggested.

"Capital idea. We'll do that. Come along, Miss Christmas. Don't be long," he called back airily. "It's rude to be late, and I am feeling a tad peckish."

"Have one of the horse's apples to tide you over," Jane called after him, turning back to Anna, who regarded her uncertainly. "I'm sorry if we disturbed you. And I'm sorry, too, for your recent loss. Tom said he'd talked with you this morning and told me . . ." She paused. "Anna, look, I'm sorry to be blunt, but of course you knew John, my brother-in-law, in Tullochbrae."

Anna nodded.

"Is he living with you? Now? In Abbotswick?"

"No, I live with John Phillips."

Jane's lips thinned. "Tom tells me after Scotland you moved to Bournemouth and settled your brother into a school there. I'm curious why you would then relocate to a little village in Devon?"

"Village life suits me. And there's a school here similar to the one in Bournemouth."

"Yes, the paper mentioned the one at Buckfastleigh. Tell me"—she frowned as Anna bent to the floor to lift the top horse blanket, a tartan of blue and green—"a little about John Phillips."

"There's not much to tell." Anna began folding the blanket into neat lengths. "A good man."

"But physically. Short? Tall? Dark? Blond?"

"Jane," Tom cautioned, startled at her intrusiveness.

"Tom, I simply don't believe this. It would be strange if John Phillips *wasn't* John Allan. Anna, you must know that my husband and I—John Allan's whole family—are anxious to find him. We thought we'd done so last year in Thornford, but then he slipped from our fingers. Why are you keeping him from us? Why are you protecting him?"

Anna's busy hands stopped. The blanket, forgotten, slipped from its folds, as she passed assessing, cautious eyes from one to the other. Something of the agony of indecision rooted her, Tom thought, as at last she responded to Jane's provocation:

"You never believed John—your John, John Allan—killed William—Boysie—did you?"

"No," Jane replied, her voice touched by surprise. "Not for a minute. Why? Did you?"

"I did. John said he did. The court said he did. And then—after a long time—I didn't believe. I knew he hadn't."

"Why," Jane pressed. "Why did you change your mind? What made you realise John hadn't killed his brother?"

"Because . . ." Anna's face seemed to bleach suddenly with misery. "Because my brother saw the killer."

"What?" The word came from Jane like a cry of despair.

Tears pricked Anna's eyes. "He didn't know what he had seen. And when *I* realised what he had seen, it was too late."

"Too late?"

"Too late to help John."

A groan rose from Jane's throat, as Tom asked, "And what had your brother seen?"

But Anna was concentrated on Jane. "You knew what Will Allan was like."

"Yes, Boysie was . . ." Jane hesitated. ". . . arrogant, nasty, snobbish. I tried in vain to like him. He didn't like me. He thought I was some sort of gold-digging colonial."

"And he was vile to my brother."

"What? Because he was mentally handicapped?"

Anna nodded, wiping at her eyes. "He would tease David for his flapping hands and taunt him for having big ears and the like—and do it in a cunning way when he thought no one was witness. This from an adult! It would put my brother in a terrible, anxious state, and when he was anxious he could explode in a temper—which became worse when he reached puberty. On the afternoon of William's . . . death, he had been getting at my brother. Davey was particularly volatile in the wake of our father's passing and then the guests and excitement around your wedding." She paused. "You knew William had been staying at Aird Cottage at Tullochbrae."

"Yes. Jamie stayed with him the eve of our wedding, while I remained at the castle. But of course, Aird Cottage is where Boysie died."

"Davey, I understood later—much later—had gone to the cottage to . . . protest? I'm not sure what—to William. I'm not sure why with his social anxiety he chose that occasion, of all occasions, but he did. It was not locked, the door was open, and . . . it was he who found your brother-in-law's body."

"David? But—"

"I know, I know," she said softly. "But you also know what John was like."

"Mirror opposite to his eldest brother." Jane looked to Tom.

"He was enormously kind to David," Anna continued, the blanket limp in her hands. "Including him in activities during school breaks and such. John had witnessed the exchange between Davey and William—"

"There was little love lost between the two brothers," Jane murmured, taking the blanket from Anna's hands and setting it on a nearby rack.

"—and followed David to Aird Cottage."

"I'm not sure I understand." Jane looked up sharply.

"John came upon David with the fireplace poker in his hand in one of the bedrooms. David was confused, frightened—"

"You mean . . ."

"John told David to run back to our cottage, making him promise to say nothing. I was in the village shopping and running errands. I wasn't back until late. By then the estate was in pandemonium. In the confusion, I barely noticed that David was even more anxious than usual. But then it was not always easy to understand his thoughts."

"John took the blame for his brother's death," Jane intoned, adding with rising indignation, "I'm sorry, Anna, but that is just simply above and beyond—"

"I know."

"But surely John knew that David, as an adolescent, would be treated less harshly by the court."

"But he would be completely separated from me. He wouldn't thrive."

"But he really made this terrible sacrifice for you, didn't he?" Tom had been observing her face, which contorted.

"Yes. Though I had no idea at the time." She paused, lifting another blanket from the pile and folding it. "We had been lovers that summer, briefly—secretly, but when he declared he had murdered his brother, I thought underneath he must be like William. I simply had to leave Tullochbrae, to go. That's why I left. I couldn't face life there as it had become.

"David was uncommunicative for a long time. His version of moody adolescence, I thought. He kept his promise to John, but then, a few years ago, provoked by I don't know what, he began to talk about that day at Tullochbrae. Strangers would find my brother a little difficult to communicate with, but I can—could—usually understand him, and after a while it dawned on me that he had been at Aird Cottage that afternoon, and had seen someone. I thought at first he meant he had seen John, and that that explained some of his mood right after William's death.

"But it wasn't John he'd witnessed. It was a ginger-haired man. A ginge, he insisted. But of course, as you both know, John isn't ginger-haired."

"No other details?" Jane's voice was urgent.

"None helpful. People with David's disability aren't at their best in recognising faces, although . . ." She took the folded blanket from Jane. "All I could gather was that David glimpsed this ginger-haired man slipping through the French doors. If you remember Aird Cottage—"

"After John's sentencing, my father-in-law in his grief had it knocked down, but I do remember, yes. The French doors in the bedroom led to a terrace near a stand of pines."

"David didn't follow. I can only imagine his confusion. At some point soon after, he must have picked up the fire poker—"

"Which is when John came into the room," Jane finished the thought.

"But did this ginger-haired man see your brother?" Tom asked.

Anna's lips pinched. "David didn't seem to know, but I was frightened that this man might have, and I thanked my mother's genes that I had obscured our origins and made it difficult for anyone to locate us."

"But most of the change was to your name," Tom pointed out.

"Yes, that's true. But David is so common a name, I thought it would easily escape notice. There might be thousands of Davids and Annas sharing homes in England, fewer Davids and Rhiannons. In addition, David wouldn't have been able to keep to a name change for himself. And I've always been Ree to him. Always was," she amended.

"But once you had an inkling Boysie's killer couldn't be John," Jane began, "surely you—"

"I did," Anna replied, anticipating her. "But I wanted to be sure before going to any authority. And I was frightened for my brother, what any press attention might do, whether the ginger-haired man would be put on alert and . . . I wrote to your mother-in-law, Jane, asking for John's address, that I might write to him, and she very kindly supplied it, without question. By then, he had been transferred from Scotland to an open prison—"

"—near Arundel," Jane murmured.

"—and was only a few months from release. I wrote and arranged to travel to see him at Ford Prison."

"It must have been a very difficult conversation," Tom said.

"It was for me. I was horrified that John had made, as you say, Mr. Christmas, this terrible sacrifice, and that there was nothing I could do that would give him back those lost years. I wondered at first if I should let it be, but he had *not* done it. He had *not* killed his brother. He was innocent! The thought that the world would always think him a murderer was unbearable." She seemed to sort through her memory. "He was changed in many ways—more solemn and serious, taciturn—but I sensed the same integrity and sweeter nature within. He was oddly accepting when I told him what David had told me, stoical—but then we were in the visit room. He had strengthened in his faith, as you know, Mr. Christmas—"

"'Tom,' please, Anna. But I suspect Sebastian—John—welcomed *you*, however unwelcome your news."

Her silence was her assent. "He had written. I never received the letters, of course. To the post office, Ree Corlett no longer existed."

"But I can't believe he was 'accepting' of this, Anna," Jane said. "Surely—"

"No, of course not. We've gone over it and over it ever since."

"*We've? We've!* Then your good man John Phillips *is* John Allan. I'm right! But why this masquerade, Anna? I don't understand."

A shadow flickered along Anna's face. "As I said, John had changed. He wanted to live a very simple and quiet life. If we brought the claim of a mentally handicapped man to the police or courts after all these years, what would it do?"

"It might launch a proper investigation!"

"And launch publicity and attention, and bring no peace, Jane. He couldn't bear a repeat of the circus around his arrest and trial all those years ago. The memory was still raw."

"And," Tom interjected, "I expect he was concerned for your well-being, particularly if this ginger-haired man had seen your brother at Tullochbrae."

Anna nodded. "We decided we would solve this puzzle

ourselves, and only then come forward and clear John's name. A very kind old gentleman who visited John in prison—"

"Colonel Northmore," Tom supplied.

"Yes, he fought with John's grandfather in the war. He made arrangements that John could live and work at Thornford Regis."

"And you moved from Bournemouth," Jane said. "But why—"

"We didn't choose to live together or marry at first because we thought that might create too much notice." Anna anticipated her. "But we wanted to be nearby, so Lady Fairhaven—"

"What! Marve? Do you mean Marve has known all along John's whereabouts?"

"Yes. Her support has been vital."

"But," Jane gasped, "John's mother, Jamie, me . . . we've been *desperate* to find him for the last four years. And we thought we had last year when we were alerted to a murder in Thornford—"

"I'm so sorry, Jane. I can understand this has brought suffering. But John very much wanted a life free of trauma, and so did I. Only if we could identify William's killer was he prepared to communicate again with his family."

"But Marve *is* family!" Jane protested. "Near enough."

"I know it's been difficult for Marguerite. But she has been marvellous to us. She's asked us no questions, made no demands, and kept our secret, as John asked her to do."

"But how—?"

"Marguerite is a trustee of the National Association of Official Prison Visitors for one thing—"

"Of course!"

"—she regularly visits at Dartmoor Prison. And she visited John, when he was at Ford. He asked for her help and she gave it willingly, helping me find a cottage in Abbotswick, arranging work as a daily to Eggescombe and as a server at the Pilgrims Inn—and when John left Thornford last year and joined me, she helped him find gardening work. He's an undergardener here on the estate, part of the time. He's been using my last name."

Tom said: "Surely he's come to Lord and Lady Fairhaven's notice."

"No. They're so rarely here, or at least Lady Fairhaven is. Lord Fairhaven comes more often, but he's paid no notice to me, a daily, and I doubt if he pays much attention to the gardening staff. It's Marguerite and the employees of the Eggescombe Trust who really manage Eggescombe Park. Besides, when Lord and Lady Fairhaven are in residence, John absents himself."

"Good God, right under our very noses!" Jane fumbled in the pocket of her trousers. "I can hardly believe it! But where is he? Where is John? In the village? I have to call Jamie." She pulled out her mobile. "Oh, no, what is it?" Her voice dropped with disappointment as she looked from her phone to Anna's face, now stiff and vaguely furtive.

"He's . . . gone."

"John? Not again. Anna, he can't have!" Jane's body slumped. "Why?" she asked in an anguished voice. "Is it because Jamie and I are here?"

"No," she said, then amended her reply, "I don't know. Yes, probably," she amended again, more firmly this time.

"Perhaps you should explain." Puzzled, Tom watched her

as she loosed the band from her hair, letting it cascade along her shoulders.

Anna paused as if to gather her thoughts. "We have racked our brains for a long time, John and I, about the identity of the ginger, going over the people at Tullochbrae at the time of William's murder. One or two of the staff had red hair, and at your wedding, Jane, a guest or two had red hair, but by the time of your brother-in-law's death, most of the wedding guests had departed. We could think of no one from David's brief description—absolutely no one—with a motive strong enough, or the character brazen enough, to—"

"And your brother could give you no other description?" Jane asked impatiently. "Height, build . . . ?"

"No." Anna shook her head. "Not that he could say.

"David lived in another Steiner community, Highdale, this one near Buckfastleigh—not far from here at all. Both John and I volunteer there. John helps them with the gardening. I often lend secretarial support, which they always seem to run short of—helping with fund-raising and such. David was very happy there. There's a hundred acres of farm and gardens and woodlands on the edge of Dartmoor, and he spent much time working on the upkeep with the other residents. He'd gained enormously in confidence. Although they're supervised as they work, they're not minded as though they're children. Last week—a week ago today—David was working in the lower vegetable garden, then went to walk up Hawkmoor Road to another garden. He would do this every day, at virtually the same time. Routine was very important to him. As you know, he was killed by a car on Hawkmoor Road, very much a speeding car, the police tell me, to have . . ." Anna looked bleak. "So hard to take in what has happened in a week."

Tom flicked a glance at Jane. "Take your time," he said to Anna.

"As you read in the paper, the police have been unable to find the car or the driver. We were allowed to bury David, however. There was a service Friday at St. Bartholomew's near Buckfastleigh. Saturday morning, I went to Highdale to retrieve David's few things, among them a tablet computer we'd given him for Christmas. He was never too interested in computers, but something about the open face and the colour of the tablet attracted him. Some games he liked to play on it, and he would watch videos. He got used to messaging me and John . . . and others, it turned out. His disability impaired his verbal abilities a little, but he could write and read at a reasonable level." She reached down for another blanket. "I happened to glance at some of the messages he had lately sent. Most were to others in the community, to some of the volunteers. A few were to old mates at the Bournemouth community, and a very few to more distant organisations—football clubs and the like. Harmless responses to matches on TV and such. But one that caught my eye was to the Daedalus Group. David's message was to ask that some group I'd never heard of—Spector? Was that it?—be considered for a concert next year at the O2 Arena."

Tom frowned. "This People's Choice concert 'Mad' Morborne, so called, was organising."

"You mean," Jane said, "your brother wrote to Oliver directly."

"He wrote to Lord Morborne's company—I know that. Morborne had been on *BBC Breakfast* last month, talking up this thing, asking viewers to email or text or tweet him—him, personally; some special address had been set up—their favourite musicians."

"But Daedalus must have received thousands and thousands of—"

"I know," Anna cut in. "But I am also certain, absolutely certain, that even though it's really staff who weed through these messages, if they weed through them at all, and it's not some cynical populist exercise, Oliver saw David's message, and read it."

"You mean," Jane said, "Oliver sent a reply."

"No. He would have been careful not to. And anyone seeing the message from David to Morborne—either at Daedalus or on David's tablet—would have thought little of it. Except for John and me."

"Why?" Tom and Jane spoke in one voice.

"Because David, sadly, despite his short-term memory challenges, was, this time, able to remember a face. At the end of his note suggesting Spector he wrote innocently, 'I've seen you before. I used to live in Scotland. In a place called Tulloch-brae. You came to a wedding there.'"

CHAPTER TWENTY

"*B*ut that's impossible!" The horse blanket fell from Jane's hand. "Olly wasn't at our wedding. He was invited, of course. One of the cousins. But he didn't come. He was at a funeral in London."

"What day was the funeral?" Tom asked.

"The day after our wedding, as it happens. Boysie should have gone to London for the funeral, too. The man who died was a friend of his and Olly's from school—Kamran Arouzi—but as Boysie was standing up for Jamie, there was just no time to get down to London." She paused. "Of course, Boysie was killed two days after our wedding. Jamie and I were en route to South America for our honeymoon. I suppose it is possible . . . but—wait!—couldn't your brother have seen Oliver at Tullochbrae at some other wedding?"

"No." Anna was adamant.

"But—"

"Jane, in the years I lived at Tullochbrae, I only recall one other wedding, and that was for one of the ghillies. David was five years younger than me, so he would have been perhaps four at the time. He wouldn't remember it."

"You're right. Jamie's parents were the last Allans to be married on the estate before Jamie and me." Jane bit along her lower lip. "Of course, Oliver would never have entered our heads. I suppose if John hadn't admitted to his brother's death, maybe—*maybe!*—some evidence that Oliver had been in Scotland would have surfaced—a train ticket or a plane ticket, a gap in his diary, a sighting somewhere on one of the roads, on the estate . . . but the police were relieved from doing any investigating once John came forwards.

"But why? We always believed, Jamie and I at least—his mother, too—that John was innocent. Whatever the differences between Boysie and John, we could not bring ourselves to believe it would end so . . ." She flicked a glance at Tom. ". . . so biblically."

"Cain and Abel."

"But a cousin?" Jane frowned. "It seems almost as . . . I can't find the word! Appalling? Shocking? Oliver and Boysie were great friends, Jamie tells me, closer than most brothers." She paused. "I can't imagine what the motive would be? And what could it be that all these years later he would come down to Devon, Anna, with the intent of harming your brother? Does John have any idea?"

Anna's movements had taken her near the window. She turned her head, as if drawn momentarily to the view. The light, northern, cool, and diffused, streamed through the curtain of her fair hair, encircling her head in a soft halo. Tom stared for the time it lasted, captivated by the ethereal, near-angelic effect, before Anna continued past. The sensation he'd had earlier, in Marguerite's garden that morning, possessed him anew. He was certain now, and impatient to ask:

"You were in the Labyrinth early Sunday morning, weren't you?"

Anna, opening her mouth to respond to Jane's question, turned slightly, glanced at him with a little stricken look. A flush mottled her throat and rose to crimson her face. "No."

"I think you were, Anna. Whatever could you have meant this morning when I offered my condolences? You said, 'Rough justice may have already prevailed.'"

"The whole village—the whole country, now—knows Morborne is dead."

"Perhaps it was the way you said it."

"Do you think that I—?"

"I wasn't accusing you."

"I've thought that I would happily have done so, if I could. He was—" The squeal of a door hinge sounding from across the stable yard distracted them.

"Roberto must be back from Totnes," Jane remarked. "That door could use an oiling. Tom, we should get the kids and move on to Marve's soon," she added, glancing at her watch. "Look, I'll have Jamie meet us there. You will come, of course." A look that brooked no rebuttal dissolved into a frown. "You said earlier you had been 'keeping out of the way.' Keeping out of the way of Jamie and me?"

"I knew you were coming to tea at Lady Fairhaven's, and I thought you might recognise me. Without John present, I couldn't—"

"My husband is going to be over the moon to see you, Anna. And then he's going to have his hopes dashed. Do you have no idea where John's gone?"

"No, none. I was going to say, Tom, that Morborne was already dead when I arrived. It was your voice I heard in the Labyrinth. I recognised it when I heard you speaking with Marguerite this morning."

"I had been saying Morning Prayers," Tom responded, troubled at her curt reply to Jane's question. Could she really be so unattuned to her lover's habits? "I thought I glimpsed someone with light-coloured hair in the faint light. What would bring you to the Labyrinth at such an early hour?"

"I followed him. Morborne. I thought he might lead me to John."

"But . . . ?"

"I thought John might be . . . dead."

"But why?" Jane stared at her, aghast.

"And then when I found Morborne dead I thought . . ."

Tom glanced at Jane. He knew exactly what she was thinking, but he no more than she wanted to acknowledge the possibility. "When you and Sebastian—John—read the text on the tablet and realised its terrible implication, what did you decide to do?" he asked instead.

Anna looked away, as if reviewing the scene in her mind's eye. "We didn't speak, really. John seemed to freeze somehow, staring, unmoving. I've never seen him like that. It frightened me terribly. Then, suddenly he got up from the table and walked out. I haven't seen him since.

"I thought perhaps he had gone straight to Eggescombe,

to root out his cousin, to show himself to you, Jane, and his brother, if that's what was necessary. It was late afternoon, and the charity event was ending. I was supposed to be on compassionate leave, but I had asked to take a shift at the Pilgrims Inn. I needed badly to keep myself occupied and the pub was expecting people to stop by on their way back to Thornford. As the evening wore on I grew more anxious. I was expecting the police to arrive at any moment, for my world to cave in again.

"But nothing. Late in the evening, Morborne came into the Pilgrims with some other men, looking hardly bothered. It was sickening to be in his presence, but I felt helpless to do anything, not knowing what had become of John. Time was called at midnight, but Morborne stayed on chatting up the barmaids. I kept my distance. When I finished I waited outside in the road. I had no idea what I was going to say or do. But he came out with Janice Sclanders, one of the staff, and went to her parents' cottage, whistling as though he hadn't a worry in the world.

"I couldn't sleep that night. John didn't return, and I couldn't contact him. He refuses to have a mobile, and it wasn't until well into the morning before I saw that his rucksack and a few other things were missing. I was frightened for what might have happened to him or . . ." Anna's voice dropped. ". . . for what he might be planning to do.

"Finally, at about five, sometime before the sun rose—I must have nodded off for a bit—I heard whistling coming down the lane beside our cottage. I expect I was fuzzy from sleep—I raced into the road in my pajamas and caught his arm. I was insane with worry and grief by that time, accusing him of killing David and demanding to know what he had done with John. He brushed me off as a madwoman, pushing me away, brutally. I cut my hand on the side of our gate. I'm surprised our neighbours weren't awoken. I dashed in, put on a plaster, got into some clothes, and found my torch. I'm not sure what I thought I was going to do. As I say, I was going out of my mind."

"You might have been in danger."

"I didn't think. I didn't care about the hour. I was going to rouse the whole household, if I had to, but . . . When I was past the Gatehouse and onto the grounds, I could see light flashing from the middle of the Labyrinth—a torchlight— and voices—"

"Did you recognise the voices?" Jane's tone was urgent.

"No. Male voices certainly. I moved on a bit, then thought one of them must surely be Morborne's. A certain haughty tone. I'd been listening to him hold court at the Pilgrims for several hours. He had only come this way perhaps ten or fif- teen minutes before me. Who else would be on Eggescombe's grounds at that hour? But the other voice was lower, indis- cernible. In my panic and dread—you must remember how dark it still was—I became certain it was John's. Somehow— in my imaginings—John had accosted his cousin and was . . ." Anna looked away.

"I ran through the maze, ran like a crazed woman. There was no light anymore from the centre, and no voices, which somehow seemed even more frightening. But when I arrived at the centre of the Labyrinth—nothing. The sky was beginning to lighten but I could see no shadow of anyone, no silhouette. I must have stood there some little time, stunned. I thought perhaps my poor brain had imagined the whole episode. Then I heard a thrashing noise of someone or something pushing through the shrubs at the edge of the Labyrinth. I tried to call out, but I think fright seized my throat. I could hear nothing but the faint sound of someone running over grass."

"Which way, which way?" Tom couldn't stop the urgency in his voice. "Did the sound seem to move towards the Hall or towards the village?"

"Towards the village. That calmed me a little. I thought, if it were John, then nothing terrible had happened, and he'd gone back to the village, to home. I turned to leave and my torchlight caught something lying on the grass in front of one of the benches. It was Morborne. The hat, the jacket . . .

"I don't know how long I stared at him. I knew he was dead." Anna stepped first into the yard. "My light caught his staring lifeless eye. Somehow I thought: Someone has killed him, someone with a powerful motive has killed him, and who would that be, other than John, who had every reason in the world to do away with this bastard, but who would be tried and convicted and spend a lifetime—another lifetime—in prison. I could feel myself about to pass out. I sank to my knees and—"

The door hinge across the yard squealed again, louder now, as Tom followed the women from the shadow of the tack room onto the warm cobbles of the stable yard. The horses set up a shuffling in the nearby stalls, as if the metallic rasp pained them. Shielding his eyes against the blaze of sunlight on the brick opposite, he glimpsed Marguerite in an awkward slumping posture—so uncharacteristic—against the door, her back to them as if she were lost in some peculiar meditation. Something, he sensed, was awry, but Max, with Miranda, burst from the shadow of the horse stalls at the moment, forestalling his concern.

"Grandmama," Max sang out.

Marguerite started, seemed to stiffen. She turned as they approached, pushing her hand through her hair and pushing her mouth into a smile that fell far short of her eyes.

"Hello, poppets," she replied with a gaiety that couldn't quite disguise her ragged breathing. "Have you come for your tea?"

"Yes, Grannie," Max enthused, then canted his head. "Are you all right? You look peaky."

"It's nothing. I was having . . . a little spell. The heat, you know."

"It's Mater who has spells," Max responded with some asperity.

"Yes, well . . ." Marguerite's eyes lifted from the children to the adults, and in them Tom could see a disturbance that made him catch his breath. Before he could respond, Marguerite said with a lightness of tone, but with eyes telegraphing urgency, "Jane, Anna, would you take Max and Miranda back to my cottage?"

"Of course," Jane responded quickly.

"You can help Jane and Anna with the tea things," Marguerite said to the children. "It'll be fun."

Both Max and Miranda frowned at her. *They're really too old,* Tom thought, *for this sort of pandering.*

"Why aren't you coming with us?" Max asked in a sulky tone.

"I'm detaining Mr. Christmas for a few moments. You won't mind, Maxie darling. I need him to help me with something."

"What? Can't I help you?"

"You can't. I need someone . . . tall. To reach, you see. Tom is taller than the rest of us."

Marguerite was improvising and not doing it awfully well. As Max opened his mouth for further protest, Jane interjected hastily, "Come on, you two. I'll race you to Marve's."

"One"—Max drew himself up to his full height, gliding off in the direction of the stable's arched entrance—"prefers not to engage in frivolous athletic activity. Come along, Miss Christmas."

"No, *you* come along," Miranda countered.

"Oh! All right. We'll both come along. Apparently we have tea to ready."

Tom sensed Marguerite sagging as they waited for the little party to turn out of the stable block onto the path to the dower house.

"What on earth's happened?" He turned back to her with not a little dread, noting her pallor.

She released a short breath and said, "Roberto's dead."

"Oh, God." Tom felt shock along his spine, and then the urgent, hopeful, hopeless question sprang from his lips. "Are you certain?"

"Yes."

"But . . . how? It seems impossible. He's so . . . fit . . . young."

"I don't know how. But one knows when someone is dead. I'm afraid, Tom, I only saw what I saw for a moment, then dashed out. I suddenly needed sun and air." She passed a hand over her brow. "Unforgivable of me."

"Not at all. We never know how we're going to react in such circumstances." Tom glanced at the heavy door to the studio, closed now against the horror. He had a ghastly presentiment, born of past experience. The winter before, in Thornford Regis, a man older than Roberto, but like him still in the prime of life, had been found unaccountably dead, sending the village into a frenzy of speculation. Men with youth and vigor don't drop dead for no good reason. And there had been no good reason. The cause had not been natural.

"I'm all right now." Marguerite's hand went to the door.

"You're not. You've had a frightful shock. What are you doing? Marguerite, it's a police matter now. Don't go in."

"I must. I can't live with the memory of me running out. I live in the country, close to nature, I see all sorts of unpleasant things—"

"The difference, Lady Fairhaven, is love."

Marguerite glanced at him, her eyes suddenly hardened. "An even better reason, then, for respect. Are you coming with me or not? I'll be wanting your prayers."

The studio interior appeared little different in arrangement than it had been on his visit the morning before, though with floodlights switched off, shape and shadow prevailed. The only light came in shafts from the open door and from a high window over the sink by the far wall—Dowager Lady

Fairhaven's destination as she picked her way past the equipment and tables and around the unfinished statue of Dionysus and Ariadne along the stone floor, which, Tom half noted, following, lacked Sunday's carpet of fine marble dust just as the air lacked that morning's scrim of floating particles. Different, too, was the quiet, now turned ominous. Only their footfalls sounded against the floor—and then, as Tom drew nearer to where Marguerite had stopped, the soft gurgle and splash of running water, as if a merry brook were running by the stables.

"Oh, my," he blurted, his attention drawn swiftly to the crumpled, near-naked figure. Marguerite was correct: One would know instantly Roberto wasn't merely asleep, though sleeping on a cold floor, in this posture, his head half under one of the long tables, was too unlikely to be credited. The artist's eyes were open, staring up, fixed and opaque, yet they more than any other aspect of him caught the little light the room had to offer; they seemed to gleam balefully. Tom bent awkwardly and tentatively felt Roberto's cheek. Cooled, but not so much so. Marguerite struggled to her knees as if she had suddenly felt the weight of her years.

"I don't understand . . ." Her voice came in an agonised whisper.

Nor did he. Tom surveyed the body but, other than the bruising noted on the chest the day before, it offered up no clues as to cause of death—no evident cuts, no new bruising, no red markings such as those on Lord Morborne that had led him to a swift conclusion about cause of death. And then, as his eyes adjusted to the thin light, he saw what hadn't been apparent before: blood, glistening blackly, pooled on the floor, half hidden behind Roberto's ear and a tumble of dark hair. His heart sank at the notion that some foolish misstep brought about this death, a slip, a trip, an awkward twist. He glanced at the tabletop above the dead man's head. The clay models that had been present the day before were tipped over. One had smashed onto the floor. Roberto fell backward? Hit the back of his head? It was possible, but the consequence—death, not injury—seemed outrageous, infuriating.

"Oh, no," Marguerite moaned when Tom gestured to the blood.

But how? he thought, rising. What had Roberto been doing when this happened? Nearby, on the arm of a battered old chair, he could see, untidily piled, the blue shirt and dark trousers Roberto had been wearing when the police had taken him from the dower house, crowned by a pair of black socks and white regulation underpants. It appeared Roberto was readying himself to resume work by returning to his uniform: shoes and chapeau and nothing in between. But his work shoes, the dust-covered trainers, sat by a pair of dress Oxfords tucked beside the old chair. Roberto's feet looked wet; they were bare, as was his head. His headdress, the white rugby shorts of the day before, was worn where rugby shorts ought to be worn, around his midsection.

"Did you know he had returned to Eggescombe?" Tom asked, his mind half occupied with the oddity of Roberto's dress.

"He called from the village, from Abbotswick." Marguerite rose shakily. "He had the police leave him there. He wanted to walk the rest of the way. I expect he couldn't bear their company, though he didn't say so."

"Then what brought you to—?"

"Here, to the stables? He wasn't answering his mobile. And I know he had it with him, because we talked while he was walking through the village," she said. "I . . . I'd forgotten to ask him if he'd like to join us for tea. I wasn't worried he didn't answer," she added, preempting Tom's next question. "Often some machine here is making a terrific racket, so I came over and . . ."

"I'm so sorry, Marguerite. So young, such talent. So much more to come in life."

"His poor father. He's already lost one child."

"Do you have a way of reaching him?"

"I have a number somewhere."

"And have you your mobile? I have mine. We'll need to call the police. Handily," he said, grimacing, "they're not far off."

He stepped nearer to her, and together they looked with sorrow upon the body of Roberto Sica in silence. Tom reached for the words to formulate a prayer, but the sound of moving water intruded on his concentration.

"Roberto couldn't possibly have had one of those decorative indoor water fountains some people find relaxing?"

"I think Roberto would have found such a thing very twee. Why would you ask such a—oh! I see. Yes, there is water running somewhere." She turned towards the sound, seeking the source in the gloom. "I know the drain in the floor by the sink is slow. Roberto mentioned it yesterday."

Tom stepped the few feet towards the sink, an old ceramic contraption with two tubs and a draining board to one side. The bright trickle wasn't of water draining, it was of water flowing, and he was right. Winking in the dim light, it slipped over the edge of the sink and streamed thinly to the sloped floor, where it contributed to a pooling around a small grille.

"A tap's been left running," he said, stepping through the water and leaning towards the sink. As he reached for the tap handle, he was arrested by a partly submerged shape magnified darkly in the rippling water. He hesitated, puzzled, his mind straining to identify the alien thing. And when he did, when his eyes travelled to the pale tether snaking from the sink, across the draining board and up the wall, he leapt away as far as any man with an injured ankle could.

CHAPTER TWENTY-ONE

"Shocking."

"That is not a worthy comment, Sergeant."

"I'm not having a laugh, Vicar. It's shocking that you think this is an accident."

"I merely presented the possibility on the phone with you to spare Lady Fairhaven's feelings. Although," Tom backtracked, "surely the possibility does exist."

"Electrical appliances don't dive into water of their own accord."

"Perhaps it got knocked—"

Detective Sergeant Blessing stopped him with a world-weary grunt. "I can understand your need for wishful thinking, sir. One murder following another in two days. Better an unrelated accident, yes?"

"Better no violent deaths at all, Sergeant."

"Well, you can't turn back time."

"Thank you for that wisdom." Tom looked down the yard, past DI Bliss and the busy scene of crime officers, to Marguerite, her face drawn, her elegant fingers tugging a horse blanket tighter around her shoulders. "It hardly seems possible."

"I thought we'd opted for foul play."

"I meant it hardly seems possible that Mr. Sica could be electrocuted."

"Did you happen to glance at the power outlet?"

"For a split second. I could see the radio didn't have one of our big British plugs."

"That it didn't. It has one of those two-pronged Europlugs. Not fused, like ours. Looks like someone pushed some item into the ground socket—"

"The killer?"

"Unlikely. People come home from the Continent with some appliance or other and can't be bothered to adapt the plug end for our system, so they nobble the ground socket and stuff the two prongs in. Highly dangerous. It's an old radio, Italian name on it. The plug looks a bit newer, though. Likely a rewiring job some time back."

"Someone was taking an awful chance, though, don't you think? Could you be certain tipping the radio into the water would have a deadly effect?"

"It does have an aura of impulse to it, I'll allow, sir."

"And it's not a copycat crime."

Blessing raised an enquiring eyebrow.

"I do glance at the occasional police procedural on television, Sergeant."

Blessing grunted disapprovingly.

Tom revisited the scene in his head. The shock, the jolt of

electricity through Roberto's body, must have thrown him hard against the table, where his head collided with a sharp corner. But the electricity, not the blow, would have killed him.

"Might I ask, Sergeant, why you and the DI decided to . . ." The expression *pick on* was entertained and swiftly discarded. ". . . to *select* Mr. Sica for more . . . intensive questioning?"

Blessing's lips thinned. "I'm not sure that's any of your business, is it, Vicar?"

"I wish it weren't so, Sergeant, but people seem to quickly attach guilt to anyone stuffed into a police car and taken away off to a police station. I've had the sensation myself."

"So I understand."

"Then you know about my late wife?"

Blessing nodded.

"Avon and Somerset CID got the wrong end of the stick then, and you got the wrong end of the stick with Roberto. I'm sorry if I'm being intrusive but wouldn't it be a courtesy to Lady Fairhaven to let her and her family know that Roberto had nothing to do with Lord Morborne's death?"

"Because Mr. Sica is dead does not mean he didn't do it. Strangle Morborne."

"If you thought he did it, you would have arrested him."

"That's as may be, sir."

Tom frowned. "I thought perhaps you were putting too much weight on the coincidence of Roberto Sica's late sister having once been Lord Morborne's lover and the two men being here at Eggescombe at the same time. It *is* only coincidence. Roberto's been living here for some time. Lord Morborne came to Eggescombe for the sole purpose of the Leaping

Lords fund-raiser. Alessandra Sica died six years ago. If Roberto wanted to take some sort of revenge, he would have—"

"Done it years ago?" Blessing shrugged. "Hatreds don't vanish, they only go underground. That's my experience. This coincidence, as you call it, presented an opportunity—isn't that possible? Besides." He rubbed at one of the many tiny eruptions on his face. "We had something more solid."

"Physical evidence?"

Blessing's battered face turned stony.

"Well, whatever it is, it can't have been strong," Tom argued, suspecting a reign of disappointment among the investigators, "or you would have brought a charge against him."

"It was you who happened across Lady Fairhaven, here, in these stables, yes?" Blessing changed the subject.

"Yes, Lady Kirkbride and I, with my daughter and Max. Lady Fairhaven invited us to tea. We found her . . ." Tom hesitated, suddenly taken by a flicker in Blessing's eyes to what was passing through his mind. "It's ridiculous to think—"

"It's not unknown—"

"I know what you're going to say, that it's not unknown for the person claiming to have stumbled across the body to have been the killer. But what on earth would Lady Fairhaven's motive be? I don't know the exact nature of their relationship, but it is at least one of affection—and most likely more. You're grasping at straws, Sergeant. Surely whoever killed Lord Morborne killed Roberto Sica—because, I suspect, Roberto posed some sort of threat."

"Which eliminates almost no one from suspicion, Vicar."

"You can eliminate the dowager countess, Sergeant," Tom

said with rising asperity, "and I'll tell you why, if you'd care to hear it."

"I'm waiting."

"Roberto was somewhat of a naturist."

"You brought that to our attention yourself. The ghost, so called, that your daughter saw."

"He also works largely unclothed. Not in the winter, I shouldn't think. But in the summer, when the sun heats up his studio."

Blessing looked to the sky. "Beginning to cloud over now."

"He does cover up—for guests who intrude into his studio, for children. I said he's *somewhat* of a naturist. He's not an exhibitionist. When Lady Kirkbride and I visited his studio yesterday, he removed a pair of rugby shorts he was wearing on his head—yes, Sergeant, on his head, to protect his hair from marble dust—and stepped into them."

"The same shorts that are on the body now."

"Exactly. It appears he had undressed to begin his work—you can see the pile of clothes on an old chair—and yet he was wearing shorts where shorts ought to be—which isn't on the head. Which suggests to me that someone interrupted him as he was about to resume his work, obliging him to pay at least lip service to modesty."

"Dowager Lady Fairhaven? Why not?"

"Sergeant, would you rush to cover up for your lover?"

Eggescombe Hall

Dear Mum,

You would think that decent, hardworking folk would have something better to do of a Monday afternoon that's not a bank holiday, but it seems there are a lot of layabouts in Abbotswick and beyond. I can see them out my window loitering in the Gatehouse forecourt this very minute expecting I don't know what from I don't know ~~whom who~~ whom. I'm surprised someone from the village hasn't set up an ice-cream stall, and when I said that very thing to the man in the village ~~ship~~ shop earlier this afternoon, his eyes lit up like a bonfire. Still, the weather looks changeable at the moment—the sky to the northeast is getting a bit dark—so anyone selling ices may well get their heads and their goods drenched. Anyway, Mum, the very nice PC who is minding the gate let me slip down to the village, which he isn't supposed to do as Eggescombe is sealed off like a castle in a snow globe, but he said that as I

*reminded him of his old mum (!), he'd let me go down the
shop to fetch some of the papers, which I've been missing.
PC Widger told me to be very ~~discrete~~ discreet not to talk
about the doings up at the Hall, but of course lots of folk in
the shop saw me at church yesterday, and I'd told the vicar
after the service where I was staying, so I couldn't very
well pretend I had just dropped out of the sky! Of course,
they were all terribly eager for news, and I was as discrete
(or is it discreet? Such a nuisance of a word!) as you please,
within reason, but it turns out they knew as much as I did!
More! I couldn't even tell them about Lord Morborne
spending the night with the barmaid, because there it was,
splashed across The Sun—"My Romp with 'Mad'
Morborne." I'm looking at it right this minute. According
to the story, Lord Morborne favoured M&S underpants! I
don't usually buy The Sun, of course, but I thought in this
instance I might give my standards leave to fall a bit. I
must say I was shocked yesterday to learn that a man of his
position would behave so wickedly, especially after
announcing his engagement to a perfectly respectable
woman in London, but he did swank about a bit—I could
see it at the barbecue supper on Saturday—so I suppose it's
not really surprising. Did you get a copy of today's
(Monday) Sun? If you did, I suppose you can see why Lord
M. might have fancied her, men being what they are.
They're never real, I said to a woman next to me in the
shop, as she was practically spilling out of her blouse—the
barmaid in the picture, I mean, not the woman in the
shop. How could a barmaid afford that sort of surgery?
Turns out her parents afforded her the surgery on her 21st*

birthday! Can you imagine, Mum? I said to the woman next to me: the handcart is very much on its way to ~~hell~~ Hades! And she agreed. Anyway, I'm told the barmaid got her termination notice sharpish. (Lord Fairhaven owns the Pilgrims Inn, I learned.) But folk say The Sun paid her £5,000 for the "exclusive" so that should tide the silly cow over. The big news is that one of the people living on the estate was taken to Totnes "to help the police with their enquiries" and you know what that may mean! It's Roberto Sica, a young artist friend of the dowager countess. No one in the shop was sure why, but I daresay one of the reporters around here will have it in the papers tomorrow, if not on telly or on some modern device or other later this afternoon. But, Mum, according to the man in the shop, who learned it from very nice PC Widger, who will probably get in trouble for letting on what he knows, the scene of crime folk found a red thread clinging to the branches of the shrubbery that makes up the Eggescombe Labyrinth. And that thread matches a jacket or a jumper found in Dowager Lady Fairhaven's house! And it belongs to Roberto Sica! 'Arry Adney's thread, a rather ~~distiquis~~ smart older gentleman in the shop said very excitedly, but no one knew what he meant. Some Greek myth apparently, though it sounded to me like the thread belonged to someone in the East End. Anyway, I'm not sure the villagers find the "arrest" very satisfying and maybe the CID didn't either, as Roberto was seen getting out of a police car at the edge of the village. Roberto isn't well known in the village. He keeps himself to himself carving things, folk say. But they are all very fond of Lady

*Fairhaven, as she does much good in the village. I told
them I met the "artist" at the Saturday supper and that he
seemed a sort of brooding type, dark brow and all, and that
there had been a bit of an "atmosphere" between him and
Lord Morborne. Eyes lit up over that, but they were much
more interested when I said that Roberto arrived at the
supper* HOLDING HANDS *with Dowager Lady Fairhaven.
That set tongues to wagging! Well, I said I supposed if
Roberto did strangle Lord Morborne he must have been
seized by a great passion! Like someone in a Georgette
Heyer novel, a lady said, which I thought rather captured
it. Perhaps he had been avenging Lady Fairhaven's
honour. But our very smart older gentleman said the
instance was more like something out of a John Webster
play, but as no one knew who John Webster was (do you,
Mum?) we passed on to other talk. No one wanted to
think that Lady Fairhaven had pitched up with someone
nasty, but no one could think of why anyone else
~~nearabouts~~ hereabouts would wish to harm Lord
Morborne though apparently, according to The Sun, he's
ticked off not a few folk in London and beyond. Of course,
many had seen that foolish video of Lord Fairhaven and
Lord M. bashing at each other in the sky like schoolboys,
but everyone here thinks Lord F. is a decent enough fellow
if a bit ~~supersilli~~ toffee-nosed. If you see Monday's Sun
you'll see the chart on page 8 of the other guests at
Eggescombe Hall this weekend, including Mr. Christmas,
who won't be best pleased when he finds out! I can't
imagine where the writer learned this, as Mr. Christmas
hadn't planned to stay past Saturday and Lady Lucinda*

fforde-Beckett and Dominic f-B. weren't expected at all!
The Sun says Lord M. and Lady L. were rowing over who
had the right to live in Morborne House in Eaton
Square—a house valued at £7 million! Everyone in the
shop thought that might set sister against brother (or half s.
against half b. in this instance), but others thought the one
who really benefits is Dominic f-B., who inherits the title
and everything that goes with it, including Morborne
House and all the art inside, but others thought it was a
bit 13th century to do in your cousin for a castle (of sorts).
Others noted that the victim's other cousin, Lord Kirkbride,
was in attendance, but I told them that Lord and Lady
Kirkbride had had Sunday lunch with us last year and
that they were very very nice and wouldn't harm a flea.
The Sun, you'll see, Mum, didn't ~~bother to~~ mention Ellen
or Mick—or me, for that matter. ~~Perhaps readers find
titled folk more interesting.~~ Just as well, I suppose.
Anyway, this may be all for naught as by the time you read
this, Lord Morborne's murderer may have been rooted out.
I hope so. I did enjoy myself at the village shop—good to be
away from Eggescombe's gloom—though our little
gathering scattered when a hawkish-looking man stepped
in. The Sun writer, someone whispered, and so I came back
to the Gatehouse. My visit with Ellen isn't quite what I
expected, I must say. I suppose we're different people than
we were years ago and all we've really got in common is
some memories of our school and London in another day,
but I think we could have got to know each other better
again if there hadn't been this unhappy incident, which
has turned everything at Eggescombe upside down.

Working in a Big House has been rather jolly and Ellen's been glad of my help which I know because she's said so, but she's come over a bit peculiar since Lord M. died. Actually, both she and Mick have just returned to the Gatehouse now, as I ~~right~~ write, which is a bit of odd timing. I should get on to the dower house anyway. Dowager Lady Fairhaven has invited me to tea! Fancy that! It's a birthday tea for Mr. C. Raised voices, Mum! I can hear Ellen and Mick right up the stairwell, as my door is open. Mum, you won't believe this. Now Roberto

Tom looked towards the dower house, its silhouetted roofline looming blackly against the pearly sky. Someone had left the front door open, he noted, but with no illumination trickling from the hall beyond, the house's entrance looked a dark cavity, a mouth in a frozen scream. No lights warmed the windows, either, despite the peculiar darkening of the late afternoon. Each window appeared as a dead black eye. It struck him that Marguerite's house looked abandoned, and for a moment crossing the gravel forecourt he felt a sickening trickle of fear. He glanced at Jamie, who had moments earlier emerged from a shortcut through the linden trees bordering the north lawn, avid—at first—with curiosity at the new flurry of activity in the park until he learned the reason for it. Now he returned Tom's glance with an anxious frown. Only Marguerite showed no sign of concern.

"Where is everyone, I wonder? Hulloo!" Jamie called as he stepped past the lintel.

When he got no answer he added in a comic voice, as if to cover his own anxiety, "And is there honey still for tea?" He poked his head through the door into the front drawing room. "Is there any tea at all?"

"Perhaps they're in the back garden visiting the chickens." Tom followed behind a silent Marguerite. With Jamie in front, they had unintentionally formed a phalanx around her.

"Then to the back garden we shall go." Jamie stepped down the passage that led to the kitchen.

It was as they approached the door that divided the front rooms from the service rooms that Tom's earlier trickle of fear surged to an adrenaline gush, setting his heart to racing. The hushed house they were passing through in shadow, a sudden skittering noise beyond the door, like that of a small animal disturbed, followed by a faint acrid whiff of sulphur as Jamie pushed through the door: It all came together in an instant and he knew before the room blazed up with light and his heart calmed what was to befall him. He almost bowed his head to the inevitable as Marguerite stepped aside, and the word in a swelling of high voices sounded:

"Surprise!"

"Are you surprised, Daddy?" Miranda asked, her face radiant in candlelight glowing from a large gateau in her small hands.

"I am *thoroughly* surprised!" He looked left and right of Miranda at Anna and Jane, who telegraphed an admixture of emotions: worry, dread, curiosity—and the strain of carrying on a charade of normalcy.

"It's too much, Marguerite. It really is." He turned to the dowager countess, who favoured him with a faltering smile and replied:

"Fun for the kiddiewinks, I think," adding *sotto voce*, "We must carry on."

"Quick, Daddy, make a wish! My arms are getting stretched."

"Give it to me, then. What a splendid birthday cake," he exclaimed striving for a jollity he in no way felt. "Look what's written on it! And what a *frightening* lot of candles!" He placed it on a cake stand on the table next to a small stack of cake plates and paused in contemplation, glancing at the faces of the others in its candle glow as they crowded around. Every year on this day, at this very moment, wishes swarmed his mind but after entertaining the possibilities, he wished as always for Miranda to be forever out of harm's way. He did so again, and never with such urgency.

"Daddy, please!"

The wax from the candles was beginning to sizzle into the cake icing. Quickly, Tom made his wish, then he bent forward into the blaze of heat and sucked in his breath, mindful that a birthday wish only comes true if blown out in a single breath. He exhaled in a noisy blast of air. The candles snuffed out smartly, leaving forty tiny wisps of smoke spiraling towards the ceiling. Everyone clapped and launched into a sweetly inharmonious chorus of "Happy Birthday."

"Daddy, what did you wish for this time?"

"That would be telling." Tom tapped the side of his nose as

Marguerite handed him a cake trowel. "Are you really sure you can bear this?" he murmured.

"A useful distraction, I think," she replied, plucking the spent candles from the cake top.

Tom could see Miranda studying him with frank appraisal. He cast her a wan smile, feeling somehow that his bonhomie was fooling no one, least of all his daughter. Jamie, meanwhile, he could see, was distracted by the presence of a stranger, unintroduced, in the room—Anna Phillips—but directed by Marguerite towards a bottle of champagne cooling in a bucket on the counter.

"Are you sure, Marve?" He heard Jamie echo his own concerns.

"A brandy might be the thing in the circumstances," she responded, "but this will do."

Jamie cast his eyes over the dowager countess's head at Tom, who had let the trowel hover over the cake.

"I say," Max piped up, reading aloud the message piped in white icing on the chocolate shell—HAPPY BIRTHDAY TOM THE GREAT—"how did you get *your* title?"

"I inherited it from my father, Iain the Great."

Maxie peered at him as he pushed the trowel into the moist flesh of the cake. "I very much doubt it."

"Marguerite, this is astonishing. How did you know?"

"I phoned your mothers yesterday when I knew you wouldn't be able to get up to Gravesend."

"And you baked it yourself?" Jamie asked.

"You needn't sound so surprised, Jamie," Marguerite said. "I'm quite capable."

"Would you like a big slice, Max?" Tom asked.

"Apparently"—Marguerite took the filled plate and handed it to Miranda with a ladies-first admonishment to Max—"when Tom was about nine and reading . . ."

"*The Boy's Book of English Kings*," Tom supplied.

". . . he was much taken with Alfred the Great," Marguerite continued. "The only king to be so named."

"Better than being 'Unready,'" Jamie grunted, pushing at the cork. "Like Ethelred."

"Can I be Miranda the Great, do you think?" Miranda asked.

"How about Miranda the Good?" Tom suggested.

"By George, I think I shall call myself Maximilian the Magnificent." Max spread his arms.

"You already have a title, my boy." Jamie grunted again. "Blast this cork!"

"Daddy had a phase where he was the Great Krimboni."

"That was not a phase," Tom said stoutly, placing a slice of gateau on another plate. "That was a job. At any rate, greatness is behind me. I'm now Tom the Terribly Ordinary or Tom the Distinctly Average . . ."

"I think not," Jane countered.

". . . or Tom the Suddenly Middle-Aged."

"Nonsense!" Jamie grunted as the cork flew from the champagne bottle with a bang, and the amber liquid poured over the neck. He raised the bottle and regarded them doubtfully, as he realised how ridiculous his next words might be:

"Well . . . cheers?"

Miranda dropped her plate on the table with an untidy

clatter. "What," she said, crossing her arms over her chest in a way that reminded him of her mother, "is going on?"

Tom had hoped to relay the fact of Roberto's death and shoo the children from the room before revealing the dark cause to Jane and Anna, but no sooner had he spoken than Max and Miranda named it with a shared glance: murder. Uncle Oliver's death had brought only a sniffy curiosity from his nephew, but now Max moved to comfort his grandmother with an embrace. Miranda cast her father a troubled frown: murder for her was never fully an abstraction. When circumstance had forced him to clarify the circumstances of her mother's death, she had absorbed it piecemeal, doubtful, questioning. But she had been only seven, her eighth birthday but days away that dark November. Now at ten, she could evince an awareness of the implications startling in its maturity.

Jane had gasped at the revelation, but it was Anna's restraint and the flash of fear in her eyes that drew Tom's attention.

Did you hear or see anything then? The words were on his lips, but Marguerite broke away, to make the unhappy phone call to Roberto's father.

"Marve, I can hardly express my sorrow," Jane called after her, "but about John—"

"It will have to wait, my dear, I'm sorry." Marguerite pushed through the door to the corridor. "Come along, you two," she added, addressing Miranda and Max. "We'll . . . amuse our-selves in the sitting room. I expect the adults want to have one of those conversations adults like to have."

"John?" Jamie regarded his wife quizzically after the chil-dren had reluctantly trotted after the dowager countess.

"I'm sorry, darling," Jane said, "proper introductions have gone missing. It gives me wifely pleasure to say 'I told you so,' but I told you so—this is Anna Phillips, who you knew as Ree Corlett."

Tom watched husband and wife exchange glances until, reaching for Anna's extended hand and beginning the cus-tomary greeting, the perplexity lifted from Jamie's expression. "Then it *is* you who . . . I'm so sorry about your brother."

"Jamie," Jane interrupted, "let's catch you up."

Jamie's composure drained like air from a punctured tyre as Anna related her story. "But why?" Jamie's voice was an-guished, "why would Olly kill my brother . . . his cousin, his friend? *Why?*"

"Why did Kamran Arouzi take his own life?" Jane glanced at her barely touched cake.

Jamie stared at her. "Do you think there's a connection?"

"I don't know." Jane dropped her plate on the table. "It just came into my head. You said yesterday in the library that of the three great friends at Shrewsbury all were now gone— Olly the last. All of them have died before their time, but what you didn't note—what we haven't taken into account—is that all of them have died in violent circumstances."

"And John? Where is my brother?" Jamie's eyes roved the kitchen as if seeking him in some hiding place. "What *is* he playing at? Ree, you can't possibly believe—"

"No, no! At least . . . not now. But when I saw Morborne's body in the Labyrinth, I couldn't keep my thoughts from John's manner the last time I saw him, the frightening silence, the coldness. As I was telling your wife and Tom, at that moment I could think of no one else who would want more to do away with Morborne. John had sacrificed himself thinking he was protecting David and me. Instead, he shielded the man who killed his brother. And my brother! And I thought—*If he has done this thing, then good! I'll do everything I can to protect him.*"

"You found something on or near Lord Morborne's body, yes?" Tom asked.

Anna flinched, hesitated. "Yes, how did you know?"

Tom flicked a glance at the Allans. "Lord Morborne was strangled, and not with someone's bare hands. He was strangled with some *thing*, but so far whatever it is has eluded the investigators. I think," he continued, "you removed something from the Labyrinth because you thought it might point at John."

Anna seemed to consider her reply. "Taking it was simple impulse. It made no sense being there at all, but . . ." She paused. "You see, my torchlight revealed a tie, of all things—a man's tie. But Morborne wasn't wearing a suit, and I panicked when I recognised the stripe pattern of the tie. It was a Shrewsbury tie."

"But—"

"I know your objection: How would I know one school tie from another? I went to a comprehensive in Deeside. But I kept one memento from that last summer at Tullochbrae, though I hid it away for years—a photograph of John taken in Shrewsbury School Chapel, wearing a tie."

"But John wouldn't have travelled around with his school tie," Jamie pointed out.

"I do know that," Anna responded with unexpected heat, "but you might imagine my state of mind!"

"Of course, I'm sorry."

"If you'll forgive the question," Tom interrupted, "was the tie around Lord Morborne's neck?"

"No," Anna replied. "I'm not sure if I could have brought myself to touch it, if it had been. It was in a little pile a foot or so away."

Jane frowned. "A reasonably intelligent killer would have taken the weapon away with him surely."

"Perhaps not if he were panicked or frenzied in some fashion," Tom countered, turning back to Anna. "You thought you had heard someone push through the bushes . . ."

"Yes."

"And then you heard me. You pushed through, too, and ran . . . towards the house, of course, yes?"

"Yes, I sensed that whoever I heard had gone in the other direction, towards the village, so I went the other way, yes, praying no one could see my head above the ha-ha—"

"And went into the Hall through the servants' entrance," Tom continued.

"How did you know?"

"I followed the path you made in the dew on the grass. Mrs. Gaunt was in the kitchen when I arrived. Was she there when you arrived?"

"I'm not sure. I didn't see her. Did she see me?"

"She says not."

"You know about the tunnel then?" Jane asked.

Anna's lips pinched. "Yes, I can see you know the rest. I've known about the tunnel between the Hall and the stable block for some time. Marguerite showed me, and I sometimes use it if the weather is poor and I'm going from the Hall to the dower house. Sometimes I take it for a lark. As I didn't want to be seen Sunday morning, the tunnel was a natural choice. I thought once I'd landed up at the stable block, I'd take one of the more secluded footpaths that lead back to the village."

"Did you intend to involve Marguerite?"

"No, I didn't. And I'm very sorry I have. Marguerite has had to make some very difficult choices in the last day, which I know is causing her distress."

"I'm not sure I understand," Tom started to say, but Anna, on her own train of thought, continued,

"Marguerite saw me come out of the tack room where the tunnel opening is located. She was coming for her early-morning ride. She could see that I was shattered, so—"

"She took you back to hers," Tom finished.

"For strong sugary tea and a little nourishment," Jane added. "Tom and I visited Marve later yesterday morning. Three people had eaten breakfast, though not together—Marve, Roberto, and you."

"And I expect she drove you back to the village," Tom said.

Anna nodded. "As I say, I was shattered. I lay down in the backseat, then slipped out of Marguerite's car and into our cottage. No one saw me, I don't think."

In the short silence that followed, Tom glanced towards the kitchen window, half noting the grey wash of the sky, his mind reviewing Anna's story. "You took the tie with you, of course."

"Yes, I—"

"And hid it in the tunnel. How do we know? Max and my daughter Miranda found it when they were exploring earlier."

Anna frowned. "I couldn't think what to do with it once I had it in hand. I didn't want it to be found, I didn't want to take it back to the cottage where it might . . . implicate John. Few know about the tunnel, and some of the bricks are loose, so—"

"Curiouser and curiouser," Jamie interrupted, digging into the right pocket of his trousers, "and I mean it. This is the tie the kids found in the tunnel." He pulled out a roll of tightly wound fabric and unfurled it—its satiny sheen caught the light. Anna recoiled. Tom regarded the striped affair with revulsion. As a murder weapon, it was a disturbing choice, at once the most commonplace of haberdashery and the most lethal.

"It very much looked like my tie," Jamie continued, "but I was sure—as I said earlier—that I had glimpsed my tie this morning in our bedroom when I was dressing. How could my tie have gone walkabout in a few hours, especially to such an odd place as the Eggescombe tunnel?

"Well, it isn't odd, but it is curious, because, you see"—he pushed his hand into his left trouser pocket—"my tie was in our bedroom after all, neatly rolled in one of the drawers.

"There are, it appears," he continued, making a swift unfurling movement with his other hand, "two ties! Now, what do you think about that?"

CHAPTER TWENTY-THREE

"Come, look at them in the window." Jamie moved across the kitchen.

The light was pallid, cooler now since they'd left the stables, but sufficient to better illuminate the ties. In Tom's estimation there was little to distinguish one from the other. Each was a blue so dark it might be black in feebler light. Each had narrow diagonal stripes of yellow and burgundy running down to the left. The fabric of each, oddly enough, appeared to have undergone some stress, the cloth, particularly at the thin end, pulled and stretched, though not so much as to suggest the force, Tom thought, that would surely be needed to throttle a man. The only marked difference was that the tie in Jamie's right hand, no surprise, showed traces of dust, evidence of its recent resting place.

"Tunnel tie." Lord Kirkbride wiggled the one in his right hand. "Bedroom tie." He wiggled the left. "The tunnel tie is the . . ." He grimaced. ". . . murder weapon. It must be. Ree—Anna, I mean—found it next to Oliver's body." He nodded to Anna. "But which one is the one Max brought down to the terrace Saturday evening for Tom to do a magic trick? Which one is really mine?"

"The tags are slightly different." Jane turned each tie over. "Same manufacturer, slightly different script in the needlework, I'd say, but—"

"I've never paid any attention to the writing on the tags."

"I thought not. Who would?"

"I'm not sure I could tell you who's made any of my ties. I know *where* I've bought some of them, but that's no help, I don't think. I might have brought either of these ties with me to Eggescombe."

"You'd know where these came from, darling. They're school ties."

"That's true. Mummy would take us to Gorringes to get kitted out, so the tie may have come from there—or it might have come from the shop at the school, but I'm not sure how that might be helpful in identification."

"Forensics might prove useful." Tom continued to study the neckware.

"Cloth has no value for fingerprints," Jane said, "but DNA analysis might be revealing."

"But I know *my* tie—whichever of these is mine—had been touched by many hands. Mine, yours, Jane's—you handed it to me when we were packing last week—Gaunt when he unpacked our clothes, Max when he retrieved the tie, you, Tom, when Max gave you the tie, yes? Dominic when he was being silly and put it around his waist, Oliver himself when . . . well, you know. Perhaps Mrs. Gaunt when she was tidying the next day, and who knows who else? Maxie doesn't seem to remember where he left it. Anyone might have handled it when we were in the drawing room Saturday evening toasting Oliver's engagement. I'm not sure how narrowing this will be for investigators.

"And then there's the other tie. Who knows what information it might yield up? And whose damned tie is it anyway? The only other Old Salopian here at Eggescombe is Oliver. And as he's unlikely to shed any light on this . . ."

"Still, darling, forensics might yield up something."

"Yes, of course. I must hand them over soon. The police'll be displeased I've kept them this long."

Tom passed his eyes from one stripey strip of cloth to the other. A glimpse of his own school tie, still tucked in a drawer at Dosh and Kate's in Gravesend, always brought back to him feelings of nostalgia—because he loved his school days—and relief, because he didn't have to wear the bloody silly thing anymore. (Though priesthood had conferred on him a different sort of neckwear.) Outside the school gates most days, he and his mates would whip their ties off and tie them around their heads. Once you were done with your school years, the only occasion to wear a school tie was at an old boys' event, as Jamie had done at Exeter; otherwise school ties fell by the wayside like comic books and roller skates. And yet, someone at Eggescombe other than Jamie, for some reason, was in possession of a Shrewsbury tie. Tom gave them both a last glance before Jamie rolled them back into his trouser pockets.

"Odd," he said, nostalgia replaced by revulsion, "somehow, it all feels like sleight of hand."

"Did you not see or hear anything?" Tom asked. They had moved into the back garden, Roberto's death fresh in their heads.

Anna hesitated. "No."

"You're certain."

"I'd not been in the tack room long when you and Jane arrived. I knew you were coming to tea, but, as I said earlier, I wanted to stay out of the way. I had no idea you would take the tunnel."

Tom studied her expression. Was she prevaricating? Who at Eggescombe would Anna be most likely to shield from scrutiny? John, of course, her lover. Was she keeping from them his true whereabouts? Had she glimpsed him at the stables? It seemed unlikely, so un-John-like, sneaking about. He gave Anna a small smile to disguise his fervid thinking. It was Hector his mind glanced on next. Hector, whom he had seen dashing across the great hall, then, a little later, arriving out of breath, in the estate office. Granted, he had been in trainers and running kit; it was the queer timing, this run in the noonday sun. If Anna had glimpsed Hector at the stables, would she keep silent? Hector's mother, the dowager countess, was her great protector.

A silence fell, broken only by the rustle of a rising breeze high in the sycamores beyond the courtyard. If anyone remained wedded to the notion that a stranger to Eggescombe had brought mayhem this weekend, that notion had died with Roberto Sica. Tom's mind roved further: Where had Lucinda and Dominic spent the last several hours? By the pool, as they said they were to do? And the staff, Gaunt and his missus? What were their routines and how, on this afternoon, might they have diverged? Even the reclusive Georgina, who seemed to have abandoned her family and guests? Did her migraines preempt any agency? And what of the police? Roberto's death sent them back to square one, he knew that, despite DS Blessing's reticence.

He looked again at Anna. "If I may ask, why did you leave Abbotswick this morning and come here? Marguerite said she hadn't been expecting you."

Anna pushed a loose strand of hair from her face. "I had to get away. A reporter from one of the London papers was being an utter pest. The others either loitered by the Gatehouse or holed up at the Pilgrims, but this one was nearly camped on our cottage doorstep."

"Andrew Macgreevy." Jane's lips twisted.

"That's the name. How did you know?"

"He's sort of my bad penny."

"He did introduce himself. He professed interest in David's death."

"He's always been a dog with a bone."

"You know him well?"

"Well, for one thing, he was an ongoing presence during the brief investigation into Boysie's death and during John's trial in Aberdeen."

"And," Tom added, "he appeared in Thornford last year after an unhappy death in the village."

"*Him!*" Anna snapped. "Then he's the man John thought might expose him in the press, and expose us to the red-haired man—to William's true killer. We lived on tenterhooks for months, but nothing—"

"My wife's doing," Jamie said.

"I know he comes across as the worst sort, but Macgreevy has his moments." Jane worried a fingernail. "He contacted me last year in London, during the incident that Tom mentioned—the one where a young woman was found dead in a taiko drum—saying that he had located John in Thornford. He gave me his word he would not write anything until John had been . . . restored to us, to the family. And then, of course, John vanished. Andrew's kept his word in the meantime, but . . ."

"He must recall a sister and brother at Tullochbrae with a situation similar to yours, Ree," Jamie said. "He's put two and two together."

"Perhaps he can be useful—Andrew, I mean," Jane murmured.

"Darling, have you lost your mind? I want John to come home of his own accord, not be run to ground by the gutter press."

"Yes, but my idea is to deflect Macgreevy's attention—away from John. Not by setting him on some wild goose chase"—Jane addressed Anna—"but towards proof of Oliver's criminal behaviour. The police seem to have had little success in finding your brother's killer, haven't they? And now all their resources have shifted to investigating Oliver's death. If Andrew had an inkling that Oliver was the hit-and-run driver—"

"But oughtn't we rightly to tell the police what Anna has told us?" Tom interrupted.

"The vicar's correct, darling," Jamie said. "It's a police matter."

"No, no! Jane is right," Anna cried. "If we tell the police everything now, they'll suspect John of Morborne's death right away. And maybe Roberto's." Her face pinched. "That he's . . . gone off somewhere only makes him look guilty."

"He's not guilty," Jane declared. "The last time, when Boysie was killed, John gave himself up immediately, and *he was innocent.*" To Tom and Jamie, she added, "Let's give John a little time. He'll come back. Of course he will."

Tom caught a flick of uncertainty in her voice. He glanced at Jamie, whose lips had pinched to a thin line.

"Besides," Jane continued, noting their doubt, "if the police chase after John, the papers will, too. On the other hand, if *Macgreevy* chases after John and *The Sun* prints a story, the police will get the wind up and *they'll* be manhunting John. However, getting Andrew chasing after Oliver as hit-and-run driver will keep him out of our hair, and he may find the proof that the police need." Jane tapped her forehead. "Genius, don't you think?"

Jamie gave her a sidelong glance. "Perhaps. But how might Olly have arranged it?"

"The hit and run? *If* he arranged it," Jane responded. "He might have simply taken the chance when he saw it. Sorry, Anna, if this is disturbing to you."

"But, darling, his hire car, in the Hall's forecourt, is pristine."

"Jamie, he set out from London in his silly Cadillac and it broke down—he said—in Salisbury."

"Which could be true."

"But that doesn't mean the hire car here is the one he hired in Salisbury. Hector! Hector knows something, I'm sure. Remember, Jamie, when we arrived on Thursday, Hector talking in the forecourt with a uniformed policeman—PC Widger? Hector said later it had something to do with Saturday's constituency meeting, but when Bliss and Blessing interviewed us in the great hall yesterday, Hector was strangely forgetful about PC Widger's mission that day, which was examining cars on behalf of the hit-and-run investigation."

"Darling, no. Hector's a busy man. He can't remember everything. You're getting a bit carried away, don't you think?" He glanced at Tom as if seeking moral support.

"Stolen a car?" Tom supplied.

"It would have to be an older model," Jamie said. "Cars are such bloody complicated machines now. Hard to break into."

"This can't be that difficult." Jane continued on her own track. "The investigators just haven't given David's death priority. Oliver had another car—a car in between his Cadillac and the car here at Eggescombe—which he . . . destroyed, or something, to cover up what he had done. He was Oliver Quinton fforde-Beckett—clever, amoral, selfish, destructive Olly—of course he would get away with it! It's all so suspicious. Olly never did lazy days in the countryside. He worked all the time. He rarely participated in the Leaping Lords, did he, Jamie?"

"Well, not this year. He wasn't at a practice this year, I don't think. And he missed the charity event we did last month in Yorkshire. I'm not sure how current his logbook would have been."

"So on this occasion, he leaves his fiancée in London and drives down to Devon days in advance—to do what?"

"Darling, it's too tawdry."

"Jamie, your cousin's done worse, much worse."

"Of course. You're right. Good Lord, Oliver must have been desperate. What on earth drove him to kill Boysie in the first place?"

"I don't mean to interrupt." Marguerite put her head around the door. "But your housekeeper has arrived at last, Tom. I'd invited her to your birthday tea. And she's with Mrs. Gaunt. They're both in a bit of a state, I would say, and asking for you."

Startled, but not concerned, Tom followed Lady Fairhaven back into the dower house through the mudroom. An empty hook claimed his attention. He had earlier asked Miranda to affirm that the ghost she had seen had been wearing white, not red. Now, breathlessly, as they were moving with some urgency, he said:

"I must ask you this, Marguerite, while it's on my mind: The red jacket that was hanging here Sunday morning, when Jane and I visited you—that's the one the police removed earlier today, yes?"

"Yes." Marguerite drew the word out.

"But Roberto wasn't wearing anything red, if he was the 'ghost' my daughter saw on the lawn that night."

Marguerite halted in her stride. A murmur of voices drifted from the corridor. She studied his face a moment. Hers was a study in resolve. "I had to choose, you see," she said finally.

"I don't quite understand."

"Anna wore the jacket, the hoodie, whatever it's called. I lent it to her in the spring on a day that had turned suddenly chilly. She forgot to bring it back and it completely slipped my mind. It's Roberto's. It's an old Arsenal jacket. Roberto is . . . was mad about football, rugby—all that. But he wasn't missing the jacket. On Sunday, when Anna went chasing after Oliver, she put it on against the cool of the morning."

"But, Marguerite, why didn't you tell the police that Anna has been wearing it, not Roberto?"

"I couldn't. I have no idea why the investigators had glommed onto the hoodie, but I couldn't tell them Anna had been wearing it yesterday morning. Any mention of Anna leads quickly to John, don't you think? And Anna has suffered too, too terribly in the last week."

"Would Roberto have known you'd lent the hoodie to Anna?"

"I'm not sure. And, of course, I can't know now."

Tom bit his lip. "You've made a kind of sacrifice, I think."

"I assumed Roberto would bear up. He was a big boy. I know he had every reason to loathe Oliver, but I didn't think—"

"I don't mean sacrificing Roberto. I mean sacrificing something of your own, something more . . . fragile."

"Ah." Marguerite's lips wavered into the shadow of a smile. "I understand. Well, my dear man, I would have been a fool if I imagined it would last forever. And in the end, it didn't. But not in quite the way I imagined."

CHAPTER TWENTY-FOUR

With growing impatience, Tom rubbed his thumb and forefinger over a waxy leaf from the potted orange tree nearest his hand, breathing in the pungent graveyard scent of upturned soil and damp foliage. Lady Fairhaven had suggested the conservatory for privacy, believing perhaps that plants living their faithful silent lives would be somehow restorative, but Tom felt the warm moist air settling along his skin more as a smothering shroud than a warm and welcoming blanket. With the afternoon ceding the sun to gathering cloud, the sky seemed to fall towards the glass panes, amplifying the sensation of confinement. The plants along the periphery fused to form a dense shadowy tangle. He might be in a walled garden at dusk, all colour leached away, but for an oasis of light wrought by a fat bulb below a lazily turning fan high in the glass dome. Under this tiny sun, the nearest leaves and branches, tendrils and petals, emerald bright, pink and orange and red, visibly curled and crept and twisted and surged forth as if in arrested attack. It was among them, in a green nook, on one of two facing white cane chairs, that Tom waited for Ellen Gaunt to speak. Madrun had stepped into the conservatory with them, but Ellen had asked if she might be alone with the vicar. He had accommodated her bowed head and silence for several moments, sensing her summoning the strength for some vital and immanent exchange. Finally, she raised her eyes from her lap where her clasped hands had been pressing against the soft folds of her white blouse, as if she were trying, literally but ineffectively, to hold herself in.

"My Mick did it, Mr. Christmas."

In her eyes, in the glittering black pupils, Tom could see a mixture of horror, entreaty, and disbelief, shocking as much for its intensity as for its actuality. His heart went out to her. There was no need to ask, *Did what?*

"Can you be certain, Mrs. Gaunt?" he asked gently, removing his hand from the orange tree. "Surely your husband had no business at the stables this afternoon."

She stared at him with mute puzzlement.

After a second, the penny dropped. "Oh, Mrs. Gaunt. You don't know, do you?"

"I know there was an accident, Vicar."

"Mr. Sica's death doesn't appear to be an accident."

Ellen's hands flew to her mouth. "No! You can't mean—?"

"I'm afraid so, Mrs. Gaunt. Police believe the electrocution deliberate." He paused as Ellen digested this newest horror. "When you referred to your husband . . . doing it, you meant, of course, Lord Morborne."

"Yes," she replied softly.

"Mrs. Gaunt, look at me. Did your husband *tell* you that he did? Did he say, *I strangled Lord Morborne?*"

She blinked. "No."

"But clearly something has brought you to that conclusion."

"My husband wasn't in our bed when I woke Sunday morning, Mr. Christmas."

"I'm not sure I see the—"

"I always rise first, always. Always have. When I opened my eyes I could see him leaving our bedroom in the Gatehouse, in the T-shirt he wears to bed—not his suit, as he would properly wear, you see."

"Yes, but—"

"And when I opened the door to the Gatehouse to go up to the Hall to start cooking breakfast, there he was! Oh, Mr. Christmas, the look on his face. I can't describe it. And he couldn't speak, couldn't get any words out. He dashed past me, up the stairs. I've never seen him in such a panic. I knew something was horribly wrong, but . . ."

"Duty called?"

She acknowledged the truth with a little nod. "Then, later, you arrived in the staff quarters, Mr. Christmas, and said that Lord Morborne had died, been murdered, I . . ."

"Has Mr. Gaunt a . . . history of violence?"

Ellen seemed to stare through him. "No. No, he doesn't—a mercy given what his father was like. But that look on his face! And then when he did arrive at the Hall to begin work, he asked me . . . *told me* not to say anything. To say, if I was asked, that we'd spent all night in the Gatehouse, as usual, that I'd gone up to the Hall at the usual hour and that he'd followed later, after he'd fetched the newspapers from the village shop as he's done since we've been here—that we honed to our usual routines."

"And he wouldn't say why, I presume."

Ellen shook her head miserably. "I felt so ashamed lying to the police. But as he's my husband—"

"I understand, Mrs. Gaunt. I do. Your loyalty is not misplaced. But wouldn't there be a question of your husband's motive? Would he—would either of you—know Lord Morborne sufficiently well to want to . . . ?" He pinched his lips over the dreaded word.

A shadow seemed to cross Ellen's face. "Not well, no. We were, Mick and I, valet-butler and cook-housekeeper to Lord Morborne's uncle, Lord Anthony fforde-Beckett, Dominic's father. It was our first appointment together. But I'm sure you've been told about the great estrangement between the late Lord Morborne—Frederick, Lord Morborne, that is— and his brother. I believe both Mick and I met Oliver at Lord Anthony's house in Ladbroke Square, perhaps once, but my memory of it isn't strong.

"I was more aware of Lord Morborne when we were in service to the Arouzi family. He'd gone to school with their son, Kamran. They were great friends and he would come around to the Arouzi house in Lowndes Square. Young Mr. Arouzi later took his own life. He was a very troubled lad."

"But more recently you've been in Lord and Lady Fairhaven's employ? Georgina and Oliver are siblings, of course."

"But we rarely saw Lord Morborne. He lived a different sort of life, didn't he. And you know he and Lord Fairhaven cared little for each other."

"Then why, if I may press the point, Mrs. Gaunt, would you think your husband had a particular . . . animus against Lord Morborne?"

Her cheeks flushed suddenly, splotchy in the unflattering light of the overhead lamp, stirred by anger or shame he could not determine. Her eyes glistened with incipient tears, and when she finally spoke, it was with a great weariness.

"You wouldn't know this, or remember: It was in the papers, but it's near thirty years ago now; you would have been a lad—but my sister, my younger sister, was raped—"

"Oh, Mrs. Gaunt . . ."

"—and murdered."

"I'm so terribly sorry." Tom shuddered. "I simply can't imagine the horror of this. You must have been very young yourself."

"I'm ten years older than my sister. She was fourteen when she was killed."

Tom's hand pushed reflexively into the coarse wicker. The girl's tender age made the crime all the more repellent. Miranda would be fourteen in a mere four years, a spell of time so fleeting he couldn't bear thinking about it.

"Her name was Kimberly. Her body was found by hikers in a hollow in a wooded area on The Wrekin. Police thought she had been lying there . . ." Ellen's face hardened as if to suppress corrosive grief. ". . . two or three days. We had been frantic with worry, my gran and I. Our grandmother brought us up, you see. 'Teenagers go missing all the time,' the police told us when we went to make a missing persons report. 'You watch. She'll be along with some lad and a guilty grin before you can say Jack Robinson.' But she wasn't like that—boys, staying out late. She was a good girl."

"I see," Tom said, not quite seeing—despite the story's piteousness—its relevance. "Was—?"

"The rapist was never found, Mr. Christmas." She seemed to anticipate his question.

"But . . . these days . . . DNA analysis . . ." Tom stumbled over the words, recalling his own experience in the wake of his wife's death—the taking of daubs, the swabbing of cheeks.

"Kimberly was killed before such a thing was common."

"But sometimes—"

"Did the police keep something, some bit of clothing tucked in a back room, that might be useful now? I wondered that years after, Mr. Christmas. I don't know. You . . ." She looked at her hands cradled in her lap. "You let yourself forget, don't you. You have to, if you're to go on."

Tom studied her strained features in the cruel light, allowing a new and certain and very ugly and unwanted awareness to seep into his soul. He paused to take a cleansing breath before giving voice to his thoughts: "You're going to tell me that Oliver fforde-Beckett—Lord Morborne—did this terrible thing. He—" The words felt like bile in his mouth. "—raped and murdered your sister."

Her eyes returned to his, her mouth sagging. "My husband is certain."

"Certain. But why—?"

"Because he was there."

"What?" Tom jerked in his chair. "You can't mean he was a participant! Mrs. Gaunt, that is . . ." He groped for an apt word—*shattering, appalling, criminal*—but she interrupted him before any fell from his lips.

"No, no! Not as a . . . as a participant. As a—" She pulled a handkerchief from under her sleeve and dabbed at her eyes. "Oh, Mr. Christmas, God has seen fit to turn my whole world upside down this weekend. I've learned the most horrible things. I'm not sure I can forget or forgive."

"Take your time."

Ellen twisted the handkerchief on her lap. "I met Mick in a graveyard."

"Oh?"

"At All Saints Wellington, near Telford. It was perhaps a year after Kimberly's death. I was working at a country hotel and taking care of my gran, who had taken a turn after Kim's death. I would go as often as I could to bring flowers to her grave. One day, I fell into conversation with a young man, Michael—Mick—who was visiting his mother's grave. She had died in childbirth." Ellen looked away. "Before long, we were married. And we've been happily married, Mr. Christmas . . . until . . ."

"Until?"

"Until Mick insisted we leave the Arouzis' employ last year and join Lord Fairhaven's household. I couldn't understand why he was so insistent. The Arouzis were very good employers. We were well established with them. I was always grateful for their kindnesses. As I said, before the Arouzis we were with Lord Anthony fforde-Beckett, Dominic's father. Mick was very young to be butler-valet. I suppose I was young to be the cook-housekeeper, but it was a household in a wretched state. Lord Anthony couldn't keep staff, and we were keen to establish ourselves.

"You may know of the . . . *theft* of Lord Anthony's wife by his brother and the trouble it caused. I'm afraid Lord Anthony behaved very badly as well. He became alcoholic, neglected his son—terrible given that his mother had virtually abandoned him to chase after his uncle—then drowned in that foolish sailing adventure. We stayed on in Ladbroke Square for a time. Dominic was still in his teens. Someone to come home to on school holidays. We had learned earlier we wouldn't be able to have children, so Dominic became . . ." She stopped, lifted an unsteady hand to her forehead. "I'm sorry, my mind has . . ."

"You were talking about how you met your husband," Tom prompted.

"Yes." She paused as if to gather her thoughts. "When I visited my sister's grave in those months after she'd died, I'd often find blooms left, small bouquets, though no name attached. Friends or schoolmates, I thought. Perhaps some lad had . . . admired her or perhaps they came from others in town who felt sorry, as it did get attention and cause strong feeling." Despair etched her features. "Mick left them, Mr. Christmas. He told me yesterday, in the kitchen garden. Kimberly had been . . . his lover. I didn't know. It never crossed my mind."

"How extraordinary. But surely someone else knew? Can you really successfully keep a relationship a secret?"

"Kim was fourteen, Mr. Christmas. Mick was nineteen."

"Oh . . ." Tom groaned, sensing already the unfolding of events. The lovers stood each the other side of that sexual Rubicon: the age of consent.

"My grandmother wouldn't have worn it, if she knew. She was a bit of a Tartar. And Mick's father was worse. He was valet to Lord Rossell, proper as you would expect to His Lordship, but brutal to his son. He would beat Mick."

"I am sorry," Tom said, pausing to reconsider Ellen's earlier testimony. "When you say your husband was *there*—at your sister's death, you mean he was . . . witness in some fashion, but—what?—too frightened, too intimidated to say or do anything?"

"Not witness—"

"I think that would be unforgivable."

"He says he and Kimberly had had a row about something—he can't remember what now. It was autumn, they had been walking on The Wrekin. They went there because it was too easy to be seen in Telford or Shrewsbury or one of the villages. There are lots of secluded places in the woods along The Wrekin. Do you know it?"

"Only in name."

"After the quarrel, Mick stalked off in a sulk, leaving my sister alone—he believed. He realised soon how stupid and immature he was being—darkness was beginning to set in. He had one of Lord Rossell's motors—which he hadn't been authorised to take and only added to his worries—and thought that if he didn't drive her, she had a very long walk off The Wrekin back into town. So he turned back to find her, and saw her aways with two boys, which he says put him off, made him jealous." She shuddered. "If only he had . . ."

"He walked away again."

She nodded. "Then he drove a time before having another pang of conscience. He went back, but he couldn't find her. He called, but nothing."

"No response?"

"The Wrekin seemed deserted. It was a school night, supper hour for many, not warm. Finally, he retraced his route to their 'secret place'—it was sheltered, he wondered if she was hiding there, making him come to her to punish him." She regarded him bleakly. "He found her there."

"Oh, my."

"Then he left her there. I don't know if I can forgive him for that, though I know the Lord says I must."

"I wonder if he can forgive himself, Mrs. Gaunt."

Her face hardened. Tom considered the agonies of being young and in love and in being terrorised by a disapproving parent. And then he had another thought:

"Why," he asked, "does your husband think Lord Morborne—well, the boy who would become the Marquess of Morborne—would be the perpetrator of this appalling crime? Could he identify him?"

Ellen shook her head. "He couldn't. Neither of them. He only glimpsed two young lads in dark clothing—but then the light was fading, wasn't it. He thought one of them might be coloured."

"Coloured? You mean . . . African or Asian?"

"Mick wasn't certain. It was growing dark."

"Then what—"

"It was the whistling, Mr. Christmas. Lord Morborne's queer whistling. Mick heard him on The Wrekin that day. And he never forgot it."

is dead! Mum, I've just spent the last little while at the dower house where Ellen is with Mr. Christmas. When I heard Roberto was dead, I dropped my pen and ran downstairs and I must have shocked Ellen and Mick with my presence. But they shocked me! Mick looked very peculiar indeed and Ellen had gone as white as a sheet! Roberto had somehow got himself electraocuted. An accident, they seemed to think, but it wasn't! Lady Kirkbride told me after Ellen went to talk to Mr. C. that the electriocution was no accident! Which made me wonder about Ellen and Mick. They were in such an awful state here at the Gatehouse—or at least Ellen was. Mick set about making tea, calm as you please! I knew something was terribly wrong—something besides Roberto's death— but Ellen wouldn't say. Finally, I said I was late to Mr. C.'s birthday tea, at which point Ellen took up my earlier suggestion to talk with Mr. C. as he is so good with folk who have troubles. ~~Of course, I'm disappointed they're talking in private.~~ *Of course, they're talking in private, as is proper in these situations, so I can't tell you, Mum, what's happened. I only tarried a moment. The dower house is lovely, more cosy, not so immense as the Hall, and*

I had a bit of the gateau (baked by Lady Fairhaven herself! Fancy!), but everybody's spirits were v. low, as you can imagine (Poor Mr. C.! Not the most cheerful of birthdays!) so I thought I might be of better use here at the Gatehouse ~~getting Mick to tell me~~ seeing to Mick. Oddest thing, Mum! Do you remember our old verger, Sebastian, who went walkabout over a year ago? Well, as I was approaching the Gatehouse, I thought I glimpsed him come out the door to the private apartments and turn into the trees by the road. But as the afternoon had turned a bit grey and I was down the road aways, I couldn't be sure, and of course it seemed so peculiar, even though I know Venice Daintrey insists she once saw him on the moor near here. But anyway, to make sure, I opened the big gate a crack to see if PC Widger was still on duty, forgetting, of course, about reporters and such. Well, Mum, by the time you get this you might see a picture of muggins here poking her head through looking not her best. Once they realised I had nothing I was going to tell the likes of them, they went back to smoking and hanging about uselessly. Anyway, PC Widger was on duty, so I asked him if he had let in anyone of Sebastian's description. No, he said. He sounded a bit offended, so I slipped through the gate to see if all was well, as he had been quite friendly and chatty before. Apparently he'd got something of a wigging from the higher-ups for saying things that have fetched up in the papers. Anyway, on the q.t., he told me what with Roberto passed on unexpectedly, poor man, the police will be taking an interest in Lord Fairhaven. Never, I said, shocked at first, as he is a peer of the realm, but of course, Mum, he and

Lord Morborne had been at each other, hadn't they—up in the sky, no less, so it stands to reason. That's what PC Widger said, as their fight on Saturday has been broadcast everywhere. ~~I wonder if I shall feel safe up at the Hall.~~ We talked on a bit, PC Widger and I. Turns out his mother-in-law is a cousin once removed of Tilly Springett's late husband who used to farm near Thornford, you remember. Anyway, his mother-in-law is a lady golf ball diver (ret'd). She would dive into the water traps at the golf courses all over the West Country and sell the balls she found! So nice to have a chat with someone about something normal! This really has been quite the oddest weekend I've ever spent, I think. Now here I am, back at the Gatehouse, at this lovely little writing desk in my room. When I got back inside there was no one here at all. I can only think Mick's gone back to the Hall, which I shall do too ~~immanen eminen~~ in a minute. At least I can be of use with the meals. I know what tonight's menu is, so I can make a start if Ellen is long with Mr. C. PC Widger has promised to post this for me. Make sure you read them in the right order!

Much love,
Madrun

CHAPTER TWENTY-FIVE

*T*om lifted the map left open on a low table in the Gatehouse sitting room. It was a detailed but—judging by the frayed folds—not a new Ordnance Survey map of Dartmoor, the bottom half expanded to set out the demarcations of the southern fringes of the moor, with web-like clusters of lines for Abbotswick and variegated squares for Eggescombe Park. Someone had spilled tea, recently it appeared—liquid pooled in a saucer by the map; the cup sat apart on a tray in its own ring of wet—leaving a damp golden splash, but marked with a whitish puckered trench as if Gaunt had forcefully traced a path through the paper with his finger along a footpath from Eggescombe up into the moor around Hryre Tor.

Tom lowered the map and looked towards Ellen, who had returned from the Gatehouse kitchen, mobile in hand. They had hurried from the dower house moments before, deflecting curiosity and concern, and now he was regretting letting himself to be drawn into such a charged matter. *You must go to the police with this*—it had been on his lips in the dower house conservatory, but Ellen sussed his reluctance and repelled it. She had sought him out because he was a priest, a counsellor, an intercessor, because the authority of his office would lead her husband down the path of righteousness, to make his confession to the police. Tom understood her suffering. She did not want to be a wife who betrayed her husband, no matter what his crime.

"You must come with me and talk to him." She had leaned towards him, her eyes beseeching. "You must. I can't . . . I can't bear to have my husband snatched away from me in front of His Lordship and pushed into a car."

And now they were in the Gatehouse and there was no Gaunt to be had. Ellen stared at him numbly from across the room; he found himself once again prepared to summon the authorities. The phone in Ellen's hand rang, piercing the tense atmosphere. "His Lordship!" She released a cry of dismay glancing at the screen. She let the instrument exhaust itself, then pressed fluttering fingers along the keys.

"He's called several times in the last hour." Surprise contended with concern on her plump features.

"Is Lord Fairhaven normally so . . . insistent?"

She gave him a sharp glance. "My husband is practised in anticipating every need."

"Surely Lord Fairhaven has your phone number, too?"

"He does." She reached into the pocket of her dark skirt. "But he hasn't called me." She looked from her mobile to Tom. "What can be so urgent?"

They were again jolted by Gaunt's phone ringing.

"Give it to me." Tom reached for the phone, his mind

struggling with a new and frightening possibility. "Hector," he said without preliminaries, steadying his voice for the falsehood to come. "This is Tom Christmas. I'm sorry to say that Gaunt has taken ill quite suddenly. I'm with Mrs. Gaunt at the moment. How may we—"

Hector, whose surprise at Tom's answering seemed to seep through the ether for a few seconds, cut him off with a fit of pique. Where was Gaunt? He was expecting him shortly to prepare preprandial drinks. And did Gaunt have the key to the wine cellar? Or Mrs. Gaunt? He had been looking for his copy of it earlier, intending to distract Dominic with a tour of his grandfather's collection of vintage claret. Most vexing. As Ellen nodded agreement, Tom told him that Mrs. Gaunt would ascertain the location of the wine-cellar key, substitute for Gaunt with the drinks trolley, and follow, in due course, with the serving of supper. Hector rang off abruptly. Tom stared at the mobile. He ought to feel aghast. He would say Lord Fairhaven was pigheaded, if he were pressed on the subject, but this fulmination over domestic minutiae seemed outlandish, a contrivance, almost a ploy.

"Not a single word about Roberto," he murmured as he handed the phone back to Ellen. "Hector must have been told by now."

"I directed the police myself to His Lordship in the estate office."

"Which is how you learned of Mr. Sica's death."

Ellen nodded. "But not of the manner."

It crossed Tom's mind: Was Gaunt protecting Hector? He tilted the map towards Ellen. "Is it possible your husband might go up onto the moor?"

She glanced at the map with mute incomprehension.

"Does he have walking shoes? Or a waterproof?" he added, conscious of the lowering sky in the window behind him.

"Mr. Christmas." Ellen found her voice. "This isn't a holiday for us. We have only our work dress. And . . ."

"And?"

"We've never taken a holiday in . . . wild places. Mick doesn't care for them."

Tom thought he knew why: Dartmoor, Exmoor, Bodmin Moor, Dark Peak—any might remind Mick of The Wrekin and the horror he witnessed that day. But he could see no such realisation dawn in Ellen's eyes. She bent to sweep the cup into its saucer and the tray into her hand, for all this a creature of habit. Running his fingers along the edge of the map, he pondered his next question:

"Mrs. Gaunt, what would you say was the state of your husband's mind when you left him here an hour ago? There had been . . . raised voices . . . ?"

"We didn't often row, Mr. Christmas." Ellen's face looked pinched. "He had put the kettle on for tea, but the water hadn't boiled before I could bear it no more and left for the dower house with Madrun."

Tom wasn't sure this answered his question. "Your husband has certainly seemed the consummate professional, at least to me this weekend—"

"He's never before been derelict in his duties." Ellen moved to a side table to collect another teacup.

"—but these terrible events must be taking a toll, whatever blame might be attached to him. He's told you the darkest secrets of his soul, Mrs. Gaunt. You're ready to believe he killed Lord Morborne. Roberto, too? What is the *it* you could not bear?"

"The weeping, the begging forgiveness, the whole horrid unimaginable story about poor, poor Kim! Everything." She stared at him. The cups rattled on the tray. "I can't *bear* what he's done. I can't bear what he *didn't* do."

"Fail to report—"

"Kim can't be brought back, but her killer could have got what he deserved! Rot in gaol for years and years. All that time living not knowing who had done this terrible thing to my sister and married to a man who did."

We have offended against Thy holy laws. We have left undone those things which we ought to have done. The words of the Morning Prayer flooded his mind.

"Perhaps, Mrs. Gaunt, he can bear it no more himself. What he ought to have done. And what he has done."

Tom turned again to the map. He imagined the man in his black jacket, striped grey trousers, and polished dress shoes trailing through the bracken and gorse, a peculiar figure next to hikers in their khakis and day-trippers in their short trousers. All that would be needed to complete the absurdity, he thought, noting a low, distant rumble of thunder, would be an unfurled umbrella. Glancing towards a half-stuffed umbrella stand in the hall, he gave a thought to a parishioner he had had in Bristol, a woman who under the duress of losing a young child to cancer went missing for several days until she was found by police wandering the Wednesday market at Wells emptied of any memory of how she had pitched up there.

And yet Gaunt had had the presence of mind to consult a map.

Had he bolted instead? But why not take a vehicle? The Gaunts, he knew, drove down to Eggescombe from London in a separate van, laden with provisions and goods for the family's fortnight in the country. The very van was parked in the stable block forecourt. But of course the police and SOCOs had been everywhere at the stables. The Gatehouse gates themselves were closed against traffic. Gaunt was on foot, somewhere. The moor—he glanced again at the OS map—a good bet. With reluctance, he said, "I wonder—again—if we shouldn't alert the police."

"Please, no."

"But Mrs. Gaunt, it was your intent in coming to me that we together should persuade your husband to go to the police, but as he seems to have vanished—"

"Please. Not the police, not yet. I can't bear it."

Tom bit his lip in indecision, looking at the pain in her eyes. Common sense decreed leaving this to the proper authorities, but his heart understood her mortification. How far could Gaunt have possibly got on foot? In under an hour? The only formally dressed man on the moor, he should be quite identifiable and easy to find. His eyes fell to the tray gripped in Ellen's hands, drawn by a glint along its silver surface. He felt a jolt of surprise.

"Why—?" He stopped himself.

"Mr. Christmas?"

"Oh . . . it's nothing." He forced his eyes from the tray. *Why were there two cups of tea? Hadn't Mrs. Gaunt fled the Gatehouse before the kettle had boiled?* Troubled by the implication that someone had joined Gaunt at the Gatehouse after Ellen and Madrun had left, he struggled to paste a reassuring smile on his face. Suddenly, finding Gaunt—discreetly, alerting no one—took on a new urgency.

"I have a suggestion, Mrs. Gaunt. You go to the Hall and carry on as you would—or as best you can. I'll find your husband and sort this out."

But how? He refrained from glancing down at his cast boot, his Welly manqué encumbering his right foot, lest he plant a seed of doubt in Ellen's mind over his ability to carry out this task. Instead, he increased the wattage of his smile, which she returned with a tremulous one. After giving him her mobile number, Ellen gathered up her bag and together they exited the Gatehouse. In the gates' shadow Tom watched her move down the road to the Hall; he pulled his mobile from his pocket and switched it on. No road crossed the moor at this deep south end; only bridleways and footpaths took people through the stark and melancholy landscape.

He had an idea.

"Fancy meeting you here." Lucinda pushed her sunglasses to her brow.

"I might say the same."

Lucinda peered at him, her eyes adjusting to the shadows under the arch of the Gatehouse entrance. She smiled coolly. Tom had watched her approach, some little urgency in her loping walk, aware that she did not see him. She was wearing a simple summer frock of creamy linen, the gathered waist of which emphasised her curves. It seemed an age ago he had gazed at her with longing, had found her conversation amusing and attractive. He felt now detached from this creature who had stirred strong feelings, but not—he had to admit—from the feelings themselves.

"Hector asked if I might fetch Gaunt." Her words echoed against the brick wall. "Trouble rousing him by phone apparently."

"An unnecessary trip, I'm afraid. I spoke with Hector a few moments ago. Gaunt's taken ill." It seemed not such an untruth now. "Did you not pass Mrs. Gaunt on your way?"

"No, I . . . I took a shortcut." She glanced towards the door to the Gatehouse apartments. "Nothing serious, I hope."

"Gaunt? A touch of something—summer flu perhaps."

"How very odd. He seemed well enough when he served us by the pool earlier."

"I expect he thinks it's his duty to carry on regardless. He seems to me rather the compleat servant."

"We call them 'staff' now."

"*We?*"

"Dominic and me. We spent the afternoon by the pool. Didn't we say so at lunch? Well"—she gestured to the dull sky outside the curve of the arch—"we were by the pool until the clouds gathered, English weather being ever fickle." Her eyes went again to the door. "Is there anything I can do, do you think?"

"For Gaunt?" Tom thought the offer faintly farcical. He doubted she ever betrayed much interest before in the well-being of "staff." "Rest is all he needs," he replied, wearying of this small talk. "You must know about Roberto."

"Of course. Awful, isn't it."

"How did you learn?"

"That he had . . . died? Oh? One of the police detectives—the one with the skin problem . . ."

"Blessing."

"—came and told us. When we were about to leave the pool."

"An interview?"

"Well, not awfully official, I don't think. The other one . . ."

"Bliss."

"—wasn't with him. I expect they'll be wanting another of those sort of gang interviews later." She grimaced. "I suppose Roberto's dying has rather taken the wind out of their investigative sails. What a terrible coincidence."

"Are you suggesting Roberto's death was accidental?"

"Wasn't it?"

"I doubt it very much."

"Oh . . . I see." Lucinda pushed at her sunglasses, which were slipping down her brow. "Then who do you think killed him?"

"The same person who killed Oliver, I should imagine."

"Oh, surely not. Such different . . . methods—if that's the word. Means? Roberto was electrocuted, I gather. 'Countess's Toyboy Death Shock.'"

Tom ignored the quip. "Did the DS tell you he had died that way?"

"Of course. Who else?"

Tom looked past the arch to the road with impatience. *Where are Jane and Jamie?* He strained to hear their approach. "Hector is aware of Roberto's death, yes?"

"I assume so."

"But you just came from him."

"Hector's in one of his moods. The atmosphere is a bit strained. I was happy to get away." She canted her head. "Why do you ask?"

"I thought he might come to the dower house to offer some sympathy to his mother."

"Is that where you've been hiding all afternoon? Not from me, I hope."

"Marguerite invited my daughter and me to tea."

"I see." Her mouth formed a moue. "I've told you why I'm here. You didn't say why you were here, at the Gatehouse. Are you a doctor as well as a priest?"

"Mrs. Gaunt asked me to see her husband."

"As bad as that?" She laughed. "Were you giving last rites?"

"Priests do perform other services." He immediately regretted his words, for Lucinda's laughter died suddenly. She looked at him sharply and asked:

"What other services?"

"I couldn't say in this instance. Gaunt had . . . fallen asleep."

Lucinda's brow knitted, sending the sunglasses cascading to her nose. She removed them. "I don't under—"

"Really, Lucinda, all Mrs. Gaunt wanted was for someone to walk her back to the Gatehouse. Too proud to express her fear, you understand. There *is* a murderer at large."

"And yet Mrs. Gaunt has been allowed to walk back to the Hall all on her own. Curious."

"She felt more confident." *I don't think I'll ever get the hang of lying.*

"Would you care to accompany me back to the Hall, Vicar?" Lucinda spun the sunglasses between her fingers.

"I'm waiting for Jane and Jamie. And here they are." The

sound of hooves heralded the sight of a man and woman each on a grey gelding, the former leading a third, a chestnut mare, by its reins.

"Are you going riding?" Lucy asked as they walked into the pale light beyond the arch. She glanced at his cast boot, then smiled. "May I come, too?"

"No," Jane replied, now within earshot.

"How unkind."

"I don't mean to be, Lucy. All we're doing is having a brief trot around the estate—"

"Looking for villains? It's going to rain, you know."

Jane flicked a helpless glance at Tom as she handed him down a pair of riding boots. "For some . . . diversion. It's been a very tense afternoon. I'm sure you've heard."

"Leaving women and children at home without menfolk?"

"I don't know what you mean."

"Tom suggested to me a moment ago that there's a murderer at large."

"We can run you back to the Hall, then." Jamie patted his horse's neck.

"Oh, don't be silly." Lucinda waved a dismissive hand. "I'll be fine. I'll take the road. I doubt some murderer is going to leap out at me from a hedge. But thank you, darling Jamie. Nice to know that chivalry isn't completely dead."

Lord Kirkbride had finessed the horse acquisition with, Tom presumed, aristocratic assurance. Only Roberto's studio—not the entire stable block—had been cordoned off by police tape, and the lone PC left to guard had seemed to buy the argument. On the phone Lady Fairhaven had cautioned him—and she was right, of course—that it was not wise to ride a horse even two days after spraining an ankle. But she needed little convincing of the urgency of the task he outlined or the practicality of the transport: By horse, they could roam quickly, efficiently, and unobtrusively over the rough open terrain of the moor in ways they couldn't on foot or by car. The boots, though: Without gripping heels, his orthopedic cast boot wouldn't do in a stirrup. He had winced pushing his foot gingerly into the beautiful leather boots. And he winced now, swaying in sync with the jogging animal beneath him, his right heel pressing into the thin metal stirrup.

Jane flicked him a concerned glance. The three of them were riding under a dark leafy canopy of sycamore trees. "You're sure you're not in pain? You've barely rested that foot since you've been here. We could find Gaunt ourselves—Jamie and I."

Tom chose his words carefully. "I'm not certain of Gaunt's state of mind, and I feel duty-bound to Mrs. Gaunt. She's in much distress. My housekeeper has apparently made claims for my powers of . . . mediation or persuasion."

Jane frowned. She leaned slightly towards him, as if to ensure she would be heard above the clattering of hooves. "You're not suggesting Gaunt's suicidal?"

"I'm afraid it has crossed my mind." Tom loosened the reins a little—it had been years since he had been on a horse. "But I can't quite . . . believe he would—"

"But why, Tom?" Jamie spoke. "His going walkabout has to

be about something more than being upset at the awful events of this weekend."

Tom considered the question as he found his body falling into the rhythm of the horse's stride. "I'm afraid I wasn't entirely candid with Marguerite when I asked for her help, and you'll understand why in a moment. Mrs. Gaunt begged me to be discreet, but I can't, if I'm going to have your help."

He glanced towards a pinhole of open sky at the end of the green corridor, dreading giving the words voice: "Mrs. Gaunt believes her husband killed Oliver."

"What?" Jane jerked at the reins, startling the horse into a sudden lurch. "Good God, why?" she called over her shoulder.

Unhappily, Tom relayed the story of Kimberly Maddick's cruel death on The Wrekin decades earlier, glancing from time to time to see both Jane's and Jamie's faces in profile stiffen, turning now and again to present to him features stamped with incredulity.

"I don't know what to say," Jane intoned when he had finished. "I am absolutely shaken at the depths of Oliver's depravity. I don't want to believe it's true, but if he's capable of murdering Boysie—even if it was in some fit of rage—and running down a mentally challenged boy with a car, then raping a young woman . . . a *girl*, my God, seems not—" She paused and addressed her husband, who had remained silent and stern. "Jamie, this must have taken place during that time when Olly's parents' marriage was in disarray. He would have to have been . . . *fifteen*."

"Are you suggesting age as a mitigating factor?"

"No! Not at all." Jane went quiet a moment. "And you say, Tom, that Gaunt was nineteen at the time."

Tom explained the reasons for Gaunt's unconscionable inaction at the crime scene. "Then about a year later, he met Ellen Maddick, as she was then. They married, then secured a position together in Anthony fforde-Beckett's household.

"The Gaunts, at least according to Ellen—although I'm not sure it's true—didn't meet Oliver properly until they were working for the Arouzis some years later. That's when he heard Oliver's distinctive whistle and, according to Mrs. Gaunt, *knew*. It's why he insisted on leaving the Arouzis' employ when a position at Lord and Lady Fairhaven's became available."

"Waiting for the moment to wreak revenge." Jamie frowned. "It's very melodramatic, Tom."

"Can it be true?" Jane asked. "*Did* Gaunt kill Oliver? And what about Roberto?"

"The motive's powerful in Oliver's case," Tom reflected.

"Roberto's murder doesn't seem to . . . to match somehow," Jamie insisted. "Why would Gaunt—?"

"Perhaps Roberto knew something or saw something important, darling."

"But why didn't he say something to the police, the idiot?"

"Because he may not have been aware of its significance."

"Or he was protecting someone," Tom added. "This is why I couldn't be completely candid with Marguerite."

"What? Do you think Roberto was protecting Marve?" Jane turned widened eyes to him.

"I hadn't thought of that. I meant I wanted to keep faith with Mrs. Gaunt. If Marguerite knew Mrs. Gaunt thought her husband responsible for these awful crimes, she wouldn't have patience for this exercise. And if Gaunt is responsible,

then he is paying a price, now, wandering in the moor. I'm wondering if he hasn't lost his mind, at least temporarily."

"Or," Jamie said, "simply running away."

Or he's running from *someone.* The second teacup in the Gatehouse sitting room flashed in his brain.

"But all this is based on the memory of someone's whistling?" Jane asked.

"I realise it seems—"

"There has to be something else, something more substantial . . . ," Jane interrupted, then paused in thought. "Does Mrs. Gaunt know what her husband used to strangle Oliver—*if* he strangled Oliver."

"I didn't think to ask."

"That would be an uncomfortable question, in any case. But if—"

"You mean," Tom said, picking up on her thought, "if Gaunt admitted to his wife that he had used a school tie—"

"Then Gaunt would be a certain candidate. After all, only we—you and I and Jamie, and Hector and the kids, of course—know about the tie hidden in the tunnel."

"And one other person, of course—Gaunt. If it's Gaunt. He could, I suppose, have pocketed the tie Max left in the drawing room Saturday evening."

"But then"—Jane looked hard at him, as she spurred her horse forward—"why are there *two* identical ties?"

CHAPTER TWENTY-SIX

*T*he somber green tunnel ended at an old wooden wicket gate half hidden in the yew hedge demarcating the northern boundary of Eggescombe Park and the margin of Devon's fertile mosaic of fields. Beyond, bleak Dartmoor curved upward like a ragged, greying brow towards a sky now dark and brooding. Tom shivered, whether from simple, sudden chill or from some unnamed fear he couldn't be certain. The moor without the blessed sun to soften its coarse carpet of bracken and gorse and warm the great outcroppings of cold granite could hold a malevolent power over an imagination—*his* imagination—stoked by a sickening dread at the violent deaths of two men and new fears for the fate of another. He fought to empty his mind from sinister thoughts—the moor as staging place of blazing-eyed, dripping-jawed hounds and wicked ritual murders—but he sensed himself not alone in his disquiet. Jane, beside him, cast him a troubled glance. Jamie was silent and grim. The horses, too, seemed to stir doubtfully, whickering and tossing their heads as if their finer senses detected something noxious in the atmosphere.

"Interesting the gate being unlatched," Jane remarked, twisting back in her saddle to remove a waterproof from its bundle. "Someone's left it open."

"It could be some intruder, though." Jamie pushed his arm into his jacket as Tom released his from the constraining strap by his saddle. "Hector's private security men may not be up to the job. After all, Anna eluded them. And so have we."

But like Jane, Tom took this negligence as a hopeful sign that Gaunt had come this way, even if this formally courteous man's failure to observe country courtesies suggested something more troubling.

Beyond the gate, a narrow grassy track appeared to twist its way up through a thin stand of stunted oak and scrubby fir trees towards a jagged crest. The air was beginning to feel weighted, thick.

"He can't have got far." Jamie gestured northward, giving his horse headway with a light kick. "I know there's a bridleway to the west, but this will take us to a designated footpath. Someone along it must have seen him."

Tugging their reins to hurry their horses, they cantered briskly up the stone-strewn, hummocky slope through the few trees reaching the wooden footpath sign in a few moments. But a glance up and down the path—north towards the higher reaches, south towards the distant verdant coombes—brought home to Tom with renewed force how swiftly with all the hikers and trippers vanished the moor regained its solemn emptiness. There was nothing to do but to press northwards, along the summer-hardened mud, through granite-flecked, desiccated grasses, rising higher into the sky, looking left and right for a solitary, eccentric figure. In such a barren landscape only the tors and beacons, weathered crowns of stone, thrust from the thin soil, should be higher than a man, but in the gloom of this darkling early evening the shadows of men and rock might easily blend into blackness.

The path dipped in a crease in the rise where they startled a bony man of middle years in a thin T-shirt, his arm elbow-deep in a backpack, his face downward in furious concentration. He started at the sight of them, the moaning wind of the moor now a cover to the beat of horses' hooves. He gestured vaguely north when asked if he had passed a man in a business suit. "Strange berk," he snapped, pulling a blazing yellow waterproof from his bundle.

Reassuring as was the man's sighting, no sign of such clothed figure on the footpath presented itself when they crested the next rise. Jamie shouted Gaunt's name, as if the man might burst from behind the single gnarled and nipped oak tree, but each call was sucked into the whipping wind. Flummoxed, disbelieving the possibility that someone could come so far on foot and vanish from the path, they separated, each taking a different direction into the wild heart of the moor. Tom, feeling the horse surge beneath him as he tugged at the reins, rode northeast, towards a castellated mass of stone, thrust like a giant's cloven toes through the moor's earthen coverlet. He bent his head, squinting against the first splatters of rain to see a spectral transformation cast upon the looming tor, Hryre Tor—he knew it from an earlier visit to the moor, the one Gaunt's finger had crossed on the OS map.

He glanced over his shoulder to catch streaks of brightness straggling through fissures in the clouds in the west sweep across the plain, silvering for a moment stone and stunted tree. He fancied he caught a movement, yes! and his heart surged, to be dashed by the dismaying sight of a beefy Dartmoor pony trotting like a thing possessed across the field of his vision—sensing with animal prescience before Tom's poorer powers could the explosion in the heavens, the violent tearing of the sky with the first jagged flash of lightning, the imminent barrage of thunder. Tom looked higher to see illuminated in the few bars of western sun a silver curtain of rain advancing swiftly from the northeast upon the tor and waited, pulling the hood over his head, for the drenching to come. But in that moment, as feeble sun and violent lightning once again conspired to blaze the great crown of stone before him, a narrow chevron of blinding white near the bottom of the tor, unnatural in its symmetry, met his eyes. He knew what it was in an instant and spurred the horse forward into the veil of rain.

"Gaunt!" he shouted, a hopeless noise against the drumming of rain, straining to keep the figure of a man, black against grey, in focus. But a vivid flash of lightning, bursting against the black clouds like a tree aflame, once more favoured him. Gaunt's white shirtfront flared. The man was seated, rigid, on one of the collapsed blocks of stone tumbled at the tor's rock-strewn hem, seemingly oblivious to the drenching pressing his hair to his head and his clothes into soggy tissue.

"Gaunt!" Tom shouted again, squeezing his fingers around the reins to halt his horse. "Gaunt," he called a third time, unnecessarily, but gratefully, flinching with a burst of pain as he removed his right foot from its stirrup. Struggling, he leaned forward, lifted his right leg and swung it over the horse's hindquarters, letting his good foot fall first to the ground, his weaker one nearly collapsing beneath him. Holding on to the reins, he hobbled forwards, the spooked horse straining against him. He said Gaunt's name gently now as he approached, conscious of the peculiarity of the man's posture in the circumstance, like that of a daydreaming parishioner in a pew. Above the pungent aroma of wet earth, he could smell wet wool, as Gaunt's suit, still buttoned like a City banker's, sagged in the growing weight of water. He called his name again, but this time Gaunt met his eyes, telegraphed a sort of mild curiosity, as if Tom were a vaguely familiar figure passed in the street, and rose from his stony seat. Tom lurched painfully to grab the man's arm, but Gaunt turned and stepped up to the next rock.

"Please don't," Tom called after him. He could tether the horse to a stunted tree to go after Gaunt, but his leg wouldn't steady him to climb. Hryre Tor was eminently climbable—he had done so one afternoon in the spring with his St. Nicholas's Men's Group—but now it was awash in rain splashing off the hard surfaces, cascading into the formation's hollows. Helplessly, Tom watched through the scrim of rain as Gaunt tread down paths beaten along the walls of the tor, climbing from rock to rock in his dress Oxfords with an almost robotic confidence, oblivious to the water-slicked surface. With fear for Gaunt's safety mounting, he jerked himself around on his good foot to survey the moor curving below to the valley that held Eggescombe, peering through the greyed air for one of the others, waving his arms in the vain hoping he could be seen as a moving object on an immutable landscape. In the middle distance, he could detect the silhouette of a figure on horseback—whom, he couldn't tell—and he flagged at it madly. In a minute Jamie thundered to a stop, dismounting in a swift, fluid motion. He was soaked below the hem of his waterproof and grim-faced.

"My ankle's buggered." Tom added the reins of Jamie's horse to his own, and gestured to the climbing figure, now moving quickly towards the top. "He's gone insensible," he added as Jamie clambered wordlessly past him onto the first rock and shouted after him, through the roar of the rainfall, "Be careful. He may have no idea where he is or what he's doing."

Tom watched with growing anxiety as Jamie followed a well-worn route among the stones towards the top of the tor, but taking each step with less assurance than the older man. When Jamie nearly slipped executing a turn, Tom pushed his hand into his pocket groping for his mobile. *This is folly.* He should have insisted to Ellen that the police be brought in at once. If only Jamie could catch Gaunt *this minute,* talk to him, and guide him back down the slopes of the tor, but he feared for Gaunt's precarious mental state. The man might lash out, jump down, react in some unpredictable ways, and take Lord Kirkbride with him. So riveted was he by the drama unfolding before his eyes, his ears failed to heed Jane's approach until her horse sounded a thump on the ground behind him and she executed a swift and precise dismount, a blur of fantastic orange rain slicker in the corner of his eyes.

"Oh, God, what are they doing!" Jane's voice penetrated the clatter of rain, now sheeting in fast cold drops, as she darted forward to the base of the tor, craning her neck to the figures silhouetted against the sky in another burst of lightning. With her hood over her head, springing slightly with anxiety, she looked from the back like a maddened bird set for flight. And then she did, flitting quickly onto the first rise in the stony path.

"Jane!" Tom called, straining to tether the whickering horses to the withered tree. "There's nothing you can do!"

"Jane! Stop!" Tom shouted now over the drumbeat of thunder with the full force of his voice, this time scrambling forward, pain darting at his leg. He stepped onto the first stone with his good foot, gingerly pulling the other after him. "Jane, for heaven's sake!" He lunged forward, trying to snatch at any part of her wet, slippery jacket, but failing as she skipped to another stone, then onto the rough, ascending path. He followed, stepping one pace behind, then two, frustrated at her progress, his eyes rising higher to Gaunt, now pushing towards the summit. The tor gleamed darkly with a slick skin of rain; Jamie appeared to slip and lose his footing along its side, sending Tom's heart leaping to his mouth and freezing Jane in a lockstep, long enough for him to lurch to within a hand's grasp, but Jamie recovered his footing swiftly at that moment, setting Jane lunging forwards and upwards again. But Tom in one last painful burst of speed grabbed her along the slick plastic of her arm and held on.

"You can't do anything, Jane!" he shouted while she struggled against him.

"Ridiculous man!" Her dark eyes flashed from under her hood. "I mean my husband, not you."

"He'll be all right," Tom said with an assurance he didn't feel.

"Gaunt or Jamie?"

"Jamie." .

"What can Gaunt possibly think he's going to do when he gets up there?"

"I don't think Gaunt really knows what he's doing."

Lightning again flared the sky. Their eyes flew to Hryre Tor's broad crown where the two figures were now illuminated like combatants on some dark battlement, Gaunt motionless, seemingly vigilant, gazing over the expanse of the moor, as if on watch for advancing troops, Jamie caught in an urgent forwards motion as if carrying to him the message that spelled their doom, before they disappeared into shadow and thunder sounded another bullet crack.

And then, as the sky blazed with another violent flash, they saw outlined the two men—Jamie and Gaunt—locked in a peculiar embrace, the taller, leaner man—Jamie—gripping the shoulders of the shorter, stockier man, pulling him, stumbling backwards into his chest. It was all too horrifyingly evident: Gaunt, whether by chance or by choice, had moved to step off the tor, to plummet most certainly to his death, dashed against the tor's unforgiving surface to the scattered rocks below. Jamie alone had saved him. Tom closed his eyes against the drilling rain and sent up a silent prayer of thanksgiving. *Thank God,* he heard Jane murmur, feeling her relax against his side.

In a moment, against the brilliance of a further burst of lightning, the two men were illuminated retracing their movements down the winding tracks worn into the tor's collapsed stones, Jamie half a step behind the other man, arms in a football stance to catch Gaunt should he lose his footing. Gaunt moved with a strange giddy pliancy, yet with the same assurance of his ascent, as if he were untroubled by the rain greasing the granite surface and pooling in the path. Jamie moved with greater caution. Jane stepped up along the path worn along a hollow of the tor, a gesture of impatience and helplessness. Tom remained behind, martyred to his bloody ankle, keeping his eyes peeled on the two figures as they emerged from the shadows of the great stones, twisted around a bend to blend back into the blackness before reemerging, more recognisable now, Gaunt a drowned creature, Jamie his patient minder. His fears tempered by relief at their proximity to safety, Tom turned to retrace his steps. Later, he wasn't certain what his consciousness registered first—the stony stare on the face of a man who had vanished from his life more than a year earlier, or the short sharp cry of terror behind him—but when he jerked his head to see, what tore past his appalled eyes was a shape, dark and scrabbling, in sharp descent, glancing against a stone outcropping and hitting the saturated, sloppy earth with a sickening thud.

CHAPTER TWENTY-SEVEN

*G*aunt's face was ghastly pale under a fringe of black hair, but he was breathing, the passage of air rasping, audible even against the drumming of the still-falling rain. A low moan emerged from his throat, and Tom noted as he placed his rolled-up waterproof under Gaunt's head the heavy lids of his eyes flutter weakly, a welcome and merciful sign of the brain's struggle for consciousness. Tom raised his hand to push back his own dripping hair and stared at his fingers black and wet with blood with a kind of disbelieving horror, a *frisson* of cradling his own murdered and bloodied wife almost four years ago. He must have gone rigid, for Jane laid a hand on his shoulder and murmured something about head wounds often appearing worse than they really were, which stilled his crashing heart as he watched her spread Jamie's waterproof around the fallen man. It was uncertain if luck appeared to have favoured Gaunt. He had fallen more than a storey, and though

Jane could find no further evidence of external bleeding, internal bleeding—along with broken bones—was the greater worry, and time was critical.

Tom's eyes jerked past Jane's shoulder to peer through the curtain of rain to the middle distance, seeking out the figure he'd glimpsed moments before, but forgotten in the horrible immediacy of Gaunt's trauma. Yes, there he was, a way back, hand stroking the still-restive horses, the hood of his waterproof monk's cowl over the familiar face. *Why is he here? Now? And so near to Gaunt?* The conjunction of events didn't bear thinking about. *And why is he tarrying down there?* Tom peeled his eyes back to Jane and Jamie. The pair faced away from the slope down to the horses, concentrated on Gaunt. In the pandemonium, they had been oblivious to anything but the twisted body of the man. Yet Tom couldn't let the figure vanish—again—not with Jane and Jamie so near. Not with the possibility he could shed some light on the tragedies of the weekend. He opened his lips to voice his news, but Gaunt's eyes flickered again, struggled to focus, then closed.

"Gaunt!" Jamie shouted as if to penetrate his consciousness. "Gaunt!"

The man's eyes fluttered open, this time with an uncertain stare; opaque, they held a dawning light of understanding. He moaned deeply, twitched; a yelp of pain followed.

"Help is coming." Jane took Gaunt's hand.

Tom studied the man's face for signs of awareness. "Do you know where you are, Gaunt? Don't speak if it's painful."

"Mr. Christmas?" Gaunt's voice came as a wondering croak, his glittering eyes struggling to take in the figures around him. "Your Ladyship . . . my lord . . . ?" He moved his head but groaned in the attempt. Instead, his eyes moved, roving the sky and its grey massings. Rain continued to fall, but with less intensity, the ominous black clouds massing now towards the west, where chance glimmers of sunlight splashed the horizon.

"The moor . . . ," Gaunt moaned. "I'm in the moor. But how—?"

"Mrs. Gaunt asked me to speak with you." Tom regarded Gaunt with an intensity he hoped telegraphed the information with which Ellen had entrusted him. "Do you remember? Your wife asked you to stay at the Gatehouse until she had fetched me. She's very, very worried about you."

Gaunt stared at him, seemed to absorb his intent, his eyes swinging wildly to the others. With evident effort, he struggled to restore his features to servantly impassivity, but somewhere pain shot along his broken body and shattered the mask.

"What did Mrs. Gaunt say, sir?" he groaned, his eyes sinking back.

"You needn't speak," Tom said, frightened at the extent of Gaunt's injuries, impatient for the arrival of the air ambulance. He flicked a glance to the sky as Jane performed a secondary survey of Gaunt's potential damage. The storm had put them in an invidious position. The cloud ceiling was so low, the theatre of the storm so vast, Devon Air Ambulance at Exeter had passed the task to the police, who were alert to Eggescombe's sudden notoriety. It was a police helicopter they were expecting.

"What did my wife . . . say?" Gaunt repeated with effort, his face suddenly riven with pain as he tried to rise.

"Gaunt." Jane leaned towards him. The wind whipped words from their mouths. "You must keep still. You may have fractured or broken something or . . ."

"But what did my wife say?" Gaunt said a third time, falling back with exhaustion.

Tom glanced at the others, then said, "She fears you have somehow . . . implicated yourself in Lord Morborne's death." Even to his own ears his words sounded unnecessarily genteel. "Mrs. Gaunt told me about her sister and how she died."

"And the police . . . ?" Gaunt's eyes roved from one to the other with new understanding.

"Their interest is inevitable."

"I can't really blame you, Gaunt, for what you did to Oliver." Jamie spoke harshly. "My cousin was a *beast*. But Roberto is quite another . . . Tom? What . . . ?"

Tom had allowed himself to be once again distracted by the figure lower down the slope. This time Jamie followed his glance, his brow furrowing as if deciding: friend or foe? The man by the horses appeared almost a silhouette, a study in hiker's khaki, head hooded, rucksack hoisted on one shoulder, walking stick in one hand. He might be anybody, but his posture, his aspect, his hand movements as he calmed the horses, were utterly recognisable. It flitted through Tom's mind, as he glimpsed Jamie grasp the full meaning of what he was witnessing, that movement, like voice, could be so very distinctive.

"Oh, my!" Jamie's voice filled with a kind of wonder as he got off his knees.

"Darling, what—?"

"It's John! Look! Down by the horses."

Jane's head twisted. Gaunt's hand slipped from hers. A small cry escaped her lips.

John had turned towards one of the horses, his face disappearing into his hood. Then, as if alerted by sudden movement, he glanced up. Jamie didn't run, as Tom half expected, but rather moved swiftly down the puddled incline with a kind of ferocious intent, oblivious to the water splashing around his legs.

"John!" he shouted into the rain and wind.

Would the other man step forward to meet his brother halfway? No. Tom was keenly aware of the stubbornness of the man he'd known for several months in Thornford as Sebastian, who'd served as his verger but slipped away from the village. John held his stance, leaning on his stick like a beardless prophet, and seemed, as Jamie approached, to bend from the waist, almost imperceptibly, with an air of something like supplication, as if conceding he could run no more. From a distance, under the dull skies, Tom could see little of the brothers' reunion. The meeting of James Allan, Viscount Kirkbride, and his younger brother, the Honourable John Sebastian Allan, after many years, appeared a model of restraint.

"Jane, go." Tom could sense her desperate indecision. "We can't do anything now but wait." He acknowledged her regretful glance and admonition to keep the patient conscious and watched her speed down the slope.

"Gaunt." He leaned into the man's ear, thinking talking the best, the only, method. "What do you last recall?"

Gaunt moaned. "Helping my wife in the kitchen after luncheon."

"You don't recall returning to the Gatehouse later with Mrs. Gaunt?"

"No."

"Do you recall having a cup of tea in the Gatehouse this afternoon—with someone other than your wife?"

"No." He groaned.

Tom studied the man's wet, streaked face closely. Did he truly not remember? Or did he choose not to? Had the last three hours vanished from his memory?

"Gaunt. Gaunt!" He raised his voice as Gaunt's eyes rolled into his head. "Your wife told me you believed for years Oliver—Lord Morborne—was responsible for your lover's death, for Kimberly's."

Gaunt's eyes rolled back. He released a long groan. "He would come around to Lowndes Square—"

"Where the Arouzis lived?"

Gaunt tried to nod.

"Don't move your head. You must keep still."

Gaunt groaned again. "From time to time, he would come. That whistling—"

"It is distinctive, but—"

"And . . . they talked . . . young Mr. Arouzi and Lord Morborne—Viscount Aldermyre, then. And Lord Kirk-bride . . . not—"

"Yes, I know, you mean Jamie's older brother, who died."

"Staff . . ." Gaunt released a long agonised moan. ". . . over-hear."

"An air ambulance should be here any minute." Tom scanned the skies. *Where is the bloody thing!*

"Young Mr. Arouzi was there."

"What? At Kimberly's assault?" Tom was taken aback, then remembered: "Mrs. Gaunt says you told her there was another boy, darker-skinned."

"I didn't tell her it was Kamran. He wasn't . . . a part of it, the rape."

"But a bystander? It's too—"

"A boy, bullied by his friend . . . memory of it affected him badly . . . drink, drugs . . . the Arouzis despaired of him . . . suicide. Morborne seemed only to thrive, to go from success to success. You would read about it in the papers . . . intolerable . . . unfair when Kimberly died . . . that way." Gaunt ran his tongue over his lips and said with sudden clarity, "I loathed Morborne. I've wanted him to die." The effort cost him. His groans deepened as he gathered breath. ". . . went into the Labyrinth yesterday morning."

"Your wife said you asked her to lie about—"

". . . bad sleep . . . lightning, thunder woke me . . . I heard whistling outside . . . went to catch him before he returned to the Hall."

"But it was still dark, Gaunt. How—?"

"Torchlight . . . from the Lab . . ."

"Labyrinth. Don't move your head. You saw Lord Morborne?"

Gaunt croaked: "Yes."

"You entered the Labyrinth . . ."

"Yes."

"When you arrived . . ."

"Dead. He was dead."

Extraordinary, Tom thought: Not many minutes after

sighting him, standing, living, at the heart of the Labyrinth, in the time it took Gaunt to round the Labyrinth, Morborne was fallen to the ground, dead? *Is he lying? Or forgetting?* He looked into the strained face. Gaunt's eyes were shut now, whether against pain or memory, it didn't matter. He must stay conscious.

"Gaunt, listen to me. Listen!" He tapped at the man's cheek. "Once, when you were a young man, you left undone something you should have done—Kimberly Maddick's murder, you should have reported it then, yes? You're not that young man anymore. You must have seen someone—some*thing,* heard something in the Labyrinth. It's not like this." He gestured towards the thrumming rain. "Sunday morning was quiet."

"Dead," Gaunt muttered.

A new sound dwarfed the rain's. Tom glanced towards the northern sky to see a helicopter emerging from the clouds above Hryre Tor.

"Why go after Lord Morborne at all yesterday morning?" he asked quickly before machine noise beat all into submission.

Gaunt's eyes opened only a slit, but in them Tom saw a glimmer of exultation. "... had him ... bang to rights ... make him suffer."

"I don't understand."

"Had his deen ..."

"His dean?"

"... nay."

"His—? You mean ... his DNA?"

Gaunt groaned horribly.

"But—" Tom pressed his ear near Gaunt's mouth as the helicopter blades whipped the air. "I don't—"

"Cigar butt . . . other things . . . collecting."

"Yes! From the lawn Saturday night." Tom was shouting now. "I don't understand."

". . . could prove . . ." Gaunt fought for breath ". . . that Morborne had murdered my Kimberly."

"But how? How? You would need . . ."

Gaunt's words were almost lost in the roar. But not quite.

The helicopter lifted slowly, as if burdened by weight, its blades hacking the air, whipping the drenched grasses around them, blasting wet wind into their faces. Tom sheltered his eyes with his hand and watched it ascend into the sky like some sinister black locust, wings thrumming, and bank into the northeast sky curdling above them still, though less violently than before. The aerial drama had passed by, now moving swiftly southwest towards the Channel where lightning now strobed weakly from the blanket of fraying cloud and thunder echoed distantly. The storm was spent. But this brought Tom only faint relief. The emergency workers who had rushed from the helicopter and attended to Gaunt with practised hands could offer no assurance that the man hadn't suffered life-threatening injury. And he remained without assurance that Gaunt was innocent of Oliver's death—and Roberto's. As he waited for the helicopter to touch down, Gaunt had grown incoherent, slipping in and out of consciousness, his voice a whisper against the machine's brutal rattle, the words lost, until finally his eyes glazed and he lost all sensibility.

Cold and wet and weary in mind and spirit, Tom found himself unable to greet John Allan—the man he had known as Sebastian John—with full gladness of heart.

"St. Nicholas remains in want of a verger," he said, feeling his smile thin and affectless.

"Would I pass the criminal records check in this instance, I wonder?" John's tone was light, but his eyes glinted with challenge.

The question was charged, and he understood John's intent: Tom had more or less inherited him as verger when he was appointed to the living of Thornford Regis the spring before, learning only later that an arrangement between a previous incumbent and an elderly but forceful parishioner had eased John into the position without the proper vetting. John was asking now if Tom thought him culpable of a more recent crime that would exclude him from service to the church.

Tom met John's eyes. Gaunt's declaration about Oliver buzzed in his brain: *He was dead.* "I don't know. Where have you been the last two days?"

"With the Benedictines at Hexham Priory."

"Would they be able to vouch for you?"

"Tom?" Jane interposed.

"I'm sorry, but you must see that if Gaunt—who loathed Oliver—is not responsible for these crimes, someone else is. Roberto's another one who loathed Oliver. But *he's* dead.

You're another, surely, Sebastian . . . John? Especially after what you've come to know about your cousin this week, and what he's done."

"Tom, I've been trying—"

"Someone might find it interesting that, well, here you are, on the moor, at the very time as Gaunt. One might think you were shadowing him, as if—"

"I've been at Hexham Priory, truly."

Tom realised he was projecting his feelings of guilt over Gaunt's dangerous condition onto his former verger and struggled with them as he struggled against the damp intractability of his trouser pocket for his mobile. "Mrs. Gaunt needs to know of her husband's condition. And," he added, tapping in the number she had given him, "we can expect, I'm sure, to be met by some very unhappy policemen."

CHAPTER TWENTY-EIGHT

The needles of hot water pricking his skin felt of ecstasy, and for a moment in the shower—only for a moment—Tom's worries and fears vanished. They had ridden back to Eggescombe swiftly, wordlessly, John taking Jane's horse, Jane riding with her husband. As Tom predicted, at the moor gate they had been met by a response car that conducted them not to the stables, as he would have thought, but to the Hall. It felt in an odd way like being marched to the headmaster's office. And indeed, when they stepped through the great oak door into the foyer, it was neither Hector nor Georgina who met them, but a glowering Detective Inspector Bliss, arms folded across his chest like a figure of Doom. He answered their anxious questions in clipped fashion: Yes, Dowager Lady Fairhaven, the children, and a woman from the village—who had no bloody business being on the estate!—had travelled from the dower house to the Hall. Of course, they were bloody safe! Yes, Mrs. Gaunt has been informed of her husband's condition. No, we've had no new word about that condition. Yes, you can put on some dry things—if you must!—but I want you all in the drawing room in short order. And you, Mr. Christmas, I want a word with you.

Bliss's word—words—had not been kind. Tom thought about them now as he turned his face to the showerhead and let the water blast his skin. They were words of blame. Alerted by the police ambulance to the activity on Dartmoor, Bliss had gone to Ellen Gaunt, who crumbled before his onslaught. Bliss learned what Tom had been told, but worse, he was less sanguine than Tom of Gaunt's innocence: He (Bliss) had a solid account of Gaunt witnessed by the stables that very afternoon. If Tom had gone to the police—despite Mrs. Gaunt's protestations— and had not gone haring off into the moors after Mr. Gaunt, their suspect would not be dangerously close to death.

Tom received this dressing down humbly. He had been wrong to take Gaunt's affairs into his own hands. The horrible sequence of events on the moor played through his mind. If he had left it to the proper authorities, Gaunt would have been found wandering in his fugue state, but unharmed other than lashed by wind and rain, suffering from exposure. Silently, as the water belted down, he sent up a prayer for Gaunt's recovery and for God to forgive his own lapse of wisdom.

But was Gaunt Oliver's murderer? He had cause, he had opportunity, and, Tom knew now, from the last agonizing moments below Hryre Tor as the helicopter descended, he had means. Everything pointed to his culpability, reinforced now by Bliss's eyewitness, who had seen Gaunt at the stables this very afternoon. He believed any man could be driven to the most heinous and messy of crimes, even the punctilious Gaunt. But he said he had found Lord Morborne already dead. Truth or lie? From the door of the shower, Tom glanced at the pile of wet, muddy clothes he'd dropped in a heap on the tiles. At home, at the vicarage, Madrun couldn't abide finding soiled clothes strewn in a heap. There was a basket for such things, thank you very much. But what would he do with them here? Stick them into a bin liner and take them to Dosh and Kate's? Have Madrun make use of Eggescombe's laundry? Much, he reckoned, depended on how many more days he and Miranda might remain Eggescombe's unwilling guests.

Odd thing about having a think in the shower. Was it the ozone? Was it the seclusion? The flow of blood to the brain? Because, suddenly, with a tiny fillip of excitement, he saw in his mind's eye the sequence of events as it had occurred in the Labyrinth that early morning—and a certain telling sequence in the aftermath. It felt a little like that moment on a certain Boxing Day, when he was nine: He'd retrieved the Rubik's Cube from the back garden, where Kate had thrown it Christmas Day in a fit of frustration, and solved the puzzle within the hour. Satisfying. And simple, once you'd got the knack. He thought back to bits of conversation the last two days. Lucinda by the pool: *Good old Gaunt.* Hector in the chapel: *The redoubtable Gaunt laundered that robe yesterday.* Ellen Gaunt in the Gatehouse: *My husband is practised in anticipating every need.* And he was, exactingly so.

But on whose behalf had Gaunt been so punctilious?

Tom's hand hovered over taps, preparatory to turning off the water: The evidence could simply be handed over to the police, but would that do the trick?

Likely not. Too many hands had spoiled the cloth.

Trick.

A trick!

Yes, a trick would be the thing to flush the killer from the ring of suspects. He turned off the water and quickly stepped out of the shower. He had to solicit the cooperation of one— no, two—people before they reached the drawing room. Which would be easy. Then he had to get the agreement of two others. This would be rather more difficult.

Tom ran his finger along his clerical collar and surveyed the drawing room. It appeared devoid of life at first glance, until he noted in the mellow evening light passing through the French doors the silhouette of a man, hands behind his back, gazing, apparently, past the terrace towards the line of trees sheltering the rain-dampened detritus of Saturday's fête. Sebastian—would he ever think of him as "John"?—had cut his long flaxen hair from the days, only last year, when he had been verger at St. Nicholas Church in Thornford. Staring at his back in its denim shirt, he recalled the suspicion that had surrounded John after a young woman, the daughter of St. Nicholas's music director, was found murdered. That he had vanished like a thief in the night from the verger's cottage before the murder's resolution had not stood him well. And when Tom thought about him in the aftermath, he made every effort to allay his disappointment at the abandonment and at the nuisance of seeking a replacement, trusting there had been good cause—some peril, some threat. John hinted as much then. Tom knew now that it was so.

He stepped into the room, placing a certain red velvet bag he'd carried with him on a table near the door. With the cast boot missing his weakened foot grazed the Aubusson, loud enough to take John from his reverie.

"No Inspector Bliss?" Tom said lightly as John turned.

"No. He escorted me here, then left rather abruptly."

DI Bliss's irritable bowel flitted through Tom's mind. He said, "He didn't seem surprised to see you earlier."

"He recognised me. We met last year in Thornford, you recall." His blue eyes focused on Tom. He looked as though his thoughts had taken him far away. "Anna's in the library, apparently, with Marguerite, Max, and your daughter. I don't know where the others are."

"At supper, perhaps. Have they been told, I wonder?"

"About me, their cousin, living under their very noses? Yes, according to the Sergeant Blessing who poked his head in."

Tom nodded as he paused to consider the effect on the family. "Look, Sebastian . . . John, I mean . . . I wanted to say I'm sorry for my . . . abruptness earlier on the moor."

"Understandable, Tom. Everyone's on edge."

"I should have better appreciated that this week has been a kind of hell for you. A new hell, perhaps it would be fair to say."

"We've lived for some few years knowing that David wasn't my brother's killer. But we've also lived looking over our shoulders. A red-haired man clocked David that day at Tulloch-brae. We never knew if a moment would come when . . ." He let his hand caress a Chinese vase as he drew nearer to Tom.

"But Oliver as Boysie's murderer never, ever entered our minds. And now he's David's killer, too."

"Are you certain—?"

"Would I have been justified in killing Oliver, do you think, Tom?" John seemed not to hear.

"You know the answer to that."

"But on the moor you thought I might have."

"I did. And, I'm sorry to say, for more than that moment. Anna told us about your mood. She said you frightened her terribly. And then, of course, you vanished. You wouldn't have been justified, but only a pious idiot would see that you weren't horribly provoked." Tom paused over a new thought. "Anna's known where you've been all along, yes?"

"She knows I go to Hexham Priory, of course she does. We live together, but I need solitude and private prayer from time to time. She was protecting me, that's all. And"—his blond eyebrows arched—"in this instance I've not been good in protecting her. I left her in the village with a bloody killer, didn't I?"

"Oliver."

"Pure selfishness on my part. But I was filled with . . . with a sort of loathing and fury I've never known, Tom. Not even after Anna visited me at Ford Prison and I learned I'd gone to prison to protect . . . a stranger, a ginger-haired man. I had to get away from Abbotswick before I lost my mind. It's really only chance that I came upon you and my brother and Jane by Hryre Tor. Father Harrowell, the abbot at Hexham, knows my story. Silence is the rule, as you know, but as abbot he gets some word of the world outside the walls and will share it if he feels it necessary. After radio reports of a second suspicious death at Eggescombe, he came and told me." John looked to a bronze clock on a sideboard as it struck half past the hour. "I was praying for the courage to . . . take on Oliver, which would mean shattering my family—again—but that chance has gone. Perhaps I should be grateful, relieved, that this cup has been taken from me."

"What cup?" Jamie stepped into the room with Jane, who was slicking damp hair back behind her ears. Tom was pleased to see he was wearing a dark lounge suit, the one he'd worn to the Old Salopians do in Exeter.

"We were talking, Tom and I, about restorative justice, I suppose you could say." John frowned at his brother's attire. "At Hexham I had been praying for guidance. We've lived in welcome anonymity for a long time, Anna and I, but if I brought accusations against Oliver, it would change our lives utterly. We'd have to give up any hope of a private life, at least for a time. All the unhappiness of the past would be dredged up. It would appall and shock our family further. You know what Father can be like. And there would be enormous doubt. Because an accusation would be based on what? A text message between a mentally challenged man and a well-known—what was Oliver? an impresario of sorts? A lie about attending a funeral? Flimsy stuff, on the surface of it. Oliver would be a formidable enemy."

"You know how Mummy and Father suffered over Boysie's murder and your confessing to it. In sacrificing yourself, you also sacrificed them—all of us, really, me, Jane—"

"It was my choice at the time, Jamie."

"But your choice also meant Oliver could go on being the bloody murderous bastard that he is! Was, rather."

"Jamie." Jane put her hand on his arm. "Not now. The prodigal's returned."

"Then where's the bloody fatted calf? I could use some supper. And where is everybody? I thought Bliss wanted us here sharpish."

"And what did you decide, John?" Jane ignored her husband.

"To recant my confession of years ago to Boysie's death. To make a charge, and take the consequences."

"Good." Jane put her arm into John's. "And you would have had our full support. You know we never believed you responsible for Boysie's death. It's more than a dozen years ago, but there will be records, witnesses—something that places Oliver at Tullochbrae in the days after our wedding. And David's death: It's fresh. We have a lead. It seems impossible this crime can't soon be traced to Oliver."

"But we'll never see Oliver in the docket." Jamie walked over to the drinks table. "I'm helping myself. Hector won't mind."

"Not seeing Oliver in the docket is what I was saying to Tom."

"You can't leave this undone," Tom said. "Take heart. You have your loving family's support."

"So incredibly good, such a great relief, to have you back." Jane transferred a wide smile from Tom to her brother-in-law. "You're so brown! All that outdoors! Your mother will approve."

"I almost called Mummy to tell her the good news." Jamie brandished a whisky decanter. "Anyone else? But—"

"But I stopped him." Jane interrupted. "I thought—"

"Thank you," John said.

"Was that to a whisky?"

"No, Jamie, to your wife. But I will have a drink. I need to speak to Anna before I—"

"Yes, where is Anna?" Jamie let the whisky splash into the glass. "And, I repeat, where is everybody?"

"But will we ever know *why* Olly did such an unforgivable thing to Boysie?" Jane asked. "That's what's so incomprehensible. Jamie, you've always said they were like brothers when they were at school."

"I think I know." John took the glass from his brother. "It's quite simple. Oliver always had a passion for music, didn't he? Couldn't play a note, I don't think—"

"Not at all," Jamie snorted, pouring another drink. "Tom? Are you sure? Darling? Jane? Drink?"

"I need a clear head," Jane replied, glancing at Tom, who thought to echo her sentiments, but changed his mind: Dutch courage.

John frowned. "Clear head? Why? And Jamie, why are you dressed like that?"

"I've run out of things to wear."

"No you haven't."

"It's my wife. She tells me what to wear."

"If only," Jane remarked.

"Never mind! My wife has an important question, and you seem to have the answer."

"Yes, as I was saying, Olly and music—"

"He thrashed about on a guitar, I recall, that year he was living with us at Bridgemary." Jamie handed Tom his drink. "I always suspected Father of tying the bloody thing to a rock and drowning it in the pond. It seemed to disappear one day.

"I suspect the real attraction of music, at least of that sort, for Oliver was—what would you call it, the scene?—the women, the excitement, the drugs. He was sent down from Oxford for some sort of disgraceful behaviour, and I think he only suffered the military to please Uncle Fred. Once he was discharged, he was off like a rocket into the thick of whatever it was in those days—organising parties at various clubs, sound-system raves in the woods, pilgrimages to dance on the beach in Brighton and in disused film studios in London, and that sort of thing. I remember Father saying to me once that Olly was a gamekeeper who wanted to be a poacher."

"I'm not sure I understand," Tom said, sipping at the amber liquid.

"He meant—and you must understand, Tom, that our father's very much from an older generation—that he thought Olly was sort of a traitor to his class."

"That's a bit strong, Jamie." Jane frowned.

"I don't think so. Not where Oliver was concerned. Father thought Olly should be giving his attention to the Morborne Trust, building it back up, instead of involving himself in clubs and raves. I don't know why Father was so disappointed because . . . John?"

"Yes?"

"Do you recall what Father used to say about the family Aunt Chris married into?"

"Ah, yes."

"'The fforde-Becketts,'" the brothers intoned, "'are a bad lot.'"

"Of course," Jamie continued, "Father would say this at breakfast from behind *The Times,* which had printed something in a diary column that met his disapproval, forgetting that Olly was at the table working his way through his muesli. Mummy would have a fit. But Father was right, in his way, wasn't he? Oliver is a bad lot. Was, rather."

"But Oliver did well enough for himself on his own," Jane pointed out. "Opening Icarus, carving out an impresario role—managing pop groups, arranging concerts—"

"You're not defending him, darling?"

"No, no. I'm only pointing out that he wasn't as profligate as his father and grandfather had been. He had some business sense, I think."

"*I* have no issue with how Olly got his money."

"Then perhaps you should." John raised an eyebrow. "Because I would more than wager that money lies at the heart of Boysie's murder. Do you remember, Jamie, about the time you and Jane were to be married, that Oliver was manoeuvring to buy that old theatre club on Villiers Street and turn it into that enormous nightclub?"

"Icarus. We were talking about it yesterday, oddly enough, Jane and I—Tom was with us. Boysie and Kamran were to be his partners in the venture, weren't they? I know Father didn't approve of it. I'm sure he got Boysie to renege. Boysie came into this money about that time, but you know Father—he wasn't going to have Boysie throw good money away or use the family name to raise capital all for some foolish scheme."

"But Icarus is a great success," Jane demurred. "It's one of the most consistently popular clubs in London. And Oliver was going to expand, with similar clubs on the Continent and the United States."

"But how did Oliver finance Icarus in the beginning? Uncle Fred's hotel scheme on Baissé drained much of what was left liquid in the Morborne Trust, didn't it?" John looked to his brother.

"Yes," Jamie replied. "The Morborne name was manure in capital markets in those days. How would Oliver have financed his share of the scheme, you ask? I expect much depended on the soundness of his two partners. The Arouzis are enormously rich—but quite conservative socially. I can't imagine Kamran's father wearing the notion of his son owning a nightclub, but it didn't matter in the end anyway, did it? Kamran took his own life, and that killed that goose and his golden egg."

"So where did Olly turn next, Jamie?"

"Boysie, I should imagine."

"I've had time to think about this at Hexham Priory. I'm sure you may be right, Jamie. Either Father got Boysie to re-nege on the scheme or Boysie had already forwarded moneys that he wished returned or Oliver wanted Boysie to loan him more money—or some financial doodah that made Oliver desperate. Perhaps Oliver owed money to criminals."

"But he wouldn't have got it from Boysie, would he? Father would have noticed any funny business in Boysie's estate after he died." Jamie paused to take a sip of his drink. "How, then, did Olly get Icarus off the ground?"

Tom held up a hand, as if he had been called upon in school. "I think I know."

Both brothers looked at him. "Really?" Jamie said.

"Dominic accused Oliver of selling works from the collec-tion at Morborne House. I understand that their great-great-grandfather was an early collector of Impressionist paintings."

Jamie frowned. "But surely word would get about. Those paintings are treasures."

"Apparently, under the guise of cleaning and restoration and new framing, Oliver had the paintings sent out and copied, returning the copies to Morborne House and selling the originals on a black market."

The Allan brothers were silent a beat. "The devil!" Jamie finally exploded.

"I gather he's done it again over the years whenever he's needed an infusion of cash. And if he was having trouble getting financing from the usual sources for this new business venture of his, the Icarii . . ."

"Probably one of the reasons he's wanted Lucy and her mother out of Morborne House," Jane said. "Someone among their friends and allies might begin to notice. But," she continued impatiently, "surely Oliver alit on that scheme *after* things went pear-shaped with Boysie."

"Well." Jamie stared into his whisky as if it yielded secrets. "David Corlett—or Phillips—identifies him at Tullochbrae shortly after our wedding." He frowned. "It's hard to think he went up with murder on his mind."

"I don't believe he did. Or perhaps that's what I want to believe."

"Why, then, didn't he want anyone to know he was travelling to Scotland? Why did he lie about being at Kamran's funeral?"

"I expect he didn't want any of the family to know *why* he was coming—all about grubby money. And it would have looked strange to appear after a wedding he had declined to attend. He'd been to Tullochbrae a few times when he was a teenager. He'd remember the private roads and paths. Aird Cottage is very near a public road. I don't think he travelled with stealth, I think he was simply being very discreet. Probably wanted to avoid Father."

Jamie made a dismissive grunt.

"I think whatever Olly asked for, Boysie refused," John continued. "They argued. And in a blind moment of rage, Oliver took the poker by the fireplace and struck Boysie a fatal blow. There was nothing to be gained by deliberately killing Boysie. There was more to lose, but it was done, and he thought he'd got away with it. Only he didn't realise he'd been witnessed by a mentally handicapped boy—"

"Whom you moved to protect—an astonishing act of sacrifice, John," Jane said.

"If there had been a proper investigation—" Jamie paused to drain his glass. "—then I suppose Oliver's being in Scotland would have been winkled out eventually. For example, he must have hired a car at Aberdeen. There would be a record. But as you had confessed to Boysie's murder, John, that ended that."

John didn't respond to the provocation. "What is difficult to understand is why it ended with such violence," he said instead. "What could Boysie have said or done that would have driven Oliver to . . . manslaughter?"

Tom and Jane exchanged glances.

"I think Tom has an idea," Jane said regarding him speculatively. "It goes—does it not?—back to a horrifying event in Shropshire more than a quarter century ago."

CHAPTER TWENTY-NINE

"Did you know Kamran Arouzi?" Tom asked Jamie.

"Only a little. I was a fair bit younger and excluded from Boysie and Oliver's circle at school. But Kamran would come to tea sometimes at Bridgemary. He boarded. We Allans were day boys." He looked over the rim of his glass. "You say Kamran was witness to this ghastly act on The Wrekin?"

"Gaunt's certain. But only as a witness."

"It's hard to imagine Kamran any way involved. I think of him as a sensitive boy. I wondered even then that he was such fast friends with the likes of Boysie and Olly. They bullied him a bit, I recall—perhaps *teased* is the word—they were champion at it—but maybe he was glad of the friendship. I'm not sure how kind people were to him at school, because he wasn't, you know, English—I mean, by birth. I remember Mummy once giving the two of them, Boysie and Olly, stick for calling him a Paki, which was ridiculous since he was Iranian—Parsi, actually."

Jane said, "Tom thinks Boysie was involved."

"But Gaunt saw only two boys, darling—Oliver and Kamran."

"Something Gaunt said to me, as we waited for help this afternoon, which suggests Oliver had taken your older brother"—Tom addressed Jamie and John—"into his confidence."

"All boys together, sharing secrets, that sort of thing," Jane added.

"What an appalling idea. And Boysie keeping such a dreadful secret?"

"If he kept it."

"What do you mean?"

"Something you could hold over someone, don't you think?"

"I expect so," Jamie replied after a moment's thought, adding, "Surely Oliver must have been . . . *shaken* in some fashion by the monstrous thing he had done. I would have been too young—you even younger, John. Did no one take notice?"

"Oliver's always seemed the height of lordly self-assurance to me, Jamie," Jane responded. "He probably was then, too. But for Kamran, perhaps it wasn't water off a duck's back. It was the beginning of a life of—"

"Inspector." Jamie interrupted his wife as Bliss lumbered into the room followed by his sergeant. "Any more news of Gaunt?"

"We've despatched Mrs. Gaunt to Torbay Hospital, which

should give you an indication of the seriousness of his condition." Bliss wore a harried frown. His eyes landed on John. "I've had an interview with Miss Phillips—"

"May I see Anna?" John interrupted.

"All in good time." Bliss gestured impatiently to his partner, who pulled a notebook and biro from his jacket pocket. "You were last seen in Abbotswick on Saturday evening around ten, having words with Lord Morborne. And then, Mr. Allan or Phillips or whatever you call yourself, you disappear for the best part of two days."

"I thought Gaunt was the—" Jamie protested, but Bliss cut him off:

"I'm leaving no stone unturned, sir. Mr. Allan, can you account for your—"

"Inspector," Tom interrupted, turning from contemplating the fireplace overmantel, the Triumph of Death, which had drawn his attention two nights before. "It doesn't matter."

"What?"

"It doesn't bloody matter where John's been the last two days."

"Would you care to lead this investigation, Vicar?"

"I would not."

"Then—"

"Look, if this were some sort of Jacobean drama, John here would do nicely on the playbill as the peer's son seeking to avenge a murder. He spent years in prison, sacrificing his youth to protect a vulnerable, mentally challenged young man and the woman he loved, when all along he was protecting a scoundrel. Who hearing his story mightn't imagine the outrage, the anger, the betrayal he might experience when he learned the truth? Who mightn't suspect him of murdering his cousin? Some, I expect, would hardly blame him.

"But he's innocent—of Oliver's murder and Roberto Sica's, too. A year and a half ago, when I was new in Thornford, I thought for a time that he might have had a hand in some violent deaths in the village. You know the ones I mean, Inspector.

"Then, too, it seemed he might have a motive, along with the opportunity. But I came to understand that he wasn't capable. Time spent in prison, I think, is thoroughly destructive for many people, but I think somehow John was . . . burnished by the experience, his Christian faith, which he seems to have had strongly from childhood"—Tom looked to both brothers for confirmation—"strengthened by the reversals of his life. He's had a cross to bear, and he's borne it well. However provoked—and he has been sorely provoked—I'm certain he would turn the other cheek."

"Bravo, Vicar!" Jamie raised his glass.

"Fine words, Mr. Christmas, but I don't share your certainty. With enough provocation—"

"Possibly, Inspector. I'm not going to debate with you. Yes, John has a strong motive. But he hadn't the opportunity, for one thing." He glanced at John, who remained unmoving. "I think you'll find, if you check, that he has a solid alibi with the good Benedictines at Hexham Priory.

"However, there's something more vital."

"And what would that be?"

"Means, Inspector. John hadn't the means to kill Oliver."

CHAPTER THIRTY

*P*riesthood was Tom's second vocation. Before he read theology at Cambridge, he had been, for a time as a young man, a professional magician, which one of his mothers (Dosh) didn't consider a proper job at all but a youthful enthusiasm gone riot. Whatever Dosh's misgivings, magicianship had focused his youthful energies, built his confidence, given him pleasure—and attracted not a few girls along the way. He maintained a sentimental attachment to it still. Illusory magic could awaken people to deeper aspects of their lives, he believed, though some in the Church treated his avocation with scepticism. He could slip in a moral lesson, too, and in this instance, in Eggescombe Hall's drawing room, for his first time, he was about to do something more.

He glanced at DI Bliss who had removed himself to the pale of the drawing room, ceding pride of place before the mantelpiece, a scowl on his face. He had been incredulous in his resistance to Tom's request. "And turn my investigation into a fairground sideshow?" he'd snapped, though Tom's intent was not at all to amuse and distract. Indeed, he had never before approached a performance of magic with such a freighted heart and, in this peculiar instance, with such uncertainty as to its effect. He found himself in the invidious position of reminding the DI of his contributions to their past investigative successes. Only then was permission grudgingly given.

He noted the others as they entered the drawing room. Dowager Lady Fairhaven, changed into dark linen trousers and a striped shirt, gave the police detectives an appraising stare, in which Tom read distaste mixed with a kind of surrender to the inevitable. Anna followed a step behind, but her eyes sought John's, lighting like two tiny beacons when they met his. He responded with a repentant smile and a gesture to join him. She declined a drink. Jamie remained the barman. But Marguerite accepted a brandy. Tom watched her raise an interrogatory eyebrow at Jamie's semi-formal dress, but she said nothing, taking a seat on the Hepplewhite sofa angled to the fireplace.

She had barely done so when Lucinda seemed to glide into the room from the hall on a breath of silvery laughter, as if responding to a private joke, followed in short order by Dominic, his lips compressed into a moue of amusement. Stopped short at the sight of the detectives, Lucinda pulled the solemn face of a naughty child caught misbehaving. As she stepped to the drinks table, Tom glanced at her. For a moment, a pink balloon of nostalgia hovered over his younger self—two days younger, but a birthday younger—and he marvelled at how swiftly passion had turned to embers. He popped the balloon. He had a confession to make, and steeling himself was the task ahead. He returned Lucinda's enigmatic smile with a tight one of his own as she took a chair. Dominic, after fetching a brandy, chose to stand behind her, as if to be on guard. Looking around, he remarked to vacant response:

"How terribly Agatha Christie," adding, "Hello, John. It's been a long time."

"Very," John responded noncommittally as Lucinda cast him and Anna a studied glance.

Of family and guests, Hector (with Bonzo) arrived last, just as the clock was striking the hour, his expression sullen, as if dinner had been a trial and he'd had more than his fill of houseguests, including the police who received his bristling, slightly truculent glance. Tom watched him slew his eyes around the unusual arrangement of bodies and land on John.

"So, you've been hiding in plain sight all these years."

"I've been living my life, Hector."

Lord Fairhaven grunted. "I'm sorry Georgina can't be here to greet you."

"Where is she?" Marguerite's tone suggested she knew very well.

"Having an early night. She suffers from migraines. Inspector"—Hector turned to Bliss—"I may have said. I trust you don't mind."

The time it took Bliss to respond—five seconds in which Madrun arrived in the room burdened with a tray of coffee things—indicated he did mind, very much, but he replied evenly: "If we have further enquiries, we'll take them up when Her Ladyship is recovered."

"In the meantime, Inspector," Hector continued in a voice rimed with new frost, taking a chair opposite his mother, "what have you planned for us this evening?"

DI Bliss replied dryly: "Mr. Christmas has prepared an entertainment, Your Lordship."

Tom watched Hector's eyebrows curl into commas of disapproval as he glanced from the inspector to Tom. "Have you really," he drawled, running his hand over Bonzo's silky head. "How interesting."

"I'm not sure *entertainment* is the suitable word." Tom looked past Hector's head to see Madrun's eyes behind her spectacles glittering at the sight of the Honourable John Sebastian Hamilton Allan. Apparently, downstairs, whoever was left there, hadn't been informed of his presence. "It's more of a lesson—a parable, if you will—wrapped in an entertainment."

The whisky Jamie had poured him earlier affording him Dutch courage was also scorching his empty stomach. Along with everyone else but Hector, he refused coffee, fearing it would only add to the internal sludge, but he wished the coffee had arrived with biscuits.

"As a few of you know," he began when most everyone had settled into a comfortable position, "I was, when I was younger, a professional magician. Conventions, fairs, boat cruises, a little television, that sort of thing. I'd been enchanted by magic since I was a child. But when I felt the call, I didn't turn my back utterly on magic—or perhaps *illusion* is the better word, as I don't want to give anyone the impression I'm doing anything supernatural." He glanced at Madrun, who frowned at him as she bent to serve Lord Fairhaven a demitasse of coffee from a tray.

"I've found that sleight of hand and illusion can be a good way of presenting a spiritual or moral lesson in a visual way. Not to put myself in the same august company, but Jesus Himself used parables—visual aids—in His ministry, and you can't say He wasn't something of a showman, although—"

"Will you be turning water into wine and producing loaves and fishes to feed the multitudes?" Dominic interrupted.

"Those I can't expect to match." Tom smiled a tight smile. "Anyway," he continued, unsure if his patter, unscripted and unrehearsed, was drawing the punters in, "on Saturday evening, Max very much wanted me to perform a certain sleight of hand, one from a category of cut-and-restored effects that always seem to appeal to children. I wasn't in a position to fulfill his wish—quite literally—because my foot was wrapped and elevated. In that instant, too, I was without my magic kit and certain paraphernalia. The—"

"If this is for Max's benefit, shouldn't the boy be here?" Hector frowned at him over the edge of his cup.

"Max and Miranda are playing Cluedo in the library, Hector," Marguerite replied in his stead. "Tom's trick may appeal to children, but this is intended as an adult gathering."

"It feels rather like we're playing Cluedo in the drawing room." Hector scowled.

"I was about to say," Tom continued, picking up the thread of his introduction, "that many magic performances, of whatever style, usually include one or two illusions where something appears to be broken or destroyed and yet is restored. I think when we see something destroyed, we experience a kind of psychic bruise, a spiritual strain, if you will. We've all, each of us, experienced life's destructive side, have we not?" He looked to them for agreement and noted a few flickers of recognition. "I don't think I need to point out that we have most profoundly experienced that side this weekend."

Tom paused to allow the truth of this to be absorbed—his eyes went to Marguerite—before appending his message: "However, there remains, as ever, the promise of healing and restoration." He smiled. "Now, I need a volunteer from the audience."

"We're hardly an 'audience,' Vicar."

"Hector, darling, *please*," Marguerite's tone was weary.

"I need," Tom began again, "a volunteer from those assembled who is wearing a suit this evening."

From the corner of his eye, he saw DI Bliss elbow DS Blessing, each of whom was wearing a dark suit, but he quickly cut in:

"Ah, Lord Kirkbride, thank you. Lord Kirkbride will do splendidly. Come forwards." Tom beckoned Jamie, who stepped beside him at the fireplace and took a military stance, hands behind back, head held high.

"Lord Kirkbride," Tom continued, "your suit is from . . . ?"

"Oh . . . Gieves and Hawkes, this one, I think. Hector and I have the same tailor, don't we, Hector?"

"Why are you all got up this evening anyway, James?" Hector glanced from his own casual trousers and open-necked shirt to Dominic impeccably, though informally, dressed in a cream polo shirt and navy trousers to John in his crumpled khakis.

"I . . . I've run out of things to wear. We were on the moor late this afternoon, some of us. Got a bit damp."

"Yes, I know." Hector's brow furrowed. Tom noted a new, wary expression settle on his face; he continued,

"And your shirt, Lord Kirkbride?"

"I'm not sure. Turnbull and Asser would be my guess. I'd have to look at the label. I suppose Jane could—"

"A mere bagatelle, my lord. Not important. And your tie?"

"School tie. Shrewsbury. I've had it forever. Well, since school, of course. It only ever gets an airing if I attend one of the Old Salopian events, as I did last week. Like my regimental tie. Only comes out of the box, so to speak, when I have a regimental do."

"And did this come 'out of the box'?" Tom asked.

"Well, it came out of a drawer—the drawer in the dresser in our room here, if that's what you mean."

"School ties—ties that bind, in a way." Tom felt something cool and metallic slip into the palm of his hand. "My tie was navy with double red stripes. I attended Gravesend Grammar, opened by Princess Beatrice in 1893. Not quite the same as being founded under Edward the Sixth—"

"Actually, Father wanted us to go to Ludgrove and to Eton, as he had, but Mother wouldn't wear it. She was from the colonies, like my wife." Jamie smiled at Jane. "And couldn't bear the idea of us being away from her. So, as Packwood Haugh and Shrewsbury were in effect only down the road . . . We were day pupils, all of us. Olly for a time, too, at Shrewsbury."

Mention of Oliver seemed to charge the atmosphere. Tom glanced about to note a certain shifting of limbs and straightening of attire. Only Lucinda sipped her coffee in unstudied casualness, while the two policemen continued to observe the proceedings with barely disguised impatience.

"What if I were to tell you, Lord Kirkbride"—Tom kept his attention on the others rather than his interlocutor—"that the tie you are wearing may have been the instrument that strangled Lord Morborne?"

All eyes hared to Jamie's neck, including Jamie's.

"What!" Bliss was the first to speak.

"Detective Inspector, I asked Lord Kirkbride—"

"I heard you, Mr. Christmas. What the bloody hell do you think you're playing at?"

"This!"

Tom splayed the palm of his hand to reveal a pair of scissors—cuticle scissors, it was true, from his shaving kit, the only ones he had available—but they would do. To a short, sharp collective gasp, followed swiftly by a noisier rendition, he pulled Jamie's tie from the confinement of his suit jacket and dug the sharp edge of the scissors into the fabric an inch below the knot. If he'd had fabric shears he could have bisected the tie in one quick snip. But three were sufficient, even though the cloth retained some damp from the moor. Before Jamie had time to simulate dismay at the desecration, Tom was holding the limpid strip of cloth up for display and Bliss was stepping forward in a bull charge.

"Where did you find that?" he snapped.

"In my dresser drawer, as I said, Detective Inspector," Jamie replied.

"Is this a confession?"

"Of course, it isn't. It's simply my tie, which I found in my drawer."

"Then"—Bliss focused his pique on Tom—"how do you know it was used on Lord Morborne?"

"Inspector," Marguerite said crossly, "do you mind? You're spoiling the effect."

"Mr. Christmas, you have tampered with evidence!"

"But Inspector, I shall restore evidence in short order. Lady Kirkbride?" Tom gestured to Jane, who stepped nearer. "And Lord Kirkbride, would you remove what's left of your tie? Thank you.

"I am sorry about your tie, Lord Kirkbride," he pattered as Jamie fiddled with the knot and whipped the stub from around his collar. "But a little prestidigitation and it should be as good as the day it hung at Gorringes. Lady Kirkbride, I wonder if you might show everyone what you have with you."

Jane displayed the soft red velvet bag trimmed with green, a legacy of his days as the Great Krimboni, which Tom had bid her fetch earlier. It was about the dimensions of *Hello!* magazine.

"Lady Kirkbride, is there anything in the bag?"

Jane opened it at one end and peered in. "Nothing," she said and without prompting turned it towards the others, the opening displayed like a wide dark mouth. "Absolutely empty."

"Now, Lord Kirkbride," Tom continued, "if you place your skinny end of the tie into the bag, and Lady Kirkbride, if you will take this portion—" Tom waved the tie's fat end in the air before handing it to Jane. "—and place it, too, into the bag . . . thank you."

Tom blew into the bag and gave it a shake. "Does anyone have a magic word they'd care to use? Anyone? Lord Fairhaven?"

Hector scowled and said tonelessly, "Abracadabra."

"No one can accuse you of originality, Hector," Lucinda laughed.

"*Abracadabra* will do nicely," Tom cut in, continuing the patter as much to alleviate his growing anxiety as to distract the audience. "It has a venerable history in magic, its origins thought to be in Aramaic, which some scholars believe was the everyday language of Jesus. During the Great Plague, Londoners posted it on their doorways to ward off illness."

"And did it?" Hector glowered over the rim of his coffee cup.

"Well, not really."

"Then I can't imagine it will be very efficacious here."

"Hector, darling, don't be disagreeable." Marguerite smiled wanly at Tom. "Carry on. You're doing splendidly. Such fun."

Tom smiled back with equally feeble wattage. "Yes, anyway . . ." He forced his cheeks into a wider performance smile. "Abracadabra!

"Now, Lord Kirkbride, all you need do is reach into the bag and you'll find your tie as good as the day it was woven." He held the bag towards Jamie, but in a swift movement withdrew it. "Would you like me to reach into the bag for you?"

As Jamie looked on with genuine perplexity, Tom answered for him. "No? Then please do reach into the bag."

With the grimace of someone about to perform a tonsillectomy on a crocodile, Jamie slid one slim hand gingerly into the velvet opening. He paused, a look of faint relief on his face, then pulled his hand back slowly, the thin end of the tie appearing first pressed between his thumb and forefinger.

"Brilliant!" he exclaimed with unnecessary good grace when he'd finished the manoeuvre, holding up the fully restored tie to a smattering of applause. "How did you do that?"

"It's magic," Tom replied.

"It isn't," Bliss countered.

"An illusion, of course." Marguerite tapped her chin thoughtfully, adding with a quicksilver smile, "But cleverly done."

"Yes, of course, an illusion. Allow me another. Lord Kirkbride, please place the restored tie into the bag. Thank you."

Tom repeated the actions of before, declined to seek a magic word from the fractious assembled, and had Jamie place his hand in the bag once again. His Lordship pulled out, one following the other, two parts of a striped tie.

"Give those to me," Bliss barked. "Have you got an evidence bag, Sergeant?"

"Not with me, no, sir," Blessing replied.

"I said, Inspector"—Tom displayed cut fabric, one piece in each hand—"this tie, which Lord Kirkbride pulled from his dresser drawer this afternoon, *may* be the tie used to strangle Lord Morborne, but I doubt it is. I think if you had it analysed you would find it cleaned in some fashion, certainly pressed." He happened to glance at Madrun whose face evinced a curious enlightenment. "With no trace of the hands it's been through but for Lord Kirkbride's and mine. The tie used to strangle Lord Morborne will, I'm sure, contain all the physical evidence you need to charge someone with his death. And that—"Tom turned towards the fireplace, glanced again at the macabre overmantel, Triumph of Death, and fished into the changing bag, "would be—"

He turned back to the audience, unfurling the undamaged neckwear. "This tie."

"You've gimmicked the bag," Hector spoke sharply. Bonzo's head rose.

"Yes, I have. One of these ties, the undamaged one, was found in the tunnel that runs between the Eggescombe Hall here and the stable block. It—"

"Tunnel?" Bliss interrupted. "What tunnel?"

"As the vicar said, Inspector, there's a tunnel—"

"I know that now. Why wasn't I told before?"

"You didn't ask." Hector bristled. "And I didn't think of it. We might open it as an attraction, but in the meantime the only one in the family with any interest in it is my son."

"And he found the tie?" Blessing spoke from the back of the room.

"Yes," Tom replied. "It was tucked behind some fallen bricks."

"Then am I to presume it was hidden by Lord Morborne's killer—someone who knew of the tunnel's existence?"

Tom could see the inspector surveying everyone in the room. "No, it was left in the tunnel by someone else," he answered.

"Who?"

"I left it." Anna spoke for the first time.

"I thought I glimpsed a fair-haired woman in the Labyrinth early Sunday morning," Tom explained.

"You're telling me this *now*?" Bliss's eyes glinted ominously.

"Forgive me, Inspector. I didn't mean to withhold. I wasn't sure if it was a trick of the light or not. Anyway, it was Anna. I followed the dew path she made to Eggescombe's service entrance."

"You were *in* the Labyrinth at the time of Lord Morborne's death? You told me nothing of this in our earlier conversation." Bliss turned his frustration onto Anna.

"She's been protecting me." John took her hand.

"You don't look like you need protecting," Lucinda purred.

"Anna thought I might have been responsible for Oliver's death," John continued, ignoring Lucinda. "Didn't you, darling Anna? It's all right to say so. I can't fault you. I would have thought the same thing. Inspector"—he preempted Bliss, who had opened his mouth to speak—"my family here all know about the time I spent in gaol for my brother's death. What Anna has known for some few years, what you learned from her earlier, but what my family—apart from my brother and sister-in-law—doesn't know is that there is good evidence that Oliver ended Boysie's life."

"What!" Hector roared. "But—"

"You can't know what it's like to realise you've spent your days in prison unwittingly protecting someone like Oliver," John cut in. "Then to learn he'd run down Anna's brother in the road."

"Really?" Dominic and Lucinda exclaimed as one.

"You seem somewhat unsurprised by *this* revelation, Hector, my dear." Marguerite—Tom could see—had been searching her son's face.

Hector's cheeks flushed. "And you, Mummy, seem unsurprised by everything."

"I spend more than a fortnight a year at Eggescombe, Hector. One learns much."

"Hector, do you know something about David's death?" John bent to stroke Bonzo, who had padded across the carpet towards the open doors.

"Of course I bloody don't!"

John flicked a glance at Anna as he unbent and continued.

"Anna knew how . . . how incandescent I was. I'd gone for a walk in the late afternoon to cool down, but then I came back to our cottage for a time. I suppose when Anna didn't find me at home later—"

"Saturday evening?" Blessing looked up from his notebook.

"I left to work a shift at the Pilgrims," Anna said, nodding. "I needed the distraction terribly. I was to have been here, to help Mrs. Gaunt, but I couldn't bear to be anywhere near Morborne."

"That evening I saw him pass our cottage window in the village with a few other men." John picked up the story. "It was getting dark, but Oliver was wearing that kufi hat you'd see in press photos. I didn't stop to think: I dashed out and shouted his name. He didn't recognise me at first, but perhaps something in my voice stopped him. He told the others to go on to the inn. Our . . . conversation was brief."

"Seeing you in Abbotswick after so many years must have rattled him." Jane frowned.

"I saw a flicker of caution in his eyes when he realised who I was, but only a flicker. Bombastic Oliver, of course: He was hardly going to be crushed by anything I, his disgraced little cousin, had to say. There were no preliminaries: I told him I was sharing my life with a woman whose brother had been killed only days earlier by a hit-and-run driver. 'Pity,' he said."

"'Pity'? That's all?" Jamie asked.

"Short shrift, but I took it as admission. A blameless person would show at least a little concern or curiosity. But there was a look in his eye—I know it—another sort of wary flicker. The night was drawing in, but there was a glow from the cottage sitting room window and I could see an uneasiness in his face. He didn't linger. You'd think he might—he hadn't seen me in a dozen years, more."

"But," Tom began, "if this . . . intelligence passed between the two of you, he must have realised that you also suspected the truth about your brother's murderer. One leads inevitably to the other, does it not?" He paused, as John nodded. "I wonder what he planned to do. You and Anna were surely a threat to him now."

"He wasn't so troubled that he didn't go to some barmaid's for the night," Jamie remarked.

"So." Bliss cleared his throat noisily. "You, Mr. Allan, bogged off to this monastery in the pitch black of Dartmoor for a bit of a think—"

"The light lingers in the summer. I had a torch. I know the moor well. I've walked it for years."

"I think we've established that there's proof that John did as he says," Tom reminded the DI.

"Did Mr. Allan tell you he was leaving?" Bliss turned to Anna. "Leave a note? Send a text?"

"John's absences don't surprise me, Inspector," Anna replied.

"But you didn't know for certain his whereabouts between—what?—seven o'clock Saturday evening and about an hour ago."

"Which is why I unthinkingly snatched up that tie—*that* tie, the one Mr. Christmas is holding in his right hand—from the Labyrinth. I recognised the tie pattern. John had gone to Shrewsbury. I know it's mad, John with his old school tie, but

I had lost my mind in those moments. I was frightened that he had—" She paused and reiterated her encounter with Oliver that Sunday before dawn.

Bliss and Blessing exchanged glances. Blessing spoke: "But once the boy—Max—came across the tie, this vital piece of evidence, so claimed, why wasn't it passed immediately to—"

"To you? Because we got rather caught up in events," Tom responded. "The moor and such."

"Much is my fault, Inspector," Jamie continued. "When I was shown the tie Max had found, I couldn't fathom how it had got into the tunnel, when I'd seen it that very morning in our bedroom—my wife's and mine—so by the time I returned from a recce of my bedroom, we were, as the vicar says, caught up in other events."

"You see," Tom explained, "this tie—this undamaged tie." He displayed it. "Was taken by Max on Saturday evening from Jamie's bedroom. He hoped that I would be able to do a trick, but I was missing, as I said, a few necessary accoutrements and I was indisposed on the terrace." Tom gestured to the open French doors through which richly filtered evening light poured. "Disappointed, Max returned indoors, here, into the drawing room and left the tie, as children do, thoughtlessly somewhere—on a chair, on a table . . ."

"Then Max must have it tucked behind that Meissen bowl over there." Marguerite gestured towards an ormolu cabinet on the other side of the room. "I noticed it after Oliver announced his engagement and thought it odd, as none of the men was dressed with any formality."

Tom glanced at her sharply. "Did you see anyone . . . pick it up? Put it in—?"

"No. I would have said by now. And I should point out"—
she turned her attention to Bliss—"that neither I nor Roberto
was witness to this aborted magic trick on the terrace. So despite your . . . attentions to him, he had no involvement in
Oliver's death, did he?"

"He claimed not."

"Claimed? You still believe otherwise."

"I understand that Mr. Sica—and you, Your Ladyship,
more or less invited Lord Morborne into the Labyrinth to
view the new statue."

"We didn't quite schedule a dawn appointment, Inspector."

"Mr. Sica was witnessed crossing the south lawn sometime
before sunrise Sunday morning."

"By a child."

"He told us, Your Ladyship, that he'd spent much of the
night working in his studio, later taking a walk in the grounds,
which contradicts your claim that he had been with you." Bliss
frowned. "And it appeared a red thread from a piece of his
clothing had caught in the branches of the Labyrinth."

"The jacket had been worn by someone else."

"We know that now." Bliss flicked a glance at Anna.

"And surely final proof of Roberto's innocence is that he's
dead." Marguerite raised her head and surveyed the room, as if
challenging anyone to contradict her.

And now, but for the whisper of the breeze billowing the
curtains on the French doors, an uncomfortable silence settled
over the room. Hector lifted his eyes from his coffee cup to
glance miserably at his mother, almost, Tom thought, as if
he was seeking succor from her—she sat directly across from
him—but she had turned her attention to a point above Tom's

head, to the Triumph of Death and its harsh, unforgiving imagery, her fine fingers tracing the curve of the brandy glass.
Ignored, Hector turned his head to his guests, but no one met
his glance, nor did anyone meet anyone else's—except Madrun, who regarded Tom from behind her glasses with a barely
suppressed avidity that he wished she would suppress. Dominic frowned in intense concentration, his long, elegant fingers
pressing a cat-like rhythm into Lucinda's shoulders until she,
drawn from her own thoughts, winced and shrugged his hands
off. Breaking the silence, she said:

"I know this sounds like something out of a detective
novel, but hasn't it been established that the *butler* did it? I
thought Gaunt had been trying to escape on the moor and
you'd assembled us here simply for a jolly sort of wrap-up."
She appealed to Bliss, who chose the moment to leave the
fringes of the drawing room and reclaim the fireplace and the
centre of the enquiry, DS Blessing following, chair in hand.

"As Dominic already told you, he *saw* Gaunt from the
Gaze Tower sneaking around the stables this very afternoon,
didn't you, darling?" Lucinda tapped Dominic's resting hand
with her fingers as her eyes followed the moving figure. "Surely
that—"

But a disdainful glance from Bliss quelled her. "The other
tie, Vicar," he said, "the one found in Lord Kirkbride's drawer,
the one you cut up—"

"Gaunt's," Tom replied, then amended, "in Gaunt's possession, I should say. For many, many years. But once upon a time
the tie was Oliver's."

"Oliver's?" Marguerite echoed. "But I don't understand . . ."

"Something sordid happened when Oliver was a student at

Shrewsbury, Lady Fairhaven, though fewer than a handful of people ever knew about it—until this weekend." Tom looked to DI Bliss. "Shall I or shall you?"

With Bliss's permission, Tom summarised events on The Wrekin more than a quarter century ago. "Of course," he added, "Oliver's role in this crime isn't absolutely certain, without proof, yes, Inspector?"

"But if Gaunt believed it so," Marguerite interjected, "then surely you have a motive."

Tom demurred. "There may be proof. What none of you know—including you, Inspector—and what Gaunt told me earlier on the moor is this: Oliver used his school tie—and you must forgive me, Jamie, for asking you to wear the thing this evening—to silence Kimberly's screams as . . . he raped her.

"You see," he continued, as one of the women—Anna—released a short, sharp cry, "he stuffed the tie in her mouth."

CHAPTER THIRTY-ONE

"*A*m I to understand," Jamie said after a moment, "that Gaunt kept the tie from this appalling incident on The Wrekin for all these years as a sort of . . . memento?"

"I'm not sure *memento* is the word," Tom responded. "Talisman? Fetish? Goad? I doubt he was thinking rationally at that moment. It was only later, quite a bit later, after certain scientific advances, that he realised it very well could contain DNA evidence. I'm not sure anyone's noticed, but he's been setting about here, this weekend, gathering other things that might contain Oliver's imprint, a glass, laundry, a facial tissue, a cigar stub."

"I saw him collect that last one." Lucinda pushed to the edge of her chair. "Well, there you have it, Inspector—Gaunt had a motive, he had the opportunity, and—now—the means. Have I got the traditional three correct? Yes? Case closed, then.

May we leave this horrid place now? Sorry, Hector, darling, Eggescombe's really quite lovely—in other circumstances."

"I think you've missed something entirely, Lucy," Jamie cut in. "There are *two* ties. As Tom's suggested, that tie—the cut-up one, the one I found in my drawer this afternoon—is the one Gaunt kept all these years. My tie is this one." He held it up. "This is the one Max pulled from my drawer Saturday evening and left in this room. This one is the tie that . . . strangled Oliver. Isn't that right, Tom?"

Tom nodded. "I think the question is—" He paused as he might in the pulpit at St. Nicholas, to reclaim the congregation's attention. "—I think the question is, how did the tie manage to travel from this drawing room to the Labyrinth between Saturday evening and the early hours of Sunday morning?"

No one responded. Silence descended again, this time like a pall, the atmosphere now charged with unease and foreboding energy. Tom found his eyes drawn helplessly to Lucinda as she resettled herself in the chair she'd been keen to vacate a moment earlier. She reached up to her shoulder to touch Dominic's hand, patting it gently, almost regretfully, and released a thin sigh. He watched her lips part, sure she was to give voice to his question, hoping that if she did, the contents might spare him humiliation, but Hector, as if unwilling to have anyone supersede him, interrupted:

"Well, it wasn't me walking about in the middle of the night with a silly bloody tie. I told you before, Inspector, that I was in bed with my wife."

"Hector, please don't take this amiss," Jane responded, "but

I would swear I saw you outside on the lawn sometime in the night. You were wearing that white terry-cloth robe of yours."

"How dare you."

"Hector, we must get to the bottom of this, if we're all going to carry on." Jane shifted impatiently on her feet. "I was going to have to tell Inspector Bliss sooner or later anyway. How can I not? I know it doesn't look good: You've never cared for Oliver and the two of you had been snapping at each other in the last days, I don't know why. We had to watch the two of you hitting each other at twenty thousand feet in the air and—"

"Oh, for God's sake." Hector's cup hit the saucer with a nasty crunch. "I couldn't sleep. I went out for some air, that's all. That's *all*," he repeated, turning his attention to Bliss. "I landed up on the terrace around . . . I don't know the time— before dawn. I sat for a while and went back to my wife."

"Hector," Lucinda drawled. "Don't put on middle-class airs. You don't share a bedroom with Georgie, never have. You sleep with Bonzo."

"Be quiet. I've had quite enough of you these last days."

"Hector, like my wife"—Jamie glanced over his whisky glass—"I don't want you take this amiss, but this afternoon you were late for our meeting in your office and you arrived . . . well, I can only describe your state as 'shambolic.'"

Lord Fairhaven was silent for the beat of a heart before his face filled with blood. He sputtered: "Are you accusing me of . . . what? what was it? *electrocuting* that . . . that . . ."

"Roberto is his name, Hector." Marguerite cut in with words as icy as her stare. "Was, rather. And he was a splendid artist with a promising future."

"Mummy, for God's sake! I'm your son. I didn't particularly care for ... Roberto." He battled a frown. "But who you choose to—"

"That's not the point, Hector," Marguerite snapped. "I think it's fairly obvious that Roberto might have seen something, witnessed something, heaven knows what, in his night wanderings and—"

"Well, he didn't bloody see *me*!"

"Lord Fairhaven." Bliss exercised a neutral tone. "Would you care to account for your movements this afternoon."

Hector exploded. "I was doing exactly what I told James and Jane and Mr. Christmas I was doing. I missed my morning run, so I thought I'd take one after lunch."

"In the heat of the day?" Bliss's tone was sceptical.

"Have you noted Eggescombe's many shade trees, Inspector?"

Bliss grunted as Blessing noisily turned a page in his notebook.

"You didn't," Tom interjected, "miss your morning run Sunday, however."

"My lord?" Bliss frowned as Hector shot Tom a daggered gaze.

"Then let me be completely frank about Sunday morning: I couldn't get back to sleep. I went out for some air. I returned to my bedroom. I still couldn't sleep. I gave up. I went for a run. I came back. Had a shower. Then found Jane at my door with unexpected news. There you have it."

"And why weren't you frank about your movements earlier?"

"I forgot ... well, it didn't seem important. I didn't think anyone had seen me anyway."

"Evidently someone had, my lord."

"Mrs. Gaunt."

"Who kept it to herself."

"I expect the Gaunts take the non-disclosure clause of their contract seriously," Hector responded airily.

"Do they now." Bliss spoke with barely suppressed fury.

"Lord Fairhaven," Tom interjected. He had been thinking of something Hector had said earlier. "You said a moment ago that Roberto did not see you on the terrace—not surprising given the darkness. But your tone seems to suggest that *you* might have seen *him*."

Hector flicked him a hateful glance. "I saw many things. The moon, the stars, the—"

"Roberto in the motion lights in all his nearly naked glory?" Marguerite suggested.

"Mummy, don't be vulgar." He placed his coffee cup on a side table. "All right, I did glimpse him. What of it?"

"And was he alone?" Bliss asked.

Hector shifted slightly in his seat. "I can't be certain. The motion sensors only light intermittently. I heard voices. Thought I did."

"And—again—you didn't care to mention this earlier?" Bliss glared at him.

"I wasn't certain. I couldn't think it mattered. It was some good time before dawn, which is apparently when Olly met his maker."

"Male voices?"

"They were at some distance, Inspector, but, yes, I would say so."

"Distinguishable?"

"Well, one of them was Roberto's. I think that should be clear by now, Inspector."

"The other, then."

"I have no idea. From the terrace it sounded like murmuring. There was, however, a sound like someone punching at someone else. The only word I could distinguish was one I won't repeat in this company, and I don't know who said it."

"Roberto's torso appeared bruised when Tom and I visited his studio with the kids yesterday," Jane remarked.

Tom added: "You, too, have bruises on your chest, Dominic. They were noticeable at the pool yesterday afternoon. Lucinda claimed you had walked into an open wardrobe in the dark."

"Did she? Well, there you go."

"I don't think Lord Fairhaven and the late Lord Morborne were the only two men exchanging blows this weekend," Tom added.

"Why would I be exchanging blows—as you put it—with Roberto?"

"You were attracted to him, and he wasn't attracted to you." Marguerite shot him a look of disbelief.

"Nonsense," Dominic snapped, raising his glass to his mouth.

"Did Roberto say nothing about these marks to you, Lady Fairhaven?" Bliss asked.

"He wasn't given to that sort of thing. I noted them, but assumed they were the consequence of his work, stone flying about and the like, although . . ." She regarded Dominic coldly now. "Of course, Roberto had been fine-polishing these last few days. No great chips of marble flying about, I shouldn't think."

"Again, nonsense. A complete fabrication." Dominic took another sip. "I spent, as I said yesterday in this company, Saturday night and Sunday morning in Lucy's room, or, rather, she in mine. Together, at any rate."

Tom caught Lucinda's eye. She had been sitting still, head bent, hair falling forwards like a curtain, concentrated on her hands in her lap, pushing rhythmically at the skin below the cuticles. Now, as she raised her head, her hair swept back and revealed once again the remarkable violet eyes, which had glazed with craving during their interlude of ill-considered passion. As they locked onto Tom's, a soft pleading crept into their folds. But he felt no want of retaliation. He had been victim of a cruel and stupid jest, yes, but the jest had precipitated something much, much crueler. His faith demanded he turn the other cheek, and he did, in his mind's eye, but he returned her gaze not with disdain or contempt, but with sorrow and pity and deep, deep regret. It was too late for discretion, however. Now he had to speak, though he would pay a price. He felt Hector's eyes upon him, Hector who had witnessed Lucinda's night movements and hazarded a guess at her destination, but he ignored Hector and looked instead at Madrun, his housekeeper and inconstant keeper of secrets. Would she keep this one? Could it be kept at all? It was her disillusionment, he thought, that would affect him most immediately and most keenly. He took in a cleansing breath, held it a moment, and he said with a rush of air:

"I have to tell you, Inspector, that it's not true that Lady Lucinda spent the entire night in her brother's room."

"Yes?" Bliss flicked him a distracted glance.

"She didn't spend it with Dominic, because—" He looked again at Lucinda who had returned to a fascination with her hands. "—because," he said again, feeling the blood creeping up past his collar as other eyes bored into him, "she spent it with me, in my room."

Bliss blinked. "You don't say. And what," he addressed Lucinda, "were you doing in Mr. Christmas's room?"

"Don't be obtuse, Inspector." Lucinda looked up and cast him a gelid eye.

"That doesn't mean I—" Dominic began, but Tom cut him off:

"There's a little more. As I later came to realise, after a cryptic conversation by the pool yesterday, Lucinda and Dominic had a certain wager—"

"Must you? Really? Must you, Vicar?" Lucinda's voice was weary.

"—a wager," Tom continued with grim determination, conscious of Madrun's eyes boring into him, "to see who might successfully bed a person of his or her choice before the night was through. I believe the notion was entertained some time Saturday evening, after Mr. Sica arrived and was introduced. Lady Lucinda soon enough won the bet." Tom could feel his face burning. "But I don't believe I'm incorrect in believing an attempt was made to even the score when, later, together, they observed Mr. Sica lit up by lightning from the moor crossing the lawn."

"Tom, I am disappointed." Lucinda tossed her hair back. "I didn't think you were the kiss-and-tell sort."

And now, the atmosphere grew heavy with a new anxiety. All eyes shifted to stare at Dominic and Lucinda, who received their scrutiny with the wary defiance of children caught with their fingers in the biscuit tin.

"Well, I lost the wager. What of it?" Dominic waved a dismissive hand. "There's no proof that I strangled Oliver."

Bliss gestured to the tie Tom was holding. "This may well provide proof once we send it for analysis."

Dominic rested his eyes on the tie a moment. His mouth sagged. The scrape of a coffee cup set on a saucer sounded loudly. "Gaunt was to have taken care of that," he said at last, his voice bleak. "I feel rather let down."

"Oh, Dominic, don't!" Lucinda cried.

"Is there any point now, Lucy? Perhaps it's best I appeal for clemency."

"I must caution you," Bliss began. "You don't have to—"

Dominic waved his hand dismissively again. "It wasn't something I set out to do. God knows I've always loathed Oliver. He's a bully and a boor and a vulgarian and a thief—and, it seems, a rapist and worse. Does anyone disagree? I thought not, though most of you don't know he's been plundering the Morborne estate by selling works from Great-Great-Grandfather's impressionist collection and siphoning the money into his own corporation.

"At any rate, if I visited Baissé at Christmas or half term—after my father died—and Olly was there, he would make my life miserable. One time he locked me in a rubbish bin. You might imagine the heat in the West Indies. I nearly asphyxiated. I never forgave him. I suppose some clever quack would say he was merely taking out his hatred of my mother on me. I don't know." Dominic shrugged. "I do know he was almost an adult when he was behaving this way, and I was a child.

"Anyway, as I say, I didn't intend any confrontation—or perhaps I should say *another* confrontation—with my dear cousin. I knew he was disposing of the estate assets and I knew that if I made sufficient fuss in London, I should be able to put a stop to these outrages. There are trust laws limiting his power to dispose of the estate's assets."

"Although," Hector interjected, "some might view it as quicker to simply remove the CEO—as Oliver was, in effect— from the family Trust, in a sort of hostile takeover."

"Hector, I had no desire for the title."

"Nonsense. You've been the presumptive heir to the mar- quessate since Fred died. Only Oliver's having a child—a le- gitimate child, I should say—would set you back a spot. And Oliver was about to have one, wasn't he?"

"I've always lived with the expectation, Hector, that Oli- ver's rampant heterosexuality would one day channel itself into some form of conventional domesticity, so you're very much barking up the wrong tree."

"Hector," Marguerite said, "do be quiet."

"It's called 'motive,' Mummy."

"I didn't have a motive." Dominic glared.

"Everyone has a motive. Wouldn't you agree, Inspector?"

"I think," Tom interposed, "what Dominic is saying is that he was driven by opportunity and strong emotion."

"Thank you, Vicar." Dominic affected a little bow. "Afterwards—after my . . . visit with Roberto—I wandered into the Labyrinth, I don't know why really. I didn't really like to return to my bedroom, having lost the wager—or at least not being able to match Lucy's success. The night air was lovely and fresh and I remembered Marguerite's—or was it Roberto's?—suggestion to Oliver to have a look at the new artwork in the Labyrinth. So I did. There was a bit of lightning in the distance still, but I thought, as sunrise wouldn't be long, to wait and see the marble in the blush of early morning. There are, as all of you know, a series of benches at the centre of the Labyrinth, and I must have nodded off on one of them for a while, as the next thing I remember seeing was someone's back silhouetted in the glow of a torch. Oliver. I recognised that ghastly hat of his. He was shining the light on the statue. He didn't see me or, rather, he hadn't. I watched him a moment in a sort of—I must say—thrall of loathing. He didn't contemplate the image of the Madonna as a connoisseur might. And it is a remarkably beautiful work. Oliver reached up with his free hand—the statue is to scale and the pedestal not tall—and began, if you will, if you can bear to hear it, my lords, ladies, and gentlemen, stroking the figure's breasts—her cold marble breasts."

Dominic's thin lips curled in revulsion. "Aghast as I was at this pervy schoolboy antic, there was worse to come: I heard him unzipping his trouser fly."

"Oh, God," Jane's murmur broke the appalled silence.

"Oh, God, indeed, and I shortly realised he was unzipping not, shall we say, to have a slash, though pissing on an exquisite work of art wouldn't be beneath him, as he has pissed, metaphorically, on the priceless works of art that Great-

Great-Grandfather so assiduously assembled early last century.

"'What are you doing,' I called out. He didn't seem the least startled to hear a voice come out of the gloom, but then it's never been easy to perturb Oliver in any sense. He's as coarse as gravel. Without turning, he told me—as he's told me before— to—" Tom watched Dominic's lip curl again. "—fuck off."

Dominic paused, seemed to stare into the middle distance, as if revisiting the scene. "I quite simply saw red—the rose madder of Jeanne Darlot's hat in Renoir's *Two Sisters on the Terrace,* now I think of it. You must know the work. No? Never mind.

"The tie was still in my hand, dangling in my palm. I had taken it, by the way, from behind a bowl, here, in this room Saturday before I went up to bed, intending to return it to Jamie, but I promptly forgot it until Roberto crossed the lawn outside. He said he had found it 'interesting' that I was wearing it as a belt. Well, never mind now." He paused again, mouth twisting. "I don't think I knew what I had done until some time afterward. I seem to have no memory of . . . garroting Oliver. I did garrote him, didn't I? I must have. Strange word, *garrote.* Spanish, I believe. And then, in a moment it seemed, there was Gaunt. Right in front of me. Good old Gaunt. A good man, really, even if he did rather let me down. I know he must have tried. He did try, didn't he?"

Tom nodded sadly. "Yes, he did. Gaunt, I think, was very much the compleat servant, almost from another age. Other than Lord Fairhaven, you're the only person in this room he's been in service to."

"He used some other tie. Fancy having the same tie with him, a Shrewsbury tie. What an unexpected flourishing of happenstance. He told *me* he had taken the tie away—Jamie's tie—laundered it—however one launders ties, only he would know—and returned it to Jamie's things. But . . ." He looked around blankly.

"Gaunt dropped Jamie's tie in the Labyrinth," Tom explained. "Startled by the sound of another person—Anna. I expect," he continued gently, "he didn't want you to be concerned, so he substituted the one he had."

And at what sacrifice, Tom wondered. Gaunt waited years to assemble evidence to shame Oliver for an ancient crime and then, good servant that he was, he sacrificed his needs to his onetime master's son's.

"And will he be all right, Gaunt?" Dominic asked.

Tom looked to DI Bliss and replied, "No one is sure. He had a very bad fall."

"A fall, eh? I must say the House of Morborne has had rather a fall this weekend, hasn't it? Hasn't it, Lucy, darling? I had no idea when you coaxed me down to Devon that the title Marquess of Morborne would pass to me so suddenly. Of course, I had no idea that it would all go so terribly, terribly wrong, and so soon. Sorry, darling.

"And I'm very sorry, Marguerite." He turned to the dowager countess, who sat rigid but for a tiny quiver in her throat, staring, her eyes black pools of anger. "I had to know what Roberto had said to the police. Nothing, as it happened—which was oddly kind, though I know he had no love for Olly, either. But he was really only biding his time. He said he would have to speak up, eventually—if the police came after

Hector, for instance—your son. He wouldn't want you hurt. It was terribly easy. He was cleaning his hands in that sink. Water had pooled on the floor. You must get the drain fixed, you know. And there was that radio, so close, on the shelf. It was an impulse. Another one, I suppose. Can you forgive me?"

"Of course I can't forgive you." Marguerite retreated deeper into the couch. "You're a monster—as was your cousin."

The bronze clock struck the half hour at her last words, a reminder of time passed in this unhappy atmosphere. Tom's eyes went to the sliver of terrace visible through the French doors, vague and dusky as the sun, long vanished behind Eggescombe Hall, now dipped below the horizon. Past the dark shroud of trees, an ice-blue southern sky was shot with the last of the pinks and golds and wisps of cloud. A summer day's passage into summer night usually held for him a hint of mystery, and he longed to be walking some wooded path alone with his thoughts. *Once more 'tis eventide*—the words of the hymn flitted through his mind—*and we, oppressed with various ills, draw near . . .* It was but the craving of a moment for Bliss broke the silence, and his reverie, with a question of Lucinda:

"You two weren't together the entire afternoon, by the pool, as you claimed earlier?"

"No." She sighed. "I'm afraid not. Dominic went off on his own. He didn't tell me where he was going. I thought he'd gone to climb the Gaze Tower again. I was immersed in a magazine. When Gaunt arrived with drinks, I told him Dominic was probably up the tower. And, of course, silly man, Gaunt dutifully climbed the tower, silver tray with drink in hand."

"And saw what Dominic later claimed he'd seen: the murderer in the stable yard, near Roberto's studio," Jane said.

"That, too, is unforgiveable," Marguerite intoned.

"Is this why I found you outside the Gatehouse earlier?" Tom asked Lucinda. "You seemed unusually concerned about Gaunt."

Lucinda flinched. "Dominic, please, your fingers are digging in too much." She edged away and addressed Tom: "Yes, it ·. . it had all become too much. I knew that Gaunt knew what had happened in the Labyrinth with Oliver, you see— Dominic told me everything when he got back that morning. He was shaking, weren't you, darling? It was horrible, but I knew Dominic didn't seek to kill horrible, nasty Olly deliberately, did you? And besides"—she shrugged—"Oliver's death seemed to solve so many problems that . . ."

Her mouth formed a little moue. "But with Roberto dead, it was simply too much. Really, Dominic, it was. I was certain Gaunt understood something about Roberto's death, too, you see. He had been up the Gaze Tower. Afterwards, when he did fetch Dominic his drink, he behaved oddly. And when he—" She gestured to Blessing. "—asked us about our movements, Dominic said we'd been together poolside but for a few minutes when he'd climbed the tower. Where he claimed to have seen Gaunt. I went—"

"To warn him? Did you go to the Gatehouse to warn Gaunt, Lucy?" Dominic asked in a voice now high and brittle. "You didn't need to. Gaunt and I had a nice cup of tea earlier. He was very understanding. Good old Gaunt."

"I don't know what I was intending to do." Lucy shifted

uneasily. "Was it to warn him? I don't know. Dominic, you seemed so unaffected by Roberto's death. I thought—"

"That I might do it again."

"Oh, Dominic, don't say that!"

Dominic's eyes were large and bright. "Well, Inspector, what shall I do? Shall I say 'I'll come quietly, Officer' and hold out my hands for the cuffs? Or do we use handcuffs in this country? Perhaps I got that from American television. Or I could make a noisy mad dash for it. What do you think? Would that do? The terrace doors are wide open. The evening light is sublime. I could disappear into it, couldn't I? Or at least try. Would that give you a satisfying ending? Of course, you'd probably catch me. Still, a breath of this fresh country air would be wonderful. What do you think?"

"Lord Morborne," Tom answered. "I think the inspector will agree with me that it's entirely up to you."

Dominic looked at him and smiled.

The Vicarage

Thornford Regis TC9 6QX

15 August

Dear Mum,

Mr. Christmas and Miranda return home to Thornford
this afternoon from their week at Gravesend. Mr. C. called
yesterday to ask would I fetch them from Totnes just before
4? I think I told you what with his ankle, he'd decided the
train was best there and back. An odd tone to his voice I
thought, Mum. I can't put my finger on it. It's really the
first time we've spoken since the events last week at
Eggescombe. There wasn't a moment to talk then, of course.
I'm still not quite sure why Lord Morborne (the present
Lord Morborne—Dominic) thought to make a dash for
the terrace after confessing in the drawing room to

strangling his cousin, but perhaps he got all caught up in the drama. I know I was all caught up in it! I can't think I've ever been witness to something quite so thrilling, but awful in its way, of course. I'm still surprised how ~~lieth~~ ~~lyth~~ limber he was. If DI Bliss and DS Blessing shed a stone or two each they might have stood a better chance of nabbing him themselves, but as it was Lord Kirkbride and his brother ran him smartly to ground on the lawn with Bonzo making quite the racket! Mr. Christmas looked to join ~~the maylay~~ them but of course his ankle wasn't recovered. Anyway, I have written you all this, haven't I? Though I didn't say, as I've only remembered it now, how put out Lord Fairhaven looked through the whole episode—a little shocked and horrified, but mostly very put out. Sulky, I suppose is the word. I noted in yesterday's Telegraph that he had withdrawn his bid to be Conservative candidate, so I expect it crossed his mind then and there in the drawing room that it was all about to go off the boil what with scandal brewing. I'm sure he's sorry now he was host to the Leaping Lords at Eggescombe as it attracted his very disagreeable in-laws—except for Lord and Lady Kirkbride who are very nice. Anyway, this is all to say that in the aftermath, no one seemed wont to linger and have ~~a natter~~ a heart-to-heart about what had happened. All the "upstairs" folk found excuses to slip away, though I think L & L Kirkbride and Mr. Christmas made a trip to the kitchens as they had had no supper. The next morning Mr. C. and Miranda were gone. I think they took a back route out of the park to avoid the reporters and

other rubberneckers outside the Gatehouse. I expect Mr. C.
thinks I'm disappointed in him, and I am, as I've said. I
think that's what must lie behind the tone in his voice. At
least he had the grace to look mortified when he confessed
in front of everyone in the drawing room to having been
with that woman the night of the murder. I know I must
set myself to be forgiving, but I worry he's taken to
misbehaving like the previous incumbent at St. Nick's, Mr.
Kinsey, AND YOU KNOW WHAT HAPPENED TO HIM,
Mum! I've told no one about Mr. Christmas's behaviour,
not even Karla. Most particularly not Karla, as she takes a
very dim view of unpriestly behaviour. I do so hate
keeping things from her, and it's been on the tip of my
tongue more than a few times, as of course everyone in the
village is avid to hear the tale of my time at Eggescombe,
including Karla who pretends to be indifferent as she
thought poorly of the Leaping Lords fund-raiser to begin
with. But of course Mr. Christmas's breaking Dominic
fforde-Beckett's alibi by admitting he was with that
woman is such an ~~ingretal~~ important part of the story, but
I've had to bite my tongue every time. Anyway, I expect
Mr. Christmas will probably say something to me about
what happened, as he likes to do that sort of thing, but I
don't know how I shall look him in the eye. We shall see at
the station this afternoon. Did you happen to see The Sun
this weekend? I chanced to glance at the top copy on the
stack at the post office yesterday and there was a lead story
about our former verger who's been living under our noses
with a different name—ANOTHER different name—in
Abbotswick the last year or so! I still can't quite believe I

*thought I saw him coming from the Gatehouse last
Monday. I suppose it was the fair hair. Sebastian wore his
long the last time I saw him, which was last year. And the
new, disgraced Lord Morborne (Dominic) wears his long,
too. At any rate, Sebastian—or John as he is called—didn't
look best pleased in the picture, which looked posed for the
paper. I can't imagine what would have made him agree to
tell his story to such an awful rag. But I'm not surprised
anymore. I must say, Mum, the scales have fallen from my
eyes about our aristocracy. I know some of them go off the
rails, but I never would have thought a peer of the realm
to steal a car! (On top of everything else, of course!) I
expect you saw that, too, in the weekend papers. I'll enclose
the clippings. It always did seem a little odd that a man as
busy and important as the late Lord Morborne would
tarry in the West Country doing much of nothing. He even
visited our very good choir director Colm Parry to invite
him out of retirement for some big pop concert next year in
London, but that was simply a ruse while he was doing a
recce on the movements of that poor young man he hit with
a car he stole at Ashburton. Such a terrible chance he took,
and so brazen! You'd think that community the young man
lived in would have supervised him more, but I suppose
they try and teach independence where they can. What if
David Phillips hadn't been as regular as clockwork in his
movements, an easy target along the road, what would
Lord Morborne have done then? But as I wrote you last
week after Ellen poured her heart out he'd done as bad.
Worse! It's all too awful, Mum. I'm not sure if knowing
after all these years who her sister's murderer was has been*

any comfort to Ellen. Poor Mick was after some recompense for Kimberly Maddick, though I don't think L. Morborne dying by his cousin's hand was what he had in mind. It'll all come out in the papers eventually, I suspect, but Mick won't have the satisfaction of seeing "Mad" Morborne before the judgement seat—the earthly one, that is. "Eye for an eye" Ellen said to me yesterday when we were up at hospital together to see Mick. Biblical that may be, I thought to myself, but I expect Mr. Christmas would find this a v. UN-Christian sentiment. I'll leave him to sort that out as Ellen will be here at the vicarage another couple of days before they move Mick to a London hospital for rehab. I still think it ~~inconcid~~ rude of the Fairhavens to rush back to London without so much as a visit to Mick or consideration for what Ellen might do in the meantime. I suppose she could have stayed in the Gatehouse, but who wants to be reminded of such unhappiness? The vicarage has lots of rooms and besides, Thornford is much closer to Torbay Hospital than Abbotswick. Nice to have her here! And so nice to be back in dear old Thornford R. where folk are as normal as normal can be, ~~except for a few~~. I don't think I shall go back to Eggescombe anytime soon, even though I never did have a chance to walk the Labyrinth which I think must surely be a bit spoiled for many folk now, though on the other hand it might well attract others—the wrong sort of course! Anyway, Mum, I best crack on. The garden wants work. It got a bit ratty while I was away, and I need to think about what to have for our supper now that Mr. C. and Miranda are to be back. I did a big shopping at Morrisons yesterday so the larder is full, which reminds me to tell you that I ran into Venice Daintrey and she told me that she had heard that the board of the Thornford Regis Amateur Dramatic Society asked Catherine Northmore to direct their next play at the village hall this autumn—and she accepted! And wasn't I ever so pleased that a Hollywood actress would volunteer her time? And didn't I think the publicity would be wonderful for the village! Well, Mum, I was ~~agas ahgas~~ floored, but I didn't show it to Venice. Catherine didn't bother to make an appearance at her father's funeral more than a year ago. She hasn't been to Thornford in yonks anyway. Besides, last I saw of her in the papers, they were considering her for the remake of Whatever Happened to Baby Jane. Do you remember that film? Surely the end of the line for any actress worth her salt! When word spreads that she's swanning in to take over the dramatics, there will be noses out of joint in the village! And I think you know some of the faces those noses are stuck to. Well, I shall keep well out of it, as is my way! I'm happy to run up some of the costumes, but that shall be my only involvement. I might see the play. "Nine Ladies" it's called. Anyway, as I say, I must crack on. Cats remain well—they seem to have survived my absence, and Daniel Swan did well enough with Bumble, considering, though he still thinks he's owed more money. I'll have a contract for him to sign next time! Love to Auntie Gwen. Glorious day!

Much love,
Madrun

P.S. I have prevailed over ScootersPlus! They were wrong. I was right! They DID send it to the wrong address. Not Thornton Curtis. Thornford Regis! If you don't have your ShopRanger Deluxe Mark IV by the time you get this letter heads will roll.

P.P.S. Mark Tucker who you know is the treasurer of the PCC tells me the Leaping Lords and the Thornford folk who parachuted raised nearly £29,000 towards the church repairs. Nine of the peers contributed £1,000 each. The late Lord Morborne's cheque bounced, however. So, on the whole, something good came of the weekend, though the big plywood thermometer outside the north porch that Mr. Christmas threatens to set on fire is still in place. The red has much shot up the tube, though!

Acknowledgments

With thanks to:

My agent: Dean Cooke

My editor: Kate Miciak

Random folk: Laura Jorstad, Priyanka Krishnan, Marietta Anastassatos, Ben Perini, Martha Leonard, Sharon Klein, Lindsey Kennedy

unRandom folk: Clark Saunders, Warren McDougall, Bradley Curran, Pierre Bédard, Michael Phillips, Janice McKenzie, Rosie Chard, Sandra Vincent, Frances-Mary Brown, Perry Holmes, Spencer Holmes

Vicky Geilas, Brian Forbes, and Skydive Manitoba (all mistakes are mine, some deliberate)

The Reverend David Treby (all mistakes are mine, none deliberate)

About the Author

C. C. BENISON has worked as a writer and editor for newspapers and magazines, as a book editor, and as a contributor to nonfiction books. A graduate of the University of Manitoba and Carleton University, he is the author of six previous novels, including *Twelve Drummers Drumming* and *Eleven Pipers Piping*. He lives in Winnepeg.

www.ccbenison.com

About the Type

This book was set in Caslon, a typeface first designed in 1722 by William Caslon. Its widespread use by most English printers in the early eighteenth century soon supplanted the Dutch typefaces that had formerly prevailed. The roman is considered a "workhorse" typeface due to its pleasant, open appearance, while the italic is exceedingly decorative.